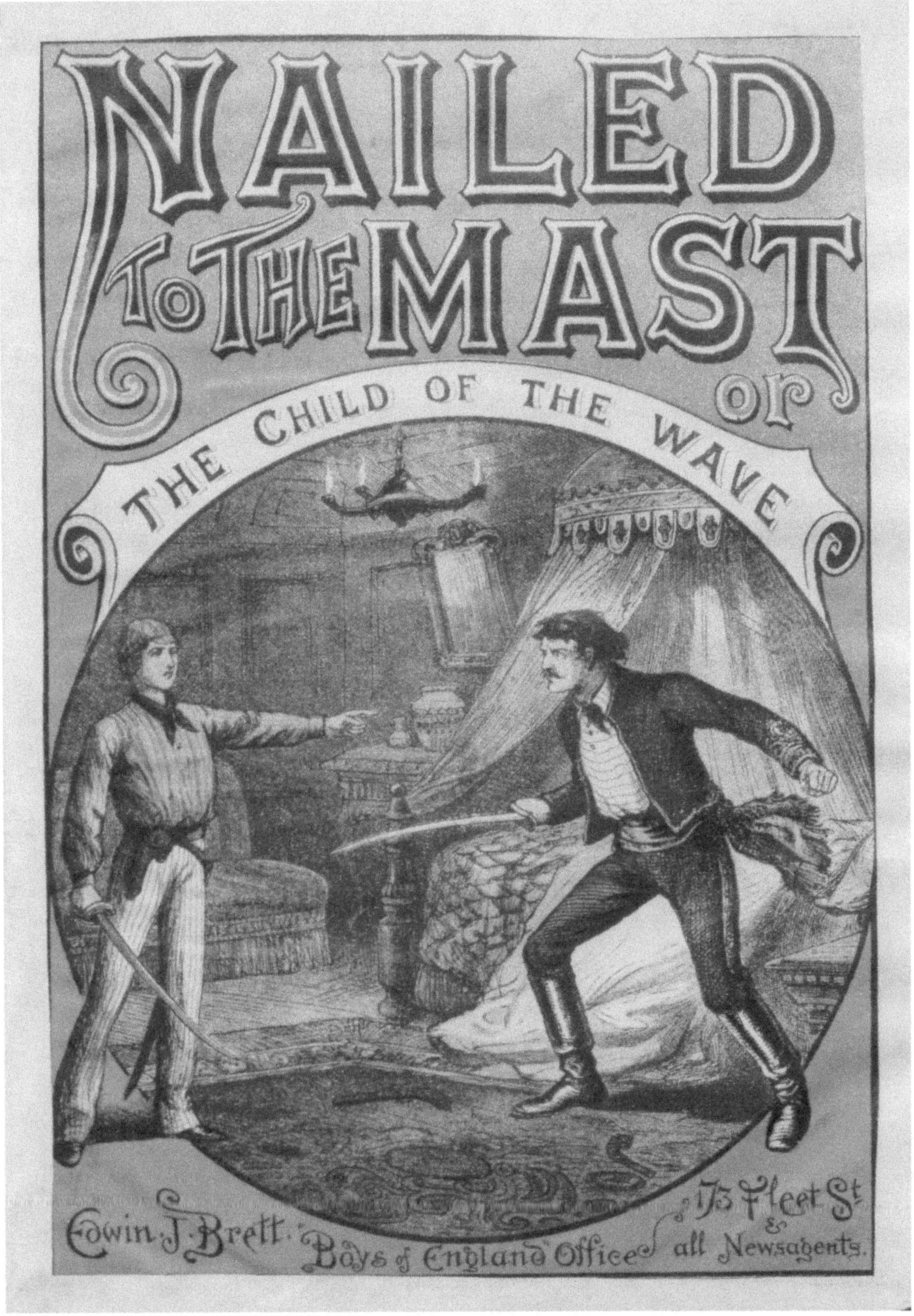

NAILED TO THE MAST

OR

THE CHILD OF THE WAVE

Edwin J. Brett. Boys of England Office 173 Fleet St. & all Newsagents.

"AT EACH STAB THE DOCTOR BOUNDED AT LEAST A FOOT FROM HIS CHAIR."

NAILED TO THE MAST;

OR,

THE CHILD OF THE WAVES.

COMPLETE.

BEAUTIFULLY ILLUSTRATED.

LONDON :

"BOYS OF ENGLAND" OFFICE, 173, FLEET STREET, E.C.,

AND ALL BOOKSELLERS.

NAILED TO THE MAST;

OR,

THE CHILD OF THE WAVES.

" 'BE CAREFUL,' SAID JACK BARNACLE, 'THE CAPTAIN NOT ONLY BARKS BUT BITES.' "

No. 1

NAILED TO THE MAST;

OR,

THE CHILD OF THE WAVES.

CHAPTER I.

NAILED TO THE MAST.

"I TELL you it's a whale, Jack Barnacle."

"And I tell you it's the sea sarpint."

"Sea sarpint!" said the first speaker, contemptuously. "Whoever heard tell of a sea sarpint out of a book?"

"I have, and lots of times I've seen 'em, too."

"You may go and tell that yarn to the marine."

"I've done that, too, lots of times when I was in the Royal Navy. But I've no time for yarn-spinning now. I shall go and report to the captain what is out there on the weather-bow, Bill Bunt."

The above conversation took place between two old sailors, who, leaning over the gunwale of the brig "Sea Breeze," had noticed something dark rising and falling in the sea some two miles from this vessel.

At first they had taken it for a patch of seaweed, such as is often found in the Caribbean Sea, but when they drew nearer they soon discovered that it was not that; and also that it appeared to be endowed with life.

The captain and mate of the "Sea Breeze" were pacing up and down the after-deck as the old sailor approached them.

"Well, Barnacle," said Captain Ireton, somewhat sharply, "what is up now?"

"Don't know, your honour, exactly," said the old man, as he touched his hat to the officers. "Bill says it's a whale, and I says it's the sea sarpint."

"Bill is more likely to be right than you are, but it is most likely that both of you are fools."

"Thank you kindly, your honour," growled Barnacle.

"Where away is it?"

"On the weather-bow, your honour."

"Mr. Daulton, go forward and see what it is."

The mate, a man nearly as old as the captain, bowed and went forward.

Whilst he is thus engaged, we may as well describe the two officers.

Captain Ireton was a man fully sixty-five years of age, with a fine, handsome face, bronzed with exposure to the weather, but very slightly wrinkled with age; and yet, handsome as his face was, it was not a pleasing one.

The lips were so tightly compressed that the muscles round the mouth were quite rigid.

Anyone would have sworn that Captain Ireton had never smiled in his life, and certainly no one on board the "Sea Breeze" had ever seen him do so, unless the first mate, Mr. Daulton, and Jack Barnacle had; for they were almost as mysterious as the captain, and they alone seemed to know all about him.

As he stood aft by the wheel, the wind blowing his snow-white hair about, he looked what he really was—a brave man, and a gallant sailor.

Lieutenant Daulton was about sixty.

His cheeks and chin were red, and deeply furrowed by time, but his whiskers, the pride of his life, were jet black; for, as true historians, we are bound to own the truth—Lieutenant James Daulton, once of the Royal Navy, the hero of many a battle, *dyed them.*

"Well, Mr. Daulton, what can you make of it?" demanded the captain, as his officer returned.

"Nothing much, sir," said the lieutenant, touching his cap in the true naval fashion to his superior officer. "It is *not* a whale; it is not the banks of seaweed so often washed off the coasts of these isles. It is either some timber washed off from Honduras, or it is part of a wreck."

"Get me my glass," said Captain Ireton. "I will examine it myself."

The sailor addressed sprang down the companion-way, and soon returned with the glass.

Captain Ireton seized it, and leaping into the rigging, fixed his glass and examined the strange object closely.

"You are right, Daulton," he said, as he sprang back on deck and closed the glass. "It is part of a wreck, and I fancy I can see someone on it; but, I fear, he or she, whichever it may be, is past our aid."

"But surely you will make the attempt to save him or her, Captain Ireton?" said the lieutenant. "You are not the man to let a fellow-creature perish, when there is the slightest chance of saving him."

"I don't see why I should put my ship out of her course."

"To do an act of mercy, captain," put in Jack Barnacle.

"Mercy?" laughed the captain. "What mercy has man or heaven ever shown to me? None. Why, then, should I show mercy to anyone?"

"Asking your pardon, captain," said Barnacle, with the greatest respect, "things I know has gone rather rough upon you sometimes, but I don't quite see that heaven was altogether to blame in the matter, or man either. Things might have been a great deal better, if— —"

"Silence!" roared the captain; "have I not told you never to speak, or even hint, about the past? Let it be buried with the dead."

"I'm dumb as a cod," growled the old sailor.

"Captain Ireton," said Lieutenant Daulton, in a firm voice, "I do not wish to allude to the past, but you were the one who began it with Barnacle just now; you know that very well."

"Yes, I was, I own it; but I knew what he was about to do."

"That is past; let it be so. Listen to me. As well as we can make out, there is a fellow-creature bound to that wreck. He or she may be alive; if so, it is our duty to save her."

"Her!" exclaimed the captain; "I will have no women on board."

"I meant *him*, for it is a hundred chances to one that it is a man. Anyway, it is a human creature; and, if there is the slightest chance of life being in it, we are as men and Christians in duty bound to save that life. All men are in God's hands, and no men more so than sailors. Death is around us at every moment. Before sunset we may be drifting like yonder unhappy wretch."

Captain Ireton turned quickly round, and said—

"Put up the helm, Mr. Daulton. I leave the ship in your charge. You can make for the wreck. I shall go below."

The captain disappeared below, and the lieutenant, taking the command of the ship, soon had her cleaving the waves in the direction of the floating piece of wreck.

"The captain must be a hard-hearted monster," said one of the men to Barnacle, "to think of leaving a poor wretch in such a position as that. Why, a heathen would not do it."

"Don't you go for to call the captain names," said Jack.

"Well, but mustn't he be? I heard you say it was a shame."

"What I says is one thing, what you says is another. But mark this, don't you go for to call the captain names. I know all about him, and the first one that speaks against Captain Ireton, will have to answer for it to Jack Barnacle, that's all."

Leaving the man perfectly cowed, the boatswain marched away.

"Humph!" remarked the man, when Barnacle was out of hearing, "it may be so. They say the devil is not so black as he is painted, so the captain may be a hangel in disguise."

They had now come so close up to the wreckage that they could plainly see that the person bound to the mast was a youth.

They now discovered, too, what had made Jack Barnacle declare it was a sea-serpent, and Bill Bunt that it was a whale.

Round the wreckage were a vast number of sharks swimming about, now snapping at each other, now at the loose parts of the wreckage, evidently trying to reach the body, and lashing the sea into a foam with their tails.

"Look at them varmints," said Bill Bunt; "I should like to have a go in at them. Maybe the skipper won't mind if we do after we have rescued that there poor chap. You might just ask, Jack Barnacle. He'll do it for you."

"Let's see first how the captain receives that which we shall find," replied Barnacle; "maybe it may not put him into the best of tempers, and he may wish to chuck the body back to feed the varmints, instead of trying to kill any on 'em."

"He couldn't be such a brute as that, surely!" exclaimed Bill.

"Couldn't he?" sneered Jack; "that's all you know about it."

At that moment the lieutenant gave the orders for the brig to be brought to, and every hand was busy. Then the boat was lowered and manned, and rowed by the side of the ship, whilst the lieutenant gave Barnacle his last instructions.

"You must be cautious, Barnacle, how you approach those devils," he said; "I have known them do the most savage things when they think they are about to be robbed of their prey.

"Give way, lads, and may you find the poor creature still alive."

The men did give way with a will, and were soon amidst the shoal of sharks.

And dreadful things they were to look upon as they swam about.

Now they would go slowly, just showing their dorsal fins above the water; then they would roll over, showing their slimy sides and white bellies, their mouths filled with horrible teeth, and their small, but most hideously vicious eyes.

They came up so close to the boat that they impeded its progress.

"Never mind the sharks, lads," cried Barnacle; "pull ahead."

They reached the wreck and found on the floating mast the body of a lad some fifteen or sixteen years of age, seemingly dead.

As he lay there, his pale face turned up to the heavens, his eyes closed so that their silken lashes fell upon his cheeks, his mouth slightly open showing his pearly teeth, and his rich brown hair

floating on the water, the rough, but tender-hearted sailors could not help feeling something in their throats, and the tears rose to their eyes.

"I say," said Barnacle, "when they had looked at the youth for a moment or two, "I fear as how it's a girl in boy's togs. If so we might as well leave her here as take her aboard of the 'Sea Breeze.'"

"Leave her here?" chorussed the men; "blowed if we do."

"Well, you see, lads," continued old Barnacle, scratching his head, "the captain goes rampageous mad at the sight of a petticoat."

"But he hasn't no cause here," argued one; "if this here be's a gal, she has had the good sense to doff the petticoats and put on the breeches. Look here, lads: if so be as it is a gal, he must not know it. The luff (lieutenant) is a good sort, and will keep the secret. We'll make a proper kind of a bunk for her for'ard, where she can be as secluded as a mouse in its hole, and she shall become the pet of the for'sal."

"It might be done that way," murmured Barnacle, who not only relished the idea himself, but saw that the men were delighted with it. "Anyway, as mortal men, we can't leave the poor critter here.

"Dead or alive we will have the poor critter aboard. If dead, we can read the sarvice over the body before we chuck it to these wretches; and if alive—boy or gal—Lieutenant Daultin ain't the man to let the captain do so fair a critter harm, even in his maddest fits. So cut away, Bill; off with the lashing and drag the body on board."

The sharks, it must be explained, had been kept off the body by the aid of spars, sails, and ropes, which had become entangled with the mast in such a manner as to form a kind of raft.

Through this the boat had to be pushed to enable Bill Bunt, who was in the stern, to reach the body.

"Make haste, Bill," cried Barnacle: "cut the lashings. These beastly varmints are coming after us, and if we let them get only a grab at the lad, we shall only save part of him, I reckon."

Bill understood this, and leaning over the side of the boat, raised his axe to strike.

Suddenly he paused, with his axe aloft, and cried out—

"Shiver my timbers, Jack Barnacle! There ain't no lashings!"

"No lashings!" exclaimed the men, in an astonished chorus.

"How the deuce, then, is the lad fastened to the wreckage?" asked Barnacle.

"Why he is NAILED TO THE MAST!"

"Nailed to the mast, impossible!" exclaimed the men, and they all leaned over to get a clear sight of the lad.

It was quite true. Slips of strong canvas had been passed tightly round each wrist and each ankle, and a fifth round the waist.

Each of these slips had then been nailed firmly to the mast with a large strong nail, so that, had the lad been washed ashore, it would have been impossible for him to have released himself, and so, if not discovered, must have perished from hunger and cold.

"There's been foul play here!" said Barnacle, in a hoarse whisper.

"Then you may bet on its being a gal. Gals are always in mischief," exclaimed one of the men.

"Hold your tongue, Peter Painter, can't you?" growled Bunt, "this here ain't no time to jest. I'll lean over and see if I can't knock out the nails."

"Do so, Bill, and I'll help the fellows to beat these sea devils off."

As Bill hacked away at the nails—a nasty job—for the boat bobbed about a good deal, and he had to take the greatest care that he did not strike off part of the lad's flesh, Jack Barnacle, with the men that could be spared from keeping the boat from drifting, beat off the sharks with oars, boathooks, and stretchers.

The ravenous brutes dashed here, there and everywhere, trying to get at their prey; but the gallant seamen kept them off, though not without danger to themselves, for the sharks often caught a stretcher close up to a man's hand, biting it in half in an easy manner, suggestive of how he would have have severed the sailor's arm could he have caught it. Suddenly Bill Bunt uttered a cry for help.

A shark, far more knowing than the rest had dived, and had come up close to the mast.

"Help, lads, help!" shouted Bill; "here's one of the fiends here!"

As he spoke the brute made a rush, and Bill struck it a heavy blow on the head with the axe. Unfortunately, sharks appear to have very little feeling.

The monster turned and made a dash at its assaulter.

Bill had not time to recover from the blow; his hand was still down.

One snap! a yell! and Bill Bunt fell backwards into the boat.

"Oh, Lord!" he groaned. "I'm done for. Curse that brute of a shark!"

"Blest if he harn't a-gone and dropped the axe," cried Peter Painter.

"And the tarnation brute has taken his hand along with it!" said another.

No sooner did Jack Barnacle hear this than he sprang forward, and seizing another axe, *leaped on to the mast,* so that he might be nearer to the lad they wished to release, and with a calmness that was really awful, began to hack away at the remaining nail—the one which held the waistband.

"Look out, Jack! look out!" screamed some of the men; "here's that there monster again!"

And sure enough there *was* the same shark making for Jack.

They all knew him by the gash on his head, which brave old Bill Bunt had given them.

Jack Barnacle turned round quite quietly, raised his axe, and just when the monster was within a few inches of his leg, brought it down with fearful force, killing the monster at one blow.

The shark made one or two struggles, and then turned on his back and floated away.

The next moment Barnacle had released the lad, placed him in the boat, and had leaped in himself.

He was about to order the men to pull back to the ship, when a weak voice from the bows called out—

"I say, Jack, don't go and leave part o' me for those varmints to eat out yonder. Its inside that thin white-bellied shark's stomach. Don't let it go for to be eaten up by *fish.* I know the rest of me would never rest in peace if that happened."

"Then, by Nelson, it shan't!" roared Barnacle. "Put about, lads, and we'll precious soon have Bill's hand aboard, shark and all."

Jack Barnacle and Bill Bunt were immense favourites with the men, and, therefore, it was with a will that they pulled after the floating shark, which was already being snapped at by its late comrades.

They reached the dead shark, beat off his cannibal brothers, and lashing it closely to the boat's stern, pulled quickly to the ship, which was now close upon them.

First the youth was lifted on board, and at once carried below, where the kind-hearted lieutenant had ordered blankets, hot-water bottles, hot brandy-and-water, and other remedies to restore half-drowned people, to be in readiness.

Then the shark was hauled—by the lieutenant's permission—on board, and ripped open.

"There it is," cried Bill Bunt, suddenly, as he made a dash forward, and seizing something out of the shark's maw, and thrusting it away quickly into his pocket. "Now I am happy and d——, I don't care."

"What do you mean by swearing in *that* manner, Bunt?" cried Lieutenant Daulton, who, although a good man, was a stern one in matters of duty.

"Please your honour it's mine," said the old sailor, quietly.

"Why don't you touch your hat when you speak to me?"

"Well, sir, it ain't quite convenient," replied Bunt, with — will the reader believe it, and yet it is true—a smile, "it ain't convenient."

"It isn't convenient!" thundered the lieutenant. "Touch your hat, sir!"

Slowly did the man look round.

Then quickly he drew his left hand from his pocket, and touched his hat with it. That done he thrust it back again in the pocket of his pea-jacket.

"What the devil do you mean, sir, by touching your hat with your left hand to me?" cried the lieutenant. "Touch it with your *right* hand."

No sooner had the order been given, than Bill Bunt plunged his hand into his pocket, and plucked out the hand which the shark had bitten off, and with the ghastly member he quietly touched his hat.

"Good heavens!" cried Lieutenant Daulton, "what is the meaning of this?"

"Not much, sir. I hit a shark, and he took my hand off."

"And you have been standing here in that horrible pain, and I have been cruelly speaking to you! Give me your hand, my brave and honest fellow!"

"Well, sir, I did not wish to part with it. I did mean to put it in my next ration of rum. But still, if your honour would like to keep it—I will give it up. There it is, your honour."

And as he spoke he quietly slapped the bitten-off hand into that of the lieutenant.

"Hang it all!" cried the lieutenant, suddenly drawing back his hand. "I did not mean *that* piece of—of death!" and he threw it down on the deck. "I meant your living hand to shake. Not the dead, useless one."

Bill Bunt picked up the separated hand, and having wiped it most carefully upon his trousers, said—

"Well, sir, maybe you are right. Only that right hand of mine helped to get me my living. Aye, and my old mother's too. Now that she is gone dead, I don't forget her. God bless her! More! Although I don't like to boast, it has done my country some service, and—and—and—hang it! I respect it—that's all!"

Tears grew in the honest fellow's eyes, and his voice became thick as he said this rough, but to our minds, touching speech.

"Hang it all, Bill!" whispered Barnacle. "*You* ain't going to clap on the pumps, Lord love yer? I knew a man out in India as had lost his harms, his heart—that was in love—his legs and his liver—that was by climate—but he did not give up."

"I ain't a giving up, Jack, but I'm hurt—I'm hurt."

"Of course you are—of course you are. Who could expect a man to lose his right hand and not be hurt?"

"Come, come, my lad, I did not mean to hurt you. I warrant me the surgeon, Mr. McTaggart, will, with the assistance of the nurse, soon put your arm into order. So go below, lads, and if the doctor will give you permission, the steward shall serve you all round with a double share of grog."

"Long life to your honour—heaven bless your honour's kindly heart," resounded on all sides, as the honest fellows went tumbling below, all trouble and fatigue being forgotten in that panacea of all evils to a sailor's mind—GROG.

CHAPTER II.

THE MYSTERY—DUMB OR NOT DUMB—ALL HANDS PIPED FOR PUNISHMENT.

CAPTAIN IRETON and his lieutenant were once more pacing up and down the after-deck on the morning after the incident we have just related happened.

"The boy is quite recovered?" demanded the captain, anxiously.

"Quite. Indeed he seems none the worse for the hardships he has passed through," replied the lieutenant. "The fact is it is simply wonderful."

"What does the doctor say about him? Does he say he has recovered?"

"Hang me if I think the doctor understands the case more than I do," said the lieutenant, rubbing the back of his head violently, a favourite action of his when puzzled; "but here comes McTaggart, and he can answer for himself."

As he spoke a tall, thin man, with high cheek bones, long, hook-like nose, and a chin like a shoe-horn, emerged from the companion-way.

His hair was a rich auburn, and very curly, ill befitting his wrinkled face. We say *his* hair, for the doctor had bought and paid for it honestly when last in London—in other words, it was a wig, and this wig, together with his shirt frill, were the pride of the doctor's life.

"Well, doctor," demanded the captain, "how is your patient this morning?"

"As well as could be expected, captain, considering that, despite my orders, he drank a double share of grog, which had been allowed him by the lieutenant, and not satisfied with that, but all the men being proud of him, gave him a share of theirs—out of pity, they said—the loons! and he drank it all until he was so tipsy they had to carry him to his bunk."

"What!" cried the captain in amazement, "do you mean to say that a boy, just having escaped from death, as it were, by a miracle, dared to get tipsy?"

"Boy! Hoot awa'! who spoke about a boy?" cried the Scot.

"I asked about a boy," replied the captain, angrily, "the boy we saved?"

"Gude faith, but I thought ye meant the gunner, Bill Bunt."

"Ah, poor fellow," sighed the captain. "I fear we have made a bad exchange there. Bunt's right hand was worth twenty powder monkeys, as I suppose this lad is."

"The lad is quite restored, thanks to my skill and his natural strength."

"To the latter more than the former, I should imagine," said the captain.

"You may think what you like, captain," replied McTaggart, drawing himself up to his full height, "but you have as much justice in doubting my skill as to think that you had a powder monkey."

"Indeed! And what do you make him out to be?"

"Well. Ah! That is I don't know," said the doctor, looking confused.

"Don't know? Lieutenant Daulton, do you know who this boy is?"

"Upon my word, captain, I have not the slightest idea."

"Not the slightest idea? What can you mean? What was the name of the ship that was wrecked?"

"I really can't say."

"From what port did she sail?"

"Really, Captain Ireton, I have not the slightest idea."

"Not the slightest idea?" exclaimed the captain, looking from one to the other of his officers in surprise. "Have you not questioned him as I ordered?"

"Everything has been done exactly as you ordered, captain," said Lieutenant Daulton, seriously, for until then he had felt much inclined to laugh, but he saw a strange light coming in the captain's eye, and a knitting of the brows which he was far from liking.

"And what answer did the boy make?"

"None whatever. I fancy that the boy must be dumb, captain."

"No, no; not a bit of that," chuckled the doctor, as he tapped the top of his snuffbox. "I thought so at first, but, ha! ha! ha! I soon discovered that he was shamming."

"Shamming, eh?" said the captain, as he clenched his teeth. "And what made you think that he was shamming, doctor? It's a bad accusation."

"I was going to visit him for the last time last night, and thinking that the poor boy might be asleep, I just pulled off my boots before I went to his hammock, and crept up to him on tip-toe."

"Well, and was he asleep?"

"It seemed so, for his eyes were closed, and he was breathing heavily, but presently the poor laddie sighed gently, and softly whispered a prayer of thanksgiving to heaven for his deliverance from such a dreadful fate. So you see he could not be dumb."

The captain turned on his heel and strode away.

"What a fool you are, McTaggart. You know his temper. The lad had better have been dumb than he should know it was shamming."

"May the di'el fly wi' me if I thought of it," replied the doctor.

At that moment the captain returned, and the doctor, stammering, said—

"You see, captain, I may have been a little bit confused, and——"

"Enough, doctor! I understand you. I want no excuses. Mr. Daulton, pass the word for the boy, and the bo'swin to pipe the crew aft. I will examine the young gentleman myself. We shall soon see if he will not answer."

The orders on board the "Sea Breeze" were as speedily obeyed as on board a man-of-war, for Captain Ireton, Lieutenant Daulton, and Boatswain Barnacle had held their respective ranks for many years in the British Navy, from which they had retired at the same time.

In a few moments the shipwrecked boy, clad in rough garments supplied by the generous sailors, but looking more beautiful than ever, was standing before the captain, on whose right and left were the officers of the ship, whilst at some distance, in a half circle, were the ship's crew, hats in hands, respectfully watching the scene, and silently expressing their admiration for their foundling.

"Now, my lad," said Captain Ireton, sharply, but not unkindly, "I have one or two questions to ask you. Be sure to answer quickly, and to the point."

A slight tremor shook the lad's frame, and he clenched his lips in a manner not unlike the captain's, but he made no answer.

"What was the name of the ship you sailed in, and from what port did she sail?"

The lad moved on his feet uneasily, but made no answer.

"Come, sir. Do you hear me speak? Answer me at once."

Still no answer.

"Look here, youngster," cried the captain, in a deep, stern voice, "you do not know yet the discipline that is used on board the 'Sea Breeze.' It will be my duty to teach it you; but I have no wish to do so in one sharp lesson. If I do, by heaven you will never forget it the longest day you live! Now answer me at once. What is your name?"

A bright flush passed over the youth's cheeks, but he made no answer.

"Fire and fury, do you dare to refuse to answer me? I *know* you are not dumb. Our good surgeon heard you speaking to yourself last night. So I will have you answer me these questions—

"What was the name of the ship you sailed in?

"From where did she come, and to where bound?

"What was she?

"If a merchant, what cargo did she carry?"

The youth hung his head down, and the tears rose to his eyes, but he did not speak.

"Come," said the lieutenant, in a gentle tone, "these questions are all simple enough, and a lad of your age, who has been some time at sea, ought to answer them readily enough. Don't tempt the captain."

"Leave him to me, Daulton," cried the captain, whose eyes flashed fire as his chest heaved with suppressed passion. "I will have no Sham Abrahams on my vessel. I will give him one more chance, and if he still refuses, punish him. If that don't bring his speech back, and I shall be mistaken if it do not, I swear I will send him adrift as we found him."

A murmur of horror ran through the ship's crew as they heard this.

"Silence, forward!" roared the captain, savagely.

"Now will you speak, and answer the questions I shall put to you?"

Again the questions were put, but with a like result.

The boy either would not, or could not answer.

"Enough of this!" thundered the captain. "You shall have your first lesson in discipline. Boatswain take that younker; seize him up to the grating; let him be stripped to the waist, and give him a dozen with the cat!"

A low murmur of discontent swelled up amongst the crew.

"Silence! or I will flog you all round!" roared the captain.

"Boatswain, do your duty."

With a heavy heart old Barnacle stepped forward, and placing his hand upon the lad's shoulder, said—

"Come, my lad, it nearly breaks my heart; but I must do my duty, you know."

The lad bowed his head as if he acquiesced in what the old sailor said, and submitted to have his clothes removed quietly.

As Barnacle did this office he whispered to the boy—

"Why don't you speak? The questions the captain axes you are simple enough. Think of the disgrace to you and pain to me if you let yourself be flogged.

"Come, whisper to me that you will speak, and I will tell the captain. He ain't bad hearted, although he is a rum one. Do speak, and make all pleasant."

These kind words brought tears to the lad's eyes.

But still he would not speak.

"Seize him up!" cried the captain, and in less than two minutes, the poor youth was lashed to the grating at the gangway.

"Boatswain, do your duty!" cried the captain. "Lieutenant Daulton, you count the blows. Doctor, stand by to watch that the lad does not die."

"Please your honour," said Barnacle, "its the gunner's place to flog the boys."

"Then let the gunner do the work."

"If you please, your honour," said one of the men, stepping forward and touching his hair, "he's down in his hammock, with his bad arm, and can't move."

This might be true, for seeing the position affairs had taken, Bill Bunt, who had been on deck, had that very moment slipped down the hatchway to his cabin.

"In that case, the boatswain must do the duty," said Captain Ireton, sternly.

The boatswain paused for a moment. Then he took up the cat, grasped the strong handle firmly with his right hand, and run the fingers of his left through the terrible lashes.

Then he glanced at the white shoulders of the boy, lifted the lash and dashed it on deck.

"If I flog that boy," he cried, "may I be —— hanged!"

If a thunderbolt had fallen on the deck of the " Sea Breeze," no one could have looked more alarmed than this speech made them.

CHAPTER III.

SHOWS HOW THE YOUTH WAS MADE TO SPEAK—THE EFFECTS OF A NAME— LIEUTENANT DAULTON IN COMMAND—THE STEEL BLOCK.

As we said before, the whole crew stood in amazement when they heard Jack Barnacle's determined speech.

Never before had such words been used on board the " Sea Breeze."

"Barnacle!" roared the captain.

"Your honour," replied Barnacle, just touching his hat.

"Will you flog that boy?"

"I'll be——"

"Barnacle," roared the lieutenant, "do you remember who you are?"

"Yes, sir, I do," replied Barnacle, steadily; "I'm bo'swain to the 'Sea Breeze,' and I am also a MAN, and the critter as lays a stripe on that there young chap's back is no man."

In one moment the men gave a cheer, and even the officers could not help smiling their approval.

But it was far otherwise with the captain.

He stamped and foamed with rage at thus being defied.

"By heavens, I'll have you seized up and flogged, too," he cried. "Strip, you rascal, strip. I'll teach you what it is to defy me. I'll show you what sort of a man the captain of the 'Sea Breeze' is——"

"Lord love your honour! I've known that this many a year," said the old man, as he began slowly to remove his jacket. "*I* don't want to be told that he's one of the bravest fellows as ever served under the Union Jack, but when he lets his passions master him, why then he is a devil.

"There," continued the old man, as he dashed his clothes down upon the deck, "now you may flog me as much as you like. You won't flog wickedness into me, and you may flog some of it out of yourself."

"For heaven's sake, Captain Ireton," whispered Mr. Daulton, "do not let old Barnacle be touched. If you do there will be mutiny on board. I have sworn to stand by you, and I will, but I freely confess if it were not for my *oath*, I would leave the quarter-deck this instant."

"Daulton!" said the captain, in low but firm tones, "you can leave me if you like, *but remember her*. If you draw back now I will curse you with my last breath, and proclaim you a coward."

"I shall not leave you, you know that, and presume upon it. Do what you like. I shall interfere no further in the matter."

Lieutenant Daulton walked to the other side of the deck, and leaning over the gunwale, turned his back upon the scene.

The men seeing this, made movements which plainly showed their approval of his conduct.

The captain could not help noticing it, and his rage grew all the greater.

He glared round at the men, watching with an eagle eye to catch the slightest covert act of insubordination, but they knew their captain too well, and, strange to say, loved him, martinet though he was, and therefore kept perfectly quiet.

"There is a spirit of mutiny aboard," cried the captain, as he drew forth a pistol, "but I think you all know me too well to think for one moment that I will give way to you. I know my duty, and I know my rights, and as I will perform one, so I will claim the other. Seize up that old mutineer."

The men moved uneasily, and no one seemed ready to step forward and do the work the captain had ordered.

Old Barnacle walked quietly to the grating, and placing a bullet between his teeth,* he put his arms in the proper position, and turning his head towards the men, said—

"Come, lads, tie me up. Do your duty as true British sailors, obey the captain, never mind *what* he orders. He knows his duty, you know *your* duty. His right is to command just as he pleases; your duty is to obey his orders whatsomever they may be. So tie me up and give me my share of pussy. I know the captain will suffer more afterwards than I shall—each cut on my back will be one on his heart."

In spite of all restraint, the men burst out into a loud cheer.

"Silence!" cried the boatswain, sternly. "Don't you know that when all hands are piped to punishment every man must remain quite quiet. You sons of sea-cooks, do the captain's bidding."

At this command one of the men stepped forward and lashed Jack Barnacle to the grating.

As this was going on Bill Bunt, who had again come up on deck, slipped up to the youth, and showing him his bandaged wrist, said—

"Look here, my lad, my name's Bill Bunt, d'ye see? I lost the flipper off this wrist saving you from the sharks. Lord love you! I *don't* begrudge it, and it ain't to throw my hand in your teeth that I speak now.

* This used to be a practice in the Navy when a man was flogged. He chewed the bullet and did not scream.

"But look at Jack Barnacle—the pride of the 'Sea Breeze'—to think that there perfect angel in white ducks should go for to be flogged because you won't speak takes my breath away.

"Speak, if it's only out of thanks for the hand as I lost. Speak, if you ain't dumb ; and if you are, I'm blest if you oughtn't to speak under such circumstances as these."

A cold shudder ran through the boy ; then, turning his head towards the captain, he said—

"Captain, cast that man's lashings off. Whip me if you like. He has done no wrong. I can speak, and so much as I may tell you I will."

Captain Ireton, although still livid with passion, was glad to see this way out of the difficulty, and at once ordered that old Barnacle and the boy should be released.

"Barnacle," he said, " you can resume your place as boatswain if you please."

"It's just as your honour pleases," said Barnacle, quietly. " I'm in the bend to follow the orders of the captain of the 'Sea Breeze,' and if you tell me to pitch myself overboard, I'll do it, but not thwack a lad as ain't in the ship's books."

"Hold your tongue, you old fool, and go back to your duty," said the captain.

Jack Barnacle touched his hat, and walked back to his station.

"Now, young fellow," said Captain Ireton, sternly, as the lad stood once more before him, " what is your name?"

"I have no name," replied the boy.

"No name! Do you think to put me off with such lies ? " cried the captain.

"It is no lie. I tell you the truth. I have no name," replied the lad, firmly.

"We will see to that presently. What was your father's name ? "

"I do not know, I never saw him," replied the boy.

"Your mother's ? "

"I do not know, she died giving me birth. That is all I can tell you."

"What are you ? "

"A sailor."

"I do not mean that. What position did you hold on board the ship in which you sailed ? "

"Next to the captain. I was—that is, when I chose to be—lieutenant."

"You, a perfect boy, a mere lad, the lieutenant of a ship ? "

"You forget I was born at sea ; for all I know I might have never been on land."

"Never been on land ! " exclaimed Lieutenant Daulton, stepping forward.

"No, sir—not that I can remember. Captain Deveril—ah ! I swore never to mention his name, and I have broken my oath," exclaimed the youth, clasping his hands in terror.

"Captain Deveril," yelled Ireton, turning livid, and throwing up his arms, he fell upon the deck in strong convulsions.

Disregarding the captain's illness, and leaving him to the care of Dr. McTaggart, Lieutenant Daulton walked straight up to the lad, and taking him by the wrist, said in a low voice—

"Boy, what do you know ? Who and what are you ? You *must* speak."

"I do not understand you. Oh, what have I done ? I was warned never to mention that name. Why should the captain become so ill ? "

"Never mind him," replied Daulton, as he held the boy at arm's length and looked him sternly in the face, " but answer me these questions. What was the name of the ship in which you were wrecked ? "

"I do not know."

"No lies. I have stood your friend up to now, but, by heaven, I will have no further prevarication. To prevaricate now is to save a villain whose life I have sworn to have. Therefore I warn you not to tempt me too far. What was the name of the ship ? "

"Believe me, sir, I do not know. I—I am not well. Give me time to think how to act. Oh! believe me, I am not to blame. I—I——"

The youth said no more, but suddenly placing his hands over his eyes, staggered, and would have fallen if Jack Barnacle had not caught him.

"Barnacle," whispered the lieutenant, " I am sorry for what has happened, but you know *his* temper, and the cause thereof. You must forgive it."

"May heaven bless him, I *do* forgive it, you know," said Barnacle.

"You must take this boy down into my cabin, and lock him up there."

"All right, your honour," said Barnacle, " it shall be done."

"No, no, no. I must go back to the bunk in which you placed me when I first came on board," cried the youth. "I left it there. I must—I must!"

The lieutenant and the boatswain exchanged looks, and then the former said—

"The boy had better go back to his bunk. He is not well, and the events of the last few hours have been enough to upset a much older head than his. But you will *watch* him Barnacle. He is too ill to be alone. You know what I mean very well. Dr. McTaggart has had the captain carried into his cabin. I must go there *at once*. When I send for you, bring the boy with you. You understand."

"I understand, your honour," said Jack. "Shall I order the dismissal to be sounded?"

"Yes, yes, and that at once. See you obey me well. This may be the end of all our troubles."

The lieutenant hurried away, and as Jack looked after him, he said—

"Pray heaven it may. I would as soon have joined with Vanderdecken, and sailed on board the 'Flying Dutchman,' as I would on board this ship, if I'd a' known all. But I've given my word, and I'll stick by it, come what may. Come, youngster," he added, as he took the youth by his arm, you and I have had a narrow squeak, that's what we've had."

"If he had had me flogged," said the boy between his teeth, "I would have *killed* him."

"Hush! hush! That there ain't a right kind of sentiment, Master—Master—Master—what is your name?"

"I tell you I don't know. But I know what I am, and that is a human creature, and no man living has a right to treat me worse than a dog. What has your captain to do with me? He let his ship be brought to whilst you and your fellows saved me. *He* ran no danger; he let *you* do that, *the coward!*"

"Come, come, come, none of that," said Jack Barnacle. "He is captain of this craft, and I'm blowed if I won't be sat upon by a Turk sooner than have one word said against him. You are ot the right grit. Keep quiet and you will be all right. Do the other thing, and I only want to remind you of this: A captain is king on board his own vessel. You don't want for friends, but be careful. The captain not only barks, but he bites. Now turn into your hammock, and say no more about it."

The boy leaped into his bunk, and pulling aside the mattress he drew forth what looked like a simple block of steel, not more than four inches long, three deep, and scarcely one in thickness.

On each side of this was a fixed ring, and to the rings was attached a chain of steel, just long enough for the boy to place it round his neck.

The chain was of most peculiar workmanship, and the block of steel was engraved over with the most fantastic figures.

The boy burnished it up as well as he could with the sleeve of his jacket.

Having done that, he kissed it reverently, slung it round his neck, and falling back on his pillow, soon was fast asleep.

"Well I'm blest," said Jack Barnacle to himself when he saw this, for it must be confessed that Jack had carried out the lieutenant's orders, and watched or *spied*—if you please to call it so—all the youth's movements.

"Well *I'm* blest. Just fancy him having that lump of steel hid away somewhere, and we not finding it. But what can be the good of it? Perhaps it's a tallerman (talisman he meant), and may save him from all sorts of trouble. At all events he's asleep now, and so I'll just puff a whiff of tobacco, and think over this strange mystery."

CHAPTER IV.

THE CAPTAIN'S CABIN—CAPTAIN IRETON'S STRANGE FEARS—HE TAKES THE
LIEUTENANT'S ADVICE—THE MYSTERY OF REVENGE.

It was late at night when Captain Ireton opened his eyes and looked round him.

He had not been laid on his bed, but had been placed on one of the ottomans in his state cabin; for, from some reason or another, Captain Ireton did not like anyone to enter his sleeping apartment except Bianco, the black cabin boy, who had to make the bed and clean the apartment.

The captain raised himself up on his elbow, and passing his hand over his eyes, muttered—

"It must have been a dream—a horrid dream. Father of heaven! have I been mad again? No, no, no! Better that it was all true—that I had had my faithful servant Barnacle lashed up to the grating than I should once more be mad. Why am I left thus alone? They cannot think me mad, and have locked me in here like a wild animal. Stay! If they think that, Daulton has removed all my weapons. I will see."

He peered into the sleeping cabin, the sides of which were decorated with all kinds of weapons of the most superb make.

"No; all is right. Then it must be that this *is* no dream, and that the fiend Deveril has been within a few miles of me.

He strode hastily to the table, and struck a small silver gong.

The door of the cabin was at once thrown open, and a little deformed negro boy, dressed in the Eastern fashion, shawl round his waist, small jacket with silver buttons, loose trousers, and red morocco shoes with turned-up toes, entered.

Making a grand salaam, Bianco awaited his master's orders.

"Bring me wine, Bianco," said Captain Ireton, eyeing the boy sharply, "and let it be of the best."

The negro made another salaam, and withdrew at once.

"This is strange," muttered the captain. "If I had gone mad again, Daulton would not have left me alone,

unless compelled to by the requirements of the ship, and most assuredly he would not let me have wine."

Here the negro returned, and having placed a crystal decanter of wine, and some finely-cut goblets on the table, was about to retire, when the captain bade him stay.

After drinking a goblet of wine, the captain asked if he had been very ill.

"Massa fell down senseless upon the deck. Massa Daulton have him brought here, and he shut himself up with massa, and we heard massa save."

"Ha!" exclaimed the captain, his brow clouding as he made a step towards the negro, looking as if he would strike him to the floor, "so you are a spy. You have been listening."

"No, massa, no," cried the trembling boy. "Me not hear one word; me only heard your cries; dat is all. Then you quiet, and the lieutenant send for the doctor. He gave you stuff to drink, and you fall asleep, and all quiet again. You sleep tree, four, five hour, and no wakey. Dr. Tagget say all right."

"Ah! I remember now," said the captain, trying to put on a light air. "Yes, yes; I have never been well since the time I had that sun-stroke. Go and ask Lieutenant Daulton to come to me here, as I desire to speak to him."

Bianca salaamed, and once more withdrew.

"Ah, Daulton," said the captain, as he held out his hand to the lieutenant when the latter entered the cabin. "My dear old friend. I know you would never desert me. Come, sit down and have some wine. Tell me, I have been ill again?"

"You have—very ill," said the lieutenant, as he tossed off a bumper of wine.

"Ah! I thought so. Did I say anything before the men?"

"You would have done so, but I carried you downstairs into the cabin. You, Barnacle, and myself are the only three who know the *true* nature of the 'Sea Breeze,' and to accomplish our plans it is necessary that no one *shall* know our secret until *he* is in our power."

"True, true. I understand you. Go on," muttered the captain.

"I need say no names. Well, if you give way to these most ungovernable fits of temper, you will let all out, and heaven only knows what may be the consequence. I have as much wrong to repay as you have, and am as hungry after revenge. Do you see me commit myself as you have done? No! The finest hound to drag down its prey is the one that makes the least noise, not the one who continually barks."

"You are right, old friend—quite right; but remember he was so dear to me."

"And was not *she* dear to me?" retorted the lieutenant.

"Yes, yes, old friend. But if I do not rescue *him*, all the hopes of a long and illustrious line are lost for ever."

"It is sad, but *we* have done our best. Are you well enough to speak on business of importance?"

"Quite. What is it?"

"The boy you would have flogged with Barnacle."

"Speak not of that. I must ask Barnacle's pardon. I was mad."

"He knows that. If you would make up for the wrong you have done him, never let it happen again. That is all he will ask."

"I will do my best. But go on. The boy who was picked up."

"Yes; there is a deep mystery about him. You must treat him kindly."

"But why would he not speak?" demanded the captain.

"I don't know. You may rely upon it he had good cause. You have tried what violence will do, and failed. Worse than failed. You have bred up a feeling akin to mutiny in the crew. You must now try kindness. The lad is brave, and has evidently good qualities in him. Make him like you. He will soon become the pet of the crew, who already look upon him as their property because they saved him. In this manner you will bind the men closer to us. Do you see?"

"You are right, old friend. Do with me as you will."

"Agreed," said the lieutenant, summoning Bianco. "Bianco, pass the word forward that the captain wants Mr. Barnacle and the lad who was saved from the wreckage. Let them come to this cabin immediately."

CHAPTER V.

EXPLANATIONS—OUR HERO BECOMES SECOND LIEUTENANT OF THE "SEA BREEZE" —THE FINGER OF FATE—THE SIGNAL OF THE "FIREBRAND."

"I WONDER what's up now," said Jack Barnacle, as he helped the lad to dress. "I say, sonny," he continued, as the lad quietly hung the steel block round his neck, and tried to conceal it beneath his shirt. "I say, sonny, what is that queer thing you have there? It ain't no hanky-panky business; no chain fudged up by some of those nigger fellows on shore by the aid of the devil, is it? If so, take my advice and chuck it overboard, for it can't do any good, and must do harm."

"It is the gift of the only friend I ever had, and I wear it for his sake," replied the youth.

"Well, just as you like. It is no business of mine, anyway, that is clear.

So come along, and see if you cannot pacify the captain. He's a good, brave gentleman. A little too fond of having his own way—but then, who isn't? and he has a right to have it."

Thus advising the lad, old Barnacle entered the captain's cabin, leading in the youth.

Starting from his chair, Captain Ireton advanced to Barnacle, and took him by the hand.

"My dear old friend," he said, "you must pardon me. I have done wrong, a great wrong. You, who have been so faithful a friend in sickness and danger, to be treated so! It is shameful, and I—I ask your pardon."

"No, no, your honour, do not speak

like that. I pray you do not. It—it didn't matter a bit. You only did what you thought right, and it was my duty to obey."

Here the old man drew away his hand from the captain's, and passed the back of it over his eyes.

"Heaven bless you, Barnacle," said the captain, and then, turning to the youth," he said, "and you, too, young sir, require an apology from me. You must forgive me. I am hasty, have had great trouble, and sometimes feel almost mad."

"You, sir, are the captain of this ship," said the youth, somewhat haughtily, "and therefore, can do what you please. I have been too used to seeing deeds of violence to be astonished at anything now."

Captain Ireton bowed coldly, and bade the lad be seated. Old Barnacle would not sit down, but stood behind the captain's chair.

"Young man," said Lieutenant Daulton, kindly, "we would not press too hard into your secrets, but still the service you have received at our hands should at all events entitle us to some knowledge as to your antecedents, and at least you might explain why you refused to speak."

"Because I am bound by a terrible oath not to reveal certain secrets which have been entrusted to me. Fearing that I might be questioned on these subjects I preferred pretending to be dumb."

"Will you tell me your name?"

"I have no name."

"Let us know what you like of your history. If you wish it to be kept a secret it shall be so. You are among friends."

The youth thought for a moment, and then spoke in a low but distinct voice, as follows—

"I have no name. I remember nothing before being on board the 'Firebrand.' There I was treated, sometimes with foolish lavishness, and sometimes the greatest sternness.

"I was well educated, but the only pleasant recollection I have is that of a thin, pale-faced man who kissed me and held me to his heart; aye, and sometimes wept over me. He died when I could not have been more than six."

Here the youth paused, and with difficulty suppressed his emotion.

"After his death all was misery. Sometimes Captain Deveril made me his favourite. I lived in his cabin; the men had orders to obey me as if I were the captain. Then, because I would not not join in his fearful orgies, or assist in the capture of vessels or slaves, he would turn upon me, and disgrace me before all the men. Sometimes he would set me in a barrel of gunpowder to which was fixed a lighted slow match.

"But why should I speak of these things? A few nights ago he attacked and captured a merchant vessel. I tried to warn her of her danger, but she did not understand, or did not heed my signals. She was taken and the crew thrown overboard—no one was spared. The next morning I was led on board the captured vessel, and nailed to the mast as you found me.

"'There,' cried Captain Deveril, 'I will not kill you. Your blood shall not stain my hands, but you shall die. The bottom of the ship has been bored through, and she must sink. You cannot escape. If I could have made you a pirate I would have done so; you should have lived to become a disgrace. But since you will be virtuous, you shall die virtuous.'

"With that he ordered the men to set all sail on the sinking ship. The helm was lashed hard up to bring her to the wind, and, in an hour I was out of sight of the 'Firebrand.'

"The night came, and with it a fearful hurricane. Directed by the hand of Providence the ship was dashed on some rocks. She parted amidships, and the mast to which I was nailed fell into the sea. I knew no more until I came to myself on board this vessel."

As the lad finished speaking he noticed that the captain was in a fearful state of excitement, his face being convulsed, and his hands working violently.

Lieutenant Daulton was pale as death, and his hands were clenched until the knuckles showed large and white through the mahogany-coloured skin.

Jack Barnacle's face for once looked savage; but he comforted himself by a huge quid of tobacco, which he thrust quickly into his right cheek, and said—

"'YOU SEEM TO KNOW A GREAT DEAL OF CAPTAIN DEVERIL'S AFFAIRS,' SAID CAPTAIN BREEZE."

No. 2

"Cuss him! That's the varmint who has caused all this trouble."

"Speak for me, Daulton; I cannot speak. Tell him what you like," said the captain.

"My lad," said Daulton, almost gaily, "I believe it *was* the hand of Providence that placed you on the mast and guided you to us. That Deveril, if I guess rightly, is a man who did my captain and myself a great deal of harm—an injury neither of us will ever forget or forgive. The ship, the 'Sea Breeze,' is owned by Captain Ireton. He has letters of marque, so that we are ranked as a man-of-war, but our purpose is really and truly to capture this fiend, whom we believe to be Deveril. If I describe him, will you tell me if it is the same man?"

"Certainly."

"He stands six feet two at least?"

"He does."

"Is well and muscularly made?"

"He is."

"He would have been handsome but for a peculiar servile look. He has a heavy black moustache which hides his mouth, but whenever enraged, he draws back his lips and discloses his teeth, fangs of a fearful and unnatural length."

"It must be the same."

"He has black hair, which he brushes low on the forehead to hide——"

"A scar that runs from the left temple to the right eyebrow," cried the lad. "It *must* be the same man!"

"It is he!" cried the captain and the lieutenant; whilst old Barnacle, who knew more of the points of the compass than of the rules of grammar, contented himself by exclaiming—

"Them's 'em. That's the dastardly son of a sea-cook."

Captain Ireton paced up and down the cabin for a few moments, and then pausing before the lad, said—

"If you met this fiend in human shape—this—this— well, we will call him Deveril at present, what would you do?"

"Kill him," replied the youth, with such energy that all were startled.

"You would?"

"Without mercy, without one thought; he killed the only man who ever loved me—the only one I ever loved. What was it for? Partly to please himself, and partly because he feared me.

"If I had consented to become a pirate he would have had me in his power. To induce me to become one he offered me the place of first mate in his ship. It was refusing that which made him determine to put me to death. Judge, then, what mercy I will show to Captain Deveril."

"Providence, indeed, hath brought you hither," cried the captain. "Our second lieutenant, Mr. Pringle, died of the yellow fever. Will you take his place? I intend to scour these seas until I have seized that terrible fiend, the captain of the 'Firebrand.'

"You have the same wish for revenge. Join us, and together we will chase this fellow until he is forced to confess his crimes, and we bring him to that punishment which he so richly deserves. Who knows but that you may wring from him the secret of your birth, and learn by that how to seek your parents."

"That, indeed, is hopeless," said the youth, "for he has never varied in one thing, and that was telling me that my parents were both dead. If I can believe what he said, I am the orphan child of a relation of his, who dying in poverty, left me to his charge. Sometimes I have believed it, sometimes I have doubted it. I know not what to think; but I thank heaven that I have escaped such a hideous companionship."

"And do you accept my offer?" demanded Captain Ireton eagerly.

"I do with pleasure."

"And you will use all your knowledge to trace out the murderous wretch?"

"I will. I live with no other thought than that."

"'Tis well. What name will you be known by?"

"Call me what you will; it matters not to me."

"We must think of this. Hush! someone comes. Come in."

The door of the cabin opened, and a petty officer entered, and touching his hat, said—

"A dark night, sir. The wind is N.N.W., and we have just sighted a sail on the weather-bow. She cannot be more than a mile away."

"Good. We will be on deck directly."

The petty officer disappeared.

"Gentlemen," said Captain Ireton, as he buckled on his sword, "what has passed between us to-night must be a secret. This gentleman I appoint my second lieutenant. If Deveril wished him to be his first lieutenant he must be a good sailor. Young man, help yourself to weapons from yonder cabinet."

This our hero did; for need we say that the youth so strangely found *is our hero*, and we assure our readers that many a startling adventure he will have before our story ends.

All being armed, the captain led the way on deck.

Night glasses were used, and all they could make out of the strange sail was that she was a large schooner.

"What do you think of her?" demanded Captain Ireton, as he placed his hand upon our hero's shoulder in almost a parental manner.

"The darkness of the night and the sea mist puzzles me a good deal," replied the youth, "but I could almost swear it is the 'Firebrand.' Perhaps she has not seen us. If we could get the weather gauge of her, we might drop down and board her."

"A good idea. Stay! You must be known to the men. Barnacle, call the men aft. I would speak to them."

The men soon assembled, and the captain addressing them, he told them that the youth they had discovered *nailed to the mast* would be their second lieutenant, and that henceforth they must obey the orders of Mr.— Here he paused, for there was no name again.

"Confound it," muttered the captain, "you must have a name. What shall I call him?"

"Call him," shouted old Barnacle, carried away with excitement. "Call him! Why, what should you call him? Did we not find him nailed to the mast? Didn't old Ocean nurse him gently, as if he were its own infant? Then what better name can you give him, until he finds his own, than the CHILD OF THE WAVES?"

"The Child of the Waves! The Child of the Waves!" shouted the men. "Three cheers for the Child of the Waves."

And they gave them, too, with hearty British goodwill.

"Hush! hush!" cried the Child, as we shall now call him. "Look yonder. *There is the sign.*"

The ship which they had seen in the darkness had heard the shout, and suddenly a *burning torch* was run to the mast-head.

"See! see!" cried the Child of the Waves. "It is as I suspected, the 'Firebrand.'"

CHAPTER VI.

THE ENGAGEMENT BETWEEN THE "SEA BREEZE" AND THE "FIREBRAND"—A DRAWN BATTLE.

As the crew of the "Sea Breeze" heard the name of the "Firebrand," they sent up a shout of joy.

"Do you think it would be advisable to get the weather gauge of the pirate, so as to prevent his sheering off? I scarcely think that it can be possible he intends fighting," said Captain Ireton to the Child of the Waves.

"I think not. Deveril means to fight. Keep all close, to set sail if necessary."

"Set sail!" cried the captain in surprise. "You do not think I would turn *from* him?"

"From him alone, no! But you do not know what this fellow is up to. You imagine that there is only one 'Firebrand.'"

"Decidedly."

"You are wrong. There are at least a dozen of them. Deveril is admiral of that pirate fleet."

Captain Ireton looked at the Child of the Waves in amazement.

"Can this be true?" he ejaculated. "If so, it will account for many strange stories I have heard."

"Just so. He gives out that there is only one 'Firebrand.' He has selected the captains of the different vessels from men as like him as possible. They imitate his manners, voice, everything, and assume his name. Thus the contradictory accounts which have so puzzled the men-of-war sent in pursuit of this pirate are accounted for.

"Now they hear he has captured a ship close to France, then within a week it is reported that he has seized a vessel off the coast of South America.

"If you could have believed it only one ship, you must have given credence to the story which he has set about, namely: that shot and steel will not injure him, and he has only to *wish* his vessel from one side of the world to another, and it is conveyed there in an instant."

"I see now how I have been deceived," muttered Captain Ireton. "But with your help I trust that I shall yet bring the villain to justice. See! We must now be within range of each other. Mr. Daulton, tell the gunner to fire one of our long guns at yonder vessel. Let him see if he can hit her in the foot."

"Ay, ay, sir," said the lieutenant, and he hurried forward.

Bang! crash!

As the smoke from the gun cleared off, the men jumped eagerly into the rigging to see if the shot had told, and they sent up a ringing cheer when they perceived by the commotion on board the pirate that it had done good execution.

The decks of the "Sea Breeze" were now cleared for action.

The guns were run out double shotted, and the men with handkerchiefs tied round their brows, naked to the waist, their canvas ducks being kept up by leather belts, in which were stuck cutlasses and pistols stood at their posts eager for the fight.

The "Firebrand" suddenly shortened sail.

Sheet after sheet was taken in until she rounded to about three hundred yards from the "Sea Breeze," when she immediately opened a fierce cannonade upon her foe.

"Aim low, and reply well, my lads," cried Captain Ireton. You know the rewards I have offered. A hundred pounds to the first man who springs upon that vessel's deck, two hundred to the man who captures the captain, dead or alive, and a thousand pounds amongst the crew if we take the vessel."

"Hurrah for Captain Ireton!" shouted the crew. "We will take the ship! we swear it."

And now a regular duel with cannon took place, both vessels trying to injure each other in the spars and rigging, so that the ships should become unmanageable, and in this they succeeded very well.

Already each vessel had received great punishment in its spars, and the "Sea Breeze," which had but so lately been one of the most graceful vessels afloat, now looked a perfect wreck.

"Captain Ireton," said our hero, "we cannot stand this much longer. The 'Firebrand' carries heavier metal than we do."

"What can be done?" demanded the captain, "I swear I will not leave him."

"No, but the best thing we can do is to board them," replied the Child of the Waves.

"Board them! It is impossible," replied the captain and Lieutenant Daulton together.

"Not a bit of it. The equatorial current is in. Put a little sail on the ship so that she may forge ahead. They will think that we are flying, or trying to escape, and will put on sail. We meet, and in an instant all hands are aboard."

"What say you, Daulton?" said the captain, "is the plan good?"

"So good that you cannot do better than take it. This boy knows this sea well."

"Then let it be done," said Captain Ireton, as he grasped the hilt of his sabre tightly. "I wish to be at close quarters with these fellows. If heaven will but give me my revenge, I will be satisfied."

"So would I," muttered Lieutenant Daulton, as he walked forward to give the orders.

But Deverill, of the "Firebrand," was a clever sea captain, and at once perceived the plan of attack.

"Out with the nettings to receive boarders," he shouted. "Stand to your guns, men, and fire rapidly. 'We will blow the 'Sea Breeze' over the water to a merry tune. Ah, ha, Monsieur Ireton, you came for revenge, and you shall have it."

So loudly did he shout this, that it

could be heard above the roar of the guns.

The nettings were triced up with the greatest swiftness, so that they were all in their places when the "Sea Breeze," carried down by the tide, drifted right against the "Firebrand."

"Fire," roared the Child of the Waves, who had arranged with Captain Ireton that directly the two ships touched the guns should pour in a broadside.

Oh! what a terrible crash there was as the hail of iron was poured into the "Firebrand."

So great was the shock that the two vessels rolled asunder and it was some minutes before they approached near enough for the grappling irons to be fixed.

At last this was done, and then, with a ringing cheer, the men of the "Sea Breeze" leaped up the nettings, trying either to cut their way through them, or to scramble over them and leap down on to the deck.

They were met with equal resolution by the pirates, who thrust their cutlasses and haul-spikes through the nettings, forcing them back.

No one thought of asking for quarter, and no one dreamed of giving it.

Our hero had been the first on board, and had fought with the fierceness of a lion.

The fore-deck was already cleared, and the pirates had gathered together on the quarter-deck, ready to receive the attack of their foes.

"Forward!" cried Captain Ireton, who led his men in person. "Forward, and cut them down."

"Halt! as you value your lives. Halt!" yelled our hero.

But the warning came too late to save the hapless crew of the "Sea Breeze."

Scarcely had the words fallen from the lips of the Child of the Waves, when the pirates opened their ranks, disclosing the muzzle of a long swivel-gun, which Deveril had slewed round.

"Fire!" roared Captain Deveril. "Fire! and blow these idiots into eternity."

The gunner applied the match, and the long swivel-gun poured forth its deadly contents amongst the devoted crew of the "Sea Breeze," mowing them down right and left.

"It is useless to advance farther," said our hero to Lieutenant Daulton, who stood by his side. Our men are dispirited. We had better get back to our own ship, and cast off the grappling irons. We may yet be able to sheer off and repair damages; for there is a light breeze springing up from the south-east."

"Can we fight our way back?" groaned the lieutenant. "I am wounded in my left arm, and Captain Ireton is shot."

As he spoke he pointed to Captain Ireton, who lay bleeding on the deck.

"You lead back the men," cried our hero, "and I will look to the captain."

Our hero at once sprang forward, and caught up the captain, supporting him with his left hand, whilst with his sabre he kept back the pirate crew.

"Cowards!" yelled Deveril, as he sprang forward, "will you let a boy keep you back?"

"Yes, Leonard Deveril," cried our hero, as he crossed swords with the pirate captain, "the boy will not only keep you back, but avenge all the wrongs you have done him."

The light of a torch flashed upon the face of our hero as he spoke, and instantly Deveril staggered back with a loud shriek, and fell flat upon the deck in a fit.

Had the crew of the "Sea Breeze" not suffered so much by the action, they had now a chance of regaining their ground; but the captain and first lieutenant being dangerously wounded, our hero, who now held the command, deemed it advisable to draw off his men.

They managed to regain the deck of the "Sea Breeze;" the grappling irons were removed, and the ships sheered off, both having received severe damage, and were glad to get a little time to refit. But the Child of the Waves determined to recommence the action as soon as morning came, and therefore set his men to work to repair the rigging.

But the "Firebrand"—the terrible, unconquerable "Firebrand"—for such was the name the pirate vessel had gained for itself—had met its match in a smaller ship, and as morning dawned, the crew of the "Sea Breeze" discovered that her foe was sailing away at full speed.

CHAPTER VII.

PERILOUS CONDITION OF CAPTAIN IRETON AND LIEUTENANT DAULTON—THE CHILD OF THE WAVES TAKES THE COMMAND OF THE "SEA BREEZE"—THE LIEUTENANT GIVES CAPTAIN BREEZE HIS SAILING ORDERS.

CAPTAIN IRETON was found to be so severely wounded that Dr. McTaggart was in the greatest fear that he would never recover.

He had received no less than three bullets in different parts of the body, two of which could not be extracted. Added to the damage caused by this, fever set in, and the captain lay upon his bed, raving like a madman, fancying himself a nobleman, and calling frequently upon his son, whom he declared he had driven from home and ruined; so that he had to be continually watched.

Lieutenant Daulton had had the upper part of his left arm smashed by a bullet; and the surgeon declared that there was no help for him but amputation.

"What," growled the fine old fellow, "do you mean to say that I and my left fin must part company, after having sailed together all these years?"

"I am afraid, my dear Lieutenant Daulton, you must have an operation performed."

For a moment the lieutenant was silent, and then uttering something which sounded like an oath, said—

"Get out your murdering tools, and see you make short work of it. It will make one more debt to be paid Captain Deveril, when I meet him. That's all."

After this the lieutenant never uttered a cry or groan, but remained unflinching until the operation was over, when he insisted upon having a stiff glass of grog; and having drank that off, rolled himself up in his bedclothes and was soon fast asleep.

Dr. McTaggart and Jack Barnacle consulted with the men about the future course of action that they should pursue, now that it was certain the captain would not be able to resume his duties for many months, if at all; whilst it was equally positive that Lieutenant Daulton would not be able to take the command.

What, then, should they do?

The wisest and best thing would have been to bear up to some proper port to refit, but this was so directly opposite to the standing orders of the captain, that they dared not do it.

Meanwhile our hero had quietly but firmly taken the command of the ship.

This he did in such a masterly manner that the whole crew were surprised.

At first they seemed rather inclined to object to obey him.

"Who was he?" they asked each other. "Not one of them—no one knew a word about him. What right had he to command them? Let Jack Barnacle, who was a full-grown man, and a proper seaman, too, do that."

But Barnacle and Bill Bunt stuck up for our hero, and pointed out to the crew how capitally he had seen to the repairing of the ship, and had not only superintended everything himself, but had worked with a will and a skill at the most difficult repairs that the oldest sailors on board had not shown.

And they and the doctor persuaded the crew into submission.

One day the "Sea Breeze," under easy sail, was flying rapidly through the water before a fair wind.

Our hero was pacing up and down the quarter-deck, when he perceived a movement in the forecastle, and presently the whole of the ship's crew, headed by Jack Barnacle and Bill Bunt, who had an iron hook, made by the armourer, affixed to his stump, in place of a hand.

When they reached the quarter-deck, Jack shouted—

"Hats off, you lubbers, and salute his honour."

At the same time he doffed his own tarpaulin-covered straw, and pulling his forelock, kicked out his left leg in the approved style.

All the others did the same with like success, saving Bill Bunt, who getting his hook hitched into a matted lock of hair, had to be assisted by one of the men before he could release it.

"Look here, yer honour," said Jack, who acted as spokesman, "we lads have been thinking over the way this here ship is to be managed. At first we thought you too young, which was natural; but we have seen the clever way in which you have managed the ship, and we have come to the conclusion that you shall act as commander until the captain or Mr. Daulton is able to take charge of her. That's what we say, isn't it, lads?"

"It is, it is, it is!" shouted the men.

"But what's the captain's name to be? We can't call him Captain Child of the Waves," said Peter Painter.

Scarcely had he said these words when Bill Bunt hitched his hook into Peter's collar, and shaking him violently, said—

"Why you lubberly son of a sea-cook, ain't you got no better manners nor that? How dare you speak on the quarter-deck, you swab? I'm a good mind just to hoist you over the gun'el, and drop you into the water to feed the fishes."

"Hold, in mercy hold, Mr. Bunt," cried the unfortunate Peter. "I didn't mean no 'arm. You know as I act as clerk to the ship, and I can't put it in the ship's books that the acting command was taken by the Child of the Waves."

"Egad! the young fellow hath reason," said Dr. McTaggart. "It never struck me before."

"But that's no stop, your honour," said Bill Bunt to our hero. "Just you order up a double share of grog, and we will christen you anything you please. You give it a name as to the drink, and we'll give you a name."

Spite of all the trouble which surrounded him, our hero could not help laughing at the oddness of the idea, and at once gave his consent.

The steward quickly appeared with the cans of grog, which the men were about to drink, when Jack Barnacle stopped them.

"Hold on, you lubbers. Ain't you got no better manners than to drink afore we've given our new skipper a name? I'm ashamed on yer. Where was you brought up? Not on board ship, I'll be sworn, but in some land-lubberly school.

"Now, here's my idea for the new skipper's name. He came on board in a breeze, he gave the foe a tidy breeze when our poor cap'en and luff came to grief, and I'll warrant he'll take us *out* of many a stiff breeze when the elements are angry, and into a stiff breeze with the foe again.

"He's just the lad to make us lots of fun in the way of fighting, and get us lots of prize money to kick up a breeze with when we go ashore. So I suggests—that is, if his honour is agreeable and willing—that he shall be known as Captain Breeze."

"Hurrah, hurrah for Captain Breeze!" shouted the men, and then tossed off their cans of grog.

"My lads," exclaimed our hero, "I am willing to accept your offer, and will act as your captain, until such time as Captain Ireton or Lieutenant Daulton can take the command. But remember this: although I am young, I am not to be played with.

"Still I am not one of those who dislike a joke, or any kind of innocent mirth. No, a light-hearted fellow always works better than a morose one; so do your duty, and then fiddle, dance and joke amongst yourselves as much as you like. *Only mind you do your duty first.* That done, you are, as far as can be compatible with duty, your own masters.

"Now the purser will give you each a stiff glass of grog; but I must ask you to give no more cheering, as you will disturb the wounded and sick."

"Then we'll give the cap'en one under our breaths," said Jack Barnacle.

And the men, waving their hats over their heads, whispered forth three hearty cheers, and then stole gently away below.

But the noise had disturbed Lieutenant Daulton, and he at once sent for our hero, who, of course, informed the lieutenant of all that had passed.

"The fellows could not have done better," said Daulton. "Besides, it was your place by right. Lord knows how soon I shall be out of my bunk, and able to do duty; and as for my lord—I mean Captain Ireton—I fear he will never be of much good."

"At all events, you can let me know whereabouts you would have me cruise, and what is the purpose of this expedition."

"The purpose of this expedition must remain a secret for the present. One day, when the Captain is well, I dare say he will let you know it, but I dare not. You know something about these pirates —their retreats and harbours ?"

"Of those I know little, or I might say nothing, for Captain Deveril would never permit me to go on shore. Still, I do know whereabouts they used to anchor their vessels and unload their plunder."

"Ah! that is something—a great deal, indeed. Well, Mr. Breeze, as that is to be your future name, your orders are simple enough. Chase this Deveril all over the world until you have driven him out of it. Spare not one of the cruel horde. *You* must know the cruel,

dastardly, bloodthirsty wretches they are."

"Indeed I do," said Captain Breeze, with a shudder. "I tell you, Mr. Daulton, that I have witnessed such horrible scenes on board the 'Firebrand,' that my heart is steeled against all mercy to Deveril and his fiendish crew. I have my own revenge to take. Fear not but that I will take it."

"Do so. Sail where you think best. If you want gold, draw for what you like. The captain would spend a hundred thousand pounds to capture that fellow Deveril, and swing him at the yard-arm. Now go; the wind is freshening up; and, from the state of the barometer, I think we shall have a gale before morning."

"Never fear, sir. I will see all snug," replied our hero.

CHAPTER VIII.

ON BOARD THE "FIREBRAND"—THE PIRATE VILLAGE—THE SPECTRAL LIGHTS ON THE LAKE.

As we said, the "Firebrand" had been terribly mauled about in the engagement; but she had not been so disabled as the "Sea Breeze," and therefore was able to take better advantage of the breeze that sprang up, and spreading her shot-torn canvas as well as she could, she sailed towards the north.

The killed were thrown overboard without the slightest ceremony; whilst the wounded were thrust into the cockpit, to be tended as well as could be by their unskilful comrades.

What repairs could be made whilst in full sail were quickly done, so that when the ship dropped anchor off a rocky island she looked pretty sound and seaworthy.

At the captain's orders the boats were lowered, the sick placed therein, and then the captain and chief mate entered, and the boat shoved off.

The men pulled in silence round a point of a rock, and then seemed to be making their way straight at the latter, but on nearer examination a low arch might be seen in the cliff; so low indeed, that as the boat shot under it the men had to stoop down until their

backs were almost on a level with the gunwale.

One or two, who were stretched upon their backs, forced the boat along with their hands, pressing against the roof and clutching any irregularities therein.

This arch ran through the rock for more than a hundred yards, and then the boat shot out into a beautiful lake surrounded by cliffs fully a thousand feet high.

No sooner did the boat appear on the placid waters than a shout arose, and from innumerable caves, hollowed out of the rock, came pouring a crowd of men, women and children.

A strange place this. It seemed as if nature had formed it for a pirate's stronghold.

The only apparent ingress to this lake was by the way we have described.

The rocks which surrounded the lake were of the most precipitous character.

The discovery of the lake was quite an accident, and came about this way—

Deveril, the pirate chief, had by some means been cast loose in a boat whilst sleeping.

Carried by the tide the boat had

drifted out at sea, and upon awaking he had found himself some miles from the rocky and uninhabited island, near which his ship had been moored for repairs.

He seized the oars, and pulled for the island.

The tide was running strongly against him, but he was a man of immense muscular power, and knowing that it was a case of life and death to him, he pulled with all his might.

But although the pirate captain managed to reach the island, the tide had carried him far off from the point where his ship had been moored ; and a storm coming on, his little boat was urged with resistless force on towards the inhospitable shore.

Thinking that his frail bark must be dashed to pieces, Deveril had thrown himself down at the bottom of his boat, giving himself up to despair.

Death he believed was near him. To escape the thought was impossible, and for the first time in his life *he believed in a future.*

But what could that future bring to him ?

Nothing but misery of the deepest kind. All hope of pardon had long since fled.

A false and treacherous friend ! A cruel foe ! A murderer ! A thief ! What hope of mercy had he ?

None !

As he raised his eyes, the white crested waves leaped up and hung over his boat, as if they were the ghosts of his victims gloating over his misery.

With a groan of the deepest despair he sank back almost insensible.

He was almost upon the rocks now. A huge wave took the boat and dashed it forward.

To Deveril's surprise there was no crash ; but he was hurried down a tunnel.

All was dark as night. He could almost fancy that he must be dead. Could death be so easy ?

Suddenly the boat shot out into the placid lake, which we have just described.

For some time Deveril remained in wonder, gazing upwards at the scud which flew over the stars.

Where could he be ?

The scene on such a night was terrible enough to make him believe that he was in another world.

But Deveril was not a man easily frightened, and he soon found out the truth of the case.

As morning broke he had landed at one of the many caves which pierced the rocks, and examined it carefully.

He soon discovered, by the structure of the rocks, that the whole island was nothing more than an exhausted volcano, which, after expending its fiery fury, had partly sunk into the sea. Time had clothed the outside of the mountain with mosses, grass, and trees, whilst the exhausted crater had been filled by the sea through the tunnel through which his boat had been so safely carried.

Deveril at once saw the advantages of the cave, and after examining it completely, once more entered his boat, passed through the tunnel, and having joined his ship, let his chief officers into the secret.

And here, in this natural stronghold, he had formed his chief rendezvous.

The sailors who joined him had to serve some years before they were admitted into this secret place ; and all those who had the secret revealed to them were bound by a fearful oath never to reveal it.

Such was the place where Captain Deveril and his crew landed, and were received with loud acclamations of joy by the inhabitants.

Passing them quickly by, Deveril made his way up some steps cut in the rock, and entered a large cave.

A cave, indeed ; but *such* a cave !

Over the mouth fell heavy velvet curtains, and the interior was furnished in the most magnificent style ; so that no London drawing-room could surpass it.

Having arrived at this place he threw himself into a handsome arm-chair, and struck a silver gong, which was instantly answered by a black slave.

" Is Gomez here ? " he demanded.

" Yez, massa, he came last night," replied the grinning negro.

" Good ! let him attend me instantly. See that a feast is spread in the banqueting hall, and when Gomez leaves me send Lucinda here."

" Yez, massa," answered the negro,

THE CHILD OF THE WAVES.

who seemed only too anxious to get out of Deveril's presence.

Springing from his seat, Captain Deveril paced up and down the cave in deep thought.

He was a tall, muscular, handsome man of about forty. But there was an evil look in his face, which made women shudder, and children run trembling from him.

If the old legend of the evil eye could be true, surely Captain Deveril had it, for he seemed to blast and ruin all good which came under his gaze, with the exception of two people who had defied his power. One was the Child of the Waves, the other Lucinda, a beautiful maiden, whom he had captured in a merchant vessel some years ago.

"Ah, Gomez," he exclaimed, as the officer he had sent for entered the cave. "What news have you?"

"Good! Two of our ships have come in laden with booty; here is the list."

"That is well; and where are the ships now?" demanded Deveril, as he took up the list and examined it.

"Gone south. They have heard, through our spies at Cape Sable, that a rich merchantman will sail from New Orleans in a little while, and they wish to intercept it."

"I wish they had waited my coming."

"You said you would be here three days earlier. They waited, and only started on the day you said."

"Gomez, you know my history? My *fate* has appeared at last."

"Ha! I am not good at riddles. Speak plainly, then I shall understand."

"I will. I have encountered *his* ship, the 'Sea Breeze.'"

"Humph!" muttered Gomez, in an uneasy manner; "but you—you conquered?"

"No."

"How? Not conquered! At all events you beat them off?"

"No. They beat me off."

"*That* is the first time that such a thing has happened to the 'Firebrand.' Where was *the boy*?"

"I told you my intention how to act to him if he refused to join us. He *did* refuse. We took a ship, bored holes in her hold, and nailed him to the mast."

"Ha, ha, ha! He's gone."

"Wait a moment. We saw the vessel sink—she struck some sunken rocks, I think. All the masts went by the board, and——"

"The boy was drowned. Good, good —very good. I always hated and dreaded him."

"Wait! Some time afterwards we met the 'Sea Breeze.' Our vessel gave the challenge. We fought. They boarded us. I swung the swivel-gun round. My deadly foe, who calls himself Ireton, was wounded. I sprung forward to complete the work so gallantly begun, when who should confront me but *the boy* Conrad!"

"Conrad!" exclaimed the other, staggering back. "I thought he was drowned."

"Aye! so I believed him. So he may be; for I know not whether it was his spirit or he had been saved. But there he was, sword in hand, to protect his—Ireton—you know—you know."

With a deep groan the pirate sank into a chair, covering his face with his hands.

For some moments Gomez seemed almost as much overcome as his chief.

Raising himself from the stupor the surprise had caused him, he went to a cabinet, and drew therefrom a flask of brandy and two goblets, which he filled to the very brim.

"Drink!" he said, as he thrust one into Deveril's hands. "That will give you courage."

"I need not courage to meet mortal man," said Deveril, as he took the goblet, "but if the dead can return——"

"They can't, or we should have lots of such visitors," replied Gomez, grimly. "Luckily, by my advice, the lad knows nothing of our secrets. Even his very name has been hidden from him. Who will believe a lad who does not know even his own name? Ha, ha, ha! Cheer up, captain. We will soon have the 'Firebrand' all trim and taut, and will blow the 'Sea Breeze' out of the water. Come, captain, let the men have a good feast, and they will be ready to meet the devil if need be."

"Go, see that it is prepared. If it be my fate to fall by *his* hand, I will at least give a good account of myself."

"That's right, captain, never say die. I warrant me *he's* gone, and a good job, too," he muttered, under his breath as he left the room; "for the captain would have made *him* second in command. Now *I* must be, and if I have the chance, it shall not be long before I am first in command."

Captain Deveril had fallen into a deep reverie, when he was aroused by a sweet, mournful voice saying—

"You sent for me, Captain Deveril. I have obeyed your orders, and am here."

Starting up the pirate beheld a lovely girl standing before him.

"So, Lucinda, you have come at last," he said, trying hard to conceal his agitation.

"It was but just now you sent for me," replied Lucinda, calmly.

"Lucinda, I have much to tell you. Sit down. You have already heard me say how I love you."

"I pray you speak no more of that," replied the girl, shrinking back.

"Listen, and interrupt me not. I am wealthy beyond many a prince. Jewels, plate, money are mine. All these I will lay at your feet if you will only become my wife."

"All the wealth in the world would not make me consent to such degradation. You boast of your wealth—that wealth has been purchased at the price of your soul. Nay! do not think to terrify me by your frowns. I fear you not. I am in your power. You may kill me, but you shall not break my spirit."

"Girl, are you mad to taunt me so? Beware! provoke me not too far, or I may use force——"

"Stand back!" cried Lucinda, as she drew a small glittering dagger from his belt, and held its point pressed to her bosom. "Dare but to place a finger on me, and I will plunge this dagger into my heart."

"Hold, hold, Lucinda! No, I would not have you hurt," cried Deveril. "Why will you treat me thus? Have I not promised that no harm shall come to you? Other captives have I had who would willingly have become the mistress of my heart and wealth. But I loved them not, and——"

"Murdered them!"

"Fire and fury, why wilt thou tempt me thus? But I will hear no more. Listen to me Lucinda: to thee have I shown such tenderness as never yet did I show to any living creature. I loved but once; but let that pass. She whom I loved was even as cruel as thou art. I swore revenge! A revenge so terrible that even I shuddered as I uttered it. But I did not shrink from the vow I had taken. She died, and her child— No, I will speak no more of this," he said, in a husky voice.

"And why? Surely such recollections must cheer such a heart as yours."

"Begone!" cried Deveril, passionately, "and see that you attend the banquet."

With a light laugh the girl turned upon her heel and bounded out of the cave.

"What madness is this?" muttered the captain of the pirates, as he paced up and down his room. Why has this girl such a power over me? I cannot tell. She alone of all human creatures hath made me feel afraid of the future. If she would love me; be mine, I would fly with her to some distant island, and try to atone for my past life—if it can be atoned for. Ha! what is that?"

He listened intently, and heard a hum of voices outside.

Deveril rushed from the cave, and discovered that all the sailors had gathered on the beach, looking in horror at the lake.

And well they might, for the surface of the water was covered with a strange and terrible appearance.

Floating hither and thither were strange blue flames of a most spectral character.

None of them were much more than three feet high, and to the superstitious sailors seemed to have the appearance of small spectres engaged in some weird dance.

"What is the meaning of this?" demanded Deveril hoarsely.

"I know not, captain," replied Gomez. "It can bode no good to us. I have heard tell of such things being seen in these seas—that is only one or two of the ghastly fires—and then wrecks are sure to strew the shores and storms to sweep the ocean. But I never heard of such a fearful sight as this."

"I can tell you," exclaimed Lucinda, stepping out of a cave. "They are the spirits of those unhappy creatures whom you have cruelly murdered. They stretch forth their hands, and call to heaven for vengeance. Be sure their prayers will be heard, and vengeance will fall upon your heads."

"Down with the witch! down with the witch!" cried the pirates, drawing their cutlasses, and rushing towards her.

Bravely Lucinda stood, facing her enemies.

"Strike," she cried, "and let me join with these spirits of your murdered victims to call down vengeance on you."

Their cutlasses were raised to strike, when Deveril sprang forward and with his sword warded off the blows.

"Ha!" he thundered, "dare you act without my orders? He who ventures to raise a finger against this maiden dies. To your room, Lucinda. Gomez, see that the men have good cheer for themselves, as such brave fellows deserve. See! the lights fade away. Bah! it is but some strange phenomenon, doubtlessly common enough in these volcanic regions. To the wine-cup, my boys. Drink and be merry, if to-morrow we die."

Seizing Lucinda by the wrists, he dragged her into the cave.

For one moment he gazed at her, his eyes glazed, his lips blue and drawn back, then tossing up his arms, he rushed away.

CHAPTER IX.

SHOWS HOW CAPTAIN BREEZE REFITTED HIS SHIP—TOUCHES AT JAMAICA, AND GOES IN SEARCH OF MORE MEN—A FIGHT IN THE DARK—BLACK BEN'S VOW OF VENGEANCE.

CAPTAIN BREEZE, the Child of the Waves, was now in actual command of the ship, and he determined that he would show the men that young as he might be he was worthy of the trust placed in him.

Some young fellows would have endeavoured to win the men's confidence by giving way to them; but not so the Child.

His method was to prove to them that he was a thorough seaman. He had all his commands carried out to the letter, and on the instant.

That done he cared not to stop the men's mirth, but rather encouraged them to be mirthful, so that they had become so fond of him that they would willingy have faced death to serve him.

Our hero knew perfectly well that Captain Deveril possessed a fleet of ships, each of which was called the "Firebrand," and built the same as the others.

Each vessel had a private signal known only by the commanders of the different "Firebrands," and then when they happened to cross each other at sea they would signal each other, and thus each would know who commanded the other vessel.

So, being fully aware of the capital organization of the pirate band, the Child knew that it would be no easy matter to overcome them, especially with the small force he had in hand.

Therefore he set about marking out a regular plan of action; the chief portion of which was to have the "Sea Breeze" thoroughly overhauled, her rigging well looked to, the number of her guns increased, and also her crew nearly doubled.

Besides these great additions, he determined to fill all the spare parts of the ship with spars of all sizes, so that after a combat at sea, he would be able to refit in a very little time.

To carry out these plans our hero altered the ship's course, and bore up for Kingston, Jamaica, where he also knew that he should be able to get extra medical skill for the captain and mate.

The "Sea Breeze" made a quick run of it, and under the skilful direction of our hero, she was soon all ataunto with her provisions and stores all on board, and as the Child of the Waves walked the white deck, and his eye wandered from the capstan, masts and spars, to the long row of bright guns, his heart leaped with delight, and his whole wish was to be once more in chase of the pirate.

But men were not so easily to be found as stores and cannon.

Somehow it had been rumoured that the "Sea Breeze" only attacked the pirates, and the sailors of Kingston, brave men as they were, knew that such combats, produced more knocks than prize-money, and they liked just the reverse.

So in spite of the large wages offered by our hero, the men only came slowly in.

Such was the state of matters on the evening when our hero was pacing the deck.

"I beg your honour's pardon," said Jack Barnacle, touching his hat as he walked up to our hero, "but I think it is time that we were fully manned."

"So do I, Barnacle," replied the Child, "but how are we to get manned? The sailors think of nothing but prize-money. They do not care for glory."

"I don't know quite so much of that, sir," replied the old man. "Still, it is only natural. You see the glory goes to the officers. Poll and Moll don't care a dump about honours. They ain't called 'my lady,' and taken to balls and parties. They're only made much of when Jack has come home with his pockets full of shiners to buy them fine ribbons and other trumpery, and to take them to the dances.

"But you hold, or rather the captain holds a Royal commission—this vessel sailing under letters of marque, so we have a right to press men."

"I do not like to press men," said our hero, impatiently. "They too often turn out wrong."

"No, I think not, sir; but there's another plan. Supposing you promise them prize-money, not only from the pirates—and if we find their hiding-places we shall make a splendid haul of it—but with the taking of French and American ships. That will fetch them. I've seen a lot of men hanging about, having a squint at the old barky, and she is a beauty and no mistake."

"Why do they not join, then?" demanded our hero, impatiently.

"You go to a rum shop with me, stand drink to the fellows, pitch 'em a yarn about the pirates' hidden treasure, also about the prize-money from the French and Yankee traders, and then stand more drink. I warrant me you will have your full complement of men to-night, and can twist the blue Peter and sail at daylight."

"You speak wisely. Get the boat ready. I will just go below and speak to the first lieutenant, and if he approves we will start at once."

Mr. Daulton listened patiently to all that our hero had to say, and then replied—

"Go on shore, my dear Breeze, and take Jack Barnacle with you. I can't go, and if I did I don't think I should be able to help you now one of my spars is shot away. Only take care that the rum doesn't get into your head, and look out for tricks."

"You need not fear, I shall keep sober, and let those beware who play tricks."

"Ah! but you may not know these fellows' tricks. Tell Barnacle to order six of our best hands to follow you in couples at a distance, so that they may enter the drink shop as if they did not belong to you. Now go, lad, and may heaven protect you. I shall crawl up on deck and see all right."

"Thank you, sir," cried the Child as he hurried away to his cabin.

Quickly changing his uniform for a thick pea-jacket, blue serge trousers, and a straw hat, he armed himself with a heavy cutlass, and a brace of pistols.

Then hastening on deck he gave Barnacle his orders about the boat and men.

In a little time all was ready, and our hero stepped into the stern sheets.

"Give way, men!"

The oars fell into the water with a slight splash, and Captain Breeze was swiftly pulled to the shore.

The night had now closed in, and the town of Kingston was all life and fun.

Directed by Barnacle, our hero made his way to one of the lowest parts of the town, and entered a drinking shop, from whence came loud sounds of laughter, the clinking of glasses, and sea songs, roared out in voices far more strong than sweet.

Entering a long low room, lighted by some candles stuck in a hoop suspended from the ceiling, our hero found some fifty sailors drinking and smoking at long deal tables, in company with their sweethearts.

For some time the conversation seemed to flag after Captain Breeze's arrival, so taking some silver from his pocket, he threw it down on the table as he called out—

"Come, lads, don't let my entrance stop your mirth. I am a sailor, and like to see all sailors happy. What ho! landlord, take this money and bring in as much punch as it will purchase. To-morrow at dawn I shall be on the seas, seeking for adventure, and it may be many a day before I come back; but when I do return it shall be with ingots of gold and bags of jewels to treat the lassies. Come, lads, come, here is the grog. Drink without fear, for I have a few more shiners in my pocket, and there is plenty more grog where that came from. Let us drink to our sweethearts and wives."

"Our sweethearts and wives," shouted the men, tossing off their grog.

"Pardon me," said a black-visaged fellow, who with some half-dozen others was seated at a small table at the darkest end of the room. "Pardon me, your honour, but if I am not mistaken you belong to the 'Sea Breeze,' now laying out in the roads?"

"You are quite right, my man, and a more taut little craft does not sail the ocean."

"Maybe. I've nought to say against that," replied the fellow. "All I say is, if she runs across Captain Deveril—or Captain Devil, as some folks call him—they are not likely to get much prize money. I have been in a fight with that fiend, and had to walk the plank. Luckily I got on a piece of rock, and was picked up after being nigh upon twenty-four hours in the water. I know him, and have had enough of him. I do not want monkey's allowance—more kicks than halfpence."

A murmur of assent ran round at this, the sailors agreeing with the last speaker.

"Tut! We had a brush with the fellow and beat him off. Made him run for it. If we had only been half as well armed as we are now, we would have brought the 'Firebrand' in here as a prize."

"That you will never do," said the man, in a most emphatic manner.

"How do you know that, my friend? You seem very decided on the point."

"I am decided on the point; for I know Captain Deveril has sworn to blow up his ship, himself, and his crew before he will surrender. I heard that when I was his prisoner."

"Well, let him blow his ship up. The sooner the better for honest men; but he cannot blow up the vast treasure he has in the rocky island, in the Caribbean Sea, or in the Barata."

The stranger made no reply, but Captain Breeze fancied he muttered an oath.

"But are there these vast hoards of treasure, sir?" asked one of the sailors, eagerly.

"Of course there are. What has become of the enormous wealth they have taken from Spanish and American traders, not to mention our own? Ay! or for that matter from any ship, friend or foe, weaker than themselves. Part is, of course, spent and passed away through their agents; but the largest part is buried in caves, of which I have a good clue."

"Bah!" said the surly man in the corner, "it's easy to say that. Wait until you do get the treasure."

But the speech of Captain Breeze had made some impression on the men, and a great deal on the women, who at once began to persuade the men to join the "Sea Breeze," and to plunder the pirates.

"But is it true, sir, that the 'Sea Breeze' means only to make war on the pirates?"

"Aye!" interrupted the surly one, "the captain of the 'Sea Breeze' has a spite against Captain Deveril, and that's because Deveril cut him out in a love affair I have heard."

"You seem to know a great deal of Captain Deveril's affairs," said Captain Breeze.

"I think most sailors in this part do. But it doesn't matter a shot to me. Join if you like, lads. The ship is a good ship, and will only be beaten after hard fighting."

"If she does not come out the conqueror," laughed our hero. "But hard fighting is a joy to a true sailor. Besides, this cruise I mean to have a slap at the French and Yankees, and I warrant me the 'Sea Breeze' will bring many a good prize into this port."

"Why, if so be that that is to be the case, and that you mean regular privateering," cried a sailor, "I'll sign articles to-night; for I'm real cleaned out—not a shot in my locker, and shiver my timbers if I don't like the cut of your jib, your honour. You have the right voice and eye for a sailor. Here's my hand on it. I'll go with you."

"Right, honest fellow. Here is half-a-guinea to drink my health with," cried Breeze.

This was too much for some twenty of the sailors, who at once pressed forward, and pledged their honour to come on board, and were every one of them anxious to "drink his honour's health;" but the surly man and his companions did not move, whilst the men of the 'Sea Breeze' noticed that the other sailors were most anxious to press these men not to join their ship.

Pleased with getting so many men to join him, our hero drew forth a bag of gold with which he had provided himself in case of such a chance, and at once began dealing out the money—it must be confessed in rather a careless manner.

The last man had just received his money, and Captain Breeze was about to call upon the others to come forward like men to join in a glorious cruise, instead of idling their time on shore, when the sharp crack of a pistol was heard, and instantly the string holding the hoop, on which were stuck the candles was cut, and the whole fell to the ground, and the lights being extinguished, the whole party was left in complete darkness.

"Men of the 'Sea Breeze' gather round your chief," shouted Barnacle. "Look out, Captain Breeze, we have got amongst the sharks. Stick together, lads, and fight to the door."

Yells, screams, the clash of steel, the quick reports of pistols, echoed through the darkened room.

Tables were overturned, forms smashed, and bottles and glasses used as weapons.

Placing his back to the wall, our hero guarded himself as well as he could with his cutlass, but he would not strike because he could not tell friend from foe.

As he tried to move towards the door, his foot kicked against something.

Instantly he stooped down and seized it, and to his joy found it was part of a torch.

Drawing himself under a table to shield him from the blows, he proceeded to light it.

Then springing up, and holding the torch aloft, he cried in a loud voice—

"Now, my lads of the 'Sea Breeze,' forward and do your duty. We can see our foes, and will let them know what we are made of."

"Hurrah!" shouted the men, and then paused in surprise, for they discovered that the men who had commenced the disturbance had all disappeared through a small window, with the exception of the surly man, and he, holding the shutters of the casement, which opened outwards, stood glaring in at them.

"You have baulked me now," he cried, as he shook his fist at Captain Breeze; "but you do not bear a charmed life, and the next time I help to nail you to the mast I will see that my cutlass is driven through your heart."

"'Tis Black Ben, the boatswain of the 'Firebrand,'" cried our hero, in surprise.

"You've hit it my lad," laughed the ruffian, "and here's my last present to you."

As he spoke he suddenly drew a pistol from his belt, and fired at Captain Breeze.

Luckily the bullet passed close to our hero's ear, burrying itself in the wall.

Seizing a pistol from Barnacle, Captain Breeze returned the shot, but could not tell with what effect, as Black Ben, at the same instant as the pistol was discharged, slammed to the shutters.

"Quick! lads; follow me," cried Breeze, as he dashed to the door. "We may still overtake them."

But not only was the door fastened securely by the lock, but the key was gone.

They knocked loudly and called for the landlord, but no one came.

"Barnacle," cried Breeze, "take a couple of hands and burst open the door."

No sooner was the order given than the old sailor had sent the door crashing.

Out rushed the seamen, determined to have revenge for what they looked upon as a stop to what was about to be a very pleasant evening—that is, one with plenty of rum and dances.

"THE LITTLE WRETCH MADE A STAB AT THE CAPTAIN."

Crash! and over went several forms and buckets, which had been placed in the passage, from which all light had disappeared.

"Take care, my lads," cried Breeze; "there is treachery here, so move with caution."

So they forced their way to the bar, where they found the negro landlord and landlady, surrounded with their servants—also natives of Africa—on their knees."

"Oh! golly, massa cap'en. Am de end ob de world come?" shrieked the negro.

"Get up, you black thief, and answer the captain properly," said Barnacle, as he gave the negro a kick of no gentle nature, making him howl with pain.

"Have mercy! have mercy! massa pirate captain, an' don't for to go to murder my ole man," cried the landlady.

"Pirate captain! you old black doll. What do you mean by that? We are none of your thievish pirates, so look up," cried Barnacle.

But the negroes set up a fearful chorus of howls, and would not listen to reason, so that our hero was about to give up all questioning in despair, when Jack Barnacle cried—

"I'll bring their dusky brains back from wool-gathering, and here's the thing to do it with."

Seizing a thick pimento stick, which he happened to see in a corner, he applied it with a will to the negro's broad shoulders.

Up sprang the negro with a howl, and would have run at Barnacle and stabbed him with a knife, only the sailor was too quick for him, and drawing quickly back, swung his pimento stick round, giving a leg cut.

This he did with such dexterity that the heavy stick cut across that most delicate part of a negro's anatomy—his shins, bringing him down to the ground roaring and yelling with pain.

"Now, you murdering ruffian, what do you mean?" demanded Barnacle, as he picked up the knife. "Get up, all of you, or I'll make each of you dance to the music of my stick on your shins."

The threat was quite enough.

Up sprang all the negroes, and began to jabber away like mad, so that nothing could be understood of what they said.

By Captain Breeze's orders the whole place was searched in the strictest manner.

Not a sign of the pirates could be found, whilst the negroes, more pacified, declared that they had believed the pirates honest sailors like the rest.

At this the sailors of the "Sea Breeze" were so indignant, that had it not been for Captain Breeze they would have set the inn on fire at once, and in their passion, even he might not have been able to check them; only, fortunately, one of the military patrols having been informed of the disturbance came round to the place.

Captain Breeze instantly informed the officer in command of what had happened.

"Humph! that confirms what I have already heard," said the officer.

"Indeed!" cried Captain Breeze, anxiously, "is there a report about the pirates?"

"Yes; the 'Firebrand' is said to be cruising between this and Cuba."

"In that case the ship must have put into one of the creeks north of this island."

"I doubt not but such is the case. On my return I shall report the matter to the commandant, who, I have no doubt will at once order out a battery of artillery, and some infantry to attack them from the shore, whilst one of the gun-boats will attack them from the sea."

Captain Breeze thought to himself—

"Much obliged for the news, Mr. Lieutenant, but if the 'Sea Breeze' is not beforehand with you it shall not be my fault."

"Will you go and report this case?" asked the young lieutenant.

"No; none of my men are badly wounded, the pirates have all escaped, and I am in a hurry to get to sea. To report would do no good——"

"Except shutting up that house of Dark Sambo's. It is one of the worst in Jamaica; but I'll keep my eye upon him. Take my advice, and watch all the men pressed from that place. They are sure to turn out bad, and now good-night, sir."

"Good-night, sir, and many thanks for your service and advice, the latter of which I shall not neglect, you may be sure. Good-night," and, bowing low, our hero hurried away.

CHAPTER X.

THE "SEA BREEZE" PUTS TO SEA—BARNACLE MAKES A GRAVE MISTAKE THROUGH
OVER ANXIETY—THE HURRICANE—A CRUEL SHOT—"WHAT'S THAT?"

No sooner did Captain Breeze arrive on board with his new hands—only half, or a little over, turning up, the rest having "sheered off," as Barnacle called it—than he hurried down to the lieutenant and reported what had happened.

"Never mind the men, my boy, although you have done well in securing so many. Clap them on the ship's books directly, and then get the anchor apeak and all sails set. Egad! if we overhaul her I'm hanged if I don't get up and have a slap at the foe."

"Never fear; if we do overhaul him he shall not escape so easily this time," laughed our hero, as he hurried on deck to give his orders.

There was no reason to call the men on deck, all were too anxious for the work.

A south-easterly breeze was blowing rather freshly over the sea, and having seen that the officers were in their proper stations, the captain gave the orders.

They were sharply given, and instantly obeyed.

The topsails came to the mastheads, and in a minute the sails were set.

Then the windlass was manned, and the chain cable came up with a clank.

A few hearty heaves, and the anchor was soon at the catheads. The head-yard was filled away, and the gallant ship began to glide through the water.

Onward sped the vessel: the night dark and without moon or stars, but the sea calm.

All eyes were turned anxiously to the coast in hopes of getting the first glimpse of the "Firebrand." Even old Barnacle did not take his usual glance at the horizon.

Our hero had been below, consulting his charts and preparing for the action, and now came up the companion-way with his night-glass in his hand, and with that peculiar, listless movement most men have when they have done all they can do, and must wait patiently until they see the result.

Suddenly his face became alarmed as he gazed out astern, where he perceived what appeared to be a dark cloud coming upon the wind.

"For heaven's sake, Mr. Barnacle," he roared out, "give the word to take in sail. Do you not see there is a hurricane coming upon us?"

The old sailor perceived his error, and in less than no time all hands had tumbled upon deck; and in a very short time most of the sails that had been set a little while before were taken in, but not all of them; and when the tempest struck the ship it ripped these sails into pieces, and heeled the vessel over nearly on her beam ends.

The wind blew fiercely, the sea rose in mountains. The heavens were ablaze with lightning, whilst the thunder kept up one deafening roar.

Wave after wave dashed over the ship, so that every man had to cling to the rigging and ringbolts.

Everybody was drenched to the skin in an instant.

"Thank heaven!" shrieked Breeze into Barnacle's ear, "the mast still stands it."

The old man made no reply, but shook his head mournfully.

"She has righted now, and bears up beautifully; but if the tempest lasts, no one can tell what may happen."

"We have no other chance, sir, than to keep her afore the wind," replied the old sailor. "If the lightning doesn't strike us it will do us good, for it shows us sometimes the state of things. Look here, sir, if that ain't Mr. Daulton yonder."

Sure enough there stood the one-armed lieutenant, holding hard on to the mizen-mast.

"This is madness," cried our hero. "I will go to him and make him go below."

"Hold hard, sir, for heaven's sake," yelled Barnacle. "Look out for this sea."

Captain Breeze had only time to throw

himself down on the deck and cling to one of the guns, when a fearful sea broke right over the vessel, deluging her decks with water, and making her tremble like a frightened horse.

As the water rushed off to leeward, a fearful flash of lightning lit up the desolate scene.

"Man overboard! It's Mr. Daulton," cried a man who had lashed himself to a gun close where the lieutenant had been standing only an instant before.

"Hold firmly to the end of this rope," cried Breeze, as he lashed one end of a coil of thin rope round his waist. "Stand by, Barnacle, and I will save him."

Before Barnacle could prevent him, our hero had leaped over the gunwale into the raging sea.

"Lord help him! he's gone," sighed the old man, as he quickly belayed the rope round a cleat. "Gone, and all my fault. Why couldn't the sea have taken on old man like me instead of a gallant young fellow just in the prime of life? Cut off like— No, it is he pulling on the rope. Quick! some of you help me to haul in our young captain."

In spite of the fearful risk they all ran, the fellows dashed forward, and in a few seconds had hauled Captain Breeze, who held Mr. Daulton in his arms, upon deck.

The lieutenant was insensible, but Breeze seemed really and truly a child of the waves; for he shook himself and sprang to his feet almost the instant his feet touched the deck.

"Hurrah! hurrah! for the Child of the Waves," shouted Barnacle.

And the men took the cry up with hearty goodwill

Scarcely had the cheering ceased than the report of a gun was heard, and a large cannon ball flew between the mizen and mainmasts, fortunately doing no harm.

"What on earth can that be?" cried the men in terror, for they could not believe it a cannon ball reaching them in such a storm.

"It is the pirate," shouted our hero. "Keep her head a little more to the wind. She must be running the same course as we are doing, and by this move we shall have the weather gauge of her, so that when this hurricane clears off, which I hope it will soon do, for the storms in this region cease almost as suddenly as they begin, we shall be able to run her down."

The men met this with a hearty cheer, and Barnacle proposed that they should fire a shot or two in the direction from whence the other had come, to try and hit the privateer.

"By no means," cried Breeze. "We might hit and sink some vessel in distress. It is only such cowardly and bloodthirsty men as the pirates who would do such a thing."

The storm seemed to have spent most of its force when the lieutenant was washed overboard, for gradually it swept away, the rain ceased, the wind fell, and the dense mist or fog was pierced by the beautiful rising moon.

Quickly the men were sent aloft to cut away the torn sails, and to make all snug for the night; for our hero rightly considered that the men would require rest after the fatigue of the storm, and so determined not to bend fresh sails till the morning.

But though the men were placed in their respective watches, he could not sleep.

In company with Jack Barnacle, who remained sadly silent, only now and then muttering that he deserved to be seized up to the gratings and receive a good round dozen, and then be dissected and put before the mast for not seeing the storm in time to save all the trouble.

The moon was now riding through the flying scud, shedding its silver light on all around.

Our hero had just been trying to console Barnacle, when turning round to come aft they paused, and pointing in that direction, with bated breath, both whispered, "WHAT'S THAT?"

CHAPTER XI.

DAVEY DUMP, THE DEFORMED DWARF—IS IT A SEA MONSTER?—DR. M'TAGGART REFUSES
TO EXPERIMENTALISE ON, OR BE EXPERIMENTED ON BY IT—"SAIL, HO!"

WELL might our hero and his companion exclaim "What's that?" for the object they beheld was horrible to a degree.

Was it human?

If not, it must be some hideous, distorted goblin come from the sea.

Slowly it crawled over the taffrail, glanced quickly to see if the man at the wheel had heard him, raised his head slowly, gazed at the moon, and then stole with a cat-like tread under one of the gun covers, where he concealed himself.

This strange figure had on its head a striped cotton night cap, and a pair of coarse canvas drawers or trousers reaching from the waist, where it was securely fastened, to the knees.

Not another garment did the little wretch have to cover his hideous body.

The head was large, and covered with matted hair of a bright red colour.

The forehead low, the eyebrows burly, and hanging over two deeply set and corpse-like eyes.

A nose flattened on his face, across which it seemed to spread almost to touch two large, sharp and pointed ears.

His mouth was one large gash, with thin, blue lips, so drawn back as to show large, fang-like teeth.

The shoulders and bust would have suited a Hercules, and become a giant, much better than this horrible little object, which did not stand more than three feet ten high.

But even the bust was spoiled by being covered with tufts of reddish hair, as were his long, ungainly arms and hands, reaching nearly down to his ankles, and his short bowed legs, scarcely twelve inches long, and his huge webbed, splay feet.

"What can it be?" whispered old Barnacle. "It must be some horrid sea monster."

"Not a bit of it, Barnacle. Sea monsters don't wear caps and trousers."

"How do you know? Asking your honour's pardon, did you ever see a merman?"

"No, nor anyone else; but I must confess I do not like the looks of the creature."

"If it ain't David Jones himself, it must be his baby," said Barnacle, sturdily.

"David Jones or not David Jones, he does not sail aboard this ship unless I know something more about him, so here goes," said Captain Breeze.

Stealing quietly up to the gun, our hero plucked off the cover suddenly.

In an instant the little wretch had sprung to his feet, plucked a knife from his waistband, and made a stab at the captain, which he had great difficulty in guarding.

Fortunately he was able to knock the little monster's arm up, and seizing his wrist, wrenched the knife away from him."

"You hideous little scoundrel," he cried, "from whence do you come, and what do you do here?"

At first the ugly dwarf struggled with all his might to release himself, and made several well-directed attempts to bite his captor—no joke with such formidable teeth, but our hero kept him off, and threatened him that unless he desisted, he would have him put into irons and flogged and thrown overboard.

Then the little wretch became perfectly quiet, and looking up at Captain Breeze, smiled. Oh! such a smile! One terrible to look upon, fearful to dream about.

By this time Barnacle had gathered the part of the watch, whose duty was not too particular to prevent them leaving their posts, around the strange creature, whom they all examined with disgust and wonder.

"Now, my man," said Captain Breeze, as kindly as he could, "where do you come from?"

"Down — dare — the sea," and he nodded his head in that direction.

"There, your honour, I told you as 'ow he was a merman," cried Barnacle.

"Avast there, mate," said Bill Bunt;

"he can't be a merman, he ain't got a tail."

"How do you know that? Mayn't he have it down his trousers, or coiled up behind?"

"He smells fishy enough for it," laughed Captain Breeze. "Come, my lad, you do not *live* in the sea."

The monster shook his head, and grinned and pointed towards the west.

"He lives in Mexico," said Dr. McTaggart. "I have often heard that the original people who inhabited that country were a deformed race, scarcely equal, if not inferior, to beasts and reptiles, and——"

But the doctor stopped his learned discourse, and sprang behind Barnacle for protection; for on hearing this remark about his beauty, the monster broke from the captain, and made a dash at the learned doctor, at the same time gnashing his teeth in a way highly suggestive of cannibalism.

"Here, hold off, you bit of fishified human nature," cried Barnacle, "or I'll strangle you."

"Do, do! It is nothing human; it is a freak of nature, and ought to be killed," cried the doctor.

"Not a bit of it, doctor. You wished to experimentalise on this young gentleman, and he wanted to do the same on you. But, come here, my man. Don't you pretend not to understand English, for you have plainly shown that you have understood what we have said."

"Hang me if that ain't both sense and logic, like a double-shotted gun," said Bunt.

"Now," continued the captain, "tell me, where do you live?"

"On a rock, dare, in de middle of the sea," grunted the boy.

"Well, if he ain't a marine monster, I'm a Dutchman," exclaimed one of the men.

"Now, my man, I will have no nonsense. Answer me truly."

"I have. In a cave—very big rock. I go sleep on rock, tempest come and wash me in the sea."

"If that is true, how is it you are not drowned?" asked the captain.

"Because I can swim. Davey Dump swim miles in any sea."

"I believe it," cried Dr. McTaggart, who had not yet got over his fright.

"So the best thing we can do is to throw the little monster back into the sea."

This was too much even for the sailors, and they burst out laughing.

"Stay, doctor," said our hero, with a sly wink. "Do you not think that such a rare specimen of the freaks of Nature as this should be preserved carefully for the sake of science?"

"No, no; most certainly not. He bites, and is dangerous. Certainly do not preserve him."

"Not in a large cask of rum, so that you could make him a present to the College of Surgeons, and lecture on him if we should return to England?"

"Well, really, I do think that might be done. Or show him alive, and——"

"Or run a pin through him, stick him on a card, and send him to the British Museum."

The subject of these pleasant remarks scowled on all, and gnashed his teeth.

"Come, come, Mr. Davey Dump, if that be your name, we will have no more of that," said the captain. "You come on board my ship, hide yourself, and when discovered try your hardest to stab me. Then you tell us falsehoods, and try to bite our worthy doctor."

"I tell no falsehoods," growled the dwarf. "I am Davey Dump, they call me so. *They are kind.*"

"They! Who are they? I do not understand what you mean. Explain."

"Men like you, with big ships. Men who come to get water from the rock, and see my mother."

"His mother! Well, I guess she must be a beauty, anyway," said one of the sailors.

"Do you know how to steer a ship home?" demanded the captain, eagerly.

A quick, shrewd look seemed to come into the creature's eyes as he glanced up and answered—

"No; don't know where I am. Might know the rock if I saw it."

"Humph! I don't quite like the looks of this fellow," whispered the captain to the doctor, who had crept round behind him.

"Like him! I should think you did not. Pitch him overboard."

"No; he had better be taken down in one of the berths," began the captain, when a cry from the crew arose.

"He shan't sleep in my berth. I know that," cried one, indignantly.

"Nor in mine! or mine! or mine!" said the others.

Here was another fix. What was to be done now?

"Hark you, my fine fellow," said the captain. "You came on board without asking me. So I feel perfectly justified in keeping you here as long as I like. Do you object to stay?"

"No, if you treat me well. If you don't, I'll——," and here he gnashed his teeth.

"Well, as you have stated yourself that you have lived on a rock, it can be no great hardship for you to sleep under the forecastle; and as your temper appears so sweet, I think, for everyone's comfort, you should be chained up there to a ring bolt. You shall have plenty to eat and drink. Do you object to that?"

"No; I'm hungry. I'm thirsty, and I am cold."

"Then come along," said our hero.

The deformed creature permitted himself to be secured with a chain to a ring bolt, and actually clutched at the sails to warm him as if they had been the greater comforts.

Then a plate of meat and bread was placed before him.

He seized the meat, and holding it in his hands, tore it with his teeth, but the bread he threw aside.

The meat despatched, a good jorum of stiff grog was handed to Davey, who at once tossed it off. Letting out a grunt of satisfaction, he coiled himself upon a sail, dragged another right over him, and appeared to go to sleep at once.

"Phew!" whistled Barnacle, "blest if I don't think he is civilised, after all, by the way he drank that grog off."

"I don't know what he is," said Bill Bunt, "but I guess he has made a change in the fortunes of this ship, either for good or bad. Mark my words, and see if I am right."

Just at that moment the men at the masthead gave out the welcome cry—

"Sail, ho!"

CHAPTER XII.

PURSUIT OF "FIREBRAND" NUMBER TWO—EXCHANGE OF SHOTS—A CRUEL AND DESPERATE DEED—A SCENE OF HORRORS.

"SAIL, HO!" What a thrill the sounds sends through every man-of-war man's heart.

The words speak to him of gallant battle, and of prize money.

He thinks little that in the "death-dealing battle" he may lose his life. He has been used to dangers, and cares not for them.

Need we say that every eye was stretched in the direction given by the look-out as that in which the ship was.

"What is she like?" demanded Captain Breeze, hailing the look-out.

"She's like—," began the man, and then stopped. "From what I can make of her, sir, she's the 'Firebrand.'"

A general shout of joy arose from the crew, and Captain Breeze, seizing his telescope from one of the midshipmen, ran up the rigging until he could get a good view of the vessel.

For some moments he watched the ship without speaking, and then closing the glass with a snap, came quickly down to the deck without saying a word.

"Well, your honour," said Jack Barnacle, anxiously, "what is she like?"

"What is she like, Mr. Barnacle?" said Breeze, quietly. "Why she is like the 'Firebrand!'"

"But is she the 'Firebrand?'"

"Most assuredly if we take her we shall find her called the 'Firebrand,' but she is not the 'Firebrand' we are after. However, we shall give chase, so please, Mr. Barnacle, to see the decks cleared for action, and make all sail, whilst I go down to see if Lieutenant Daulton has any orders to give."

"Ay, ay, sir," replied Barnacle, and placing his boatswain's whistle to his lips, he blew some shrill notes.

"Mr. Barnacle," roared Captain Breeze, standing on the companion-ladder, do you forget that you are a lieutenant and not an officer."

"Ay, ay, sir," growled the discomfited ex-boatswain, as he put up his whistle, and then he muttered to himself, "smash my skylights if I shall ever be able to forget the boatswain, and remember I'm a hofficer.

"All hands make sail.

"Let stunsails low and aloft.

"Shake all the reefs out."

Sail after sail was soon spread out, until the gallant ship flew through the sea, making the foam hiss and fly round her sharp bows.

"We are nearing her fast," said Captain Breeze, as he watched the other vessel.

"Yes, sir," said Barnacle, "but what is she doing now? She's taking in sail. Hooray! she's going to fight."

"Mr. Barnacle, would you kindly remember that you *are* an officer on the quarter-deck?"

"I'll try, sir, but it's werry hard to a man who has been so many years a boatswain."

"Mr. Bunt, Mr. Bunt," cried our hero, "what are you doing there?"

The cause of this exclamation was, that Bill Bunt, forgetting that he was an officer, had stripped himself down to the waist, and was serving the guns as he had done when he was a gunner.

"Ay, ay, sir," shouted the gunner, "we are all ready for 'em. I double-shotted the guns."

"That was the office of Mr. Smith. You are a quarter-deck officer."

"Lor! so I be," said the gunner as he scratched his head. "Here, one of you fellows, help me on with my jacket, and look here, Mr. Smith, look well to them three guns."

"She is trying our rate of sailing," Captain Breeze said, "and he finds that we are too strong for her. Fire a gun, and run up our colours."

This was done, the gunner noticing well where the shot fell, so that he might tell when the vessel would be within range.

"Bang!"

The other ship returned the shot in defiance, and then a black ball—or rather what seemed like one—was run up to the mast head.

As it touched the track it slowly unfurled itself to the wind, and showed a large black flag, on which was embroidered a flaming torch or firebrand, so ingeniously wrought that the flare of fire close by the torch represented a skull, the flames and smoke appearing like flowing hair."

"It *is* the 'Firebrand,'" shouted a number of the men.

"Order," cried our hero, sternly.

"Is it the 'Firebrand,' sir?" asked Barnacle, humbly; for this proof of our hero standing no nonsense had worked a good effect upon the crew all round.

"I have told you it is the 'Firebrand,' but not the one commanded by the pirate Deveril. But we will have her. She cannot outsail us, and we will never leave her until we have sunk or captured her."

Rapidly the two ships cut through the water, but it was evident the "Sea Breeze" beat the other vessel on whatever tack she went, and the pirate captain tried all he could to escape.

At last, finding escape hopeless, he bore up for some small rocky islands, about a league and a half distant.

"What on earth can the fellow be after?" muttered our hero. "He must know that these islands cannot be approached by a ship within a mile, owing to the coral reefs.

"Stay, those are the islands that Deveril used to steer for after he had taken a rich prize, and then I was always imprisoned in the cabin until the ship was well out to sea again. There is some mystery here which I must see to. Mr. Smith, are we within range yet?"

"I think we are, sir."

"Then give her one of our long bow-chasers, and fire high, to see if you can carry away some of her spars," cried Captain Breeze.

The gun was trained with great care, and at the word "fire!" a bright flash shot from the prow of the ship, a fearful explosion, and then a dense cloud of smoke was blown over the sea.

All eyes were turned to see what damage, if any, had been done to the foe.

She was still dancing merrily over the sea, but the men were busy doing something to one of her gunwales, showing that the shot had told on the hull instead of the rigging.

"Hurrah! my lads," cried the captain, "we are within range of her. Now keep up the game."

But the "Firebrand," although not inclined to fight, was certainly not willing to receive the iron compliments which were being poured into her without *some* return; and, therefore, replied with good aim from her long swivel gun, with which she managed to kill several of the crew of the "Sea Breeze," besides doing no little damage to her hull.

"Confound it," cried Captain Breeze, as he leaped forward, "cannot some of you silence that gun? Stand on one side, and let me train the gun. I warrant I make it tell."

The men drew respectfully on one side, and the gun was trained by our hero with great care.

"When you are ready, sir, just give the word, and I will apply the match," said Bunt, who had once more forgotten his promotion, and was all anxiety to play the gunner.

"Steady! Wait until the ship rises! Steady! Fire!"

A terrific explosion followed, for both ships had fired at the same time, and both with success.

Captain Breeze had remained stooping, so that he might the quicker see the effect of the shot.

The smoke soon rising, he saw that his shot had been so well aimed that it had dismounted the swivel gun, and killed at least a dozen of the crew.

"Hurrah, my brave men! we have silenced that piece of metal at all events," cried Breeze.

"And the bit of metal they sent us would have silenced your honour, had you raised your head; for it passed within a foot of you. As it is, it has done enough mischief."

"Mischief! where?" exclaimed Captain Breeze, looking round in horror.

"There, your honour," said the man, and to his amazement Captain Breeze beheld Bunt dead.

"Dead!" he gasped.

"Yes, your honour. The shot passed over you, and struck him full in the chest."

"Let him be carried below," said Captain Breeze in a tremulous voice. "He was a good friend to me, who never had but one friend until I came on board this ship."

For a moment he covered his face with his hands, and the sailors noticed that the hot tears started in his eyes.

A womanly act, some men may say, but the sailors did not think so, and from that moment the Child of the Waves became, to most of them, a greater favourite than before.

It was only a momentary weakness, for in a few seconds he had dashed the tear-drops away, and with eyes flashing with fire had again addressed himself to the men.

"Lads, stick to your guns!

"Remember that every shot will be so much towards avenging the death of an honest man, and bringing confusion on those blood-thirsty rascals."

"Mr. Smith," he continued, turning to the gunner, "fire high. We must have that ship, and I fear she knows some creek into which she can sail, and for which we draw too much water; therefore, cripple her, and you shall have five pounds for every spar that falls.

"All right, your honour, trust to me," cried the gunner. "Bear a hand, there, and we'll soon let 'em know the game we are arter."

And now the bow-chasers kept up a perfect roar, which was replied to by the pirate with two small guns which they managed to bring aft.

But the wind falling suddenly the smoke hung about the ships. A perfect veil was thus drawn up between them, so that neither could tell the exact position of the other.

"Cease firing, there," cried the captain. We cannot see where to aim. The wind is sure to freshen up in a minute. Double shot the guns, so as to be able to pour in a good salute when the smoke blows off."

Anxiously the men waited for the smoke to rise, so that the battle might be renewed.

"Here comes the wind at last," cried Captain Breeze. "Now, then, keep a sharp look-out, and be ready with——

"Down with the helm! Stand by the royal halyards; hands aloft, clew up royals, lay out there and furl them."

In an instant all hands were busily at work; not in trying to heap destruction on the pirate ship, but to save their own, for on the smoke rising, Captain Breeze found that his ship had drifted close upon a coral reef—so close that it seemed impossible that she could be saved.

As to the pirate ship, her doom was settled, for as the vessel wore round she went crashing upon the rocks.

So close were the two vessels that the crews could plainly see each other's faces.

The captain of the pirate vessel leaped up in the rigging and uttered a shout of defiance.

"So ho," he cried, "you are not dead. Nailed to a mast and thrown into the sea, you have escaped. What ho, there! give them a broadside as our parting salute!"

"Down on your faces all of you," thundered the Child of the Waves, and only just in time: for scarcely had the men touched the deck than a hail of iron from the "Firebrand" came sweeping over them, cutting away some of the standing rigging, and splinting some of the spars.

"Up, boys, and give them *our* parting salute," shouted Captain Breeze, who alone had stood up, and strange to say, was unwounded by even a splinter.

"I know you, Walter Savage," he cried, turning to the pirate captain, and if you *do* escape, and your patron saint, the Father of Sins, *may* save you, tell Captain Deveril that I am alive, well, and happy; that I have taken two oaths: one that I will discover the mystery which hangs over my birth, the other that I will never rest until I have destroyed every 'Firebrand' in the sea.

"Fire!"

A fearful crash! for the "Sea Breeze" had poured a broadside into the devoted vessel, which she could not approach to board because of the breakers.

The smoke hid the "Firebrand" some moments from their view; but the awful shrieks that went up—up, as it seemed to heaven, shrieks for mercy and pardon—served to show them the fearful havoc they had committed.

The order to swing the yards round was given.

All dreaded to look upon the sight that must meet their eyes when they next were able to look upon the coral reef.

The "Sea Breeze" was a capital ship, and being well handled, answered well to helm and sails, and having been brought round was soon out of danger of the reef, and then all eyes were turned to see what had become of the "Firebrand."

The hull was still there, but the mast and rigging had gone, and hung over the sides.

One boat alone remained whole, and in this Walter Savage, followed by his crew—not more than twenty remaining —were preparing to take their departure from the ship.

As he stood on the ship's side, he raised his clenched hand on high, as if swearing to have revenge.

Then he pointed down to the deck as he glanced at the "Sea Breeze," and appeared to utter a contemptuous laugh.

At the same moment thin curls of blue smoke were seen to issue from the hold.

"Bah!" laughed our hero, as he saw him get into the boat which was rowed to the rocky island, "he thinks we have come after the plunder only. No, we have rid the sea of one 'Firebrand,' and it shall not be my fault if we do not rid it of all the others.

"Lower the boats there; we will go on board the pirate ship. Perchance we may find something useful to us there, and then as *they* can cross the coral reefs, so can *we*, and we can fight as well on land as at sea."

The boats were lowered and manned, our hero taking the command of the first.

As they pulled towards the wreck, they saw the pirates land on the rocky island.

The pirate captain, Walter Savage, waved his hand in contempt to the boats of the "Sea Breeze," and seemed by his signs to ask them to board the wreck.

"Back-water, back-water for your lives!" cried our hero, suddenly. "The villain has set the ship on fire, and the magazine will blow up."

With all speed the men backed water, and then turning the boats, pulled as quickly away as they could from the wreck.

The pirates, who had in the most cool manner stove in their boat when they had landed, stood watching the scene in silence.

"Lay on your oars, men," cried our

hero. "We are quite far enough away to be safe."

Scarcely had he said the word than a loud explosion rent the air.

A huge cloud of black smoke, mingled with tongues of lurid flame, shot up from the ill-fated "Firebrand," and those who observed it closely noticed that dark objects were in it.

The men lay upon their oars, and watched the dreadful scene in horrified silence.

The dark cloud spread out over the sky at the top, whilst the lower part cleared away.

And then there came an *awful rain.*

A rain of the torn and bleeding limbs of human creatures.

Hands, arms, legs, heads, trunks all came splashing into the water, some falling even into the boats of the "Sea Breeze."

These were quickly examined, and were found to be those of negroes.

"The inhuman wretches," cried the captain. "They were running a cargo of slaves."

"There can be no doubt about it, your honour," said Barnacle, shaking his head.

A general cry of rage and horror arose from the ship's crew at this wanton cruelty.

"Sooner than we should give the poor wretches their liberty, they have blown them up," exclaimed Captain Breeze.

"May the Lord send them varmints a death quite as bad or wusser," said Barnacle.

"Amen!" replied the crew solemnly, and raised their hats.

"Pull to the 'Sea Breeze,'" said the captain. "We can do no good here. Stay!"

He had turned to have one more glance at the "Firebrand," which was now in a blaze, and had fancied he had seen something alive moving amidst the smoke and flame.

He fixed his eyes on the spot, and watched intently the place.

"It *is* a man moving in the flames," he cried "Give way, men, and pull towards the burning ship. If we can save one fellow-creature all our trouble will be well repaid."

"Give way, men, and pull with a will."

The gallant sailors strained every muscle, so that in a few moments the boat shot alongside the burning ship.

The heat and smoke scorched and nearly blinded the men.

At last our hero, standing up in the stern sheets of the boat, beheld a dark figure crouching down on the taffrail of the ship to avoid the flames which rushed in volumes over his head.

"Leap! leap!" cried the Child of the Waves. "We will save you."

The man neither moved nor spoke.

"I fear the poor creature is suffocated," said our hero. "Jump, jump, I tell you," he cried again. "It is your only chance to save your life. Jump at once."

The figure half rose, and muttered some guttural sounds, and then stretching out its arm pointed to the sea.

Our hero glanced down, and saw that the ocean was crowded with sharks.

"Keep the boat well in, my lads. Peters, hook on with the boat-hook. Now, steady all."

Before the men knew his intention, Captain Breeze leaped from the boat and caught the stern of the burning ship with one hand.

He then hauled himself gently up, and in a few seconds was standing on the burning deck.

The sight there was something awful.

Dead bodies, so disfigured that it was almost impossible to know they were human, were everywhere.

The hold of the ship was one mass of fire, and the stench of burned flesh was fearful.

To seize the unfortunate wretch by the arm, and lower him into the boat, was the work of an instant, and then our hero sprang back himself.

"Shove off, men, and make to the 'Sea Breeze' as soon as you can," he said.

The rescued creature was an African, and now that he was out of danger, he became insensible.

He was hoisted on board the "Sea Breeze" with the greatest tenderness, and passed down into the cockpit for the treatment of Dr. McTaggart.

But the sickening sights which were to meet the gaze of the crew of the "Sea Breeze" were not over.

The men leaned over the gunwale of

the ship, and watched with horror and disgust the shoals of sharks which were snapping at the limbs of the dead negroes, just as carp in a pond snap up flies and bread crumbs.

"Why doesn't the skipper give orders to weigh and get out of this infernal place?" said one.

"If he doesn't do it soon I shall be as sick as a Cockney at sea."

"And I shall go as foolish as a sailor on land," retorted Peter Painter, who was a Cockney.

"Hold your tongue, you counter-jumper," growled the other. "Don't you know—— But here comes the captain on deck. I guess it will be 'all hands make sail now.'"

But it was not all hands make sail; for the boatswain piped all hands aft.

The men tumbled aft as quickly as they could, and stood in a semi-circle before the captain.

Captain Breeze was pale as death, but perfectly calm, and not a muscle of his face moved.

For a few moments there was a dead silence, and then the captain spoke in a deep voice—

"My men, you have witnessed to-day's terrible work. Not our's the blame. We have done our duty, and if we could have relieved those poor wretches from their chains we should have done so."

"Ay! that we would, your honour. There ain't a mother's son amongst us as wouldn't."

"I do not doubt you, my brave fellow," said the captain, smiling at the grim old seaman who had caused the interruption. "Not in this ship, I trust, could a man be found to sanction such awful work, let alone to take a part in it. We had driven these villains on shore, and would have taken their ship from them in a hand-to-hand fight, let the odds have been what they might, had they remained out at sea. But they, like all bad men, were cowards, and shrank from the encounter."

"They knew better than to stay for us, the murdering villains," broke in the grim old quartermaster.

"You are right, they did; but with all their cunning they shall not escape us."

"They shall not! they shall not!" roared the men, clenching their fists.

"They *shall* not, I swear!" continued the captain, with emphasis. "I have been compelled to see many fearful deeds performed whilst I was a captive amongst those wretches; but never such a scene as this. Look at our fellow-creatures being devoured by the monsters of the deep. These men look upon a negro as so much goods—I know he is a man and a brother. An English clergyman aptly called the negro 'God's image carved in ebony.' He was right; they are like ourselves, carved in the same likeness. But what is the black-ness of the skin to that of the soul? These poor negroes were truly to me as brothers. The villains who doomed them to that cruel death are black inside—they are made in the likeness of the Fiend."

"They are, they are!" yelled the men. "We will never spare one when we meet them."

"That is what I want you to promise me," said our hero. "Swear by the remains of the victims of these wretches that henceforth you will devote your lives to their destruction, that on shore or at sea you will still do your best to bring them to justice, and for that pur-pose will employ all and every means in your power, either open fight or strata-gem. Swear!"

"We swear; by the dead victims here around us we swear!"

Captain Breeze glanced round, and he at once noticed that some of the men he had obtained at Dark Sambo's turned rather pale at this oath, and did not take it very readily. He, therefore, de-termined to keep a sharp look-out upon them.

But now he had done all he could, and to have complained would have been useless.

So he gave orders for the "Sea Breeze" to stand out to sea to refit her broken rigging, whilst he consulted with the other officers upon their plan of action.

CHAPTER XIII.

OUR HERO DETERMINES TO LAND ON THE ROCKY ISLE—DAVEY EVINCES HIS DISLIKE TO THE DOCTOR—HE BECOMES TRACTABLE TO CAPTAIN BREEZE—THE DOCTOR'S DILEMMA—THE START.

CAPTAIN IRETON, Lieutenant Daulton, and Captain Breeze were seated in the chief cabin, consulting as to the best way to attack the pirates.

"They have stove in their boats, and they cannot escape," said Breeze. "I vote that I land with a number of our people, and hunt them up amongst the rocks."

"It would be a dangerous act," said Captain Ireton, who was still unable to leave his bed; "for these men are up to all kinds of warfare. Besides, why should you risk your young life in such desperate work? True, you have good cause to hate this Deveril; but no reason, such as I have, to seek such dire revenge."

"I know not that, sir. It is every-one's duty to try to bring so cruel a wretch to justice. Besides, if I had him in my power he might reveal the mystery of my birth. That there is a mystery, and one that greatly affects him, I am sure."

"Ah!" cried Captain Ireton, "can it be possible that— But no, no, that can never be. No fortune will ever smile upon my path again."

His voice grew weaker as he spoke, and his head sunk forward upon his chest.

"Say no more, say no more," said Daulton, quickly, "the captain has one of his dark fits upon him. He will neither speak nor listen to us now."

"Do you, Mr. Daulton, think that the plan is good?" asked our hero.

"I do. That it will want the greatest caution no one can doubt, for as the captain has said, these men know every method of warfare, be it by land or sea."

"That is what I think," replied Captain Breeze. "I have told you that I was never permitted to join in any of their land expeditions. At sea I was compelled to learn all the duties of an officer, for I knew Captain Deveril wished me to become the second in command. Had I done so I believe he would have loved me."

"Pah! Deveril love you. He only loved to blast. His kiss was like an adder's sting—Death."

"It may be so. I knew him to be a villain, lieutenant. And now, if you please, I will start at once."

"With all my heart, lad; but do not be rash. I believe there was a purpose why you were sent on board this ship, and that purpose you will carry out. Go, and may heaven defend you."

They shook hands heartily, and our hero sprang up the companion-ladder deck, and gave the orders for the boats to be lowered.

"Look here, your honour, there's something the matter with Davey the dwarf," said Jack Barnacle.

"I will go and speak to him," said our hero.

"Then there is the black fellow as we saved off the burning ship. He's all right now."

"He may be of service to us. I will go and see him presently. See that the boats are well manned, and that the men are fully armed. We may have dangerous work before this adventure is over."

Captain Breeze walked forward, and found the hideous-looking little dwarf tugging and pulling at his chain with all his might, sometimes in his passion even taking it between his teeth, which were long and sharp, like those of an ourang-outang, and biting it in fearful rage.

Several sailors stood by, laughing and teazing the unfortunate little wretch.

"What are you doing there, men?" demanded the captain. "Do you think this poor creature is an object to be laughed at?"

"Ax pardon, your honour," said one of the sailors, "but he has been going on so."

"Please to attend to your business," replied Captain Breeze, sternly. "I will not have this poor creature teazed."

The men, who by this time knew our

hero was not to be played with, touched their hats and walked away.

"Now, then, Master Davey," said the captain, kindly, "what's the matter with you?"

The dwarf left off for a moment, but remained silent.

"Will you not speak to me? Believe me I have no wish to illtreat you, or let others do so."

The sharp eyes of the dwarf were raised for a moment to Captain Breeze's face.

His thin blue lips parted, showing his horrible teeth and large flat tongue.

Then once more he commenced his mad endeavours to break his chain.

"Listen to me, Davey," said Captain Breeze, "and if you answer me I may set you free."

"I will be set free," roared the dwarf. "What right have you to chain me up here?"

"The right of self-preservation," replied our hero. "Harkee, my young friend! I believe you are in league with Captain Deveril, the pirate. Do not think that I believe your story about being washed off the rock, for I do not. Now, if you will confess all to me, I will protect you."

"I know nothing of Captain Deveril," growled the dwarf. "I hate mankind, they all hate me, and I hate them. I want my liberty, and nothing more. Let me go, I can swim ashore."

"You forget the sharks, my young friend," said Captain Breeze; "they might stop you."

"The sharks won't touch me. Let me go; I will go," and here the dwarf again began his furious prancings.

"It is not the slightest good speaking to the little monster," said Dr. McTaggart, walking up and taking a pinch of snuff, as he examined the dwarf much after the manner a naturalist might examine a strange animal. "I have been trying to argue with him the whole of the morning, but could not make him stir. I think a whip——"

The doctor could say no more, for incautiously he had approached within the length of the dwarf's chain, and the little wretch with one bound was upon him, and had seized him by the nape of his neck.

The doctor uttered a fearful shriek, and with a desperate effort tore himself free and fled, leaving his wig—for he wore one—in the dwarf's possession.

In spite of all he could do, Captain Breeze could not help laughing; but at the same time he plainly saw that Master Davey Dump must be checked a little.

So, pretending to be very angry, he ordered the boatswain to pipe all hands up."

"Listen to me, Master Davey," he said, sternly. If my men had had their way you would have been flung into the sea. I saved you, and this is the return you make. You see, the men are getting all ready for you to be flogged; if, however, you will promise to be tractable I will not have you punished."

The little brute seemed struck with this argument, and remained silent a moment.

Then he threw down his chain, and, turning to our hero, said—

"What would you have me do? How can I love men when all hate me? No one loves me but my mother, and you would keep me away from her!"

"Does your mother live on yonder rock?" asked our hero.

"Yes."

"If I take you to the rock will you guide me to her?" demanded the captain.

"What do you want to go to her for?" demanded the other, suspiciously.

"To do her no harm. Tell me, do you know anything of the pirates who haunt these islands?"

"I know sailors come to my mother for charms, that is all I know. I know not what they may be. I know *they* are kind to me."

"A pretty broad hint that," thought Captain Breeze. "At all events it is one I will take. Listen, Master Davey! I will let you free; I will trust in you, and I will be kind to you. You shall guide me to your mother, and I give you my word that I will do her no harm. You understand that?"

The dwarf nodded his head, and Captain Breeze continued—

"But at the same time I warn you that at the least attempt at trickery I will blow your brains out. Do you understand that?"

Again the dwarf nodded.

"And you consent to those terms? If so you shall have a good meal before we start."

"I agree. Let me have the food."

Our hero gave orders that the dwarf should be fed, and then went below to see after the negro, who had been saved from the burning ship; but far from finding him as well as Barnacle had declared him, he found the man raving in delirium, speaking some African language.

Then came the most solemn part of the duty of a captain.

The burial of the dead.

Poor Bunt! All the old crew of the "Sea Breeze" loved him, and the officers knew that there was not a better or a braver seaman to be found in the world; and many an eye grew moist as the sailors talked in whispers of the gallant and kindly actions he had done.

The ship's bell was tolling out the summons to the crew, and officers were gathered on the quarter-deck.

The grating on which the body lay, sewn in a hammock and covered with a flag, was rested on the lee gangway, with the feet projecting a little over the gunwale.

In a solemn tone our hero read the funeral service, all standing with uncovered heads.

At one part of the service one of the sailors draws the flag away from the body.

Then at the solemn words "we commit his body to the deep," the grating is shoved over into the sea.

A heavy splash, and the hammock being loaded with shot, the body sinks out of sight in an instant

All sailors are glad to get rid of a dead body, believing that it brings ill-luck; and, therefore, the spirits of the men were greatly improved when they saw the last of their old messmate, and even the captain seemed relieved.

He went himself and released the dwarf, and took him to the boat which he himself was to occupy.

To his amazement he found Dr. McTaggart seated in the stern sheets.

"Why surely, my dear doctor, you do not mean to accompany the expedition?"

"In truth I do, captain. I have heard that there are rare plants to be found on these rocks."

"I guess the only things we are likely to find on that island are blows," said the captain, grimly.

"That has nothing to do with me. I am not a combatant, but a man of science."

"I doubt whether the pirates, if we are lucky enough to come up with them, will care much about that. But you can do what you like. Here, Peters, help Master Davey Dump in."

"Davey Dump," screamed the doctor, "You surely do not mean to tell me that you intend to take that little wretch with you?"

"In good truth I do, doctor, and I look upon it he will be of great service."

"But you will not have the little wild beast in this boat?"

"Indeed, but I shall," replied our hero, who, truth to tell, enjoyed the doctor's fears.

So did Master Davey, for, with a horrible yell he leaped into the boat.

With another, but a different kind of yell the doctor leaped out of it, trying to jump into another boat; but he was not so agile as Davey, and fell into the water.

In spite of all discipline the men burst out into roars of laughter.

"A shark! A shark! A shark!" yelled the men, as the doctor's head bobbed up.

"Yah! help me! help me!" roared the unfortunate doctor, holding up his arms.

But the men were laughing so heartily that they could not assist him.

Down he went again, and the laughter grew louder, until Captain Breeze called out—

"Are you mad to let a man drown or be eaten by sharks? Have you forgotten the scene we witnessed when the slaves were blown up?"

In an instant all the men were silent, and the next time Dr. McTaggart appeared, so many boathooks and hands were stretched forth to save him, that his clothes were almost torn off his body.

"Oh, my clothes! You will not leave a particle of them on my body," he yelled.

"Never mind, doctor, laughed Breeze. "I do not think we shall meet many ladies."

"'OH, MY CLOTHES!' YELLED THE DOCTOR. 'YOU WILL NOT LEAVE A PARTICLE OF THEM ON MY BODY.'"

"But the tails of my coat have gone! Was it the sharks that bit 'em off?"

"I should rather think it was," said the coxswain, as he unhooked one of the tails from the boathook he held, which had been the real destroyer of the doctor's garments. To see them there devouring creatures around you was something awful."

"Oh, lor! and what a narrow escape I have had," cried the doctor, with a shudder.

"Worsur nor you think for," said the coxswain; "but you fought like an angel."

"Did I," cried the doctor, delighted, "did I? Then you see what it is to be scientific."

"The way you landed this here shark in the eyes, and that there 'tother in the jaw, I should think that it rather was science."

"Did I? Verily in my youth I did practice boxing——"

"Silence, there," cried our hero, for he thought the joke had gone too far. "Never mind your clothes, doctor; there will be less of them to dry. Give way, there, and keep all the boats well together."

CHAPTER XIV.

THE SEARCH OF THE ISLAND—STRANGE DISAPPEARANCE OF DR. M'TAGGART AND PETER PAINTER—THE WITCH OF THE ROCK.

SLOWLY the boats pulled towards the shore.

They passed the remains of the burned vessel, now high and dry on the coral reef, on which she had struck, and pulled straight to the rocky islands.

They pulled about for a proper landing place, in spite of the repeated assurance that there *was* no proper landing place from Davey Dump.

At last they let the little man have his way, and pulled up to the side of a rock on which they were able to land; but not without some difficulty, for the tide being low, the rock was some feet out of the water. However, they scrambled on shore, and leaving two or three men in each boat, ordered them to keep at least twenty yards from the shore, and to hold themselves in readiness should they hear any alarm.

Then the party set forth.

They crawled all round the rocks, and caused many a sea bird to fly out to sea uttering its wild screech.

They tried to climb to the top of the rock but failed—utterly failed.

Do what they would, they could not find the trace of a living creature; and our hero at last gave the word to return to the boats.

"Now then, lads," he said, as he reached the boats, "let me go through the muster roll."

The men stood ready, and answered one after the other to their names—save two.

"Doctor McTaggart!" cried the captain again and again, *but no answer came.*

"Who saw the doctor last?" demanded Captain Breeze.

"I think I did," said one of the men. "When we were up by the deep gulley up yonder, the doctor bribed Peter Painter to go with him to seek for a mirrabulous, confabulous, daisycuss, or something like that, which he had heard grew upon these rocks."

"And did that fool go with him?" demanded our hero, sternly.

"I rather think he took the two pounds, and slipped away with the doctor."

At this the men could not help laughing, but Captain Breeze was in no humour for mirth.

"Silence!" he cried. "Do you not know that we are most likely standing on a mine? Those pirates I still believe to be hidden on this island. Where, I cannot say, but I shall keep the ship close to this rock to discover them, and to prevent them receiving any relief from their comrades."

"What can we do now, sir?" demanded Barnacle.

"I scarce can say. I wish I had ordered the doctor out of the boats."

"He did get out of one of the boats,

sir, at all events," said Barnacle, with a grin.

"I pray you be quiet. Let me think for a moment. Where is Davey?"

"I'm here," said Davey, standing forward.

"Davey, do you know where my two missing men have gone?" asked Captain Breeze.

"No; my mother might."

"Your mother! Do you mean to say that she has led them away from us?"

"No; but she has wondrous charms to find out all sorts of things."

"Tut! I do not believe such nonsense," replied the captain, impatiently. "Still," he added to himself, "I may as well go with this dwarf and see the old woman. Come, Davey, lead the way, and we will go and see your mother."

"You must go alone with me," growled Davey. "I dare not take more than one person."

"And why not?"

"Because she would curse me and wither me up like the branches of elm she sells to the sailors," replied Davey; "so you must come alone with me, or not at all."

"Be it as you will," said our hero, "I will go with you alone. But listen to me, Master Davey. If I catch you attempting to play any tricks upon me, I will blow that ugly head of yours to pieces."

Captain Breeze gave orders to his men to remain on the shore, and then started off with the dwarf.

Climbing over rugged rocks, passing along such narrow ledges, that if our hero had not been used to climbing, he would have been unable to follow, the dwarf danced along as if it were the easiest path in the world.

Now and then he would pause and look behind to see if our hero was following.

"Come on, come on," he croaked. "We shall soon be there. Oh, yes, very soon."

"The sooner the better," muttered Captain Breeze. "Your mother must be as agile as a cat if she climbs this mountain often. Or, perhaps, she goes in for the proper witch's steed—a broom."

At length they reached a deep fissure in the rock, at the brink of which Davey paused.

With his eyes lit up with a most malignant light, his thin blue lips drawn back in a horrible smile, showing his hideous teeth, he stretched forth one hand and pointed down the fissure.

This fissure was not much more than six feet wide at the top, but seemed to be much wider at the bottom, where the sea beat in with such force that the spray reached the place where our hero stood.

The rocks, which were evidently of volcanic formation, had taken the most fantastic forms, and the captain could scarcely believe but that art had lent its aid to nature.

Here and there a jutting piece of rock resembled a horribly grotesque head, no doubt the work of accident; but the two peculiar pebbles which formed the eyes, our hero had no doubt had been placed there purposely by someone who wished to increase the weirdness of the place.

"Why do you pause here?" said Breeze. "It is not a pretty spot, nor a pleasant one."

"No; it is not a pleasant one. This is the way that the wicked spirits come to my mother."

"A most fit path. But I wish to go to your worthy mother, and I am not afraid; so I would ask you to proceed at once, as time presses."

"Follow me," replied the dwarf, and he led the way to a spot where an elm tree grew, overhanging the chasm.

A weird-looking tree, with twisted, leafless branches, and scathed with lightning.

"This is my staircase," chuckled the dwarf. "Follow me, *unless you fear*."

"Go on, I have no fear," replied Captain Breeze, impatiently.

From a hollow in the trunk of the tree the dwarf drew a rope, at the middle of which was an iron ring.

He passed the middle of the rope round the tree, threading one end through the ring.

"Follow!" he said, and seizing that half of the rope which had been passed through the ring, at once descended to a narrow ledge of rock about twenty feet below.

Here the little wretch looked up, and

uttered a scream like that of a screech-owl.

"Come down," he cried. "She is at home, and expects you, so make haste."

"Expects me!" thought Captain Breeze. "If she does she must indeed be a witch, for I never expected to be here."

Swinging himself down by the rope, the captain was soon standing by the dwarf.

Then the artful little wretch took hold of that half of the rope which had not been passed through the ring.

He pulled it gently, and, of course, the ring slipped away; and in a few seconds he had unfastened the rope from the tree, and coiled it round his arm.

Our hero now discovered that they had reached the mouth of a small cave.

"Follow me!" said the dwarf, and he passed into the cave; and the next moment they were in total darkness.

"Listen," said Davey. "She is holding a conversation with the fiend. Do you hear the spirits?"

Captain Breeze did listen, and could plainly hear what appeared to be the roaring of an immense furnace.

There was also a rushing, roaring sound, which he attributed to the sea and the wind, as they beat and raved round the rocks.

"Hush! she calls," cried the dwarf.

Sure enough there was a peculiar call, followed by an elvish laugh.

Then, in a cracked voice, was chanted—

" Close to my portal,
    Stands a strange mortal.
Mother's or father's love never he knew ;
    Myst'ry hangs round him,
    Foes would have drowned him—
Dark was the day, that the first breath he drew.
    Enter the witch's cave,
    Child of the darkening wave !
    Ask what question you dare,
    But be warned, and beware !"

It must be confessed that Captain Breeze was a little taken aback at hearing himself so accurately described by a person he had never before seen in all his life.

"Ha, ha!" grinned the dwarf, "I told you that she knew you. *Will you enter now?*"

"Why should I refuse?" replied our hero. "Give me your hand and guide me, for I cannot see an inch before me."

"Wait; I will soon have a light," said the dwarf, and almost at the same instant he appeared with a flaming torch in his hand.

How he had gained it our hero could not tell.

By the light of this torch he was able to examine the cave.

It was a low vaulted passage, with many strange twists and turns.

The walls were decorated with bones and skulls, both human and of beasts.

Skeletons of the osprey, gull, albatross, and other ocean birds were arranged so as to make them appear to be swooping down to fish out the eyes of human creatures, or rather human skeletons, who were put in the position of drowned sailors, and the bills of birds thrust into the eyeless sockets.

"What think you of our cave?" grinned the dwarf. "Is it not beautiful?"

"Whose horrible work is that?" demanded Captain Breeze, with a shudder.

"*That* horrible work. Do you call that horrible work? I call it beautiful. It is all done by the spirits. But come, I must not keep the Witch of the Rock waiting, or she will be angry."

Leading the way, he passed down to the end of the cave, and here there was a long narrow passage, sloping downwards.

Down this they went until they reached another small cave.

Here, seated on the skull of a gigantic bison, was a woman who appeared not much over sixty.

Her face bore traces of once having been beautiful, although now it was as cadaverous as that of a corpse.

Her long hair reached down far below her waist, but it had lost the gloss of the raven's wing, and was now a grizzled grey, and hung in loose, wild locks about her shoulders.

She was dressed in a long robe of some coarse blue stuff.

She cast a sharp glance at the captain as he entered the cave.

This cave was decorated in the same way as the other was, only that there were more human skeletons here.

In different parts of the room were stuffed sea monsters, hideous and disgusting to look at.

"Child of the Waves," cried the hag, as the captain entered this terrible place, "what wouldst thou have with the Witch of the Rock ?"

"In truth, good mother, I scarcely know," replied our hero; "but first let me know—since I am told that you have such wonderful powers to read the past, present, and future—where are my doctor and man, Dr. McTaggart and Peter Painter ?"

"They are where you will never see them again," muttered the hag, and then burst into a shrill laugh.

"Woman," cried Captain Breeze, "if you know what has become of them I charge you tell me ! Nay, mock me not, for I shall hold you answerable for their lives !"

"Hold *me* answerable !" laughed the crone. "Bah ! do you not know that I have power to call up spirits from the deep who would rend you limb from limb to protect me ?"

"I should like to see these same spirits," replied the captain, laughing.

"Scoff not, Conrad of the Wave," said the witch.

"Ah, Conrad ! Then that is my true name ?" demanded Captain Breeze.

"Was it not by that name the man who reared you called you ?"

"Sometimes. But to the purpose, good mother. Where are the two missing men ?"

"Dead !" replied the woman.

"Dead ! And who killed them ? By heaven, I will have revenge !"

"Revenge ! Ha, ha, ha ! This is always the cry with you men of blood. Have revenge upon this island, for that killed them."

"How can that be ? Speak plainly ; I like not riddles."

"Well, Conrad of the Waves, for so I will call you until I may breathe your right name——"

"My right name ! Then you know it ? Wherefore should you not tell it to me ?"

"My lips are sealed with a terrible oath. I dare not yet reveal it."

"Do you know who were my parents, when I was born, my country ?"

"Aye ! I know all, but dare not reveal my knowledge. This much I can tell you though : You were born on board a pirate ship. From the moment of your birth you were doomed to a pirate's life. The oath was taken—I saw it given—a

fearful oath. Your mother died, or she, too, would have been forced to take it."

"Dared they attempt to give such an oath to a dying woman ?" exclaimed Breeze.

"He who administered the oath cared little about dying women."

"And this monster of inhumanity was Deveril ?" cried our hero.

"Ask me no more ! My lips, I tell you, are sealed. I dare not speak further !"

"Be it so ! But I can guess, and until I have proof that it is not so, I shall hold that monster answerable for the death of my mother. By heavens ! he shall pay me with his life."

"More slaying, more blood, more of the devil's dance," laughed the crone. "But you would learn my power to tell you what has become of your men. Davey, the caldron."

Davey, who had been caressing a villainous-looking, black goat, started up, and, moving to a corner, produced therefrom a caldron about a foot and a half in diameter.

This was fastened by a hook to a chain, which ran over a pulley fixed in the roof.

"Do you see that iron ring in the floor ?" demanded the Witch of the Rock.

"I do !" replied the Child of the Waves.

"Seize it, and pull it with all your might."

Captain Breeze took hold of the ring, and after some little difficulty managed to pull up a flat stone about two feet square, disclosing a well-like hole, from which came a thick mist, smelling strongly of sulphur.

Meanwhile the witch had thrown into the caldron a lot of dried sticks, powders, and other ingredients.

Captain Breeze, in spite of his incredulity, could not help being interested in her actions.

When the caldron was half full, by the witch's orders, Davey slung it over the hole.

As the dwarf lowered it rapidly, the witch stood close to the hole, seeming to treat the sulphurous fumes with the greatest impunity ; indeed, they seemed to excite in her a strange frenzy.

Her eyes grew brighter, her body

quivered, her limbs seemed to become more agile.

She waved her arms to and fro, and as she chanted a strange wild song, moved in a weird dance.

What she chanted the captain could not make out, for it was in Indian.

Suddenly she set up a most awful scream, and as she foamed at the mouth, cried—

"Beelzebub, spirit of fire, thou hast heard me, and thou hast plucked the burning brand from Tophet to light the magic caldron! I thank thee. Draw up the caldron."

Instantly the dwarf set to work.

The vapour grew thicker, and the witch's antics more frantic.

Up came the caldron at last, and to our hero's astonishment, its contents were all ablaze.

No sooner had the caldron been lifted up about a foot over the hole, than the Witch of the Rock slipped an iron grating over the latter, and on this the caldron was lowered.

Then the witch cast in a number of herbs, and as she did so, sang the following chant—

> "Spirits of the vasty deep,
> Ye who never rest or sleep,
> Spirits of the hidden fire,
> Causing pestilence most dire.
> Spirits of the earthly bed,
> Where there slumbereth the dead.
> Spirits of intrenchant air
> Hither all your powers bear."

Scarcely had the witch concluded this incantation than there seemed to be an explosion in the well beneath the caldron, and livid flashes of fire sprang from the hole.

"Now—now do you believe my powers?" cried the witch.

"No, I do not," said Captain Breeze, quietly. "If you can call up the spirits of my men, whom you declare to be dead, I may be tempted to believe in you."

"I cannot show you them as spectres, but you shall hear their voices," replied the witch.

"Be it so! That at least will be some relief."

The witch ran through some more incantations, and then called out in a loud voice—

"Answer me! Spirits of the lost ones, come! come! come! Are you here?"

"We are!"

In spite of all his incredulity, our hero could not help being startled, for the voices were undoubtedly those of Dr. McTaggart and Peter Painter.

"Ask what questions you will," said the witch, "they are bound to reply."

"Is it true that you are dead?" demanded Captain Breeze.

An awful groaning and wailing succeeded the question, and then came the answer, "Yes."

"Can I find your bodies?"

"No."

"Why not?"

"They are consumed with fire. Begone! Quit this unlucky island and torture us no more."

"Ask no more questions," said the witch; "trouble not the departed."

"I will at all events see if they be the departed," cried Captain Breeze as he sprang past the witch, and dashed at the side of the cave from which the voices had seemed to come.

Vainly he tried to discover some secret hiding-place.

He struck the rock with the butt end of his pistol, but it seemed quite solid.

Not one hollow place could he find.

"You still doubt me," laughed the witch, "and yet I would do you good."

"How would you do me good?" demanded Captain Breeze.

"By giving you good advice. Quit the sea. You were born on it; if you remain on it a month longer, you will die on it. Be warned in time. The book of fate is open unto me. I read there is a terrible destiny for you, unless you relinquish this foolish pursuit of the 'Firebrand.'"

"Ha! you know the name of the ship I seek!"

"I do. I also know you will never capture her. Think not that I am interested in the advice I give you. What care I if you should fall a victim to Deveril's hate, or that he should perish by your hand? So that blood be shed, I care not. Still you have been kind to my boy"—here she pointed to the hideous little Davey—"and I will give you good advice: quit the sea. Have nought to do with Captain Ireton or his friend Daulton. Take my advice and thou mayest be happy; reject it and death will be thy lot."

"Then death will be my lot," replied our hero, firmly, "for I will never quit Captain Ireton until I have avenged his wrongs, and punished the cruel Deveril or his wickedness."

"On your own head be the blood that is shed," cried the witch. "Begone, and leave me."

"No. I am still not satisfied about my men. If they are dead, as you say, how did they die?"

"Your friend the doctor would climb the rocks to seek for plants. This rock is full of traps formed by nature."

"Traps formed by nature? I do not understand you. Traps for what?"

"Men, fools—but they are mostly the same—anything. Look here."

As she spoke, she hobbled to a corner of the cave, and pulled away a stone from the floor.

This stone left a hole much smaller than the one down which the caldron had been lowered, but of the same character.

"Look down there, but cover thy mouth up with thine hands, for the fumes from this well are most deadly."

Covering his mouth and nostrils with his hand, our hero leaned over and gazed down the hole.

Far, far down he saw what appeared to be a river of molten metal.

"Ha, ha!" cried the witch. "I tell you, Conrad of the Waves, this island is full of mysteries."

"To me this seems but little of a mystery," said our hero, quietly.

"How? No mystery where fire flows like a river underneath the earth?"

"No; this island is a volcano."

"Stubborn in heart, proud of knowledge, scorner of the hidden secrets which bind the world, begone! I can teach you no more. The day will come when you will return to implore the Witch of the Rock to help you. Then she will be deaf to your prayers. Begone!"

"And this Davey—your son. Is he to go with me?" asked our hero.

The woman paused for a moment as if to consider, and then said—

"Yes, lest you fall into one of those wells as your men did. But let Davey come back to me when he has seen you to your boats. He shall join you to-morrow, and bring with him a piece of elm to guard your ship from wreck."

"I want not your elm. Good seamanship, a firm trust in Providence, and a courageous heart will keep my ship afloat. I have no dealings with such as you to ward off fate. If what you say be true—which I do not believe—then are you in league with the devil; if not, then you are an impostor, and in both cases I had better be free of you."

Captain Breeze turned to leave the place, when the old woman sprang forward and caught him by the arm.

"Stay, Conrad!" she cried, "you will not take my advice. Be it so; why should I care? Your life is little to me. But, my boy, shall he go with you?"

"If you like; I know no worse place where he could be brought up than here."

"True! He shall sail with you. Farewell! Remember the words I have said."

Wrapping her cloak around her, the witch curled herself up in a corner.

"It's no use speaking to her now," said the dwarf, "she would not answer anyone. Come, I will show you the way back to the boats."

He made his way from the cave, the Child of the Waves following him.

Davey, with wonderful precision, threw the rope over the gnarled elm, keeping the iron ring in his hand.

Then passing the end of that half of the rope which had passed over the tree through the ring, he drew the latter tightly up to the trunk.

Up the rope both Captain Breeze and Davey climbed, and then the latter took the way down to the boats, where our hero inquired if the doctor and Peter had turned up.

Receiving an answer in the negative, he, with much sorrow, returned to his ship, leaving Master Davey to go back to his mother.

THE ATTACK ON THE SMUGGLERS' CAVE.

CHAPTER XV.

SHOWS HOW DR. M'TAGGART'S LOVE OF ORCHIDS PLACED HIM IN A TERRIBLE FIX, AND EXPLAINS SOME OF THE WITCH'S MYSTERIES.

WE must now return to Dr. McTaggart and Peter Painter, who had started off in order, as the doctor hoped, to find new specimens of plant life to enrich science.

"Peter," said the doctor, as they went crawling over the rocks, "I have heard that these rocks abound in strange and wonderful specimens of orchids."

"Horkids! What's a horkid? I know that it is precious horkid crawling over these here rocks."

"Dear me, dear me, friend Peter, your ignorance is very distressing."

"So is this here crawling about, your honour. Twice have I nearly slipped down big holes."

"Of a truth this rock is extremely rugged, being of volcanic formation. The holes of which you speak seem almost as deep as wells. I wish we had brought a long rope with us, I would then have lowered you down one of them, so that you could have examined it."

"Lor' a mercy, sir! I wouldn't go down one of them holes for a hundred pounds."

"And why not, good Peter? Who knows what you might discern?"

"Ah! indeed, that is true. Who could tell what I might see? Why, they smell of nothing but brimstone and sulphur. It's my belief that they open into the infernal regions, and I should not be surprised if we came on a legion of devils soon."

"Tut, Peter, you are ignorant indeed. But see, down on that rocky ledge yonder? There's an orchid. An orchid, Peter, is a plant of the order *Orchidaceæ*. Some have curious and beautiful leaves only, whilst others bear lovely flowers, having rare fragrance."

"I daresay it's all right, your honour, but to my thinking, the fragrance of a good stiff glass of grog is worth all the smells of all the flowers ever known."

"You are indeed extremely ignorant, Peter, and a lover of drink as well. I must have that flower."

"Must, your honour! Then I'm blest if I know how you will get it," said Peter.

The doctor looked first at Painter, and then at the plant.

It was certainly no easy thing to reach, for the person who would gather the plant must climb down the face of the rock, holding on by the cracks, and finding a foothold as best he could.

"Peter," said the doctor, after a moment's consideration, "I want that flower."

"Well, your honour," replied Peter, "I'm sure I wishes as how your honour may get it."

"Peter, I will give two guineas for that flower—two guineas directly I have it in my hand."

"Two guineas for that there weed!" exclaimed Peter in surprise, looking first at the flower, and then at the doctor. "Your honour cannot be in earnest?"

"I am indeed, Peter; and what is more, you shall have a bottle of rum when we return aboard."

Peter said no more, but began buttoning up his jacket, as if determined to try.

But, as he approached the verge of the precipice, his courage failed him, and he drew back.

"It can't be done, sir," he said. "Now, if we had a rope we might try."

"Let us consider the matter," said the doctor, laying down full length on his stomach, so that his head and shoulders protruded over the precipice. "Do you think that you could crawl down by that ledge, and clinging on with one hand, gather it with the other?"

Peter was now as anxious to get the flower as the doctor.

Not because of the scientific value of the specimen, but for the guineas and rum.

So putting himself by the side of the doctor, he stretched his head over the precipice, and looked down.

"No, your honour, it could not be done. We had better return to the boat, and get a rope and——"

"*If you attempt to rise we will hurl you into the gulf below*," said a stern voice, and instantly a heavy foot was placed upon Peter's back, and another on the doctor's.

Fear held them both motionless; but even if they had had courage enough to struggle, it would have been useless, for the position they were in deprived them of all strength; whilst the heavy foot on each seemed endowed with almost superhuman weight.

Peter was the first to recover the power of speech, but he trembled so that what he said was scarcely audible.

"Oh, oh! No, no! Please, Mister Devil," he stammered, "don't come for to go for to hurt us. We ben't doing no harm. Please let me get up. I feels quite sick, looking down this place."

"You will feel worse when you are *thrown* down that place."

"Oh! please don't hurt. I'll do anything you like, only don't do that."

"If you value your life, keep still and remain silent—*silent as the grave.*"

"I won't say another word. You may do with me what you like, only do not hurt me."

"Friends," began the doctor, but ceased, for at the sound of his voice, he was seized by the ankles, and his feet quickly elevated, so that his head shot over the precipice.

"For mercy sake, do not let go," he shrieked, as he shut his eyes. "Do not let go, or I shall be precipitated down the precipice."

"One word more, and I thrust you down," replied the voice, and at the same moment the doctor was thrust forward half a foot, as if the threat was about to be carried into instant execution.

The doctor screwed up his eyes tighter, and groaned fearfully.

To his great relief he was once more laid on the ground.

"Close your eyes," said the stern voice; "attempt to look round, and your fate is sealed."

The two men closed their eyes, as if they were never to open them again.

Their arms were then drawn back and securely fastened behind them.

Then they were carefully blindfolded, and a running noose placed round each of their necks.

"Oh, lor! oh, lor! if they ain't a-going to hang us," groaned Peter.

"Keep silent," said the voice, sternly. "Now, my lads, *up with them.*"

At these words, so like an order to run them up to a tree, the doctor yelled.

"Gag that old idiot. If he resists, knock in his teeth with the butt of your pistol."

"I will be silent, indeed I will. I only——"

The doctor said no more, for a handkerchief was forced into his mouth, and rammed firmly therein with the barrel of a pistol.

"I don't think he will make much noise now," growled the man who had done this act.

"Bring them along," replied the gruff voice. "Listen, prisoners, round each of your necks is a running noose, so that if you attempt to run away you will be instantly strangled. At each of your heads is a pistol, so that if you make the slightest resistance your brains will be blown out. Now march."

As well as the doctor could make out, they were taken into a narrow passage, which sloped downwards.

Now and then he could hear large boulders of rock being rolled away from openings, and when they had passed through the rocks were rolled back again.

In this way they proceeded until they arrived at a small cave, where, from a few words that were said, the doctor, who had now recovered a great deal from his fear, gathered that the leader of the party had left to consult with someone.

Presently he heard him return and converse with a comrade in whispers.

But the doctor could not make out what he spoke about, all he heard was—

"He is here—alone—seize him—she will not permit it—keep still—deceive."

"These brutes are up to some cruel work," thought the doctor. "They must be the pirates."

Presently the doctor and Peter heard a confused sound of voices and then they were commanded—the doctor being ungagged for the purpose—to repeat certain phrases in a loud voice.

These phrases were dictated to them in whispers, and ran thus—

"*We are*," then the man who held them captive, groaned and shrieked.

After this the prisoners were made to say, "*yes*," then "*no*," and afterwards, "*they are consumed with fire. Begone! quit this unlucky island and torture us no more*." All answers which our hero had received in the witch's cave.

The truth was, the pirates who were in league with the witch, had made their prisoners answer from behind a trap in the witch's cave.

No sooner had our hero gone, than the trap was opened, and Walter Savage followed by one of his men entered the cave.

"How now, Elspie," cried the pirate, furiously, "is this what you promised me?"

"Aye!" replied the old woman, leaning on her staff, and looking at him scornfully.

"How can that be? Did you not promise me that you would lay a trap to catch this Conrad?"

"And have I not done so?"

"No; you have let him depart without injury. What service have you done us?"

"Much. It would have been better if you had not seized these men. I tell you, Walter Savage, that that boy Conrad is fated to kill Deveril, to break up your band, destroy your ships and seize your wealth."

"Confusion!" cried the pirate, "you tell me that, and yet you let the viper escape?"

"And who could have stopped him?" demanded the witch with a shrill laugh.

"I would—I and my men."

"Bah! I tell you that not forty such men as you could have stopped him. I know you are fearless of death, but I warn you, avoid the Child of the Waves. He was deprived of a mother's care almost as soon as he drew breath, and entrusted to those who wished him dead. Yet he lived and throve, even making the man to whom his very sight was poison, at last almost love him. Mark you this: the man who slays Conrad of the Waves will not live twelve hours to boast of the deed."

"And why not, good mother?" demanded the sailor, who in spite of knowing some of the deceptions the witch used, yet was a firm believer in her supernatural powers. "Does he bear a charmed life?"

"Why need you ask? Have you not known him stand where shot and shell have been flying thick as hail, and yet be untouched? Has he not beaten off and greatly injured the 'Firebrand' commanded by Deveril, and has he not defeated you?"

"But can nought be done to rid us of this dangerous youth? We cannot—will not stand tamely by, and know that he is planning our ruin. Tell us, good Elspie, are there no means by which we can overthrow the charm or spell which protects him?"

"It may be done; but not now. Hark! I hear my dainty Davey calling. Begone! Take your prisoners to the inner lake. Tell Deveril all that has happened. I warrant me he will not be pleased with the news; but he must e'en make the best of it. Say that he must make a grand banquet for to-night, for I and my dainty Davey intend to sup with him. Begone."

And the old crone threw herself down on her bed of sea-moss and seal-skins, turning her face to the side of the cave.

The pirate knew from experience that it would be useless to try and draw another word from her, and so left her cave to conduct his prisoners to the presence of Captain Deveril.

CHAPTER XVI.

CAPTAIN DEVERIL'S PLANS—A PIRATE'S BANQUET AND ROUGH JUSTICE—THE DOCTOR AND PETER PAINTER FORCED TO JOIN THE BAND.

THE cave of Captain Deveril was one blaze of dazzling light.

Tables were groaning under plates of massive gold and silver, holding rich dainties.

Decanters of cut crystal, containing different coloured wines, sparkled under the light, and the walls were hung round with the richest stuffs, so that the cave looked like a palace.

The pirates were lounging about, conversing at the entrance to the cave, smoking and laughing.

"Basta ! " cried a Spaniard, "this is bad news about Savage—all the slaves lost."

"Yes. Do you know how the chief took it ? " demanded another.

"As he does most things at first— calmly ! But when he has his opportunity his revenge will be fearful. Savage had better make haste and redeem his laurels, or he will pay dearly."

"See ! " cried another, "what light is that on the lake ? Is it another spectral light ? "

"No ; that is the Witch of the Rock, old Elspie, crossing the lake in her skiff. But those spectral lights were fearful to behold."

"Bah ! The captain declares that he has often seen them in this place. You know that this island is a volcano. Even now, at some places, a stick shoved into the crevices of the rock will take fire. These lights, so said Captain Deveril, are only gases which escape through the water, and catch fire when they reach the air."

"It may be so ; but I doubt it," said another. "If the captain knew all about this, why was he so terror-stricken ? "

"Caramba ! José, you ask a fellow too much. Do you not know that at times the captain goes nearly mad ? Some say he sees visions — horrible phantoms, and hears voices in the air. We all know that when he is in a rage he speaks the wildest nonsense, and is capable of killing his best friend——"

"Even if it were Sebastian Largo," said a deep voice.

The men turned round quickly, and beheld Captain Deveril standing behind them.

"Ha, ha ! " he laughed, "those who have to deal with Captain Deveril should be most cautious in their speech. See to it, my friends. To-night all is forgiven—look to the future."

Smiling significantly, the pirate strode down to the landing-place, where Elspie's skiff had already arrived.

Elspie had changed her dress.

She now wore a long flowing robe of black velveteen, which was embroidered with mystical signs in silver. A band of the same precious metal, formed as a snake, clasped her waist, and she wore bracelets and a necklet of the same pattern ; whilst on her head was a crown formed of two serpents twisted together.

Her only attendant was her "dainty Davey," who was decked out in a fantastic dress of black velvet, on which were wrought red flames, so that the little wretch appeared to be standing in the midst of flames.

"How now, Elspie ? " said the pirate chief. "What news do you bring me ? "

"None that is good. Would that you would be guided by me, and in disguise quit this place ! I warn you, Walter Deveril, that your fate is near at hand. Conrad, the Child of the Waves, will conquer you."

"I pray you, good mother, speak not like that before the men."

"No ; why need you warn me of that ? Have I ever betrayed your secret ? "

"No."

"I blame you not, Walter Deveril. You were born amidst bloodshed and— but let that pass. If you are still determined to lead this life, I still must help you. But be warned that treachery is around you."

"Do you mean that my men would mutiny ? " exclaimed Deveril.

"I warn you to beware of them. But you have more to speak to me about ? "

"Lucinda."

"Ah ! does the wind lie in that quarter ? Is the beautiful Pauline forgotten ? Bah ! men were ever the same changeable creatures. A pretty face holds them in chains until another one comes to banish it, and the last is always the fairest."

"You wrong me, mother. I shall ever remember and love Pauline ; but——"

"You love Lucinda also ! Listen to me, Walter Deveril. You have sworn that you would avenge my wrongs on him who now calls himself Ireton. On that condition I have helped you. As for this girl, Lucinda—wed her if you will. I care not for her ; but you must not—shall not, forego your oath to me against Ireton."

"Doubt me not, good mother. It shall be done, even as you desire. Ireton shall die."

"It is well; but the boy—Conrad must be spared. Your hand must not be raised against him."

"But he has sworn to have my life. Surely I may strike in self-defence?"

"Yes; but not otherwise. To-morrow you must leave this rock by the secret channel. Call all your fleet together, and go south. Ireton will follow you. You can, with all your ships, fall on and crush him. Davey will go on board the 'Sea Breeze,' and give you the private signals when they are required."

"Ah! Davey appears to have made a great mess over his going on board the 'Breeze' in the storm."

"He did his best; and who but Davey would have been able to reach the ship in such weather? But we have spoken enough. Here, take this scroll. In it you will find a plan laid down on which you must act. Now to the banquet. See that you do not displease the men. Be jovial, and make them laugh."

"I will do my best; but Lucinda? If I leave the rock, she must——"

"Remain here until you return in triumph. Fear not; in your absence I will take her in hand. Trust me, I will make her pliable to your will. Now let the horns be blown."

At a signal from the pirate chief, a dozen men took up as many shells, and, putting them to their lips, made the caves and crags echo forth a most dismal sound—wild, weird, and melancholy—but so loud, that it was plainly heard by the crew of the "Sea Breeze," who immediately put it down to supernatural causes, for all the sailors had come to the conclusion that the rock was inhabited by evil spirits.

The pirates came pouring out of the caves which formed their sleeping apartments, and were soon seated at the festal board, at the head of which presided their chief, having the Witch of the Rock on his right hand.

The fun grew fast and furious. Songs were yelled forth, and spirits and wine drank like water, until the natural consequences followed—quarrels.

Most of these the pirate chief was able to put down almost directly by a word, until the fellow called José commenced twitting Walter Savage with having lost his ship.

"Methinks, good Captain Savage," laughed the fellow, "this good cheer must taste rather unpleasant to you, when you remember how much of our property you have lost."

"Your property!" replied the other, with a sneer; "a beggarly Spaniard talks of *his* property. A cigarette and a water melon are the riches of a Spaniard."

"Basta! dare you say that I have not as much right to property as you have? Caramba! we freebooters of the sea have equal claims to the booty which they capture. Have we not, brothers?"

"We have, we have," cried the others.

"Yes, we, out of kindness, let the drones feed with the bees, even an idle wretch as you are, José, we permit to have a share, although we know that you are too great a coward to strike a blow," said Savage.

"St. Iago! thou shalt see if I am too great a coward to strike a blow," yelled José. "Take that."

Before anyone could seize the infuriated Spaniard, he had drawn a knife and plunged it into Walter Savage's heart.

A yell of rage arose from the crew of Savage's vessel, who immediately leapt to their feet, and drawing their knives, fell upon the Spaniard's friends.

Fearful blows were given on both sides, and many would have been killed but for Deveril.

Springing from his seat, he snatched a couple of pistols from his belt, and fired them over the heads of the combatants.

Then bounding forward, he used the butt-ends of his pistols with such good effect, that he stretched several of the men senseless on the ground.

"How now, ye hounds!" he yelled. "Dare you resist my authority! Put up your knives, or I will slay every one of you. Ah! Senor José, that weapon of yours has done too much mischief already. Thou art ever too free with thy tongue and thy knife. I must find means to make both harmless. Down with the knife, I say."

As he spoke, he brought the butt of one of his pistols down on the unfortunate Spaniard's right wrist with such force that he smashed the bones.

The other combatants perceiving this,

quickly put up their knives and drew back.

"Gomez!" cried Deveril, "pick me out half-a-dozen officers. Let someone go and bring hither the prisoners. They shall see that we are not the lawless band they think us. It may be a good lesson for them."

The men, who had now cooled down, quickly resumed their places at the board.

Presently some of the men led in Dr. McTaggart, and Peter Painter, still blindfolded.

The unhappy prisoners were placed at the end of the table.

At a sign from their chief two men stood behind the prisoners, and so far unfastened the bandages which covered their eyes, that they could be removed in an instant.

Then every man drew forth a pistol and pointed it towards the roof of the cave, and at a signal from Deveril fired, at the same time uttering a fearful yell.

As the pistols exploded the bandages were snatched from the eyes of the prisoners, who were so surprised at the uproar and the sudden change from total darkness into a blaze of light, that they both fell to the ground, screaming out that they were shot.

"Arise!" cried Deveril, sternly, "arise and learn a little justice of the free brothers of the ocean."

More dead than alive the doctor and Peter Painter crawled to their feet.

"Let the judges stand forth," said Deveril, sternly, and his lieutenant led forth the six officers he had selected as judges.

"Gentlemen," said Deveril, quietly, "you saw the disturbance just now?"

"We did," cried the six men.

"A worthy, a noble officer who has done us much service, but met with a misfortune lately, was twitted with that misfortune—a thing quite against our rules. Our captain bore it patiently, replying with a jest. The prisoner, Spanish José, stabbed him to the heart. A common seaman stabs an officer of high rank. What is his punishment?"

"Death!" cried the six men.

"What have you to say in defence, José?" asked Deveril, coolly.

"Nothing! If I were to speak for an hour, you would not pardon me."

"You are right, I should not. Let the execution be carried out at once."

Four of the sailors caught hold of Spanish José to secure him.

But, in spite of his wound, the fellow threw them off, and looking defiantly round, said—

"Curse you, keep your hands off me. I am wounded, and this, my right hand is useless, but my left can still deal a heavy blow. Do you think I fear death?"

"No, no, none of us fear death," shouted the pirates.

"I am not so sure about that," said Spanish José, with a grim smile, as he looked at some.

The men laughed, and it must be confessed that one or two hung their heads and looked remarkably foolish.

"Never mind, lads," laughed the doomed man gaily, "I will show you how to die."

"I guess you can do that better than teach us how to live," said one, with a laugh.

"You lie, you lubber," cried Spanish José, sternly, "and had I time to spare I would teach you a lesson that you would not forget as long as you lived. But I have no time to waste on such as you. Who ever saw me lag behind when the order was given to board? Who ever knew me draw back when a comrade was in danger, or money to be had for blows? Answer me that, mates. Am I a coward to skulk when danger's in the way?"

"No, no, no, you were always ready to fight," shouted the men.

"Ever! I fear no death. Captain Deveril, you have doomed me, I do not complain."

"It would be useless if you did," replied the captain, grimly, "you know that."

"Yes, and you are right. Having such a lot of demons to control, you could not do otherwise. Besides, you would not if you could. You have the two necessary qualities to make a good captain of pirates, an utter disregard of another's suffering, for you love cruelty. Your other quality is your love of power and wealth. You have no heart, yet I think you have still a little touch of honour left."

Captain Deveril puffed the smoke

from his cigar, and bowed to the compliment.

"That being so, I have one favour to ask. It will cost nothing, and only delay my execution a few minutes. Will you grant it to me?"

"I have no wish to hurry your execution," replied Deveril, calmly. "If I were in your place, however, I should like to get the matter over as soon as possible, knowing it must take place sooner or later."

"I do not mean to ask you for my life. I want to drink to the prosperity of the band, and health and happiness to my comrades, and I wish then that they should drink me a merry voyage. That done, I should like to die by my own hand. I will place myself on the verge of the rock hanging over the lake, and, with a pistol, fire *as near the heart as possible.* If I do not kill myself by the shot, I shall fall into the lake and trouble you no more."

"A strange request," said Deveril, sneeringly, "and one that it would be scarcely wise to grant."

"Do you refuse me?" cried the man, in bitter tones. "Are you afraid?"

"No, I will grant your request. But the toasts must be short. I have no time to waste."

"And shall I be permitted to be my own executioner? I would not cause a comrade another sin, for I know that they have sins enough to answer for without adding to the score."

"Yes; but mark this, *I* will see that it is carried out. Now to your drinking bout."

"Hurrah! comrades," cried José, who seemed, in the pleasure of drinking, to have quite forgotten that he was soon to die. "Come, fill your glasses to the brim. No water—in rum and brandy alone shall such toasts be drunk. Ha! Pedro, thou hast by thy side a large goblet. Give it here, and I will drink out of it. This, you know, is my last drink but one, and I swear by all the devils it shall be a good one!"

"Take care, José, how you swear by them," said the fellow as he passed the goblet; "you'll be in their claws soon, and they may make you pay dearly for using their names so freely."

"Bah! I fear them not. They cannot be more wicked or cruel than the present company."

At this doubtful compliment the men roared with laughter, as at a good joke.

"Come, captain, let the prisoners carouse with us," cried the bravo. "I dare say I shall meet them soon, and I should like them to be friends."

"They shall drink with you. Fill up the prisoners' glasses."

"I would rather not——," began the doctor, when a fierce look from Deveril stopped him.

"Drink it—drink it doctor, or he will order us out to be shot like the Spaniard," whispered Peter.

Dr. McTaggart saw that this was only too true, and therefore seized the goblet.

"Comrades," cried Spanish José, raising his cup in the air, "I drink this toast. I might almost call it a loving-cup—or a stirrup-cup would be better, for I am about to take a long journey! Before I go I would wish you all success in life; after life you are sure to get your deserts."

At this terrible joke the men laughed loudly, and cried, "Bravo, José!"

"But I will be brief. I and the captain have never been great friends. The fault may have been mine, or it may have been his. I do not pretend to know, and I have no time to discuss the question; but I hope to argue it out with him when we meet another time in another place, which I trust will be soon. So, comrades, here's to you, and may you give the Devil the slip!"

Shouting with laughter, and applauding the speech, the men drank the toast.

"Fill again," said Deveril quietly, "I must return that, I think."

The men did so; and Deveril, holding his goblet aloft, said—

"José, we have not been good friends, for the reason that you possess many of those qualities you have been good enough to accord to me. But you are ambitious, and would do anything to gain your ends. I know that you have long wished to create a mutiny against me. You have failed. I have foiled you. Revenge is sweet to you even as power, and to revenge yourself upon Captain Savage, who had warned me of your plots, you picked a quarrel with him and stabbed him. If we do meet in another world—and it is possible we shall—I will punish you again. As it is,

I wish you a speedy journey, and thank you for your wishes."

The pirates drank again with loud shouts of applause.

"Now comes the last toast," cried José. "Fill up your glasses, and this time we will drink *in flames!*"

"Mercy, Peter," groaned the doctor, who had been compelled to join the last drink, although it had nearly choked him. "Mercy! Peter, these be real devils indeed. Drink in flames!"

Peter Painter, who had never yet turned pale at the sight of a drink, did at this.

The goblets were filled with spirits, and then the lights were all put out but one.

From this one light the men lit splinters of wood, with which they ignited the spirits in their goblets.

As the spirits flared up, and filled the cave with its livid light, the pirates, as they stood up with glasses raised, looked like a troop of ghosts, so that one could have almost thought that some of the spirits of the old pirates who had fought under Morgan and Blackband, had returned to the cave to indulge in one of their old orgies.

A terrible scene, and one that made Peter and the doctor tremble, especially when they had two large burning goblets placed before them.

"Here's wishing José a safe and speedy journey," cried Deveril. "Hip, hip, hurrah!"

"Hip, hip, hurrah!" shouted the men, and, lifting the flaming goblets to their lips, by a quick puff of their lips they blew out the fire, and then quaffed off the heated liquor.

The doctor and Peter did not perceive this trick.

Closing their eyes they made a frantic endeavour to quaff the flaming liquor.

But no sooner had it reached their lips than the flames singed their hair, eyebrows, and noses, whilst their lips were burned horribly.

The pirates shouted with laughter, whilst Deveril cried—

"Drink, slaves—drink! Drink, or you shall accompany José on his voyage!"

Again the goblets were raised.

As they raised them a third time, a voice whispered in their ears—

"Blow the spirit out quickly, and then drink—that is the way."

Pain and fear had made them quick to grasp at the slightest chance, and they managed, as bidden, so well that even the pirates were deceived, and a murmur of applause ran round the room.

"Oh, lor'! oh, lor'!" cried Peter, as the tears ran down his cheeks and he placed one hand to his mouth and the other on his stomach. "I've burned my inside out, I know I have! I shall never be able to eat or drink again, I know I shall not—I know I never shall. Oh, oh!"

"What cheer, messmate!" shouted José, who was convulsed with laughter. "Never mind about the future—think of the present! Ha, ha, ha! I am never going to eat or drink again; still, I do not mind it. Come, let us have another cup of fire; it warms the heart!"

"Mercy! mercy!" roared the doctor. "I could not drink another to save my life. I have not a bit of skin left in my mouth! Oh! kind gentlemen, I do pray you excuse me!"

"You have had your last drink, José," said Deveril, quietly. "Keep your word like a gentleman."

"Basta! I forgot that," laughed José, as he rolled up a cigarette and lit it. "I am ready."

Puffing at his cigarette, he led the way to the overhanging rock.

Placing himself on the verge of the precipice, the fellow turned round, and, in a careless tone, said—

"Will any gentleman oblige me with a pistol. I do not want one that misses fire—a good one."

In an instant, in the most obliging manner, some twenty were offered him.

"Hold!" cried Deveril, "for such a purpose my pistol shall alone be used."

José took the weapon, examined and cocked it.

Seeing that it was in good condition, he threw away his cigarette, and, bowing, said—

"Gentlemen," holding the pistol carelessly pointed to his breast, "I said I would shoot as near to the heart as I could, and I will keep my word. Mark this, I did not say *my* heart, and thus I carry out my word."

"SPRINGING FROM HIS SEAT, DEVERIL SNATCHED A COUPLE OF PISTOLS FROM
HIS BELT AND FIRED THEM OVER THE HEADS OF THE COMBATANTS."

In a second his whole manner changed, and, rapidly turning the pistol round, he fired at Deveril, aiming straight at his heart.

Most of the pirates started back with amazement, and called out to each other to draw their pistols, and shoot the wretch down.

But Deveril stood unmoved, his eyes fixed upon the would-be assassin, and his arms folded.

"It was lucky I suspected this, and gave him a pistol loaded with powder only," he muttered to himself, and then aloud, "Fool! know you not that I have a charmed life? Have you not seen me on the deck of my ship when bullets have been flying round me, and sabres flashed on every side; yet never hath death laid his icy hand on me?

"No! Until I have fulfilled my duty, no bullet can injure me. But now—now I take my revenge."

Quickly drawing a pistol, he presented it at the man; but before he could pull the trigger, José turned swiftly and plunged head foremost into the lake.

"Lights! lights!" cried Captain Deveril. "Down, some of you, to the water's edge, and shoot him as he rises. Twenty pounds to the man who kills him."

Torches were lit and raised aloft, tar-barrels were set on fire and floated out on the lake, boats were launched, but, do all they could, they saw no trace of José.

The Spaniard was never seen to rise even by those who had seen and watched the place where he dived?"

"The rascal has plunged into some hole," said Deveril, as he joined Elspie on the rock when the search was given up. "If I had found him I would have burned him alive."

"I am ill at ease," muttered Elspie, "I know what José was. He would not have dared to act as he did if it had not been for others higher in command. No, I tell you, beware."

"Fear not, Elspie, I have no dread of any man. But the youth, Conrad——"

"Ha, ha, ha!" laughed the witch, shrilly. "You *know* he will be your fate—your death."

"Come! or I may forget what I owe thee. Methinks I have little to thank thee for. It was thy cursed tongue, thy promptings and prophecies that have made me what I am."

"Aye, Walter Deveril, and yet thou dost not know all. Listen! Conrad's hand shall not strike the blow which shall lay thee low, but he will cause it. Thou shalt cause Captain Ireton's death. *That* thou must do, or be for ever accursed—remember, accursed!"

"How am I to know that the story is true?" demanded Deveril; "where are the proofs?"

"Thou hast had proofs enough, I trow. Have you lost the tablet?"

"No, I have it. Yes, I must believe it. Fear not, Elspie, my old nurse, I will obey you. But I must go in and make the men get into a good humour after such a scene as that which has been acted to-night, for they want careful treatment."

As he spoke he strode into the cave, where he found the men all seated around the table, drinking and laughing heartily, the cause of their amusement being Peter Painter and Dr. McTaggart, who were seated at the end of the table, the doctor warbling forth a comic song, being compelled thereunto by Peter Painter, who had a small knife, with the point of which he spurred on the doctor every time he seemed about to stop.

This was no wilful cruelty on the part of Peter, he being forced to do what he was doing by a black-bearded gentleman, who held a pistol close to his temple.

The doctor made a pause between each syllable to look round him, and at each pause, the pirate with the pistol pushed its muzzle close to Peter's temple.

Under these circumstances as, self-preservation is the first law of nature, Peter at once plunged the knife into the unfortunate doctor's flank, and at each stab the doctor shouted "oh," and bounded at least a foot from his chair, so that there can be little wonder, that the pirates laughed.

Even Deveril laughed, a rare thing for him to do, and was so much amused that he waited until the end of the song, which finished by a deep dig of the knife by Peter, and a still deeper groan from the doctor, whose head sank forward on the table.

"Encore! encore!" roared the men.

"Hold!" cried Deveril, advancing;

" what right have you to let these men eat and drink with us at the same board. Are you mad? Have you forgotten the rules of our order?"

" We meant no harm, captain," grumbled one of the men, "*you* let them drink with us."

" Aye, to please José's whim — the fancy of a dying man—but not to make them one of us. Now, we have only two ways left open to us, and these are to make them brothers or to kill them. Which shall it be, my lads? Will you have them as companions, or will you not?"

" They shall be our brothers," shouted one burly fellow; "we want a doctor, and the other will make us food for powder for the enemy. Let them join us."

" Ay, aye, let them join us," shouted the others.

" Gentlemen," said Deveril quietly, " you have heard what my good fellows declare, you are to join us, or be shot.

" Choose, gentlemen; I give you five minutes to decide."

" I'll join, I'll join, Mr. Pirate," cried Peter, who had turned deadly pale at the idea of being shot.

" Peter, Peter," groaned the unhappy doctor, "do you know what you are saying? Oh! that I had never left the boats, and gone in search of orchids."

" But, doctor," replied Peter, "if we do not join them we shall be shot."

" And if we join them and are taken by our countrymen, we shall be hanged," replied McTaggart.

" Just so, doctor, but if we join the pirates we may not be taken for some time, therefore we may have a long time to live; but if we refuse, we know these gentlemen will carry out their threats with the greatest despatch. No, doctor, I shall join."

" Now, doctor," cried Deveril, "will you join us?

" Yes, or no?"

" Yes, yes, I will join," groaned the doctor "and may heaven have mercy on me."

" Lead them away, and see that they are properly treated," cried Deveril.

The prisoners were led into another cave, where they were stripped of all their clothes, and then were compelled to leap into two hogsheads containing a jet black fluid.

" Down with you," cried the man who had taken charge of the operation, "down under the fluid, heads and all. If you attempt to rise above the surface I'll dash your brains out with the butt-end of my pistol.

" Down!" and he emphasised the last word with a heavy crack on the heads of the prisoners, compelling them to plunge beneath the surface, where they were forced to remain for fully a minute, when they were permitted to climb out of their inky baths.

They were then placed before a roaring fire, the heat of which acted so quickly on the liquid that it dried in a few minutes, and no African negro was ever blacker than Dr. McTaggart and Peter Painter.

" Now dress yourselves in these clothes," said the man, throwing to each a common suit of sailor's clothes.

When they had obeyed, a man stepped forward and cropped Peter's hair quite short. They would have done the same for the doctor, only as he was as bald as a billiard ball, they were unable.

The prisoners were then led back to the chief cave, where they were compelled to take the most fearful oaths of faithfulness to the pirate band.

" Listen!" cried Deveril; "do not think that all the ceremonies you have gone through in taking the oath of fidelity have been for fun!"

" I don't," groaned the doctor.

" Everything has a meaning in it, which you will better understand when you are admitted fully into the brotherhood. At present you will only be told one or two things. Be sure that you are attentive to what I say, for if you, after this, make a mistake, no excuse will save you from the punishment I shall visit upon you."

" We are attentive; we will not forget," said Peter, quickly.

" The reason you have been dyed black is to disguise you should you meet any old friends."

" Verily thou hast done that to perfection," said the doctor. "My own mother would not know me."

" It also is a safeguard against your running away. For if you did so, we should very easily trace you, and once in our power your doom would be death by torture!"

"Oh, lor!" ejaculated Peter Painter.

"At present you will be treated as servants. McTaggart, your business will be to wait on me, be my surgeon, my valet, in fact, anything I please.

"You, Peter, will attend on Captain Gomez. Neither of you will have arms of any kind until you have proved your faithfulness to the brotherhood. Then, step by step, you will be promoted until you are full-fledged pirates. Now, men, to our pleasures."

The pirates shouted, and in a little time the wildest fun and most exuberant hilarity again prevailed.

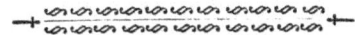

CHAPTER XVII.

THE MYSTERIOUS APPEARANCE OF THE VOLCANO—OUR HERO SAVES A MAN, AND RECEIVES SOME STRANGE INFORMATION.

CAPTAIN BREEZE and some of his officers stood upon the quarter-deck of the "Sea Breeze," closely scanning the island, to which their attention had been called soon after dark by the strange appearance it had assumed.

As we have already said, the island was in truth nothing more than an exhausted volcano.

But as the darkness closed in, a lurid light seemed to rise from the crater.

"The volcano seems springing into activity again, captain," said one of the officers.

"Them there fiery mountains are like women — there ain't any trusting on them. Don't you think, sir, that we had better stand more out to sea?" said old Jack Barnacle.

"Not until I know more about the mountain," said Captain Breeze. "Go below, Mr. Barnacle, and ask Mr. Daulton if he can come on deck for a few moments, as I wish to see him."

Down below scuttled old Barnacle, and soon returned with the lieutenant.

"Look yonder, Mr. Daulton," said our hero. "Can you explain that phenomenon?"

"The volcano must be about to become active again," was the reply.

"No; I do not think it is that," replied our hero; "but rather that is the work of the pirates. Probably they have done this to deceive us; but we know they landed there, and at present we cannot discover any way they could have left the place.

"Mr. Barnacle, see that the cutter is lowered. I shall pull nearer to the island."

The order was given and carried out.

"I'll take care of the ship whilst you are away," said Lieutenant Daulton. "But, my dear boy, be cautious. Take Barnacle with you; he is an old sailor, and may be useful. And above all, do not venture too close to the island; be cautious, for those wretches are as cruel as they are treacherous."

"Fear not; I will take care," replied our hero as he leaped into the boat. "Give way, men, and pull steadily and quietly."

As the boat approached the island, the light from the volcano became stronger.

The night was a dark one, neither moon nor stars to be seen; but although the sky looked so threatening, the water was perfectly calm.

The sailors pulled close into the island, and keeping under the shadow of some rocks, remained perfectly motionless.

And now, upon the still night air, arose wild yells and shrieks, as if a band of fiends had broken loose, and were carrying on the most diabolical revels.

The sailors turned pale as they heard these fearful sounds; and one or two breathed a prayer, for they fully believed that the noise was made by evil spirits.

"What do you think of this, sir?" asked Barnacle. "Blessed if I don't think they are fiends."

"Fiends in human shape, Barnacle," said our hero. "The noise is made by the pirates. I would give something if I knew how I could get at them; but it shall go hard if I don't find their secret out, and destroy this nest of vipers. Stay! what is that in the water over there? Surely it is someone swimming?"

"Not a bit of it, sir; it's some large fish. The back of a shark most likely."

"No—hush! it is a man. Did you not hear that cry for help? Give way, lads, and pull to him."

"Take care, sir — take care, for heaven's sake," said Barnacle; "this may be a snare."

"I know not if it be. I only know that I see that the man is sinking, and I must save him."

The men pulled to the object our hero had seen, and leaning over the side of the boat, Captain Breeze had only just time to seize the man—for it was a man—by the collar to prevent his sinking for the last time.

They pulled him into the boat, and as they did so, his right hand struck the gunwale. The fellow uttered a shrill cry of pain, and fell back insensible.

"The poor wretch has had his wrist broken," said Captain Breeze. "Here, one of you, pass that bottle of brandy here. Mr. Barnacle, you must steer, whilst I will look after this poor fellow."

"Aye, aye, sir! But which way shall I steer?" demanded Jack Barnacle.

"To the ship. This fellow may be able to tell us the mystery of the rock."

The men pulled back to the ship, and the half-drowned man—whom our readers have doubtless recognised as Spanish José—was at once placed in a hammock, where he was carefully attended to by our hero.

In about an hour's time the man was sufficiently recovered to be cross-questioned.

He stared blankly around him, and refused to answer any questions until he knew where and in whose hands he was, and what was the name of the ship he was in.

"Caramba!" he exclaimed, "and is it possible with my smashed wrist that I swam to this ship? Basta! but it was a brave thing to do. Still I have no remembrance of it."

"You did not swim to the ship," replied Captain Breeze. "I had a boat pulled in shore. I saved you."

"Humph! I do not recollect that more than the other," said the man.

"You are a pirate?"

"No," replied José, with a quick glance at our hero, "I am not a pirate."

"Then who are you? Are you one of their captives escaped?"

"No — yes — that is perhaps so," replied José; then after a pause, he went on—

"Captain, if you will grant me a free pardon, and give me your word that I shall not be punished for my past deeds, I will tell you the whole truth, and put vast wealth into your hands."

"How can I promise you that? How can I tell what terrible deeds you have done?—for I believe that *you are* a pirate, in spite of all you may say.

"If you will carry out your word, however, I will not hand you over to justice, but use what interest I possess in the proper quarters to gain your pardon. Will that do?"

"It must," said the man, after a short reflection. Then suddenly looking up, he said—

"You do not know me? I am Spanish José, boatswain to Gomez."

"Ah! I have heard of you; but I only knew the men who sailed with Deveril."

"Yes; you were kept as close as a rat in a trap. I have tried to find out who you are, but have failed. Do you know? Ah! I thought not."

"Never mind about my birth; but tell me how you came into the water."

"Give me a cigarette and I will do so," said the Spaniard, quietly.

Our hero rolled him up a cigarette. The Spaniard lit it, and, leaning back in his hammock, related all about the pirates' banquet, the quarrel, and his escape from execution.

"Then you mean to tell me that in the centre of this island there is a lake, in the caves round which the pirates live?"

"Beyond a doubt. Did I not tell you that I have only just escaped from there?"

"Yes; but you did not tell me how," replied Captain Breeze.

"May I ask, captain, what you would do if I showed you the way to this lake?"

"I would at once attack the place and destroy this nest of hornets."

"Basta! but you would not find that so easy to do.

"Listen, senor. I could take you to the entrance of this inland lake; but then you would not be able to enter it. Sunken rocks are strewed everywhere, and only a few of the pirates even know how to pilot a boat into the narrow channel.

"Again, the channel is well guarded, and Deveril has a force five times as large as you could bring."

"Are there not any other means of entering the pirates' stronghold?" asked our hero.

"Yes; but they are kept strictly secret. Even I never had one shown to me, save the one I have told you about."

"How, then, did you escape?"

"I will tell you the truth. I discovered one secret passage. I made the discovery purely by accident, and I doubt much if even Captain Deveril knows it. But although, as I have found, it is most useful to escape by, or to spy upon the pirates' actions, it would not be of the slightest use to attack by."

"Will you show me the way?"

"Can you swim?—can you dive?"

"Yes; there is scarcely anything which I cannot do in the water. You know, I was born at sea."

"So I have heard; but I doubt it. Well, senor, let a boat be manned and alongside an hour before dawn. Have the oars muffled, be ready to start with me, and I will be your guide to the pirates' secret cave."

"It shall be done. And now I will go and see that all is prepared."

CHAPTER XVIII.

A STRANGE EXPEDITION—THE GOBLIN CAVE—OUR HERO ALONE AMONGST THE PIRATES.

IT was pitch dark when the boat was manned and lowered.

Then José and our hero, dressed in light canvas suits and close caps, such as fishermen wear, stepped into the boat, and the order was given for the men to give way.

"You take the rudder lines, captain, and I will tell you how to steer," said José.

"Very well," replied Captain Breeze. "Give way, men. Pull steadily and noiselessly."

Through the dark waters shot the boat, José keeping his eyes fixed upon the huge rock, and now and then waving his hand to larboard or starboard, as he wished the boat to be steered.

At last they were close under a part of the volcanic island, where the mountain rose up to a tremendous height, and was smooth and perfectly perpendicular.

"In with your oars, men," whispered José. "Keep quite still; you must remain here until we return."

"Avast, there!" growled Jack Barnacle; "you can't land on a place like that."

"Don't you fret yourself," said José, quietly. "I know what I am about."

"Captain," said honest Barnacle, placing his hand upon our hero, "don't you go for to do anything rash. How do we know if what this fellow says may not be false?

"How do you know that this here ain't a trap? What proof is there that he ain't a-going to lead you to destruction? I say let us pull back to the ship, and if you must go after any adventures of this kind, do it in the broad daylight, not in a night like this, when it is as black as pitch."

The sailors evidently agreed to this, and even our hero could not help looking doubtful.

"Come at the daytime!" replied José, scornfully. "Come to your death, you mean! This expedition must be undertaken at night, or not at all. Senor, I do not blame you for doubting me; it is natural, but, in this case, wrong. That there is much danger in this expedition, I admit.

"If we are taken by the pirates, it will mean death for me, but I do not think Deveril would let you be hurt; he likes you too well."

"Strikes me he has a rum way of showing his liking!" growled Barnacle. "If he nails people he likes to a mast, I should like to know what he does to those he does not like. You take my advice, sir—don't you go."

"Deveril must have been mad when he did that," said José, "for I know that he does not wish to kill you, Captain Breeze—if not out of love, for some other reason. Therefore, you would not be put to death. On the other hand, if I am taken, I shall be tortured to death. But I will not press you further. If you will not go, let us return to the ship."

"I will go with you; but mark this, if I discover that you are about to betray me——"

"Put a bullet through me. I shall deserve it, and you will be right to do so. Now, are you ready, for we are near the pirate's home?"

"Yes; I am quite ready. Tell me what I am to do."

"Dive down as deep as you can, and swim some twenty strokes under water towards that rock, and then rise to the surface. I will go first. Now, are you ready, and do you understand what you have to do?"

"Perfectly."

"Very well; follow me."

The fellow stooped down, and seemed to slip into the water like an eel, making scarcely a splash.

In an instant he had disappeared, and in another our hero followed him.

Down, down, down they went, and then Captain Breeze made his way to the rock, which, to his surprise, although he was a quick swimmer under water, he did not touch before he was compelled to rise to the surface by want of breath.

He reached the surface of the water, and gazed around in amazement.

To what strange place had he come?

All around him was completely dark—so much so that he could not even see the glimmer of the water. When he had plunged into the sea, there had been a slight southerly breeze; now there was not a breath of air.

The sky, it was true, had been dark; still, clouds could be seen as they rushed along—now not the slightest cloud or glimmer of the faintest light could be seen.

The atmosphere was close and oppressive, and the smell of the iodine of the sea tremendous.

All this our hero had discovered in a minute, and, treading water, he remained almost stationary, gazing around him.

"Is that you, captain?" said a voice close by him, causing him to start; for although he knew the voice to be that of José, who only spoke in a whisper, yet it sounded hollow, and there were strange noises in the air, which had a horrible, ghastly effect.

"Yes; I am here. What horrible place is this to which you have brought me?"

"Horrible! I warrant me you never saw a more magnificent one in your life."

"It may be so, for at present I cannot see a thing. How cold the water is!"

"Yes. We had better take a rest. Keep where you are, and whistle softly, so that I may know where to swim to you, guided by the sound."

Our hero did as he was told, and in a little time he felt José seize his arm.

"That is well. Now swim with me; or, better still, take the end of this scarf, turn over on your back and float, and I will draw you to the landing place."

The captain seized the scarf, and José, holding the other end in his teeth, towed him to a rock.

"Scramble up here. I will get a light soon, and then if you do not confess that I have brought you to a natural palace, I shall indeed be surprised.

José crawled up the rocks, and presently the captain could hear him hard at work with a flint and steel.

A flash, and he had lighted a maroon or blue light, which gave forth a strange glare.

Captain Breeze looked round him in astonishment, for the sight he beheld was one of the most beautiful and weird that the most fantastical brain could imagine.

He found they had entered a large natural cave, which appeared to have no exit or entrance.

The walls were irregular, and the projections and deep indentures took hideous goblin forms under the blue light. Crystals were imbedded in some places, and sparkled like diamonds, whilst from the ceiling long stalactites of various hues hung, giving the place a beautiful but goblin appearance.

José remained for some moments perfectly silent, watching his companion and enjoying his look of wonder.

"It is indeed a terribly beautiful place," said Captain Breeze at last.

"Basta! you say rightly. When I look at this place I wonder how it is people can refuse to believe in goblins and gnomes.

"This island abounds in strange caves and strange sights. Deveril and others say that it is an extinct volcano, and I do not doubt it, for, see, here are large pits full of sulphur. Sometimes ghostly shadows are seen flitting about the lake. How do we know what kind of creatures lived down here when this mountain was all ablaze?"

"Tut, tut!" said the irate captain, "nothing could live in fire."

"I doubt that," said José; "the air has birds; the water, fishes; the surface of the earth, animals; and far down in the bowels of the earth, worms.

"Why, then, should fire be the only element wherein life cannot exist?

"They may have been demons, goblins, gnomes, imps, or whatever you like to call them, but I believe that they did exist, and these caves are their handiwork."

"I do not believe there were any devils in this mountain until the pirates took possession of it," said our hero, "and worse demons than they are could not be found."

"You may be right," replied José, "but I like to think differently. But we must start on our journey.

"Remember that you must not use your pistol but as a last resource. Trust to your knife and sword; the sound of a pistol shot would alarm the whole place, and we should have the pirates down upon us at once."

"How did you find out this place?" demanded our hero.

"By accident when diving; having found my way into the cave I managed to find my way out again. I returned, bringing lights with me, so that I could examine the cave well. I tried the walls, and at last found another opening below water-mark, which let me reach the sea."

"It was a bold undertaking," said our hero.

"Yes, and not at all a pleasant one at first. However, I had long known that Deveril would sooner or later destroy me. He had made up his mind to do so, as he suspected me. Therefore, it became necessary that I should plan means to escape. I brought provisions, knives, and other things I thought I might want, into this cave, and concealed them here.

"But you must be sure to mark the place where we shall emerge from the water, for we may have to dive in hurriedly, and if you miss the opening and are seized, then it will be all up with you. Now, are you ready?"

"Yes, lead on."

"Remember that the opening which leads into the lake is exactly opposite the one which leads into the sea. Now follow."

Again they dived, and passed through another submarine passage, and on rising, Captain Breeze found himself in the inland lake amongst the pirates.

CHAPTER XIX.

THE CHILD OF THE WAVES SEES LUCINDA FOR THE FIRST TIME—LOVE'S POWER—A DARING UNDERTAKING, AND A BOLD RESOLVE.

"KEEP close to the rock," whispered José, "and do not even make a splash. Stay! here is a ledge where you can cling. So. Look round and tell me what you think of this."

"This is indeed most remarkable. And where is this entrance you spoke about?"

"Yonder do you see a small tunnel only some six feet broad, and some three feet above the water?"

"Yes."

"That is the way the boats enter. The ship remains in a kind of land-locked bay outside."

"But there must be other entrances?" exclaimed the captain. "Deveril would never trust himself to a place from which there was no escape."

"There are many secret ways into the place, I have no doubt," said José, "but Deveril is the only one who knows nearly all of them; and that he does not know all, is proved by his not knowing about this one.

"One or two of the captains know some of the ways, and they are bound by the most awful vows never to reveal these secrets to any but the most trustworthy of their crews.

"To be found searching the mountain is *death* by the law of the band.

"But now, senor, what do you wish to do?"

"I wish to examine the rock," said the captain, coolly, as he drew himself out of the water. "I must find out some means of entering this place. To see it as we have seen it, is of no good. Will you show me the way?"

"Caramba! it is showing you the way to my death," muttered José. "I did not bargain for this."

"If you are afraid you need not go. I will lead no man into danger against his will."

"Stay behind! Not I, senor. I must die one time or the other, so come along. Only you must let me lead the way, and whatever you see do not be surprised, and don't make the slightest noise.

"Remember, the pirates we have to deal with are more devils than men."

Captain Breeze nodded his head. "Go on," he said.

Crawling carefully up the rock, José had just reached the platform, when he paused and made a sign to the captain to remain quiet and keep where he was.

Captain Breeze saw José draw his long knife, and then glide on to the platform like a snake, and wriggle along until he reached a place where stood a sentinel.

His musket leant against a rock, and he himself was half-stupefied with drink —for the guard in the pirate home was very carelessly kept, it being believed that no enemy could penetrate into the stronghold.

José first carefully removed the priming from the man's gun, and then raised himself up on his feet.

Grasping the long knife tightly, he, in an instant, plunged it into the man's back.

Not even a groan escaped the unhappy wretch, and José coolly let him slip down upon some rocks below.

"Now, senor, we are pretty safe. Will you follow me?" said the Spaniard.

"Great heavens! you have killed the man," said Captain Breeze, in horror.

"Yes, senor, there was nothing else for it. But why are you so horrified? You would have cut him down or blown him to pieces in battle——"

"Yes, in fair fight, but not stabbed him in the back," replied our hero.

"Bah! you are too particular. Now, senor, I think you cannot doubt my truthfulness, and can trust me. You see yonder entrance to a cave from which a light is gleaming?"

"Yes. What place is that?"

"That is the chief banqueting hall, and from there lead the chambers of Captain Deveril, and his chief officers and favourites. There also a great portion of his treasures are kept."

Captain Breeze thought for a moment, and then examined his pistols and saw that they had not been damaged.

"I will lead the way," he said quietly, and then approached the mouth of the cave, using the greatest caution.

The large cave was deserted, and the lamps burned low.

Taking one of the lamps, our hero examined the place, and was greatly astonished at the costliness with which it had been fitted up.

Pushing aside the curtain which hung at one end of the cave, he entered a most beautiful little apartment, fitted up in a style more like an Eastern harem than a pirate's cave.

Two large standards, some six feet high, and made of the purest silver, stood at the back of the cave.

On each of them was placed a silver lamp, which gave forth a soft, tender light, at the same time emitting a pleasant perfume.

But between these standards was an object which drew our hero's attention from everything else.

It was a small couch hung with blue silk, and on it reclined a most beautiful maiden fast asleep.

"José," whispered our hero, as he caught the arm of his companion, and pointed at the sleeper, "who is that?"

"Caramba, senor. She is as great a mystery as you were. She is the Senora Lucinda. Where she came from, no one knows. All we are sure of is this: The captain loves her with all his heart."

" And she, can she, so fair a creature, so innocent-looking, love this Deveril ? "

" Love ! Does the dove love the serpent—the canary the cat ? But she is in his power *and must*."

" You do not mean to say that he has dared to force this beautiful girl to marriage ? "

" Well, I know not that, senor ; but I have heard the people most about him say that she scorns him—treats him as if he were the slave and not she."

" She a slave ? It is impossible ! She has the mien and beauty of an empress," cried our hero.

" Basta ! So have many of the goat girls in Andalusia. Still, I admit that the lady Lucinda is beautiful—very beautiful.

" But let us go, senor, she seems waking. If she should scream and we were found here, nothing on earth could save us."

But the captain heeded him not.

Fear had never penetrated his heart, but love now made it tremble.

He stood like one entranced, gazing on the young girl's beautiful face; and just as she was about to open her eyes, he leaned over and kissed her.

Uttering a low scream, the maiden started up, snatched a small sharp dagger from beneath the pillow, and aimed a desperate blow at Captain Breeze, who had scarcely time to step back and avoid it.

" Villain !" she cried, " have I not told thee that I would sooner die a hundred deaths than bear your caresses ? "

" I pray you, pardon me, sweet maiden. I am not he whom you so much dread. Sooner than harm you, I would die ; and before anyone should offer you harm, I would sacrifice my life to save you."

The maiden gazed in wonder at Captain Breeze.

Passing her hands over her eyes, she said in tones of bewilderment—

" Can this be true, or is it some dream sent to torment me ? Who art thou ? "

" One who will be thy slave if thou wilt let me," replied our hero, passionately, as he knelt by the couch.

" Away !" exclaimed the girl. " Has Captain Deveril become so mean that he would entrap me by such base artifices ? And you—you bear an open, honest face, which should be an index to an honest heart, why should you falsify nature ? Begone ! and torment me no more ! "

" Lady," replied Captain Breeze, " you mistake me. I am no friend of this villain Deveril, but his deadly enemy."

" Can this be true ? No ! it cannot be. If you were his enemy, you dare not venture here."

" It is because I am his enemy that I am here," replied our hero. " I have sworn either to kill him, or to bring him to justice. Tell me how I can serve you, and it shall be done."

" Serve me ! Oh ! it is impossible. I am a prisoner amongst these vile wretches. To save my life I had to swear a fearful oath that I would not divulge their secrets until I was permitted by Captain Deveril. I am in his power, and until he dies must remain his prisoner."

" You were compelled to take the oath," urged our hero, " therefore it is not binding on you."

" I dare not betray them—neither dare I venture to escape. I am in his power."

" Yes ; but against your will. Tell me, you cannot say you are his willing captive ? "

" No ! Oh, no ! I am not that. Oh ! if you knew how I shudder when I think of my fate."

" You shudder at this bondage, and yet you dare not break it ? "

" I dare not—I cannot."

" I cannot understand you," cried Captain Breeze. " I know this Deveril well ; know what a strange and fearful power he has over all those with whom he is connected, but only the base and vile would willingly remain with him. It cannot be that you love him."

" I love him ? I hate, abhor him ! Oh ! you cannot tell the depth of the loathing I feel for him. I shudder at his touch. I tremble at his approach as at that of some venomous snake.

" Love him ! Behold this dagger. I have it near me night and day, and if he were to offer me violence, I would strike it into his heart, or into mine own."

Captain Breeze looked with the profoundest admiration at the beautiful girl, an admiration so perceptible that Lucinda's eyes dropped before his, and her cheeks became suffused with blushes.

" Maiden," cried the captain, " I know not who you are, but I love you. Tell me that I may hope, when I have forced you from this thraldom, one day to call you mine ; and I swear that I will never rest until I have claimed you as my own.

" Nay, do not shrink from me. I know that my passion has carried me away, and that my boldness may frighten you, but not mine the fault, but rather your beauty, fair lady. Do not turn away from me ; give me but some faint hope, and I will pledge my life to rescue you."

" Most noble and generous stranger," replied Lucinda, blushing, as she cast down her eyes, " I know not who you are, neither do I know whence you come ; but your noble offer to help one so friendless and forlorn as I, shows that you have a brave and honest heart.

" I do accept your offer ; and, in proof that he who gains my freedom will receive my life-long gratitude, and that I will do all I can to repay him, I give you this ring. When I am free return it to me, and ask what you will. If it be in my power, it shall be granted."

" Sweetest maiden," cried our hero, as he took the ring, and, kneeling, kissed the hand that gave it, " I need not tell you what the reward will be that I shall ask, for all the treasures of the world would be valueless to me if I had not your love. I will keep this ring as my greatest treasure. Do you keep this one, and sometimes, as you gaze upon it, think of me," and he placed a ring upon her finger.

" I pray you, sir, depart. If Elspie should find you here, she would arouse the men, and your death would be certain."

" Caramba ! senor, are you mad to delay like this when every moment is fraught with danger ?" cried José, who had been standing in a shadowy part of the cave, and had, in consequence, been hitherto unobserved by the maiden.

" Ah ! that is José the pirate," cried Lucinda, shrinking back ; " I am betrayed."

" No, senora. It is true I am José, but I am no longer a pirate. I am now an honest man, and the deadly enemy of the pirates. I now serve under Captain Conrad Breeze."

" Conrad," ejaculated Lucinda. " Surely I have heard Elspie and Deveril speak of a youth called Conrad ? Are you the Conrad of whom they spoke ? "

" I am," replied our hero. " But I must not linger longer in this place, although I fain would remain by you for ever. My birth is shrouded in mystery ; but time will dispel the clouds that have o'ershawowed my life. Already gleams of light have pierced the gloom, and I doubt not that I shall be able soon to force the fiend Deveril to disclose all. Till then, sweet angel, fare you well."

One kiss he snatched from the shrinking girl, and then hurried from the room.

" Basta ! senor, you have made a good thing of this," said José, sneeringly. " You came here to conquer, and are conquered. You are a captive to love, and I suppose now will go back to the ship as melancholy as all lovers do. The senora is beautiful, but methinks you have bid rather too high a price for her, and——"

" Silence ! " said Conrad, sternly. " Breathe not a word against that lady, or I become your foe."

" By Jove ! this is a case of love at first sight. Well, senor, I do not care. Do as you will. I will just take a few of these golden cups, and then we will return to the ship."

" Do what you will. I doubt not but that you have as much right to the plate as Deveril."

" If it came to a matter of *right*," laughed José, " I don't think any of us would have much to claim on that score. But as we have to swim to the boats, I will take the smallest, and——"

" Peace ! Take what you wish. Which is Deveril's apartment ? "

" That yonder. But why, senor ? You surely would not go into the lion's den ? "

" I intend to see Deveril—perhaps to speak to him—at all events, to leave him some proof that I have been here."

" You must be mad—the captain always sleeps well armed. A brace of pistols are always by his side, and he never misses aim. Be warned, senor, and do not attempt this dangerous game."

" I tell you that I will see Deveril. Will you come with me ? "

" Come with you ! I ? faith, not I ! No, no, senor ; I know the captain too well. When I face him again it shall be with a score or two of valiant men at my back; but until then I will keep out of his way."

"Do as you will. Go, when you have completed your work, to the place that leads to the cave by which we entered this place. There await me. I shall not be long."

"That is, if you return at all," growled José. "I tell you it is certain death."

"I do not think so," replied our hero, quietly. "If you should hear any firing, wait until you are in danger, then go at once."

Drawing his cutlass, our hero strode into the pirate's private apartment.

CHAPTER XX.

THE SLEEP OF SIN—A TROUBLED CONSCIENCE —CONRAD CONFRONTS DEVERIL— THE TEMPTATION REJECTED—THE COMBAT—A TERRIBLE BLOW.

CONRAD, the Child, of the Waves, found the pirate's apartment fitted up much in the same manner as the state cabin of a yacht.

The cave was illuminated by a silver swing lamp, which was suspended from the roof.

Stretched on the couch was the pirate, Deveril, asleep; but in no easy sleep, such as comes to those who have a clear conscience, but a slumber wherein hideous dreams passed through the heated brain.

By the side of the bed were two silver-mounted pistols and a heavy cutlass.

Cautiously Conrad removed the pistols, drew the bullets, and then replaced the weapons.

Having done this, he approached a writing-table, and, taking pen, ink, and paper, wrote the following note—

"From Conrad, the Child of the Waves, to the villain, Captain Walter Deveril.

"Be prepared to meet your fate. I have sworn to destroy you, and I will keep my word.

"Much that you have hidden I have had revealed to me. Heaven has placed in my hands the means to pursue you and punish you, and I have sworn never to rest until I have rid the world of so vile a fiend.

"Beware how you treat the maiden who is in your power, for I warn you that you shall soon be called to account, and be forced to atone for your sins.

"Adieu, we shall meet again soon."

Having finished writing this, he placed it on the table by Deveril's bedside, and, as he did so, the pirate tossed about and breathed our hero's name.

"Conrad!" he exclaimed. "Yes;

where is your son? Ha, ha, ha! Think you to frighten me? I tell you, Ireton, that I loved her. Bah! What is that you say—treachery? Well, call it what you like, I care not. Fear! I have no fear. My soul is too far steeped in sin. Nothing can save me. I will go on bravely to the last, and risk all for revenge."

"Unhappy wretch," thought Conrad; "how powerfully, even in your sleep, you argue in favour of virtue. You have wealth and power, it is true; but all the wealth in the world would not purchase you one moment's peace of mind."

"So you are the Earl of Bellchambers?" continued the sleeping pirate. "Ha, ha, ha! *You* are the last of your race! Ho, ho, ho! The name of which you are so proud will be extinct. The title dies with you!

"Ah! you would grasp my throat! Back, or I will strike you! I killed him? No; *you killed him*—killed him by your infernal pride! Fancy a father plotting against his son out of pride! Ha! ha! ha!"

Conrad shrank back in horror as he heard these mysterious words.

But suddenly the pirate's tone changed, and something like contrition and awe rang in them as he cried—

"Pauline! Pauline! I loved you—heaven alone knows how dearly! I could not bear to see you happy with another; but I spared him from death for your sake, and——

"Back—back, I say! Why do you torment me thus? Away, fiends! In vain you try to tear me down and frighten me! Know ye not that my soul knows no fear ?   I see the flames—fierce serpents dart out their fiery stings at me, but I will not yield !   Oh ! mercy, mercy, mercy !"

As he spoke the last words his face became perfectly horrible from its expression of agony.

The features worked in convulsions, the complexion became livid, and huge beads of perspiration stood out on his forehead.

Clasping his hands, he sprang up on his couch, and gazed wildly round.

Then Conrad noticed, as the coverlet was thrown back, that the pirate captain was in full dress.

As Deveril's eyes fell upon Conrad, he gave a convulsive start and grasped his pistols.

"Am I still dreaming ? " he murmured in a low voice.   "Are you one of the phantoms that haunt my sleep ? Begone, I fear you not !   If I be doomed to perdition, I will meet my fate boldly like a man—not like a whining coward."

" I am no spirit, but the youth whom you would in your passion have so foully murdered.   See, I am flesh and blood, for I have written that letter by your side, and Conrad pointed to the letter he had written.

" For what purpose have you ventured here, then ?" demanded Deveril.   " Know you not that I hate you ? "

" Yes ; and that you would do much to compass my death.   Still, I have no fear of you."

" No fear of me ? " said Deveril, as he levelled one of his pistols at our hero. " You know I am a dead shot."

" Yes," replied the Child of the Waves, coolly ; " that is why I unloaded those pistols.   I knew if you awoke and saw me at your writing-table you would fire upon me."

Deveril examined the pistols, and when he found that our hero had spoken the truth, he dashed them down in his rage, and leaping from the bed seized his cutlass.

" This, at least will not fail me," he exclaimed as he drew it.   " Rash boy, you are in my power ! "

" Not so, Walter Deveril," replied Conrad, drawing his sword ; " as you know, I am skilled in fence.   But before we strike a blow I would speak to you."

"If you would speak, speak quickly.

But I will give you some advice first, and one more chance."

" Speak, but do not think to frighten me from my purpose.   Nothing can turn me."

" Boy ! " cried Deveril, " you know not what a fearful struggle it costs me to speak as calmly to you even as I do now.   But I never flinch from what I have sworn to perform, and I have taken an oath that when I had you in my power, before I raised my hand against you, I would give you *one* more chance."

" That time has now arrived."

" You are very positive," replied Conrad with a sneer.   " I pray you go on and dispatch."

" I am not sure how you gained an entrance to this place, but I *am* assured of one thing—unless you agree to my terms, you shall not leave it alive."

" That may be.   But it is not, I presume, the subject about which you wish to speak ?   Go on."

" Conrad—for I will call you by your name, now, though for purposes of my own I would have for ever concealed it from you—my feelings have not always been against you.

" Had you listened to me I would have made you leader of this band, and at my death you should have inherited all my wealth."

" Do you think that I would receive wealth so gained ?" cried Conrad proudly. " Never ! "

" Listen, boy, to my wrongs.

" I was once as proud of my good name as any noble in the world, and loved—ah ! how I loved.   Well, fortune smiled upon me, and I married my beloved one.   To me life then seemed a happy dream, but there was a serpent in my paradise.

" In an unlucky hour I met the Earl of Bellchambers.   He professed friendship for me, and advanced me money to purchase a ship and trade, for I had been brought up a sailor.

" I trusted him and sailed away with a light heart, hoping to win fortune for her I loved and our babe.   But he, the noble earl, this gentleman beseiged my wife's heart, won her, and I returned to find my home desolate, my wife, my child gone from me."

" Can this be true ?   Did you not seek

out the cowardly ruffian and avenge your wrongs?"

"I would have done so, but he knew of my return, accused me of piracy, declared me his debtor, and set the law to work against me."

"Can such villainy really exist?" exclaimed Conrad.

"Ay, boy! But hear the sequel, and blame me if you can. I had to fly, but not alone.

"One night, aided by some dare-devil fellows, I carried off my wife and child, bore them on board this ship, and become what I had been accused of being—

"A pirate.

"Now, Conrad, you know what made me the wretch I am. Can you blame me?"

"You have had much to bear, but if the earl treated you so cruelly, is that a reason that you should declare war on all mankind? No! the more you should have felt for others."

"I—I feel for others? I, the wronged and deceived? I, the jeered and scoffed at? No! I have declared war against all mankind. Tell me, Conrad, will you join me? Our life is one of daring, suited to a bold spirit like yours. Be my lieutenant, Conrad. By your aid I will seize the 'Sea Breeze,' and rechristen her the 'Firebrand,' and you shall be her captain."

"No; I am no traitor. When you had me cast into the sea, the crew of the 'Sea Breeze' saved me. I am now their captain, I have sworn with them that I will destroy this nest of pirates, and I will keep my word. I pity, but cannot pardon you."

"Boy, beware, lest you tempt me too far."

"Tut! I fear you not. Had I fear in my heart do you think I should be here?"

"Conrad, you know not the terribleness of my wrongs. You have not loved."

"Not loved!" cried Conrad, and then stopped and flushed red.

"Ah! is it so?" exclaimed Deveril. "And yet when you sailed with me you never saw a female. But love comes in a minute, and grows swifter than the forest bine. Stay!" he cried, quickly, "where did you get that ring?"

As he spoke he pointed to the ring which Lucinda had given the Child of the Waves.

So suddenly was this question put that Conrad became confused, and flushed more than ever.

"Ah!" exclaimed Deveril, his brow becoming black as midnight, "can this be so? Are you and yours ever to cross my path and blight my dearest hopes? Boy, answer me at once—how did you come by that ring?"

"By what right do you dare question me? I refuse to answer you. It is mine, and I will keep it."

Foam flecks came upon Deveril's livid lips, and he trembled with passion, although he endeavoured to be calm.

"Conrad, I *know* where that ring came from. It was Lucinda's. Tell me, did she give it you, or did you steal it?"

"Steal it!" cried Conrad, indignantly, as he grasped his cutlass tighter.

"*So she gave it you?*" hissed Deveril, between his teeth. "You viper! you have poisoned my life, and yet I have spared you, and now you would tear Lucinda from me. But I am used to misfortune and hardships. Listen, Conrad—do as I have told you, join as my lieutenant, betray the 'Sea Breeze' into my hands, and Lucinda shall become your bride."

"Do you think that I am as base as you are? Think you that Lucinda could love one who was a traitor? No! she would spurn me from her. If she did not I would cease to love her. I tell you, Walter Deveril, that there can be no terms but war between us. I have sworn to avenge the outrages you have committed, I have pledged my word to release Lucinda, and it shall be done."

"Ah! say you so?" cried Deveril, "Thus, then, will I end your hopes."

Springing forward with the swiftness of lightning, he brought his sword down with a fearful cut at our hero's head, but the Child of the Waves was too quick for him, and a fearful combat ensued.

Deveril had more strength than his opponent; in skill the combatants were equal; but Conrad had the advantage of coolness, for the pirate chief fought with the utmost rashness.

Neither of them breathed a word.

Foot to foot, eyes fixed upon eyes, the two fought.

At last Deveril became mad with rage at being baffled, and springing forward to make a furious blow, his foot slipped, and he fell prostrate on the ground, his sword slipping from his grasp.

In an instant Conrad was upon him, his foot placed firmly on the fallen pirate's chest, and his sword's point at his heart.

In another moment Deveril's life would have been ended; but some curtains at the end of the room were thrust on one side and Elspie, the Witch of the Rock, rushed forward, and seizing our hero's arm, exclaimed—

"Hold—hold! rash youth. You know not who it is you would slay."

"Unhand me!" cried Conrad. "I know too well the nature of the cruel reptile I have beneath my foot. He is no man to claim mercy. He is a devil."

"Strike if you will," exclaimed Elspie with a shrill laugh as she released his arm, "strike! and KILL YOUR FATHER!"

CHAPTER XXI.

CONRAD REMAINS FIRM—DEVERIL'S DECEIT—BLACK BEN AND CONRAD IN THE DEATH STRUGGLE.

As Conrad heard these words he reeled back as if struck by some terrible blow.

The blood flew to his temples, and he almost fell to the ground.

"'Tis false!" he cried at last. "I will not believe it. No father would treat his child as Walter Deveril has treated me. No father would try to take his son's life and drag him down to sin."

"A father who has been well-treated would not," replied Elspie with a diabolic grin. "You forget how your father has been treated by your mother. Ha, ha, ha, ha! a fine madame who——"

"Silence!" cried Conrad. "I will not hear one word said against my mother. I know not if your story be true; but if it be it is no fit one for a son's ears. I will not listen."

"Will not listen," roared Deveril as he sprang to his feet, and clutching one of his pistols, hastily rammed a bullet into it. "But you shall listen. That you are my son I now must own, although I would willingly have hidden it from you, for in you I behold my disgrace. But now that your are owned as my child I claim your obedience.

"Put down that sword, and thank heaven that you have not to answer for a father's blood. Put down the sword."

"Never!" cried Conrad. "I have nothing to thank you for. He who could love or respect such a fiend would share his crimes. I'll have none of it."

"Say you so?" roared Deveril. "Methinks I will soon make you sing another tune. Once more I ask you, is it to be peace or war? Pause ere you answer, for you are now in my power."

"If I were at the stake, and you held the flaming torch to ignite the faggots, I would spit at and defy you.

"Then your blood be upon your own head," cried Deveril; and levelling his pistol at our hero he fired.

His aim, however, was bad, and Conrad was unhurt, but the discharge of the pistol re-echoed like thunder through the caves, and at once alarmed the pirates, who came swarming out like bees from a hive.

Deveril snatched up his cutlass and attacked Conrad with all his might.

The Child of the Waves perceived the danger he was in.

The pirates were now all fully awake and alarmed; whilst Deveril's attack was of so violent a nature, that he dared not turn and fly, or the pirate would have cut him down.

Deveril rained down fearful blows, whilst Conrad only guarded them, until, in his rage, his antagonist left himself open, and our hero slashed him across the forehead, and that so deeply, that in a few seconds he was blinded with blood.

In rushed a number of pirates, headed by Black Ben.

"Fire and fury!" yelled Deveril, trying to wipe the blood out of his eyes. "Seize that young whelp. He has blinded me. Cut him to pieces. Show him no mercy, he has betrayed us."

"BEFORE THEY COULD REACH IT THE CANISTER BURST INTO FLAMES."

For some moments the men stood as if unable to realise what had happened, and then they made a rush at Conrad.

But our hero had marked his opportunity, and as they made the rush he slipped aside, and then, slashing with his sword in every direction, cut his way through the crowd.

Having done so, he dashed as quickly as he could towards the lake, determined to dive in at once and try to pass into the hidden cave, and from there reach the ship.

But fleet as he was, there was one behind him still faster, and that was Black Ben.

"So ho!" he cried, as he clapped his hand upon our hero's shoulder, just as he was about to spring into the lake, "do you remember Dark Sambo's inn at Kingston? I told you that I would have revenge then, and by heaven I will."

As he spoke he placed the muzzle of a pistol to our hero's head.

Throwing up his arm, Conrad dashed the pistol on one side at the moment it exploded.

The bullet whistled past his ear, and struck one of the pirates full in the heart.

Turning quickly on Black Ben, Conrad aimed a blow at him with his cutlass, which the pirate guarded admirably with his pistol; but the blade of the cutlass, striking on the lock of the firearm, broke off short at the hilt.

The latter Conrad dashed with such violence into the face of Ben, that the villain reeled back and fell.

Then drawing his pistols, which up to now he had not used, our hero shot down the two nearest pirates, and was once more about to plunge into the lake when Black Ben leapt to his feet, and throwing his arms around him, tried to drag him back.

"No, no, my hearty," he said, with a fiendish laugh. "You don't escape me that way. It's no good struggling. I would only release my hold in death, and then I'd hold you."

"Then try it," cried our hero, as grappling with Black Ben, he dragged him one pace nearer the brink of the cliff. "Try it, and believe me I will cling to you until we one or both are dead."

One struggle, and the next moment both of them had fallen into the water.

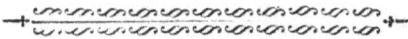

CHAPTER XXII.

A COMBAT ON AND UNDER THE LAKE—CONRAD OVERHEARS THE PIRATE'S SPEECH—OUR HERO RETURNS TO THE "SEA BREEZE."

DOWN—down—down they sank to a fearful death, as it seemed to both Conrad and Black Ben, for they would neither of them give up, and clutched each other firmly.

But at last they were obliged to rise, as if by mutual consent, to take breath, and then they struggled on the top of the waters.

The whole of the caves were lit up now, for the pirates were climbing about the rocks with torches in their hands, waving them about, so as to show a light on the waters of the lake, in hopes of saving Black Ben and seizing our hero.

Black Ben called loudly for help.

Grasping the pirate by the throat, Conrad plunged again, and the struggle once more commenced beneath the surface.

He grappled the villain, and would not let him rise, although Black Ben, quite forgetting his vow that he would never release our hero until death, and not even then, would have been very glad to shake him off.

At last the pirate's grip relaxed, and he struggled to rise, but Conrad held him fast.

As he felt the pirate grow weaker, our hero held him with only one hand, whilst with the other he drew his knife and plunged it into the villain's heart.

Then he released his hold, and the body floated upwards to the surface.

Swimming under the water until he touched the rocks, Conrad then ventured to rise, and to his delight found that he had come up under the shelter of an overhanging rock.

He had scarcely reached this place when he heard the shouts of the pirates that they had discovered the body of their companion.

Conrad watched the pirates as they bore Black Ben's body over the rocky pathway, and laid it at the feet of Deveril, who, with a blood-stained kerchief bound round his brow, stood leaning on his sword, pale and trembling with rage.

"See!" he cried, "see! my brave hearts. Here lies one of your boldest and most daring comrades, dead. Cursed be the hand that slew him. The hand was that of one I would have made one of your leaders, and loved as a son.

"How has he repaid this kindness? By baulking all our plans. He has betrayed us to our old enemy, the captain of the 'Sea Breeze,' and set the bloodhounds of the law upon our heels.

"He stole into my chamber in the dead of night to murder me. See how the traitorous hound has hacked me."

As he spoke he tore off the bandage from his forehead, and the ghastly wound gaped forth afresh, and the blood once more flowed over his cheeks.

A cry of rage rose from the men, and one and all called loudly for vengeance.

"Revenge — revenge!" they cried. "We will be revenged upon the traitor."

"Stay! he may be dead already," said Deveril. "Think you that Black Ben would have fallen so easy a victim to a stripling? No! he has, I doubt not, killed the viper who has stung us; but it would be cowardly on our part if we did not avenge his death, and it shall be done—that is if you have the courage to follow me."

"We have and we will. Long live Captain Deveril! Death to our foes!" roared the pirates.

"'Tis well, my gallant men; you shall have your way, and trust me I will lead you on to victory."

"Hurrah!" shouted the pirates. "Long live Captain Deveril, who always gains the day!"

"Listen, my men: To avenge the death of Black Ben, we must take the 'Sea Breeze.' The crew may join us, but the captain and officers shall swing at the yard-arm or walk the plank. Will you swear to follow me—to conquer or die?"

"We will—we will," shouted the men.

"This, then is my plan—

"To-morrow we keep quite still, and as night approaches we will signal the 'Firebrand,' to stand in near, and at midnight to attack the 'Sea Breeze.'

"At the same time we will leave this place in our boats. In the midst of the confusion of a sea fight and in the darkness our approach will not be noticed, and we shall swoop down upon them like eagles on wood pigeons."

A hearty shout met this proposition, and then Captain Deveril continued—

"And now, my brave fellows, see to your arms; have all in readiness, for I doubt not that the fight will be desperate.

"I know Ireton well. He is a man of the greatest courage and resolution. He will fight to the last, and—mark this— *he must be taken alive.*

"Death would be a relief to him—a relief that he shall not have. Remorse gnaws at his heartstrings. Day by day I will see him suffer. He would have slain me—I will let him live that he may suffer more."

The diabolic idea evidently pleased the men, for they shouted with delight, and then dispersed.

Keeping close under the rocks the Child of the Waves crept along until he reached the spot where he guessed the submarine cavern to be, and then dived.

To his delight he found the cave at once, and in a very little time was out in the sea, swimming swiftly and silently towards the boat, in which he beheld a strange scene being enacted.

Standing up in the boat was old Jack Barnacle, his jacket thrown off, and his waistcoat being torn off in a great fury, whilst at the bottom of the boat was José, held down by a couple of powerful seamen.

"Lay still, you warmint," said one of the men, giving José a heavy tap on the head with his fist; "if you don't I'll give you something that will make you."

"*Angeles demonios!*" hissed José, "what have I done to be treated like this? Is it my fault that your captain would thrust his head into the lion's mouth? I tell you I stayed as long as I dared, but when I heard the pistols fired I knew that it was all up with him, and I made off at once."

"Yes," growled old Barnacle, who was now nearly undressed, "like a cowardly furrener as you are, you sneaked off. Do you think an Englishman would go and leave his captain in distress? No, he'd scorn the action.

"I don't know if you have told me the truth, but I'm going to see, and if I find that you have deceived us, why, then, the Lord have mercy on you, that's all I can say, for I won't."

"What are you going to do?" gasped José. "I tell you if you venture into that place now you will be killed."

"Maybe I shall, but that's neither here nor there. I'm going, and if I do not come back, it strikes me that it will be the worse for you."

"Basta!" cried the Spaniard, "but this is too much. Not only have I to take that mad young fellow into the pirates' home, but when he will not be guided by me—when he scorns my advice, and does all I tell him not to do—I am to be made answerable for that.

"Now this old fool will go and thrust his head into the lion's jaws, and if the lion snaps his head off I am to be punished for it."

"I don't say you will be," replied Barnacle, quietly, "only I do not think that some of my mates may not be too pleasant if the young captain and myself do not come back; but that I leave to them."

Barnacle was about to dive into the water when the Child of the Waves, who had swam so quietly towards the boat that his men had not heard him, called out—

"Hold hard there, Barnacle. You need not take a bath to-night, for I am here."

"By all that is fortunate, it is the captain," cried Barnacle. "All hands to man the ropes and help the captain on board. Here you are, sir. Hurrah! my lads; give three cheers for Captain Breeze."

The men gave a hearty cheer before our hero could stop them; but as soon as he could do so, he commanded them to keep silence, and pull at once to the "Sea Breeze."

José was released, and apologies for the rough treatment he had received made to him, which had the effect of dispersing his just indignation, and in a little time they were all safe on board the ship, where our hero at once had an interview with Captain Ireton, and told him all that had happened.

When the captain and Lieutenant Daulton heard the news, they glanced quickly at each other.

"Can this be Conrad?" said Lieutenant Daulton, in a whisper.

"Hush," replied the captain, in the same low tone, "I think he must be, but until we are certain we will not speak openly. Deveril might have placed a lad in the place of the one we seek, so as to deceive us."

The lieutenant nodded his head, and then asked our hero—

"And what plans have you formed now?"

"My plans are these," replied Conrad. "No one but ourselves shall know of this intended attack upon the pirates; but quietly myself and Barnacle will get all ready for war.

"I shall at nightfall man the boats with picked crews, and pull to the island. José shall act as pilot, and we will force our way into the lake and commence the attack at once.

"In the meanwhile you can have the boarding nettings rigged up, the guns double shotted, the small arms loaded, and the cutlasses placed round the capstan, so that the 'Firebrand,' as she sails up, shall think that no watch is being kept."

"Ah, I see!" cried the lieutenant, "it will make her careless about the way she attacks."

"Exactly; she will creep up close to you, and most likely you will be able to rake her fore and aft. While you engage the ship, I shall be attacking the pirates on the island."

"I trust that you will be in time to save my old friend, Dr. McTaggart, and that foolish fellow, Peter Painter," said Captain Ireton.

"I doubt not that they are safe, and that we shall rescue them," said Conrad.

"Ah! my dear boy, you know not the cruelty of Deveril," replied Captain Ireton. "If you come across him, spare him not. *Believe me, he is not your father.*

"The mystery of your birth shall be cleared up, and whether it turns out to your honour or otherwise, I promise you fortune. I am rich—and I swear that if you slay this monster you shall have all I possess."

"Pardon me, Captain Ireton," said Conrad, as he drew himself up haughtily, "I am no hired assassin. I certainly shall not spare Captain Deveril when next I have an encounter with him, but it shall never be said that I slew him for the sake of gold."

"Bravo!" cried Lieutenant Daulton. "You are no son of that scoundrel; he could not have so noble a child.

"And now, Captain Ireton, you turn in, as we shall soon have some precious hot work to look after."

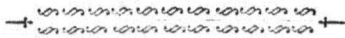

CHAPTER XXIII.

LOLO THE NEGRO ATTEMPTS TO BETRAY CONRAD'S PLANS TO DEVERIL—CONRAD'S MERCIFUL SENTENCE.

As night drew in the men on board the "Sea Breeze" were busily engaged getting ready for the attack on the pirates.

José was most busy and energetic.

He set to work with a will, and by his knowledge of the pirate's ways of fighting, was able to give our hero some capital advice.

The hour for starting was approaching; the men had gathered together on the foredeck in little groups, talking in whispers.

Conrad was passing forward when José placed his hand upon his arm.

"Hist, senor! I would speak to you! Come aft and lean over the taffrail, as if watching the currents, so that no one may notice us."

Conrad at once turned and walked aft with the Spaniard, doing exactly as he had requested.

"You have a negro on board whom you saved from one of Deveril's ships," whispered José.

"I have. What about the fellow? I think fear has turned his brain."

"Bah! The fellow knows what he is about," replied the Spaniard in tones so nearly contemptuous, that our hero turned quickly upon him, and demanded sharply—

"What do you mean?"

"I mean that the fellow is a traitor— a creature of Deveril's. I have seen him with the chief often."

"But he himself told us that he was one of the slaves," replied our hero.

"Told you so? There is only one thing that Lolo is more ready with than his knife—that is, his tongue, when lying is in the way. I tell you the man is a scoundrel and a spy! He was left on that ship so that he might be taken on board this one, and so play the spy upon your actions."

"Can this be true?"

"As true as I am standing here. Lolo is the best pilot the pirates have. He is as cute a villain as ever drew breath, and— hist! see him. By heaven! he bears witness that my words are right."

As he spoke, the dusky form of Lolo glided to the side of the ship, and our hero saw him hastily place something like a small canister upon the gunwale, and then rapidly creep back to the fore-hatch and dive below.

"This means mischief!" said Conrad, and he and José hurried forward to examine the canister; but before they could reach it, it burst into flames, giving forth a bright blue light.

One push and the canister was sent into the sea, wherein it floated some time before it was extinguished.

"What treacherous purpose could the fellow wish to serve by this?" asked Conrad.

"He was, doubtless, signalling to the pirates. No doubt he has discovered all your plans, and in this manner has warned Deveril of the intended attack.

"Take my advice, senor. Have the fellow brought up on deck, and then run him up to the yard-arm. That is the only way to stop his tricks."

Conrad thought for a few moments, and then said—

"No; that must not be done. I have another use for the fellow. Go, José, and have him brought before me. Barnacle, pass the word for all the men to assemble aft. Let no noise be made, or lights shown. The people on the island may not have seen the signal, and we may yet take them by surprise."

"It would astonish me if they had not seen it. But it matters little now. The deed is done, and we must make the best of it," grumbled José, as he departed to obey Conrad's orders.

The men were all assembled on the quarter-deck, when José appeared, dragging Lolo after him.

"What for massa bring me here?" squealed the negro. Poor Lolo done nothing wrong."

"Hold your tongue, you black scoundrel!" said José, or I'll run my knife into your dusky carcase. You know very well what you have done. We saw you light the maroon."

"Up then, some of you and get a whip on to the yard-arm," said Conrad.

Two of the men flew up the rigging, and soon the end of a rope, with a hangman's noose, was lowered on to the deck.

Lolo watched all these preparations with a dull, sullen look, evidently pretending that he did not understand what was about to happen.

Fixing a stern gaze upon the negro, Conrad said—

"Put the noose round the fellow's neck, and then let the rope be manned!"

No sooner did the negro feel the rope round his neck, than he altered his tactics.

Dropping on his knees, and clasping his hands, he exclaimed in tones of abject fear—

"Oh, massa captain, massa captain. Don't just go and kill the poor ole nigger man. He do you no harm—he berry, *berry* innocent. He be your slave and follow you like a dog—only let him live."

"You say you are innocent?" replied Conrad sternly. "If you be so, tell me why you lit that blue light."

"Blue light, massa captain?" demanded Lolo, as if in surprise. "What blue light? I see no light."

As the rascal said this he gazed round, as if looking for the light.

"Come, come, you cannot deceive me! I saw you light it," said Conrad.

"But, massa captain, where we get blue light? we no hab blue lights."

"Men at the rope, stand by and await the word of command!" shouted Conrad.

The men did as commanded, and that with such a right good will, that the negro was jerked upon his feet.

"Marcy, marcy!" he roared. "Don't go hang poor old negro, and he will tell all. I did light lily bit of blue fire just to show Captain Deveril that you intend giving him a visit; but not much blue fire."

"Silence! You confess, then that you meant to betray us?"

"No, massa, not exactly that. You see I Captain Deveril's slave, and he make me do just what he please. He say, through his lieutenant, Captain Savage, ' you stop on board the ship and let dem take you prisoner. Dey no hurt black man. Dey tink him new slave and treat him kindly. Den you watch them and betray them.'

"What could I do? I forced to obey my massa, or he beat and kill me. Dat why I burn the blue light."

"Can this be true?" whispered Conrad to José.

"It may be; but negroes are all such liars that it is safest not to believe them. Let us hang the fellow, and have done with it. We must be on the safe side then."

"Impossible! Listen to me, Lolo. You say you only acted as your master commanded."

"Dat true. Poor ole nigger must obey his master, you know."

"But Deveril is no longer your master. *I* am your master now. Do you understand that?"

"Yes, massa. I understand it."

"Now, will you swear to serve me faithfully if I spare your life?"

"Yes, massa. I swear do all you tell me, massa. Onny spare my life."

"Take off the noose, and let him be put in irons. Until the business of this night is over he must not be permitted to be at large. Now, my men, let the boats be manned, and we will start at once for the pirates' isle."

CHAPTER XXIV.

THE ATTACK AND CAPTURE OF THE PIRATES' STRONGHOLD—DEVERIL'S STRANGE ESCAPE—ELSPIE'S REVENGE.

GUIDED by José, the boats pulled with muffled oars to the entrance of the tunnel through which the pirates gained access to the lake.

Here the oars were shipped and, using the greatest caution, the boats were forced into the tunnel.

"Steady — steady!" whispered José. "I believe we shall surprise them after all."

Scarcely had he said these words than the boats shot out into the lake, and at the same moment a hundred fires seemed lighted amongst the rocks, whilst the pirates, who had not failed to see the signal made by Lolo, sprang from their places of concealment amongst the rocks, and poured a well-directed volley at the boats.

"Out oars," cried Conrad, "and pull for your lives to the shore. We must engage them hand to hand."

Answering their leader's call with a hearty cheer, the men pulled with all their might, and as the boats touched the landing-place, they sprang ashore with such determination that the pirates were forced to give way.

In the midst of the fight the pirate captain's tall figure could be seen.

"Drive the rascals into the sea," he thundered. "Stand close and we must conquer. They shall not escape us now. They are caught in a trap."

"Forward, my men!" cried Conrad. "Keep close together. Don't throw away your fire. Bravely done, lads! See, the cowardly rascals give way."

"Stand firm, men—stand firm," yelled Deveril, as he saw his followers wavering. By heavens, I will cut the first man down who dares turn his back upon the foe.

"Cowards! do you think you can escape death by yielding? No! you will be taken prisoners to Kingston, and there hanged.

"Strike for life and liberty. Let us die sword in hand, sooner than yield."

"Stand, Deveril — stand and cross swords with me," cried Conrad, who had been vainly trying to reach the pirate.

"Coward! would you urge on your men and yet fly yourself?"

"I am no coward, as you well know," shouted Deveril; "but I will not cross swords with you, for I have her in my power whom you hold dearer than life."

"See!" cried Conrad to his men, "the coward flies me. Turn, Deveril, if you have the heart of a man—shield not yourself under this paltry excuse."

But it was evident that Deveril would not combat with Conrad.

Springing from rock to rock, he was ever fiercely engaging the foe, but always avoiding our hero, who at last gave up the pursuit in despair, and turned his whole energies to the conquering of the pirates, who seemed now considerably disheartened.

They fled from Conrad in fear, for like all such men, they were superstitious to a degree; and remembering the mystery of his birth, his marvellous escape from the death to which Deveril had doomed him when he had him nailed to the mast, his strange appearance in the cave and escape therefrom, made them think that he was more than mortal.

And now the panic spread everywhere.

Some of the pirates flung away their weapons, and plunged into the lake; others climbed the rocks and concealed themselves in the cave; others again yielded themselves prisoners.

The battle was over, and the crew of the "Sea Breeze," as they waved their cutlasses aloft, rent the air with their cries of victory.

"Be not too sure that our victory is complete," shouted José. "This place is as full of secret hiding-places as a rabbit warren is full of burrows. Keep together, or we may find ourselves in an ambuscade, or a trap of some kind. Let us make sure that the pirates are really beaten, and then hurrah for the plunder."

Cautiously they advanced to the caves, but found them deserted, save by some of the wounded pirates, who had crept there to die, and who made the air dismal with their moans.

Leading his men forward, our hero made for the sleeping chamber of Lucinda; but as his foot was on the threshold, a deep, stern voice, which he knew to be Deveril's, cried—

"Back, Conrad! Dare to place one foot in this chamber, and I will fire this train and blow us all into eternity. Hold up your torch, and look ere you venture another step."

Conrad paused, and holding up his torch, found that Deveril had piled a heap of kegs containing gunpowder in the middle of the room.

To these he had laid a train, leading from the very back of the cave to the kegs.

The pirate captain stood near the bed.

His left arm supported the inanimate form of Lucinda, whilst in his right hand he grasped a torch ready to fire the train.

"Ha, ha, ha!" he laughed, as he pointed to the casks of powder, "there is a barrier, methinks, no one will venture to pass.

"Ho, ho! Master Conrad, did you think to snatch my beautiful bride from me? But you have failed. If I fire the train she will perish with us.

"Now advance if you dare!"

"Monster, you dare not do so foul a deed. If you have one spark of generous feeling in your heart, let the maiden go. Then I will meet you hand to hand, and trust our quarrel into the hands of heaven. Think that if you do this deed of horror, even the men whom you have led to crime will shudder when they hear your name pronounced."

"Talk not to me, boy, of fame and reputation. These phantoms which tickle the sickly pride of some men are as naught to me. I let my passions and my pleasures rule me. Life is too short to wait on dreams. I grasp the real, and leave the ideal for fools."

At this moment Lucinda roused herself from her fainting fit.

Pushing back her hair, she gazed wildly around, until her eyes falling on the Child of the Waves, she stretched forth her hands, and called to him wildly to save her.

"Back!" cried Deveril, as our hero was about to spring forward. "You will

not? Then take the consequences," and so saying, he hurled the flaming brand upon the train.

Scarcely had he done so, when he tore the silken hangings on one side, touched a spring in the wall, and a door flew open.

Still bearing the terrified girl, he dashed through the door, and closed it after him with a loud crash.

Conrad would have followed him, but José and some of the sailors seized him and dragged him from the cave.

Scarcely had they reached the outer air, when a terrific explosion took place, shaking the whole mountain to its foundation, and throwing down large boulders of stone and rock, which fell crashing into the lake.

The sailors reeled and fell about like drunken men, and it was some time before they could compose themselves to speak.

"The monster! to have destroyed that beautiful girl," cried our hero.

"Be not so sure that he has done so, senor," said José. "This is some trick of Deveril's. He loved the pleasures of this world too much to quit them sooner than he could help. No, no, senor; depend upon it he had the means of escape ready to his hand."

"It may be so," sighed Conrad; "heaven grant that you are right. But the smoke has cleared away, and we can search the cave."

They found that only a portion of the gunpowder had exploded, so by our hero's orders, the kegs which were still whole, were rolled out on to the platform, and thrown into the lake.

The chamber was one mass of ruins.

Our hero found in it a small gold locket, which on opening, he discovered contained the portraits of a lady and gentleman, from whose likeness to Lucinda, he doubted not were her parents.

This he hastily hid in his breast-pocket, and then continued his search for Lucinda.

This was no easy task, for the explosion had brought down a tremendous quantity of stone, which quite covered the back of the cave.

After great toil it was cleared away, but to discover the secret spring baffled them all.

At last they had to give up the search, and rest contented with the certainty that Deveril had got away with Lucinda.

That the beautiful maiden had escaped so terrible a death was a great consolation to Conrad; but, at the same time, he dreaded to think what might be her fate.

But now the men pressed on eagerly to ransack the place.

They had heard wonderful stories about the wealth of the "Wolves of the Waves," but had never, in their wildest dreams, imagined that it was so vast as it turned out to be.

Gold and silver plate in abundance; chests of money of all nations; jewels, bars of silver and gold, besides other valuables, in the shape of silks and velvets.

The men hailed each new discovery of treasure with loud shouts of joy.

Conrad alone seemed sad, and he, sword in hand, crept up the rocks, and peeped into all the caverns he could find in hopes of discovering Deveril's hiding-place.

It was a dangerous task, for who could tell how many of the pirates might be concealed in these dismal places, where a sudden blow could be delivered before a man was aware of the presence of a foe.

But Conrad feared no danger, and boldly continued his search, having ordered José to sound a horn directly the wealth had been collected and stowed away in the boats.

He had just climbed a rock, and was about to enter a cave, when a gleam of light flashed from it.

It was from a torch, and grasping his sword tightly, he rushed in, hoping that he had come upon Deveril.

Stretched on the ground was the body of the hideous dwarf, Davey Dump, who had been shot by one of the seamen during the fray.

Over him was leaning Elspie, the Witch of the Rock, wringing her hands and bemoaning his fate.

"Thou art gone," she wailed—"thou who alone, in all the world, loved Elspie. Cursed be the bullet which struck thee. Oh, thou art gone, and with thee my greatest hopes of revenge."

At the word "revenge," her eyes gleamed with a fierce light, and she clutched the hilt of a dagger she carried in her sash.

"Revenge—aye, revenge! Why should I not have it now? The wild people on the mainland sacrifice their enemies over the dead bodies of those they have loved. The priests and medicine men declare that the spirits of the sacrificed will be the servants of the beloved ones in the other world. Can it be true? I know not, but it may.

"It shall be done," she continued, after a moment's thought, and she leaped to her feet, plucking forth her dagger.

Conrad remained quite motionless.

She crept to the farther end of the cave.

Never had he seen anything more terribly fiendish than this old woman. Her hands trembled with rage, her eyes gleamed with the fierce fire of madness, and as she convulsively clutched the dagger, she chuckled with delight.

Leaning over something which, as far as our hero could make out, appeared to be two dirty heaps of feathers, she muttered—

"Ah, ha! you came to this island for much good, my friends. You shall attend upon my little imp. Come. At all events, Conrad shall not rescue you."

To our hero's horror, the old beldam seized one of the bundles, and hauled it to the side of the dwarf's body, and then returned to fetch the other.

Whilst she was thus engaged, Conrad leaned forward, and as well as he could, without risk of discovery, examined the strange object which lay groaning by the dead dwarf.

In was in shape like a man, but was clothed in feathers, and where the feathers had been scratched off the skin appeared quite black.

The unfortunate creature, whatever it was, was tightly bound and gagged. It was evidently aware of the fate that threatened it, for it groaned and gasped, seeming to be pleading for mercy.

Conrad drew back as the old woman dragged forth the second creature, so that she should not discover his presence; but he saw this second creature was like the first one.

"Now!" cried the witch, baring her thin, but powerful arm. "Now I will tell you the news. The pirates are beaten. Your friends of the "Sea Breeze" are within call of you, and would come to your help. Ha, ha, ha!

how you writhe about. Oh, I like to see your agony. It does my heart good. You must die to keep my boy company."

She raised her hand to strike, when Conrad dashed forward, and wrenching the dagger from her grasp, dashed her away from her intended victims.

"Cruel and vengeful woman!" he cried, "fly hence lest I forget your sex, and strike you to the ground."

Like some poisonous reptile, foiled of its prey, the witch crept close to the wall, until she reached the mouth of the cave, and then she paused, and cried—

"Conrad, I have stood between you and vengeance—between you and death. I did this for no love of you, but to prevent one, whom I had once dearly loved, from further sin. But now he may do his worst.

"Beware! you have crossed my path, and old Elspie, the witch of the mountain, blights all who dare do that. Beware! beware!"

Conrad sprang forward to seize her, but she rushed away, and when he reached the mouth of the cave, he could not see a trace of her.

At that moment the notes of a horn told him that the boats were loaded, and ready to return to the ship, so cutting the prisoner's bonds and ungagging them, he bade them follow him.

"Praised be the Lord, I am free at last!" cried one. "If ever I go a-looking for *orchards* among the rocks, may I be taken by *cannon-boils* and eaten alive."

"*Orchids*, Peter, not *orchards*. The word is pronounced *awrkid*, and I presume you mean cannibals when you say cannon-boils."

"I daresay I do. I know that the hawkids are well named, as they are most hawkid to get. If seeking science leads men into these kind of scrapes, I thank heaven I know nothing of science."

Conrad turned and gazed at the two in astonishment.

"Why, as I live, you must be Dr. McTaggart and Peter Painter!" he cried.

"We are, and—why it's the Child of the Waves!" cried the doctor; "but this tar and these feathers have almost blinded us. But is it true the pirates are beaten?"

"Yes; but we are close upon the boats now. Let me think what had better be done. I should not like the men to see you in that state, doctor; they would never respect you afterwards."

"Really, my dear boy, I can do without their respect. I will not stay five minutes longer in this accursed place than I can help. So let us get down to the boats."

"Stay, stay! Do I not tell you that you need have no fear now? See, here are two of the pirates that have been killed. Take their boat cloaks and straw hats, they will make you look a little more presentable; and when on board you can slip down into my cabin, and hide there until you are restored to a proper state for society."

The doctor and Peter gladly availed themselves of the disguises, and were soon seated in the boat by Conrad's side.

Out through the tunnel, and once more on the open sea.

The men, by Conrad's orders, pulled back towards the ship as noiselessly as they had left her.

They were within some fifty yards of the vessel, when Conrad, in a low, clear tone, said—

"Cease rowing! There is something wrong with the ship. By heavens! WHILST WE HAVE SEIZED THE PIRATE'S STRONGHOLD, I FEAR THEY HAVE SEIZED THE SHIP!"

CHAPTER XXV.

THE "SEA BREEZE" IN THE HANDS OF THE PIRATES—STRATAGEM—THE TRAITOR GOMEZ AND HIS PLOTS—CONRAD COUNTERPLOTS.

THE whole party now became convinced that there was something wrong on board the ship; for although there was no great noise, there was a confused humming sound, and lights were seen flitting about the lower decks.

"I think we had better lay off and see what those fellows are about," suggested Jack Barnacle.

"No; I think not," said our hero, quietly; "the tide will carry us right down to the ship, and we will creep up the vessel's side, and be on deck, perhaps, before they see us. Now, lads, in with your oars, and, remember, not a word must be spoken. Thank heaven, the night is dark."

When the boats were a dozen yards or so from the ship, a voice, which our hero did not know, hailed them.

Conrad was about to give the order for the boats to dash forward, when José placed his hand upon his arm, and motioning him to be silent, replied in Spanish—

"Do you not know us? We have come off to see if you had seized the ship. Satanas! but we have had hot work with the fools who thought they could take our stronghold. Is the ship ours?"

"Yes," replied the other. "We took her without firing a shot. It was planned beautifully. But we have orders not to make the least noise, so come up quietly, and I will report you to the captain."

"Let me go first," said José, in a whisper to Conrad. "There has been treachery here, and we should meet treachery with treachery. Here, throw a rope," he continued, to the man on deck.

The rope was thrown, and in two seconds more José was on deck.

The next moment he had plunged his knife into the heart of the watch.

"Now, my lads, up, up, as quickly as you can!" he whispered.

The men of the "Sea Breeze" needed no further orders. They were eager for the strife.

Up they silently climbed, and were soon standing on the fore-deck of the "Sea Breeze."

"Keep close to me, and do not speak," whispered Conrad to his men, as he advanced aft.

He had not gone far before his foot kicked against what he fancied to be a dead body; but the deep groan the fellow gave showed our hero that he was alive.

Stooping down he examined the man,

and found that he was bound both hand and foot.

"Hist, friend!" he whispered in the man's ear. "Who are you? Tell me your name."

"Bill Jones."

"Do not cry or speak loudly. Do you not know me?"

"No. How should I? But I suppose you are one of the murdering crew who got aboard of us under false colours? Kill me right out, for I won't join you, as I am an honest man!"

"Jones, my good fellow, I am Captain Breeze."

"Captain Breeze! Thank heaven!"

"Hist, hist! We have beaten the pirates on the island. What has happened here?"

"Mutiny!"

"Mutiny?"

"Yes; the men we got at the drinking shop at Kingston were all pirates. Directly you were well away, the murdering villains crept about. They murdered a man suddenly, overcame the others, and bound them hand and foot."

"I will cut your bonds. There, and take this knife, release as many of the men as you can, and tell them that we intend retaking the ship.

"Barnacle! Take some men with you, and see that the priming of the cannons be all damped, so that they cannot be turned upon us. Stop, do not damp the swivel guns, but let a number of our men guard them."

"Ay, ay, your honour. It shall be done."

"Now, José, let us creep round the deck and release all the men we can."

Conrad and José did this, and to their delight found only two pirates on watch, and these were so drunk, that they were easily disarmed, bound, and gagged.

As they released one of the bound sailors, and whispered in his ear who they were, he said, addressing Conrad—

"Go to the captain, sir. If they have not murdered him yet they will soon do so. Hark to the noise they are making."

A dull roar came up the hatches, accompanied with shouts of brutal laughter.

"That's their way, sir," said the sailor. "They'll drink themselves mad, and then they will torture and kill all the prisoners who will not join them."

"Keep as silent as you can," said Conrad. "If we can recapture the ship without the people on the island knowing that we have done so, we might entrap Deveril on board. Keep round the hatchways all of you. José and Jack Barnacle, look to your weapons, and follow me. But mind, whatever you see or hear, you must not do anything until you have orders from me."

Creeping down the companion-ladder, Conrad found the door of the chief cabin open, and glancing in, he beheld a sight that made his blood boil.

The splendid cabin was full of pirates, drinking and smoking at their ease.

All had evidently drank more than was good for them, and many lay upon the floor of the cabin.

At the head of the table sat Pedro Gomez.

Round him were several of the piratical officers, whom our hero knew, having seen them on board the "Firebrand," which Deveril had commanded in person.

As Conrad and his companions glanced into the cabin a song had just finished, and the pirates were uproarious in their applause.

"By all that is evil, that was a good song!" shouted one of the men. "Another—we'll have another."

"The song was good, the spirits and the wine are better; but how about Deveril? Has he beaten the fellows who went to the island?" cried another of the pirates.

"To be sure he has," returned Gomez. "Did he not say that if there was danger he would make us the private signal—the blue light?"

"Yes, but has he done so, and did we miss it?" inquired the first speaker.

"We miss it? No!" cried Gomez. "Did I not see the watch set? and when I do that, all is safe. But hark ye, lads; do you not think that we have had enough of this fellow Deveril? We have the best of it now, and could get rid of him easily."

"How?" asked one of the fellows. "For myself I would gladly get rid of him, for he plays the lord too strongly for me. He is the cat and we are the mice. If we could bell the cat, all would be well; but who is to bell the cat?"

"He is no cat," replied Gomez, with scorn. "He is a tiger! But we are not either mice. I do not wish to *bell* this cat, as you say. I wish to silence him."

"Take care, Gomez, he is a strong and brave man," said one of the officers, in a low voice. "Some of the men love him, and would die to serve him."

"I know that. Let them *die* to serve us as well as him, and so they shall," and here the fellow placed his hand upon his long Spanish knife, and smiled meaningly.

"Well, if you have a good plot, I am ready to join you," said another; "but mind, we must have no failure. So tell us the plot at once."

"It is simple. We have captured the 'Sea Breeze' without the loss of one man."

"That is what you think," thought our hero, as he grasped his cutlass tighter.

"All the men on board this ship, as far as I know, hate Deveril," Gomez went on. "Is that true?"

"It is—it is," shouted most of the men, whilst the rest looked undecided.

"I thought so, my lads," laughed Gomez, "and that is why I selected you. The men on board the old 'Firebrand' lean mostly towards Deveril. But there, a straw will turn them, and make them come over to us. The 'Firebrand,' as you know, is to wait at the north of the Volcanic Island ready, in case of necessity, to take the captain and his followers off."

"True."

"Well, the captain has evidently beaten this Conrad, or he would have signalled for us. Therefore, he will not leave the island. To-morrow we will sail up to the 'Firebrand.' We will speak to her fairly, and all that, until we are on board, and then we will capture her."

"Capital, capital!" cried the wretches, who, now that they saw a good chance of success, were *all* willing to join Gomez.

"Good! I thought you would soon see my plan. Well, then we shall have two ships instead of one. Those who are against us we can silence with the pirates' gag."

Here the wretch drew his finger across his throat.

"Good, good, we understand. Go on—go on," applauded the pirates.

"Well, then we turn our attention to Deveril. Ha, ha, ha, ha! We will make him go down on his knees and ask pardon of all of us. We will score his back with the lash, as he has done to many a better man than he. Then, lads, we will divide his gold amongst us."

CHAPTER XXVI.

THE PIRATES' ORGIE IS BROUGHT TO A VERY SUDDEN CONCLUSION BY JACK BARNACLE—THE PIRATES AT BAY.

THE pirates now turned their attention to another song, and more drinking, and then once more proceeded to business, which was disturbed by a loud snoring from one of the standing bed places.

"Who is making that infernal noise?" shouted Gomez. "Haul the fellow out of that bunk."

No sooner said than done.

A dozen willing hands were stretched forward, and the slumberer, who was no other than the treacherous negro, Lolo, was pulled from behind the curtains, and fell with a heavy crash upon the cabin floor.

"Ah, you sons of sea cooks!" screamed the negro, springing up and seizing his long knife. "What you do dat for? By golly! I make some of you smart for dat."

But the negro's threat was only met by a shout of laughter.

"Oh, you scoundrels!" he cried. "Wait till I see massa Deveril. I let him know how you treat poor lilly nigger which I save for massa Deveril's cabin boy. He make you pay for all this."

"Don't be too sure of that, Devilskin," laughed Gomez. "He may have to beg mercy of us. But what have you to find fault with? Because we chose to cut off that little wretched black imp's head? Is that what is the matter?"

"Matter! Dat bery much de matter. Hadn't he learned to cook in de French fashion? to wait at table like the true genelem negro? Warn't he like de boy massa Deveril used to hab?"

"Yes, very much so. You mean the lad the captain threw into the sea one morning because he had made his coffee too weak? I don't think that showed much love."

"Massa Deveril very hasty man. But he very sorry afterwards, when he find no one cook as well as Sambo. Ebbry morning at his breakfast I hear massa say—'Ah, pity I lost my temper, 'cause now I lose Sambo, and no one cook or wait at table like him.' Den he lose him temper again, and he trow the dishes at my head. Golly! I anxious to get anodder Sambo, and you go kill him."

"And serve the little beggar right," growled one of the pirates.. "Didn't he run his knife into the calf of my leg, when I was strapping up Captain Ireton. Of course, I cut his weazand."

Conrad shuddered when he heard the fate of poor little Biancho, for he could not doubt but that it was the little negro cabin boy who had been murdered, and he determined that his murderer should pay dearly for his crime.

"That's enough, Lolo," said Gomez. "You must know that I am your master now."

"You my massa?" screamed the negro. "No one my massa but massa Deveril."

"Bah! you fool. Had you not been so good a pilot, he would have precious soon served you as he did Sambo. Be a man, Lolo, and do as we are going to do."

"And what is that?" asked Lolo.

"Declare ourselves free—a band of brothers. Of course, there must be someone in command, and so I shall be your captain. We will take Deveril and torture him until he gives up his gold and jewels."

"By the powers, to my thinking he has a sacret that is worth all of thim," said an Irishman.

"And what 'sacret' may that be, Pat?" asked Gomez.

"About this Captain Ireton, and——" here he dropped his voice, "the Earl of Bellchambers."

"And what do *you* know about that?" demanded Gomez. "Deveril would never speak about it."

"Troth! I know that; but there are more ways of killing a dog than hanging him, and more ways of learning a secret than axing the owner of it what it is."

"And how did you trace this out?" demanded the other.

"Oh, very aisy, by putting two and two together. Why did Captain Ireton always pursue Deveril? Why, when in the papers was noticed the strange disappearance of the Earl of Bellchambers and his steward, did Deveril always run a muck, and treat us all round worse than one would treat a pig?"

"That all depends upon who the pig may belong to, Pat. If the owner were an Irishman he would treat it as one of the family, and the captain at the best of times never did *that*."

"Sure, and your right. At all events, I say let us get the secret out of this Ireton."

"Bravo, Paddy! Bravo, Paddy!" echoed through the cabin.

Lolo had been toying with his knife ominously, and when he heard these speeches, he drew it cautiously, and hid the blade up his sleeve.

"A good thought," shouted Gomez. "Bring the prisoners here, we will have some fun with them."

Conrad grasped one of his pistols, and pale with anxiety, awaited the order of Gomez to be carried out.

In doing so he did not notice Lolo glide up close to Gomez's chair.

The door of an inner cabin was opened, and from it were dragged Captain Ireton and Lieutenant Daulton.

Both were bound hand and foot, and bore proof of being badly wounded.

Conrad's blood boiled as he saw his kind friends hauled along, and thrown on one of the couches.

"So," cried Gomez, as he scowled at the prisoners, "I hope now you are convinced that I am the master of this vessel. You see all your plans have failed."

"I see that villainy in this case has been triumphant," replied Captain Ireton, calmly. "I have done my best to punish the miscreants of the ocean, and avenge my own private wrongs. I shall not draw back in paying the highest price a

man can for anything—his life. You can kill me. I have no more to say."

"Kill you! Bah! we have no need to ask your permission to do *that*. We want to know the cause of the quarrel between you and Deveril; also what is the connection between you and the Earl of Bellchambers."

Captain Ireton started.

"I know not," he said, "how much of my secret you may have learned from Deveril; but from me you shall learn nothing."

"Ho, ho! say you so? I think I will make you speak differently to that. Bring hither a bayonet, and heat it in yonder fire. We will put out one eye first, and *see* if that makes you *see* how to answer our questions better."

A shout of laughter greeted this play of words.

Turning to Lieutenant Daulton, Gomez exclaimed—

"You may not have so many scruples, and may know your captain's secret. If you will let us know it, and join us, you shall go free."

"Belay there," cried Daulton, "you may do what you like with this old carcass, but don't think that I could ever join with such scoundrels as you are. As for betraying the captain's secrets, why I'd sooner be roasted alive first!"

"Then, by heaven! you shall have your own way," roared Gomez. "Listen fool! If you do not tell us what the secret is, the punishment you have mentioned shall be awarded to you!"

"Do what you like," growled the lieutenant, "you'll not draw a word from me."

"Stay!" cried Captain Ireton quickly. "I will not have my old friend suffer for me. Should he choose to answer your questions, I give him my consent."

"Then I do not take it," cried Lieutenant Daulton. "There's only one person living whom I would impart the secret to. Deveril knows it, and the only man to whom I would make known the secret is the Child of the Waves."

"Deveril! Bah! he is as good as dead, and so is the Child of the Waves."

"Traitor!" cried Lolo, as he sprang forward, and plunged his knife into Gomez's breast. "Thus do I avenge my master!"

Gomez sprang from his seat, and

staggered back, placing his hand over the wound.

"Scoundrel!" he cried, "you have killed me. Seize him, my men; I will not die until I see the black devil killed!"

"Stand back," exclaimed the negro. "Stand back. Lolo not the sort of person who will sell him life cheap. Gomez one big rascal as lead you all astray. Captain Deveril—him all safe. I have private signal wid him. Fore I go sleep see rocket go up, know dat he triumphant as he always be.

"Dis Child ob de Waves, he be Child under de Waves by dis time. Captain Deveril be aboard de 'Firebrand,' and come here precious soon to see what you after. Pretty lads you look den! All down on your knees begging mussy."

"'Tis false!" gasped Gomez. "Stand to your colours, lads. Do not be deceived by that scoundrel!"

"'Tis true," returned Lolo. "I heard boat alongside just now. It be Captin Deveril and some man come to ax you what you do."

"You speak falsely, you black scoundrel!" shouted Jack Barnacle, unable to stand any more of the black man's palaver. "The men as come aboard were those of the 'Sea Breeze,' with the Child of the Waves in command, after having burned your nest of hornets out of that hiding-place of yours."

Had a thunderbolt fallen in the midst of the pirates, they could not have looked more startled as Barnacle dashed into their midst.

But as our hero, followed by José, entered the cabin, they seized their weapons, and stood on the defensive.

CHAPTER XXVII.

SHOWS HOW CONRAD CONQUERED THE PIRATES—THE FLIGHT OF THE "FIREBRAND."

"GENTLEMEN," said Conrad, bowing politely, "what Lieutenant Barnacle has told you is quite correct. Not only have I taken the island, but all the treasures which had been hoarded there by Captain Deveril.

"The ship is mine, and you are all my prisoners. Surrender, and you shall be treated well until I hand you over to the authorities at Kingston."

"Surrender!" cried Gomez. "Never! I am wounded to the death, yet I have life enough in me to lead my men on to conquer or die. Up, my brave lads! If you surrender, the gallows will be your fate! Thus do I begin the game."

Seizing a pistol he fired at our hero, who would have been shot through the head had he not quickly stooped.

The bullet, however, served its fatal purpose, striking José in the breast.

In an instant all was confusion.

The noise brought a number of Conrad's men to his and Jack Barnacle's aid.

The pirates sprang upon their foes with the desperation of lions at bay.

Conrad cut his way through the pirates until he had reached Gomez, and then, with a few quick strokes, despatched the villain

Turning round, he snatched a pistol from the wall, and killed a pirate, who was about to cleave Captain Ireton's head—the captain and Lieutenant Daulton having been released by our hero—and then he threw himself into the mêlée.

At last the pirates found that they were overmatched, and tried to make for the deck.

"At them, lads!" cried Conrad. "No quarter! We will not spare one of them. It is not revenge we seek, but justice!"

The men answered with a ringing cheer, and in a few minutes not one of the pirates were alive.

Then Conrad turned to Captain Ireton and Lieutenant Daulton, and grasping their hands said—

"I am thankful that I returned in time to save you. But how came it, Mr. Daulton, that so bad a watch was kept?"

"In good truth, my dear boy," cried the lieutenant, "we were deceived by this black scoundrel."

Here he gave the body of Lolo a severe kick.

"JOSE PLUNGED HIS KNIFE INTO THE HEART OF THE WATCH."

"He pretended he could hear the cries of victory from your party, and, somehow, when the watch was called, it fell to the lot of those scoundrels whom you brought from Kingston to form it—that is, the greater part of it.

"Well, the captain and I had just turned in for an hour, when we heard a noise upon deck.

"Up we sprang; but no sooner had we done so than we were knocked down senseless, for that black rascal, Lolo, had crept into our cabin, and had placed a man beside each of our bunks, armed with marlin spikes to dash our brains out if we resisted them."

"The villains!" cried Conrad. "But they have received their just reward."

"Well, we were bound, as you see," went on the lieutenant, "and then thrown into our bunks, and left there whilst these villains revelled in drink. Then we were dragged forth, no doubt, to be killed; but, fortunately, you arrived in time to save us."

"My dear, dear boy," said Captain Ireton as he placed his hand affectionately on our hero's shoulder, "you have done us a service which we can never repay.

"Heaven only knows how things may end; but from this moment I declare that you shall be to me as a son, and should the rightful heir to my fortune not be discovered, you shall be my heir."

"Don't make any mistake, Ireton," said Lieutenant Daulton, gravely! "the right heir to your estates is discovered. I should have owned him long ago; but there, each man must look after his business in his own way.

"Still, captain, if you don't think it time to tell this noble youth your history it is my opinion that you are making a great mistake."

"Not now—not now," said Captain Ireton, as he pressed his hand upon his heart. "You forget that I have many sins to confess when I make a clean breast of it. Let the cabin be cleared of the dead."

The sailors quickly removed the bodies, which were consigned to the deep.

Then the boats, which had awaited alongside, were hauled up, and the treasure brought on board.

Great was the delight of the crew as they saw the masses of glittering gold and gems.

They shouted and danced round the treasure.

In the excitement of the moment, Conrad quite forgot the doctor and Peter Painter; but they were unable any longer to stand the cold in the boat, and, therefore, climbing up the ship's side, they endeavoured to creep below unperceived by the crew.

This they failed to do, however.

"Hallo!" cried one of the sailors, catching sight of them. "Here are two more of them pirates. Just lend us a hand, Bill, and we'll take 'em afore the cap'n."

The doctor and Peter Painter were pounced upon and hauled up before Captain Ireton.

"Why, what horrid monsters have we here?" exclaimed the latter.

"Don't you know me, Captain Ireton?" groaned the doctor. "I am Dr. McTaggart."

"By all that is wonderful, it is the doctor," shouted Lieutenant Daulton. "Why, doctor, what is the meaning of this disguise?" and he burst into a shout of laughter.

"You may laugh," said the doctor, ruefully; "but it is no laughing matter to us. The wretches not only made us take an oath to become pirates, but dipped us in some horrid stuff that turned us as black as negroes.

"And that wasn't all," joined in Peter. "Because we could not dance and sing to make them laugh, they tarred and feathered us, and then wanted to compel us to fight like two game cocks.

"But we wouldn't do it, so we were tied up as if we were fowls trussed for cooking, and had it not been for Captain Breeze, the old witch would have killed us."

In spite of all they could do, the men and officers could not help laughing at this statement; but Conrad checked them as soon as he could.

"Silence, men! silence!" he cried. "We should never laugh at another's suffering; and the present time least of all, for have we not escaped from a fearful fate?

"Had these pirates remained sober, and kept strict watch, they would have been able to beat us off at least; and, perhaps, with the aid of our big guns to have taken us prisoners, in which case I shudder to think of our fates."

"So do I," groaned Peter Painter. "Oh, you may laugh, lads; but you do not know what it is to fall in with those brutes. I do. I shall not sit down with any comfort for a month to come, and the sight of a pair of sea-boots will make every bone in me ache.

"Oh, doctor! doctor! is there no way by which we can get rid of this tar and these feathers?"

"We must be bathed in grease——" began the doctor, when Peter set up a howl."

"Bathed in *Greece!*" he yelled. "Shall we have to remain in this wretched condition until we get back to Europe, and then we shall have to go all the way down the Mediterranean Sea, and——"

"Nay, nay," said the doctor, betrayed into laughter, even in his misery by his fellow-sufferer's ignorance. "I mean, not bathed in the waters of Helicon, but in a bath made from the fat of animals which will——"

"Bang!" and a large cannon-ball passed over the quarter-deck, killing two sailors who had been stationed near the wheel.

In an instant everybody was on the alert, and our hero sprang up the rigging and gazed in the direction from which the shot had come.

The daylight was breaking, and to his surprise he beheld the "Firebrand" sailing away to the south.

"Quick, lads, quick!" he cried. "Bring the guns to bear upon her whilst we heave up the anchor. Mr. Barnacle, please to make all sail you possibly can after that vessel. If we take her, we shall have destroyed the worst nest of pirates that ever existed."

"Please, your honour," said the gunner, "all the guns, except the swivel ones, have had their primings damped."

"Confusion!" cried Conrad. "I had forgotten that. It was done by my orders. But we will pursue that vessel as far as we can. She does not know our disabled state, and is evidently flying us. Therefore, clap on all sail, Mr. Barnacle. Gunner, see that the guns are put in order as quickly as possible."

"Aye, aye, sir."

"She is about to show her colours," said Captain Ireton. "I suppose it will be the old 'Firebrand.'"

"No, it is not," said Lieutenant Daulton. "*It is a woman's scarf.*"

Conrad could scarcely suppress a cry of rage and despair, for he knew the scarf at once.

It was Lucinda's, and he knew that it had been run up to the mast-head as a signal to him.

He knew that she must be upon that ship, and in the power of his hated rival, Deveril.

CHAPTER XXVIII.

TIDINGS OF THE "FIREBRAND" ARE DISCOVERED IN A HORRIBLE MANNER.

To pursue the "Firebrand" was not only impossible, but also it would have been folly to have done so, for the guns of the "Sea Breeze" were for the present useless, and the crew worn out with the hard night's work, and many of them were badly wounded.

Therefore, in spite of the disappointment and rage he felt at being obliged to let Deveril escape, Conrad came to the conclusion that it was the only thing to be done under the circumstances.

For some moments he stood watching the "Firebrand," and noticed that directly Deveril perceived that sail was

being set in the "Sea Breeze," he crowded on all sail to his own vessel, causing her to dash through the water at a tremendous rate.

"It is no good, Barnacle," said Conrad, sadly. "I do not think we could over-turn her, even if this boom were not broken, for she is a regular clipper, and has the start of us."

"You are right, sir, and we should lose a lot of time in getting the guns in order—not to mention how our crew has been knocked about. What orders shall I give, sir?"

"Let the ship be brought to, and a number of the men set to repair the damages. Dr. McTaggart must see to the wounded. Let the armourer attend well to the weapons, and tell off some of the men to stow away the booty we have taken from the pirates. At all events, I have kept my word in one thing. I have seized the pirate's treasure, and when it is divided, every man on board will be rich."

"I'll keep that dark, sir, just at present," said Barnacle, with a grin. "The fellows already are thinking too much about it, and are busying their heads about what their shares will be, when they ought to be thinking of something else."

"No; Barnacle, do not do that. Tell the men there will be a good share for each of them; but the money will only be paid when the 'Firebrand' yonder is ours, and Deveril either our prisoner or dead. That will keep them to their work."

Conrad was right.

The men were delighted to hear that they would all be well-off when the object of the voyage was accomplished, and set to work with a will, so that in less time than one could almost have thought possible, the "Sea Breeze" had weighed anchor, and was cruising down south in search of the "Firebrand."

Now and then she would give chase to some suspicious-looking vessel, and great was the disappointment when they overhauled it, to discover that it was not the one they sought.

Of all ships they passed within speaking distance of, they inquired about the "Firebrand;" but the merchantmen seemed so afraid of the terrible name the pirates had made, that they appeared fearful of giving any information about the ship; or if they did, it was so vague that little good could be made of it.

The reason of their acting thus—acting, as we may say, against their own interests, was the terrible revenge that Deveril had boasted he had taken upon all crews who had dared to give information about him to his foes.

More! he declared that in many ships he had spies—first-rate seamen, who not only performed their duties well, but managed generally to become favourites with the officers and crews of the vessels.

This done, these scoundrels would manage, by agents at the different ports where they touched, to let Deveril know all of the merchant captains' movements, the destination of the ships; and if any of the commanders had dared to give information against the "Firebrand," their ships were sure to be attacked, and the captains and crews brutally murdered.

That being the case, vexed as Conrad was at the merchant captains, he could not be surprised.

Days and weeks passed, and still no news of the pirates.

They had sailed so far south, that they had reached the vicinity of the Aurora Islands, and yet they had not obtained a glance of the "Firebrand."

It was a beautiful evening, a light wind was blowing from the east, gently moving the vessel through the water.

Lieutenant Daulton, who was now able to attend to his duties, was pacing the quarter-deck by the side of Conrad, both of them in no very happy frame of mind.

"I knew we were coming too far south," growled the lieutenant. "I can't make out, my boy, what could have led you to make such a mistake."

"Do not call it a mistake until you know it to be so," replied Conrad. "I have had good reasons for what I have done.

"Although when I was on board Deveril's ship I was kept ignorant of many things, yet they could not prevent me from studying his character, and hearing him speak about some of his ambitions.

"One of these was that if fortune turned against him, he would make for San Francisco, and amongst the rough miners and gamblers, try his hand at any villainy.

"Idle or harmless, Deveril will never permit himself to be. I firmly believe that he has committed so many horrible crimes, that he is now urged on, as if by some devil, to deeper excesses.

"He does not face repentance. His only way to bury in forgetfulness the past is by being ever at work at evil."

"If you think that he has doubled the Cape and sailed for San Francisco, why not follow?"

"All in good time. Deveril will not go empty handed to a place like San

Francisco. His plan is to carry as much wealth as he can, so as to bribe the desperadoes of the gambling tables to join him. I do not think he has had time to do that yet.

"But see—what was that flashed white over there in the sunset?"

"An albatross. I saw the flash of its wings," replied Daulton.

"That was no albatross, or bird of any sort. It looked to me like a white flag."

Conrad and Lieutenant Daulton gazed westward intently.

"See, there it goes again," cried Daulton.

"I feel certain it is a boat in distress," exclaimed Conrad; "but we are bearing down upon it. Why do they not pull towards us? This wind is so light that we have little more than steering way on the ship."

"I can't make it out," replied Daulton.

"Here, boy," cried Conrad to one of the ship's boys. "Fetch me my glass."

The boy tumbled down below, and presently returning with the glass, handed it to the captain.

No sooner had Conrad received it than he scrambled up the rigging and carefully examined the object, which had caught his and the lieutenant's attention.

"It is a boat," he shouted to Daulton; "but it appears to have neither sails nor oars. I can see a man, and I *think* a woman in it. Let one of the boats be manned, and we will pull to them."

The boat was manned and lowered, and the crew of the "Sea Breeze" stood anxiously watching it, as it pulled towards the other craft.

"Give way, men—give way. The poor creatures see us coming," cried Conrad. "Great heavens! how could they have come out so far to sea? They must have been shipwrecked."

"May be, your honour, it is some of Captain Deveril's work," said an old sailor.

"By all that is cruel!" exclaimed our hero, "it looks like it. Give way, men —pull with a will, we are close upon them."

The honest sailors needed no further urging to put forth their strength than to know there were fellow-creatures in sore distress awaiting their help. They pulled with such a will that the tough oars bent again.

No sooner had the boats been grappled together than Conrad leaped into the other.

Oh, what a fearful sight met his gaze!

Stretched upon one of the seats, his head resting upon the gunwale was a man, haggard and pale; his long hair pulled over his eyes; his lips black with fever, and his clothes splashed with blood.

Conrad thought that he had never seen a more horrible sight until he turned his gaze to the stern sheets of the boat, and there he did behold one more horrible.

Huddled up in a bundle, looking like a heap of rags, was a woman.

Her arms and face bore evidence of brutal violence.

Her dishevelled hair, which had once been very beautiful, now hung loosely over her shoulders, and was matted with salt from the sea spray.

Her face bore marks of mature beauty; but it had lost that Divine spark—*the spark of intellect.*

She was mad.

There could be no doubt of that; her eyes glared with a strange but meaningless light.

Her lips were wreathed in hideous smiles, that made our hero shudder as she gibbered at him.

In one hand she grasped a flask that had, at one time, contained water, but which was now quite dry; nevertheless, she now and then raised it to her cracked lips, and sucked at it as if it could quench the thirst that was consuming her.

In the other hand was a small locket, in which was the likeness of a fair-haired boy, at which now and then she would glance, seeming on those occasions to recover something of her lost mind, for the wild eyes would soften, and the dreadful smile fade into a look of sadness, and she would moan as if heartbroken.

Suddenly looking around, she pointed to the "Sea Breeze," as she whispered in a hoarse voice—

"A ship! a ship! a ship!"

Then the man, who had sat in horrible stillness, almost mechanically raised his hand, and waved a white handkerchief.

"Gracious powers! what has caused all this?" cried Conrad, in horror.

The man made no reply, but after waving his handkerchief for a time, let it fall by his side, and remained quite passive.

The woman, as she heard Conrad's voice, laughed as if in the greatest merriment, and then, springing to her feet, would have flung herself into the water had not our hero seized her.

"Let me go! let me go!" she screamed. "There is blood upon your hands. You struck down my fair-haired boy when he came to my help. Monster! cruel wretch! let me die!"

"Avast there!" said one of the sailors, as he caught her arms. "This here honourable gentleman ain't one of the murderous crew as you fell amongst, if I am not mistaken. He's a true-hearted gentleman. Come, missus, you're with honest British sailors, and ain't got nothing to fear."

There was something in the tone of the honest tar's voice, and the look of his bronzed face, that seemed to give the mad woman confidence, for she allowed herself to be lifted into the other boat, when they wrapped her up in a boat cloak, and gave her some weak spirits and water, and a biscuit soaked therein.

Then Conrad turned his attention to the man, and touching him on the shoulder, said—

"Come, old fellow, you are safe now. In a little time you will be on board the 'Sea Breeze,' and then you will soon be cured."

"The 'Sea Breeze!'" cried the man. "No, no; I must not go there."

"But, indeed, you must," said Conrad, good-naturedly, as he took the man's arm. "Come, put your foot there, and I will assist you into our boat."

"Put my foot where?" demanded the man.

"On yonder thwart, and then on the gunwale."

"But I cannot see!" yelled the man, madly. "I am blind!"

"Blind!" cried Conrad. "Blind!"

"Yes, he—he put my eyes out, killed my boy, and then turned me adrift, with my wife, in an open boat."

"Who could have done this cruel action?" cried Conrad.

"Who? Who but the Wolf of the Waves, Walter Deveril, the captain of the 'Firebrand.'"

Throwing up his arms, the unhappy wretch uttered a wild yell, and fell back senseless.

Catching him in his arms, Conrad lifted him into the other boat, which was then rowed back to the "Sea Breeze."

CHAPTER XXIX.

A TERRIBLE DEATH-BED—A STRANGE CONFESSION—A MYSTERY EXPLAINED.

GOOD food and careful attendance did much for the woman who had been found in the boat; but the man sank gradually, and Dr. McTaggart had at last to announce that all his skill was useless, for the poor fellow was dying.

This, in the kindest words, he conveyed to the unfortunate man, who met the sad news bravely.

"It can't be helped," he muttered; "and, after all, what is the good of a battered old hulk like mine? Better sheer off, and get into dock. But which dock? That ain't so nice a reflection."

"Brother," said Dr. McTaggart, "there is always hope."

"Now, didn't you say just now there was no hope?" asked the man, quickly. "I ain't to be put off with tricks and gammon. If you think that you are going to take me in, why, then, I'll tell you you won't. If I want to speak out, I'll speak out. If I don't want to speak out, I won't speak out. I know you want to get hold of Captain Deveril. Well, I don't mind that, and maybe I will help you."

"By doing it you will render a great service to my friends. More than you can think."

"More than I can think?" said the man, with a peculiar sneer. "Maybe I know more than others think. You see that I am not a greenhorn. I've sailed the wide seas for many and many a year, and learned a lot of things—aye, but not so much as I learned on land. No, no."

"My good fellow," said the doctor, "believe me, you cannot live. What you have to say you had better say at once, if you have any last requests or bequests to make."

"Bequests! No, I have not. Deveril has all the wealth I ever made. Aye! I served that man faithfully, and this is the way he has repaid me. Where is Phemy?"

"Phemy! Who is Phemy? Do you mean the woman who was discovered with you in the boat?"

"Yes," replied the man. "She is my wife."

"Your wife!"

"Aye, my wife! Ah! I shall never look upon her face again."

"You forget you will see each other in Heaven," said Conrad, who was standing by.

"Heaven! What chance of seeing Heaven have I?" screamed the dying man. "Who is that who speaks such words? Water, water! Give me water! I burn! I burn!"

Starting from his seat Conrad raised the dying man's head, and placed a cup of water to his lips.

"Ah, that is better," muttered the unfortunate wretch, as he sank back upon his pillow. "That cools me—cools me. Would that I had never drank anything stronger. Tut! I am a child to speak like that. Let's be jolly! What, ho! there she goes. All hands make sail. Now, Blurty Ben, train the gun well. Fire! Ha, ha, ha! She has lowered her flag at the first shot, and the prize is ours. Three cheers, boys, for the merry night we'll have."

And so the poor wretch raved on through the fleeting hours, until the "light before death" came, and he struggled to rise.

"Keep still—keep still!" said the doctor, gently.

"No, no; I have much to tell—much to tell. Where—where is Phemy? My Phemy, bring her here?"

"May she come, doctor?" Conrad asked.

"In good truth, I do not know what to say. It cannot do him harm, but—"

"Do you think it will do *her* harm?" demanded Conrad.

"It may bring her back to her senses; but she may either go raving mad, or sink into idiotcy."

"It is a fearful alternative! What shall be done? I do not like to act without your advice."

"Phemy, Phemy!" cried the sick man. "You were cruel to me once, but you loved me afterwards. I know you did. Oh, Phemy! Phemy! Phemy!"

The doctor thought for a moment, and then, as he felt the patient's pulse, said—

"Heaven only knows if I am right or wrong. Let the woman be brought here."

Conrad left the cabin, returning with the woman in a short time.

The poor creature had improved in bodily health, as we have already said; but her mind seemed quite gone, and she laughed and grinned at her dying husband, evidently not recognising him.

"Is she here?" gasped the man, stretching forth his hands and feeling about.

"Yes, she is here," replied Conrad, as he led the woman up to the cot side, and placed her hand in that of the man.

"Phemy!" he called in a feeble tone, as he pressed her hand to his lips. "Phemy, why do you not speak to me? Do you not know me? I am your husband, George—George Dale?"

The sound of his voice seemed at first to call the woman's mind back, for she passed her hand over her brow, and gazed quickly round.

But the flicker of returning sense soon fled, and once more she sank into listlessness.

At this moment Conrad and the doctor were both startled by the appearance of Captain Ireton at the cabin door.

He was pale as a ghost, and both Conrad and the doctor would have hurried to his assistance, thinking him ill; but he motioned them back, and signalled them to be quiet.

Cautiously he crept across the cabin, and concealed himself behind one of the bulkheads.

"Phemy—Phemy, kiss me!" cried the dying man. "Do you not recognise me?"

Once more the woman seemed startled and at last leaned over him.

Feeling her face near him he passed his hands slowly and gently over her features.

This seemed to call her back to her senses. The touch had awakened the memory of days long past, and the mind once more recovered its sway.

One long cry of desolation and then the the poor woman flung herself upon her husband's breast.

"George! George! my life — my love!" she cried. "What have I done? Where have I been?"

"Hush! hush! Phemy!" whispered the man. "Keep close to me. I am so—so cold!"

"George, you are ill. But you will be better, soon, love. Tell me you will. I will nurse you, dear one, and we will fly to some place where I will work for you, and we will forget the past."

"Forget the past, impossible! Would that we could. Oh, Phemy, my wife, I am dying!"

"Dying!" shrieked the unhappy woman. "Oh, Heaven! I shall go mad! You must not leave me, George. Think, darling! Our little boy has been taken from us. Merciful powers! I can hear his shriek as that monster Deveril tore him from me, and hurled him into the sea. George! George! Do not leave me in this cold world alone. Who will be kind to me save you? Kind! Have I deserved kindness or mercy? I —I who——"

The unfortunate creature could say no more; but burst into a flood of tears.

"Be calm—be calm!" said Dr. McTaggart, kindly, as he gently raised the woman. "Do not despair. Heaven will raise up friends for you!"

"Heaven raise up friends for me?" cried the woman, bitterly. "No, I have sinned too deeply."

"Not so," said the good old doctor, "repentance never comes too late in this world. Come, kneel with me, and let us pray for your husband's fleeting soul."

The woman dropped on her knees, and with the doctor offered up a prayer.

So touched was Conrad by the scene, that moving away from the cot where he had stood unperceived by the woman since she had recovered her senses, he joined the captain behind the bulkhead.

"Phemy," whispered George Dale, "that has done me good. I—I am going fast. I—I have not breath to confess. Confess for me. I will press your hand as you go on—to show that you are right——"

"But who shall I confess to, George, dear?" said the woman.

"The doctor; the good, kind, gentle doctor," gasped George Dale.

The woman paused for a moment, and then, in a low voice, began her confession.

"When I was about twenty-four I was in the service of a naval officer named Daulton. He was as good and kind a gentleman as ever lived, and his daughter, Miss Pauline, was as beautiful as an angel."

Here the woman paused, sobs seeming to choke her utterance.

By a desperate effort she recovered her composure, and went on—

"Lieutenant Daulton's great friend was Captain Ireton, a rich, proud and haughty man, who had a son as gentle as his father was passionate.

"Need I say that the young people loved each other. The captain found it out and refused his consent to their union. He quarrelled with his friend, and they separated. Then came a Captain Deveril on the scene; he, too, loved Pauline, and proposed to her. She hated him. But young Ireton liked him, and taking the cruel wretch into his confidence, confessed that he and Pauline had been secretly married, and that soon the young wife would become a mother.

"Concealing his rage at this news the villain counselled flight, and offered to take the young couple abroad in his ship. Foolishly they took his advice, and I accompanied my young mistress. We escaped, and had not been more than a week at sea, when my mistress was confined of a fine boy. Two days after, she died.

"Then the fiend Deveril threw off the mask. He treated young Ireton as a slave. He confessed that he was a pirate, and, having gained the Gulf of Mexico, hauled up the black flag, and commenced a life, the very thought of which makes me shudder.

"My husband, George Dale, was one of the officers of the piratical craft. He protected me, and I loved him, and we were married.   Young Mr. Ireton's child we protected as much as we could ; but to save it from death we had to swear—his father had to do so, also—that we would never let the child know who were its relations, or even what was its name.

"Young Mr. Ireton used to teach the child, for he was a great scholar. He was unfit for the sea, and we soon saw that he was dying from rough usage and a broken heart. He entrusted the child with a kind of amulet made of steel, and some one told the captain of the fact.

"He was furious, and to save the child I swore that I had thrown the thing overboard ; but I knew that the child had hidden it away. The captain never forgave me, or my husband, for liking the child, and soon after he sent us aboard another of his ships.

"I cannot relate the horrible deeds I have witnessed—nay, more, in which I have been compelled to take a share. Time went on, and at last the pirates' isle was taken, and we were hurried on board one of our ships. The captain with the maiden, Lucinda, came on board, and we sailed away. My husband quarrelled with the captain, declaring that the officer leading the attacking party was no other than Conrad—the boy he had so ill-treated.

"You say you can swear to it," cried Deveril—"that you saw him ? Well, you shall never see him again.'

"Then the fiend had my husband's eyes put out. I tried to save him. My fair-haired, my only child, was torn from me, and thrown into the waves. I went mad. I know no more—no more. May heaven pardon me, and aid me to bear the punishment that has already fallen on me.

"Is this all true, George Dale ?" asked Dr. McTaggart, in a low, kind voice.

"Yes, sir ; every word of it," groaned the dying man. "Oh, that Captain Ireton were here to forgive me ! "

"He is here, George Dale," said Captain Ireton, stepping forth from his place of concealment—"here, and to forgive you."

The blind man bent his head forward to listen eagerly, and then whispered—

"To forgive me ? "

"Yes ; far be it from me to judge others—I, who have sinned so deeply myself. I thought that this Deveril was a friend. I helped him to purchase the 'Privateer.' I placed you in her as boatswain ; for although I had retired from the sea, I loved it still, and took great delight and interest in it."

"I know—I know," groaned the man.

"How he returned my kindness you are aware. My wretched pride made me quarrel with my oldest and truest friend. I am of noble birth ; he had raised himself from a common sailor. We had fought side by side. We left the Navy together.

"But I forgot all that when I found that my boy loved his daughter. And yet I loved the girl as my own child. But I thought that it was a shame that Daulton's common blood should mingle with mine.

"Truly, I have been punished, and I forgive you."

"Would that Lieutenant Daulton were here to do the same," groaned the man.

"Keep quiet and wait. I will prove to you that heaven is merciful."

With bent down head Captain Ireton left the cabin.

Conrad, overcome with wonder at the news which he had just learned, remained still concealed behind the bulkhead, almost unable to realise the fact that the mystery of his birth had been cleared up.

Captain Ireton soon returned with Lieutenant Daulton.

"Jim—Jim Daulton—my old friend," said Ireton, "there are two people who helped to work our ruin. Look how their evil deeds have come home to them ! My pride has been fearfully punished. I know you will forgive them, for you instantly forgave me, and joined with me in pursuing this monster, Deveril. Come, forgive yon dying wretch whilst there is yet time."

"George Dale, may heaven forgive you as I do ! " said Daulton, as he walked up to the cot.

"Heaven is indeed merciful ! " said Dale, stretching forth his hands.

The lieutenant placed his hand in those of the dying man, who pressed it eagerly to his lips.

" Forgive—her—too—Mr. Daulton. Forgive—my—wife. She was not to blame."

" Yes. I forgive her also. Fear not for her. She shall not want."

No sooner did the woman hear this than she dropped upon her knees by the side of the bed, and burying her face in the clothes, wept bitterly, as if her heart would break.

One long and dreadful pause, and then Dr. McTaggart led the poor creature from the cabin.

All was over.

George Dale had departed this life.

No word was uttered by the captain or lieutenant; but as if by mutual consent, they led Conrad into their cabin, and having locked the door, Lieutenant Daulton produced a decanter of spirits and three glasses.

Filling the latter, he motioned Captain Ireton to take up his.

The two old men raised their glasses, and each putting a hand upon one of Conrad's shoulders, said, with one accord—

" To our grandson—Conrad Ireton," and then drank off the brandy.

Conrad was too affected to speak, and he sank back on one of the settees, and burying his face in his hands, burst into tears.

" Cheer up—cheer up, Conrad, my lad," said Lieutenant Daulton, patting him on the back. " Why, lad, ain't it a comfort to know that you do come of honest parents—that you are not the son of that rascal, Deveril—but the grandson of a real live——"

" Hush ! Until Deveril is dead I will not have that mentioned," interrupted Captain Ireton.

" A real live British sailor—that is what I was going to say," said Lieutenant Daulton, with a gulp, as if he were trying to swallow something.

" Yes, I am indeed proud," said Conrad, as he shook the old man's hand. " But our work is not done. I will never rest until I have brought that fiend, Deveril, to justice, or have slain him with my own hand."

" And so you shall," cried Daulton, slapping his hand upon the table. " Give up the chase ! Not while we have blood in our veins, or a shot in our locker ; not if it goes on twenty years,

and I am alive. But something tells me that it will not be long before we are quits with him."

" I trust for the sake of others, that it may be so, for Deveril, while he lives, will never cease to do evil," said Captain Ireton. " But this steel case, Conrad. Have you it with you ? "

" Yes," replied our hero. " I will fetch it."

He left the cabin, and soon returned with the steel casket.

It was a peculiar-looking piece of workmanship, seeming to have no opening ; but Captain Ireton no sooner took it in his hands, than he touched, a spring, and immediately a lid flew up, disclosing a small cavity.

In this was a gold locket, containing the portraits of a lady and gentleman, at the sight of which both Ireton and Daulton bent their heads, and passed their hands hurriedly over their eyes.

Then Captain Ireton drew a small roll of paper forth, and opened it.

" This," he said, " is in my dear boy's writing. I will read it."

It ran as follows—

" I, Conrad Ireton, feeling that my death is close at hand, do hereby declare that I have been slowly tortured to death by Walter Deveril, captain of the ' Firebrand.' I have entrusted this casket to my son Conrad, who is an officer on board this ship. He does not know I am his father. If I were to tell him he would be murdered. Perhaps his having no name may be noticed, and, in heaven's good time, lead to his being recognised. To aid this, I have tatooed upon his arm, above the elbow, his motto, and my dead wife's and my initials, P. D. and C. I.

" (Signed)   CONRAD IRETON."

Without saying a word Conrad rolled up his sleeve, and displayed the initials tatooed in blue above the elbow.

" My dear boy," cried Captain Ireton, " it needed not that proof. Jim Daulton here can tell you that you had not been long on board this ship before I saw a likeness in you, both to my son and his daughter. Still, we dared not speak. We watched you, and saw with delight your noble conduct. Hence we placed you in the command which you now hold.

"Come, Daulton, embrace our grandson and drink his health. We must forget the past, and as soon as we have completed this—I was going to say vengeance, but I will not use that word—this act of justice against Deveril, we will return to old England."

"Embrace him! Aye, that will I. He's got the bright, fearless eye of his mother. My poor girl—but there—we will let that pass."

"Come on deck now," said Captain Ireton. "We must announce this good news to the men, and let them join in our happiness."

No sooner were they on deck than the order was given for all men to come aft.

The men stood in a semi-circle, and removed their hats.

"My men," said Captain Ireton, "a sad death has happened on board this ship. The man whom we found in the boat is dead. Before dying he, or rather his wife, for such the woman who was rescued with him is, made a startling confession. It has been the cause of my recognising Captain Breeze, as you have beeen used to call him, as my grandson."

The men were too astonished to shout, but the buzz of pleasurable surprise that arose showed that they were delighted at the news.

"Yes, my lads," continued Captain Ireton, "my son ran off with Lieutenant Daulton's daughter. It matters not how it happened—but happen it did—that the fiend Deveril managed to obtain their child, whilst he caused my son's death.

"To recover the child and avenge his father's death, I and my old friend Daulton, whose wrongs have been equal to mine, have pursued this Deveril all over the world.

"We have punished him severely, but still he has escaped us. How long he will do so, I cannot tell ; but I pledge myself that I will not give up the search until Deveril is brought to justice."

"And I pledge myself by the same oath," cried Jim Daulton.

"And I swear I will never rest until I have avenged my father's cruel death," exclaimed Conrad.

"Come, my hearties ! " cried old Jack Barnacle, "don't let us stand behind. Let us all swear that whilst the 'Fire brand' is afloat, and that monster Deveril is alive, we won't rest either. Remember how many of your messmates have been killed by the fellow. Think of the murders and ravages he has committed, and join with me in swearing vengeance."

"We do—we do," cried the crew.

"I thank you, my men, with all my heart," exclaimed Captain Ireton. "Steward, let each man have a good can of grog immediately, and serve the officers with a stiff glass each. Be quick ! "

"Aye, aye, sir ! " said the steward, as he rushed off with his assistants, and in a remarkably short space of time each one—officers and men—were supplied with a good jorum of that liquid which sailors love so much.

"Now, lads," cried Captain Ireton, "drink this toast with me, and mind—no heel taps : *Death to Deveril, and destruction to the 'Firebrand !'*"

"Death to Deveril, and destruction to the 'Firebrand !'" shouted the crew.

And every glass and mug was emptied.

CHAPTER XXX.

CONRAD UNDERTAKES A STRANGE AND SECRET ADVENTURE.

ABOUT the sixth or seventh day after that on which the scene described in our last chapter had happened, the "Sea Breeze" spoke a merchant vessel and Conrad learned that a ship, which answered to the description of the "Firebrand," had been chased by a sloop-of-war, and had made her escape through the Straits of Magellan, and must now be cruising in the Pacific Ocean.

All sail was immediately made, and the "Sea Breeze," after some stormy weather, passed through the Straits, and steering northward, crept up the coast of Chili, carefully examining each creek and bay where they thought Deveril might have careened his ship, which they doubted not, was in great need of repair; but no signs of the pirates could be seen.

Again Lieutenant Daulton was for turning back; but Conrad was determined to hold on until they reached San Francisco.

So on they went until they reached the group of islands known as Los Angeles, when, to our hero's delight, the joyful cry, "Sail ho!" was heard from the masthead.

It was the "Firebrand;" there was no doubting that; but how were they to reach her? for to our hero's annoyance, not to say rage, he discovered that a long reef of coral ran between the two ships.

The "Firebrand" had either purposely, or by accident, taken up this position; and knowing that she could not be touched, she quietly shortened sail, and brought too.

Then up went the pirate flag, and at the peak the scarf of Lucinda, making our hero almost mad with frenzy.

The vessels were so far apart that they were beyond range of cannon shot; whilst those who knew the islands best, assured our hero that he would be at least a couple of days before he could sail round the reef, as the wind was very light, and the reef extended many miles north and south.

"We had better start closer into the main," said Lieutenant Daulton; "for if a storm were to arise, we should go upon those rocks. Take my advice, and let us make what sail we can."

Conrad thought for a moment, and then examined the horizon.

"It looks rather dark and nasty out to windward," he said; "but that storm will not reach us until the morning. We must risk it, for I have a plan I must carry out."

"As you will—as you will; but do not blame me if anything happens," growled the old lieutenant, as he walked away.

Night soon closed in, dark and rather stormy.

But Conrad had formed a plan, which he would not give up to please anyone.

The night wore on, and Captain Ireton and Lieutenant Daulton had retired to rest, when Conrad came on to the quarter-deck, and met Barnacle.

"Is all ready, Barnacle?" he demanded, in a low whisper.

"All ready, sir," replied the old sailor.

"You and the other fellows are well armed?" inquired Conrad.

"Yes, sir; each has a couple of braces of pistols, and a cutlass."

"Good. Then let us be off at once. Are the men in the boat?"

"They have been in a good ten minutes, sir."

"It is well; let us get in also, and be off. You have told the second mate that should I be asked for, he can say where I have gone?"

"Yes, sir."

Cautiously the two crept to the side of the vessel, and seizing a rope, slid down it into a small boat, which was moored at the side of the vessel, and in which four men were seated.

Conrad threw himself into the stern sheets, and Barnacle took the helm.

"Give way, men, but no noise," was the order, and the boat was soon shoved off.

When they were clear of the ship, the men pulled strongly and steadily, but also noiselessly, towards the coral reef, which they reached in about half-an-hour.

"In oars," was the order given in a low tone, "and then all spring upon the reef."

The command was obeyed.

The men then lifted the boat out of the water, and placing it on their shoulders, tramped over the reef.

This was no easy task, and one or two of the sailors had some nasty falls, until Barnacle suggested that he and Conrad should walk in advance of those who carried the boat, and pick out the best way for them to go.

This being done, they managed to cross the reef in safety, and then they beheld the "Firebrand" at anchor about a mile away.

Once more the boat was launched, and the men resumed their seats.

"Give way!" and the boat glided away like a phantom barque.

"Hist!" said Conrad, as they approached the vessel, "what is that?"

A strain of sweet melody floated over the water, and then a woman's voice sang a plaintive song.

It was Lucinda's voice.

As the song finished, the boat glided under the stern of the "Firebrand," and was at once made fast to the rudder.

Then Conrad, assisted by Barnacle, fixed a rope-ladder to the sill of the stern-ports, which were open, and placing one foot on the ladder, turned and whispered to the old sailor—

"Remember! you must not come on board unless I call you."

The next instant he had climbed up to the open stern ports, and was gazing into the state cabin.

CHAPTER XXXI.

THE STATE CABIN OF THE "FIREBRAND"—A LOVE SCENE HAS A TERRIBLE INTERRUPTION—DEVERIL AT BAY—THE MARK MISSED—ESCAPE FROM THE "FIREBRAND."

ON one of the rich couches, in the state cabin was stretched Lucinda, beautifully dressed; and as she touched the lute which she held in her hand, her taper fingers flashed with gems.

Letting the lute slip from her fingers, she covered her face with her hands, and sighed deeply.

"Ah, Conrad, Conrad!" she murmured, "shall I ever behold thee again?"

"I am here, darling Lucinda," cried Conrad, as he leaped through the port-hole.

With a slight scream, Lucinda sprang from the couch as her lover threw himself at her feet.

"Oh, why did you come? Why did you come?" cried Lucinda. "Why have you run this risk?"

"To see—to save you," cried Conrad, passionately as he caught the young girl's hand, and covered it with kisses. "Fly with me. The 'Sea Breeze' is at the other side of the reef. I have a boat close by the stern of this ship. I will lower you out of window. Then we can bid defiance to Deveril."

At first the girl seemed as if she would go.

She made one step towards the stern-ports and then paused.

"I cannot go with you. I dare not!" she cried.

"Dare not?"

"No. I dare not break my oath," she sobbed. "Go! go, I beseech you—go! If you are discovered here he will kill me! Oh, you know not how I am watched and guarded!"

"But why submit to this treatment when you can escape?"

"Do not ask me—do not press me! That we shall meet again and be happy, I feel sure; but I cannot go with you now. Listen, Conrad! I know that Captain Deveril must be in San Francisco in a few weeks. He is about to take the lead of a most desperate band of gamblers and banditti. Oh, Conrad, save me—save me from this horrid man!"

"I will. Fly with me. Think, dear one—think what your life has been, surrounded by those ruffians, who never show mercy to honour or life. Fly with me!"

"I dare not! My oath!"

"Your oath is not binding!" said Conrad. "It was forced from you. Come!"

The girl yielded, and our hero, catching her up in his arms, was bearing her to the port-holes, when a silken curtain was dashed on one side, and Deveril, holding a pistol in each hand stood before them.

"Hold!" he cried. "I have witnessed—have overheard all. By my honour, Master Conrad, you have become a practical lover in a marvellously short time! Old Ireton and his parasite, Daulton, must have altered since I knew them, to be such apt tutors. But I am here now to save you from such men. You are my prisoner!"

"Your prisoner?" cried our hero, trying to draw a pistol, but being prevented by Lucinda, who clung tightly round his neck and shielded him with her body.

"Aye, my prisoner. Attempt to draw that pistol and I will shoot BOTH of you!"

"Coward!" cried Conrad. "Dare you to point a pistol at this maiden?"

"Aye, Master Conrad, I dare; and what is more, to use it, if a coward who has wronged me, dares to use the lass as a shield for his own cowardly heart," said Deveril, sneeringly. "Stand aside, Lucinda, so that I may face this villain as does become a man!"

"No, no. It shall not—must not be," cried Lucinda, passionately. "I will not quit my hold! Oh, Conrad, if you love me, fly! He will let you pass if you will go in peace."

"I, go in peace?" cried Conrad. "Never! Leave me, darling, free to cope with this man; and may heaven judge between us if he does not let me pass."

"Let you pass? No!" thundered Deveril. "I will not let you return to the 'Sea Breeze,' and betray my secrets to my foes. You, my son, to betray his father!"

"You are no father of mine. Heaven has spared me that horrible shame."

"Have a care what you say. I have proofs that what I say is true."

"It is false, you have no such proofs; you are a cruel wretch—thou hast broken all ties, human and divine, and I have proofs that you are not related to me."

"You!" sneered Deveril. "What proofs can you have? You who were brought up not even to know your name."

"Listen! The proofs were supplied by your own cruelty."

"By my cruelty!" exclaimed Deveril. "Have a care. I like not such terms."

"Aye, by your cruelty. By your orders George Dale, who had served you but too faithfully, had his eyes plucked out. You cast his only child into the sea."

"How know you all this? What traitor could have told you it?"

"Be patient, and you shall hear more. Not content with this—the blind man and his wife—whose brain had been turned by trouble—were placed in a boat, with no provisions but a few biscuits and a flask of water. Then the boat, which had neither oars nor sails, was cast adrift."

"Ha, ha, ha!" laughed Deveril. "You know the story well, very well, although I cannot tell how you managed to get hold of it. Yes; they chose to disobey me; they boasted that they knew too many of my secrets. So I silenced them."

"You did not silence them. Guided by Providence, the boat drifted miles and miles, until it was sighted by the 'Sea Breeze.'"

"Impossible!" yelled Deveril, turning deadly pale. "I say it is not true."

"And I say it is perfectly true."

"The boat you may have found; but the man and woman must have been dead."

"The unhappy victims of your cruelty were alive. They were taken on board and treated with all care and kindness. George Dale's wife confessed all she knew about you, and related my history."

"Confusion! And are all my plots and plans to be thus overthrown? No; I have you in my power. What, then should I care? Angels, or devils, have guarded me up to this—I neither know nor care which—but they will continue to do the same."

Wretched man! I could almost find it in my heart to pity you!" exclaimed Conrad.

"I need not your pity!" replied Deveril. "I confess you are Ireton's grandchild and also Daulton's. I confess that I entrapped the pretty turtle doves — your father and mother — on board my ship, and carried them off out of revenge, for I had loved your mother. Had she lived she would have become my wife."

Here Deveril's voice seemed to break, and he remained silent for a moment.

"She was most happy in her death," said Conrad, "inasmuch as she escaped from you."

"Boy!" cried the pirate, "the love I bore her saved you. But now I am like a lion at bay, and I cast off all memory of the past. What has love been to me? A ruin! I love but one thing now, and that is—revenge."

"My darling Lucinda, do not shudder and tremble so," whispered Conrad. "Bad as he is, he would not hurt thee."

Deveril could not have heard what our hero whispered; but his jealous eyes caught sight of the closer embrace, and it aroused his passions.

"I have borne this too long," he cried passionately. "Unhand that girl and render yourself my prisoner."

"Never!"

"You refuse to surrender?"

"I do."

"What ho, there! Treason! treason!" shouted Captain Deveril

Quickly placing Lucinda on a couch, Conrad dashed to the cabin door to fasten it, for the noise upon deck told him that the captain's cries had been heard.

His hand was nearly on the bolt, when a sliding door was thrust on one side, and Elspie, the Witch of the Rock, appeared before him.

At the very moment she appeared, Deveril, taking advantage of our hero's back being turned, discharged a pistol at him.

Luckily Conrad had sprung on one side when he saw the witch, and the bullet flew wide of its mark, and striking Elspie on the left shoulder, shattered her arm.

As Elspie sank to the floor with a loud scream, Conrad, with the true instinct of a man, sprang forward, and lifted her tenderly on to a couch.

The unhappy woman opened her eyes as she was laid down, and closing them again, said with a shudder—

"You—you—Conrad Ireton—to help me?"

It was only a few seconds that Conrad had been with the wounded woman; but when he turned round, to his horror he discovered that Lucinda had been carried off, and that a number of pirates —armed to the teeth—guarded the door and the stern-ports.

Amongst them stood Deveril, a smile of fiendish triumph on his face.

"So, Master Conrad, you are caught at last," he said. "Now, sir, yield quietly! Promise me that you will obey me in all things, and that you will help me to capture the 'Sea Breeze,' and you shall be my lieutenant. If you refuse——"

"Well, and if I refuse?" said Conrad, as he placed his hands carelessly on the butts of his pistols.

"You shall not live an hour longer!" exclaimed Deveril, "but shall die, suffering the greatest torments I can contrive."

"Better torments and death than dishonour," replied Conrad, contemptuously.

"Do you refuse my offer? Remember, one word from me, and you are doomed to death!"

"You doom me to death! If it is the will of God, I must die, But should He will that I should live, you nor all your band can kill me. Thus do I prove it."

Swiftly snatching the pistols from his belt, he fired one at Deveril, who had to leap on one side, or the bullet would have struck him in the forehead. As it was it grazed his temple, and carried away the tip of the left ear.

The other pistol Conrad discharged at the pirates round Deveril, and that with such good effect that two of the rascals were mortally wounded.

Hurling one of the discharged pistols at his foes, our hero drew his cutlass.

"Death to the pirates! Hurrah for Captain Ireton!" he cried, as he threw himself upon the ruffians.

Deveril sprang to meet him, but received such a severe cut on the neck, that had he not worn a steel gorget, it must have decapitated him.

As it was the blow was given with such force, that he was struck to the ground.

Sweeping his sword round, Conrad dashed on, and, at last, sprang upon the sill of the stern-ports.

Turning round he faced Deveril, and cried, in tones of thunder—

"From your own lips, Walter Deveril, I have heard you confess the secret of my birth. Henceforth, I will never show you the slightest mercy! Beware how you treat Lucinda! For each insult or injury she receives, I will exact a fearful account. Beware!"

"Shoot the traitor!" yelled Deveril.

A dozen pistols were hastily presented at our hero, but the bullets flew harmlessly by him.

Bursting out into a loud laugh, Conrad waved his cutlass on high, as he cried—

"Farewell, Deveril! but not for long. We shall soon meet again, and then I may have my friends with me. When that happens, *we shall part, never to meet again.*"

Then turning quickly round, he plunged into the sea.

"Quick, lads, quick!" roared Deveril. "A thousand pounds to him who kills that traitor. To the deck some of you, and fire upon him as he swims. He cannot—he shall not escape!"

"'FORGET THE PAST? IMPOSSIBLE! OH, PHEMY, MY WIFE, I AM DYING!' CRIED THE MAN."

CHAPTER XXXII.

A FIERCE STRUGGLE ON A CORAL REEF—SAVED BY LIGHTNING—THE DISAPPEARANCE OF THE "FIREBRAND."

OUR hero knew that the pirates would keep a sharp look out for him, and, therefore, swam under water as much as he could.

Now and then he was forced to appear above the surface, and whenever he did so the pirates fired at him.

They failed to hit him, however.

At last, as he rose, he heard voices close to him, and, to his joy, found that it was old Barnacle and the boat's crew.

"Here I am, Barnacle," he cried. "Pull this way, old boy, and take me in. Would I had had some fifty good fellows with me. The 'Firebrand' would have been ours before this."

"And you might have had fifty good fellows with you if you had liked," growled Barnacle; "they would have come quickly enough. But no—you must go alone, and give orders that no one was to come on board, whatever they might hear."

"Look here, sir; it's all precious fine to talk about giving orders, but the carrying out of them orders depends upon what they are."

"Give orders for the men to follow you into danger, and I warrant there's not a man or boy who won't obey. But just as you say—'When your hear guns going off, and know that I am fighting against odds of something like twenty to one, you run off and keep out of danger,' and I'm blest if he'd be a true British sailor that would follow your orders."

"Nonsense, Barnacle," said Conrad, peevishly. "A sailor should always obey orders, whatever they are."

"Well, I shouldn't have done so. I was just going to order my men to board the 'Firebrand.'"

"Board the 'Firebrand' with only five men?" cried Conrad, laughing, in spite of himself.

"And why not, sir? If one could get aboard alone, I think five might."

"Oh, I forgot that, but then I crept on board. Ah! what was that? Surely they are not firing from the 'Sea Breeze.'"

The men laid upon their oars, and listened; then old Barnacle called out, loudly—

"Pull away, my hearties. That is no cannon firing, but distant thunder. The storm will be down upon us in no time; and only to think that we should be on the lee of a coral reef."

"Do you think that there is much danger?" asked Conrad in a whisper.

"Danger!" growled the old man. "There is more than danger—there is certain death!"

"Hush — hush! do not speak so loudly, you will discourage the men."

"They are not the sort to be discouraged. Hark! now the 'Sea Breeze' is firing. I know what it is. They hear the roar of the storm better than we do, and having discovered our absence from the ship, have had the guns fired to call us back."

The night had now grown pitch dark, and the wind began to moan and sigh in a most melancholy way, foretelling the fierceness of the approaching storm.

They had almost reached the reef, when a stern voice called out to them—

"Hold there! If you do not cease rowing, I will give the order to fire."

"If it ain't them there cursed pirates, I am a Dutchman," growled Barnacle.

"Lean down, men," ordered Conrad in a whisper.

"Why do you not answer?" demanded the voice. "If you do not do so at once, I will order my men to fire."

"Fire!" replied Conrad, "and we will return it."

The answer was a volley which, owing to the precautions our hero had taken, passed harmlessly over him, and his men.

"Fire!" cried Conrad sharply, and with a cheer, his followers leaped up, and from their pistols poured in a murderous fire on the crew of the pursuing boat.

At that moment, the "Sea Breeze's" boat grated against the coral reef.

"Out all, and haul the boat up,"

ordered Conrad, at the same time helping the men.

"Quick," he continued, as they pulled the boat higher up. "Hand over your pistols and ammunition to Mr. Barnacle and myself. Then up with the boat on your shoulders, and make as fast as you can to the other side of the reef. We will follow slowly, and keep these bloodhounds back.

Scarcely had the men hoisted up their boat, and Barnacle and Conrad loaded their pistols, than the boat of the "Firebrand" also reached the reef.

"Moor her to the reef, one of you," cried the leader, "and the rest follow me. We will make short work of those fellows."

A vivid flash of lightning showed that the crew of the "Firebrand" boat consisted now that some had been killed, of only eight men and their leader, so that there were not very great odds against our hero and his followers.

But then they had to carry their boat across the reef, and if it got in any way damaged, even if they overcame the men of the "Firebrand," nothing but a miserable death awaited them, for the tide was already rising around the coral reef.

Taking as good aim as the glimmer of the lightning, which now flickered in the sky, would let him, Conrad shot at the fellow who held the painter of the boat.

The shot took terrible effect.

The man threw up his arms and fell back into the boat, which, being released fell off from the reef, and drifted out to sea.

"Confusion!" roared the leader of the pirates. "Our boat has gone. Stick to them, my lads. We must have their boat or we are lost. Follow me, and remember you are fighting for life and death!"

"Then take the last," said old Barnacle, grimly, as he sent a bullet through the fellow's heart.

The pirates fired, and Barnacle received a nasty wound in the fleshy part of his left leg; but the old man did not fall, but hurled his discharged pistol with such good aim and force at the man who had wounded him that the lock caught him full on the temple, and he fell senseless on the rocks. Once again

had our hero loaded ; but as he saw the pirates draw back, he did not fire, for he was determined not to throw away a shot.

Meanwhile, the people on board the "Sea Breeze" had kept up a constant cannonade to show Conrad the way to steer to the ship, and the sailors, who carried the boat, pushed on as rapidly as they could.

The pirates were desperate.

If Conrad and his men got off with the boat, they must be drowned, therefore, they determined to risk all.

"Come along, lads," cried the boldest. "Better die like men, shots whizzing, steel flashing, the din of strife around us, than die howling on a rock. Follow me! We must conquer or perish."

"Stoop down, Barnacle, stoop down close to the rock," whispered Conrad. "It will give them less to aim at. You take the two first—leave me the two second—the others we must meet sword in hand."

Swiftly as this was said, the pirates were close upon them almost before they could carry out their arrangements.

"Fire!" cried Conrad.

Barnacle fired both his pistols, bringing down the foremost fellow, but the other one, at whom he aimed, still came on.

Then Conrad fired, and brought down his two men with deadly effect.

"Out with your cutlass, Barnacle," cried our hero.

With all the force and fierceness of desperation the combatants met.

The lightning, which was now flashing vividly, seemed to play upon their blades, whilst the thunder made awful music to this struggle of death.

Conrad, by his great skill, speedily overcame one of the three remaining pirates, and drove his sword through his heart.

A few moments later he had stretched another at his feet, dead.

He then turned to see how it fared with Barnacle, and, to his horror, beheld the old man's wounded leg give way under him, so that he sank on one knee, and was quite at the mercy of his foe, who, with a wild cry of triumph, raised his cutlass aloft.

"Pause, villain," cried Conrad, "and I will grant you his life."

"No!" thundered the man.

Conrad sprang forward; but a vivid flash of lightning, for the moment, blinded him.

Almost at the same time there came a crash of thunder, so loud, so fearful, that the very reef seemed to shake.

Confused by the vividness of the lightning, and almost stunned by the concussion caused to his brain by the roar of the thunder, Conrad stood, his sword fallen at his feet, and his hands clasped over his eyes.

At last he recollected himself, and removing his hands, gazed around.

Could he have been struck blind?

As the horrible thought entered his head, he strained his eyes to try if he could see some object.

No; he was not blind. He could see, for as another flash of lightning came, he distinguished old Barnacle, lying face downwards, on the reef, and by his side was the pirate, who seemed to be crouching down in fear.

Could the wretch have had time to slay the old sailor?

"Barnacle, dear old Barnacle," Conrad called out, as he picked up his sword and hurried towards the old sailor; but when he was within a few feet of the old man, he paused.

What could be the smell of sulphur mingled with that of burning cloth and leather which assailed his nostrils?

With a cry of horror, he once more called on the faithful old sailor.

"May the Lord deliver us!" he at last heard the old man groan. "I'm dead, and in—"

"Thank heaven, my faithful old friend!" exclaimed our hero, as he sprang to the old man's side. "Quick! we must not tarry here. To the boat—to the boat!"

With the greatest difficulty he helped the old man to rise.

"Stay one moment," said our hero. "I promised this fellow, if he spared you, I would grant him his life, and I will keep my word."

"He did not spare me," said the old man solemnly. "It was the Lord's will!"

Conrad knelt down by the pirate's side, and turned him over just as a flash of lightning lit up the scene.

No sooner did our hero behold the fellow's face than he started up in horror.

It was black and charred, as if it had been in a furnace.

The fellow's clothes were smouldering.

"Come along—come along, Barnacle," cried Conrad, shuddering, "the poor wretch has been struck by lightning."

"I know it—I know it," gasped Barnacle. "I saw the blue flame come down from the sky and run down his sword blade, just for all the world like a fiery snake. Then I had such a blow that it stunned me, and I knew no more until I heard your voice calling on me."

"Come, we must hurry. The men must have the boat in the water, for I can hear them shouting to us to make haste. Hasten, hasten! or we are lost."

They soon reached the boat, and found that the serf was now breaking so heavily on the reef that it was with difficulty that they could get the boat out.

The four sailors pulled with all their might, Conrad steered, and Barnacle kept bailing out the water that washed into the boat as they went.

"They managed to reach the "Sea Breeze," and gain her deck, although the boat, which had served them so bravely, was stove in and lost."

"Where have you been, my dear boy?" cried the captain and lieutenant, embracing their grandson.

"To see Deveril," Conrad replied. "But this is no time to tell yarns. Is all prepared against the hurricane?"

"All, my dear boy, so go below, and I and Daulton will take charge of the ship."

But our hero would not hear of such a thing.

He would remain on deck, and watch the gallant fight the ship made with the storm.

At last the storm subsided, just as morning dawned.

Then, spy-glass in hand, Conrad sprang up the rigging, and scanned the sea.

"May heaven have mercy on Lucinda!" he groaned. "THE 'FIRE-BRAND' HAS DISAPPEARED."

CHAPTER XXXIII.

THE "FIREBRAND" APPEARS AGAIN—THE PURSUIT—A RUNNING FIGHT—DESTRUCTION OF THE PIRATE SHIP.

ALL on board believed that the "Firebrand" must have gone down in the storm—all save our hero, and he would not believe it; for he knew that, with all his faults, Deveril was a first-rate sailor.

The "Firebrand" was well-built and well-found, therefore, she had every chance of escaping, being in a less dangerous position than the "Sea Breeze."

But where could she be?"

This was a question that no one could answer, and our hero suggested that, in a fit of ungovernable rage, the pirate had set sail, and been driven before the storm, determined to disappear at all risks, but this no one would believe.

Still, such was the case, as the reader will speedily learn.

Give up the chase until he knew the fate of the "Firebrand," Conrad would not.

The "Sea Breeze" was sailed round the reef, and cruised about where the pirate ship had been, but no trace of the vessel could be seen.

So Conrad came to the conclusion that, with his wonderful luck, Deveril had escaped in the manner he suspected, and determined to follow him up at all hazards.

Of course, Lieutenant Daulton grumbled at this "madness," as he chose to call it; he had always been a grumbler, and now that he had recovered his grandson, he grumbled all the more.

Captain Ireton, on the other hand, had always been a fiercely passionate man; but now that Conrad had been found, and the fate of his son discovered, he had become most genial, only losing his temper when Conrad was contradicted.

"Conrad was, and must be, right," contended the old man; and so, as Ireton was owner of the ship and all that it contained, our hero was permitted to do as he liked.

They had cleared the islands of Los Angeles, and were standing due north, when they ran into a bank of sea fog, so dense that they were obliged to take in all sail, excepting enough to keep way on the ship.

"Better have the bell sounded, hadn't I, sir?" asked Barnacle of Conrad.

"Well, I hardly think it is necessary," replied our hero. "There was no ship in sight when we ran into this wretched fog."

"That's true, sir; but the ship might have come down with the fog."

"You are right, Barnacle. It might have done so. Hark! what was that?"

They halted suddenly and listened.

Now that the fall of their footsteps had ceased, not a sound was to be heard, the heavy fog preventing even the splash of the sea against the ship being heard.

So dreadful did this death-like stillness seem, that Barnacle was about to speak, when Conrad laid his hand upon his arm, and stopped him.

"Listen!" he whispered. "It *is* the sound of a ship's bell, and that of a ship not a mile from us."

"By the Lord Harry it is," said Barnacle. "There it goes again."

Clanging through the mist, came the sound of a ship's bell, its deep tones appearing muffled, because of a fog.

"How far do you think her away?" demanded Conrad.

"That's hard to tell in this weather," replied the old sailor. "You see, sound travels so very slowly through a mist. But anyway, she cannot be far off, or we should not hear the bell."

"Call up Captain Ireton and Lieutenant Daulton," said Conrad. "I would consult with them over this."

Captain Ireton and Lieutenant Daulton were soon on the deck of the vessel, listening to the boom of the bell.

"It may be some trader," said Daulton. "We had better keep clear of her, or we may collide."

"No," said Conrad. "Something tells me that from that ship we shall have news of the 'Firebrand;' so we will steer towards her."

"That is very dangerous!" said Captain Ireton.

"It may be so," replied Conrad. "Still it must be done. I *will* capture that ship."

"Yes, yes, dear boy," said Ireton. "I wish it as much as you do; but why run against another ship in the fog. *That* will not help us."

"My dear grandfather," replied Conrad, taking the old man's hand, "I know what I am about to say may seem foolish to you; but still I must say it. I feel certain that we are about to learn some news of the 'Firebrand,' and that news will be of such a nature, that it will lead to our capturing that vessel."

"Pray heaven that your prophecy proves true," replied Captain Ireton; "but be it as it may, to you I entrust all; for something tells me that you are destined to revenge your parent's death. Hark! what is that?"

A strange murmur, as if of men quarrelling, came dull and dimly through the mist, and then arose a wild yell of agony that made all on board the "Sea Breeze" stop speaking, and gaze into each other's faces in horror.

"The bell of the ship has ceased," said Daulton, in a whisper.

They strained their ears to catch the slightest sound; but all was *dreadfully* still.

"What could it mean?" demanded our hero.

"It ain't natural," said Barnacle. "I've heard of this sort of thing before. Take my advice, sir, and let us cast anchor; if we go on, we shall only drift to destruction. That cry was from some spirits who would lure us on to a rock. It ain't natural, I say."

"Nonsense!" said Conrad. "I fear, though, that in one thing you are right. If we followed that cry, we should go to destruction, for it is my belief that the ship has run upon some rocks. So, Barnacle, keep her away, and have a sharp watch kept."

"Aye, aye, sir."

Slowly the "Sea Breeze" drifted on, and every man on board strained his eyes in the direction from which the sounds had come.

"Look yonder!"

Such was the cry that suddenly arose from the crew of the "Sea Breeze," as through the fog, a dull red light arose.

It grew brighter and brighter, until at last one broad red glare revealed a ship on fire.

As the red flames rushed up, those on board the "Sea Breeze" could see that she was a fine merchant vessel; her tall masts and taper spars were distinctly visible against the lurid light.

As it grew brighter and brighter, another ship could be seen, standing a little off from the burning one, and with one accord, they shouted—

"The 'Firebrand!'"

Yes; there she was, her black hull shown up by the flames from the unfortunate merchant vessel, to which, no doubt, she had been guided by the ringing of the bell.

To take the merchantman by surprise in the fog had been easy work.

This done the ship had been plundered, the crew massacred, and then the vessel had been given over to the flames.

"What can we do now?" exclaimed Lieutenant Daulton. "The unhappy wretches, who once formed the crew of that ship, have ere this been massacred, and cast into the sea. They are past all help, neither can we save the ship."

"But we can avenge her crew," cried Conrad, eagerly. "These rascals shall not escape us scot-free."

"But how are we to get at them? The wind is so light that our vessel scarcely moves, and the 'Firebrand' has the weather gauge of us. If the breeze would only freshen, we might manage to get up with her; but even then it would be more likely she would slip by us."

"Let the boats be lowered and manned," cried Conrad. "Place a cannonade in the bows of each boat, and we will attempt to board the pirate. At all events, Captain Deveril shall not have it to boast that we have been so near to him without paying him some attention."

The men gave a ringing cheer, and rushed to the boats.

The cheer was heard by the crew of the "Firebrand," who had evidently been too occupied with their booty to notice the "Sea Breeze;" but now she discovered her foe, and at once a cannon was run out, and a shot fired in defiance, to which, by Conrad's orders, the "Sea

Breeze " answered with one of her long bow chasers.

"There goes the hated signal," said Captain Ireton, as the pirate flag was hoisted, "and there goes that scarf. What can the fellow mean by that ? I never knew him do that till of late."

Conrad made no answer; but he looked that his cutlass was ready to his grip, and that his pistols were well primed ; and then taking an affectionate farewell of his grandparents, leaped into the launch, and gave orders for the attack.

"If I'm not mistaken, sir," said old Barnacle, who had command of the pinnace, "the weather is about to change. Do you see the disturbance of the mist over yonder ? That looks as if there was a wind coming up ; and if so, we had better have remained on board the 'Sea Breeze,' for the ship will come down on that wind, and perhaps be alongside of the 'Firebrand' before they know where they are.

"Never mind, Barnacle ; at all events it will show Deveril that we do not mean to let him escape if we can help it. Give way, lads. Fifty pounds to the first man who is upon the 'Firebrand's' deck, and a hundred pounds to the crew of the first boat that reaches her."

"Hurrah ! hurrah ! hurrah ! " shouted the men, and they bent to the oars with such a will, that the boats fairly flew through the water.

The cheer was answered by a shot from the "Firebrand," which took effect on the pinnace, cutting four of the oars in half, and carrying away the stern, besides killing two men.

The other boats had to pull to the assistance of Barnacle and his companions, who were now struggling in the sea.

This gave the "Firebrand" more time to prepare for action.

Boarding nettings were fixed up, and the guns were double shotted.

"He means fighting this time," said old Barnacle, who was now seated by our hero.

"Yes, and we shall not have an easy victory," replied Conrad, calmly.

"I wish we were on equal terms with him—that is, ship to ship. This boarding is always nasty work, and he has a large and desperate crew on board."

"Bang ! crash ! "

Another shot, and three men in the launch were sent to their last accounts.

Conrad and old Barnacle were spattered with the poor fellows' blood, and the whole crew were thrown into confusion.

At the same moment Deveril leaped upon the gunwale of his ship, and waved his sword in defiance.

"Curse that fellow's impudence," said old Barnacle; "but I should like to get a good cut at him. He's no coward with all his faults ; and, by jingo, what's he up to now ? He ain't a-going to cut and run, surely ? "

The last exclamation was caused by a change in the demeanour of the "Firebrand."

Scarcely had Deveril waved his sword, when he leaped hastily back on deck, and the next moment all sail was being set on the "Firebrand."

Slowly, but with increasing speed, the "Firebrand" began to make headway, steering to keep clear of the boats as much as possible.

"By all that's unholy, she's bringing a breeze down with her," cried Barnacle. "What can she be up to now ?"

"Up to now," exclaimed our hero, stamping with rage. "Why, fortune has turned against us, and has taken the side of the pirates. She knows we have taken most of the men out of the 'Sea Breeze,' and now the wind has freshened she is bearing up to attack the vessel whilst we are away."

"May I go to Davey Jones's locker if it ain't true," said Barnacle, slapping his knee.

Our hero gave the order for the return of the boats, and also that they should, if chance offered, treat the "Firebrand" with a taste of their cannonades.

"Give way lads," he cried. "The 'Sea Breeze' that we have sailed in so long is in danger, and we will never let it be said that we did not strain every nerve and muscle to save our old ship."

The men answered with a cheer, and bent to their oars with a will.

The "Firebrand" came steadily on, taking care to keep wide of the boats, now and then pitching a shot in among them, and doing no little damage.

The boats answered as well as they could from their cannonades, whilst they still strove to reach their ship before the foe could do so.

"By the Lord Harry, she will do us now," exclaimed Barnacle, almost crying with rage. "To think that the very winds should assist that rascal."

"Stay a moment, Barnacle," exclaimed our hero. "Look, look! the winds do not assist him. See how the sails fall flat against the masts. The wind has chopped, and here comes a spanking breeze from another quarter. The 'Sea Breeze' will get that first, and will come up with it in fine style."

It was true. The wind had chopped round as if by magic, and was now as much in favour of the "Sea Breeze," as it had before been in favour of the "Firebrand."

"Hurrah! my lads," shouted our hero. "We are safe now. Here comes the 'Sea Breeze,' spanking along at a fine rate, and the mist is being blown away, as she brings the breeze with her. Be sharp, lads, and pull for our ship as quickly as you can. Every minute she loses in picking us up, gives the pirates a better chance of escape. See, they are preparing to fly even now."

This was perfectly true.

Availing himself of the way which was still on his ship, Deveril had brought her head round and set every stitch of canvas to "woo the wind" that was coming up.

In the meantime he had run out the long stern chasers, with which he kept up a murderous fire on the retreating boats.

"Confound that fellow," said Barnacle, as he looked through his spy-glass at the "Firebrand."

"What fellow?" demanded Conrad.

"Captain Deveril," replied the old sailor; "he is pointing one of those guns himself, and I must say he does it jolly well, too, although he always aims it at this boat. There it goes again."

Crash! A cannon ball had struck the launch, killing three men, and wounding many others, and cutting the boat down to the water's edge.

"Pull men—pull for your lives!" shouted Conrad, as he sprang up and took the place of one of the men who had been slain. "Pull, or we shall go down before we can reach the ship."

There was no need to urge the men.

All saw their danger, and they pulled with all their might, whilst those who were not at the oars bailed out the water with their straw hats.

Still, they were sinking fast, and had scarcely reached the side of the 'Sea Breeze,' when the boat went down, leaving them struggling in the water, where many must have perished, had it not been for the arrival of the other boats to their aid, and the assistance given by the ship, which was hove to for that purpose.

Swiftly and cleverly as all this was carried out, it gave Deveril time which was invaluable to him.

The breeze which had now freshened considerably, had reached his vessel, and had sent him spanking along at a good rate.

But no sooner had the men been got out of the boats—all of which were in a sinking state from the murderous fire they had been subjected to, and were, therefore, abandoned—than all sail was made, and the pursuit of the "Firebrand" was once more commenced.

But the pirate captain was a first-class seaman, and had managed his ship so well that she, in the light wind, was likely to escape at last; but suddenly the breeze began to freshen, and then it became evident that the "Sea Breeze" was coming up with the "Firebrand," hand over hand.

"Quick, lads," cried Conrad, whose pale face, flashing eyes, and compressed lips showed that he was determined that this day should be an eventful one. "Quick, lads, and get that eighteen-pounder gun on to the main deck. If we could only carry away some of the 'Firebrand's' spars, we should be all right."

"Aye, aye, sir," answered the men, and soon the gun was in position, and pouring in round shot at the "Firebrand."

Still, fortune seemed to favour the pirate, for although some of the shot hulled him, not a spar, rope, or sail was touched.

"It's my belief that fellow is in league with the devil!" growled Barnacle.

Captain Deveril had run out his stern chasers, and was making a vigorous reply to his foe, doing no little damage to her hull.

"He cannot hold on much longer," said Captain Ireton. We are on a lee shore almost. He must tack. You see that low line yonder?"

"Yes," replied our hero; "that must be the coast of Lower California."

"You are right, my dear boy, it is," replied Ireton. "It is the Cape Monteroy, one of the most dangerous points of this coast. His vessel draws less water than ours, and he may have some wild notion of standing in as close as possible to the shore, where we cannot follow him, and, as we have no boats to cut him out, so escape us."

"Perhaps, as you heard him say he was determined to go to San Francisco," said Daulton, "he intends to land all his wealth and crew on the coast—sailors, such as he has with him, would make capital bandits."

"He must be mad if he does think of that," said Ireton. "The chances are ten to one that if he attempts that, he will be wrecked."

"No, no!" cried our hero, as he thought of Lucinda. "I do not believe even those desperate wretches would attempt so foolhardy a thing as that."

At this point the conversation was cut short by a round shot shattering a gun-carriage, and killing two of the men who had been "serving" the gun.

"By heaven! I will stand this no longer," cried our hero. "Come what may, we will destroy the 'Firebrand' to-night. Mr. Daulton," he continued, "you see to the sailing of the vessel. Keep every stitch of canvas on her. I will see to the working of the guns. Bravo, my lads! revenge your mates. Down with the pirates!"

Springing forward, Conrad helped the men as if he had been a common gunner, and with such precision did he aim the guns, that the pirate was greatly damaged.

Still she held on her course, and replied with the greatest vigour.

But now the rocky coast, on which the waves were beating violently, was plainly in view; and it was soon seen that both vessels must alter their courses, or rush right on a rocky promontory where they would be dashed to pieces.

This Lieutenant Daulton pointed out to Conrad, and advised him at once to stand out to sea, as the gale was becoming stronger and stronger.

But Conrad would not listen to this;

for by some lucky shots he had so crippled the pirate, that he was fast gaining on her.

Nearer and nearer did the vessels approach the shore, until at last, Conrad had to give the order "about ship."

As the yards were swung round, and the helm put up, our hero could not suppress a cry of rage, for the "Firebrand" still held on her course, standing closer into the shore, Deveril evidently knowing the little bay thoroughly.

As the pirates saw their foe go round, they sent up a cheer of defiance, and fired some parting shots at them, which, although at long range, Conrad determined to return.

The ship was brought to an anchor, and the sails taken in.

Then our hero ordered the starboard cannon to be loaded and double shotted.

Good aim was taken, and then the order given to fire.

Crash! With a roar like thunder the guns belched forth their deadly contents, and with fatal effects.

The yells that arose from the pirate vessel told a terrible story of the slain, whilst some of the spars came rattling down on the deck.

The man at the helm—the wheel, both had gone; and the ship, having lost all guidance, swung round and dashed upon a sunken rock.

At another time, had it been in open combat, the crew of the "Sea Breeze" would have been overjoyed at their victory; but there was something so terrible in this end of the "Firebrand," that they witnessed its destruction in deep silence.

"She's done for; there go her masts. Phew, they may cut the rigging away as much as they like, and heave the guns overboard, but that won't help 'em," said old Barnacle. "Just see how the water is rushing into her. See! she's heeling over."

Conrad stood horror bound.

What had he done?

By his last order he had driven the ship upon the rocks, and had doomed *all* in her to destruction, and Lucinda was on board.

"This is terrible!" cried Captain Ireton, as he covered his face with his hands. "If I had a boat I would try to help the poor wretches."

This he said, alluding to many of the pirates, who had been knocked into the sea by the falling masts and spars, and were vainly struggling against the current that was beating them to death.

All on board the "Sea Breeze" were intently watching the pirate.

They saw the boats lowered, and a number of good-sized chests placed in them.

Then the sailors came with their hammock sacks well filled, and placed them in the boats.

All this was done under Deveril's direction, who walked the decks with the greatest coolness, as if he had just gained a battle instead of losing one.

Then when all was ready, Deveril went below and soon returned, dragging Lucinda after him.

The girl was evidently struggling, and as she reached the side of the vessel, she attempted to cast herself into the sea; but Deveril held her with a grip like iron.

She was placed in a boat, and once more Deveril descended into the ship's hold, returning in a few minutes.

He leaped into the boat, in which Lucinda had been placed, and which was at once shoved off, and the other boats followed it towards the rock-bound coast.

"He has escaped us again," said Captain Ireton, regretfully. "He, no doubt, knows this coast so well, that he will find a passage for the boats through those rocks, which no other man could.

"See! he has set the vessel on fire! There goes the last of the 'Firebrands.' But who was that woman he had with him? Conrad, what is this? Are you wounded? Speak to me."

Conrad made no reply.

He had watched the fearful scene as well as he could for some time.

His face was white as a ghost, and the cold perspiration stood in heavy drops upon his forehead.

As the flames rose out of the hold of the "Firebrand," he uttered a deep groan, and fell back senseless in Captain Ireton's arms.

CHAPTER XXXIV.

CONRAD HEARS A DESPERATE PLOT, AND FORMS A DANGEROUS RESOLUTION—THE BODEGA ESCOVEDO.

WHEN Conrad recovered his senses, he found himself in a pleasant house, built much after the Spanish style, with a verandah overlooking the sea; and upon inquiry he discovered that he was at a villa some miles from San Francisco, which Mr. Ireton had purchased.

He also learned that he had had a severe attack of brain fever, and that, in his delirium, he had used the name of Lucinda so often, that Captain Ireton and Daulton had become suspicious, and had questioned José upon the matter.

He had related the little he knew of the affair, at the same time stating that if anyone knew who the lady was it was old Elspie.

Finding that his grand-parents knew this much, Conrad quickly told them the rest, and in a little time had persuaded both of the old men to sanction his love for Lucinda, provided she should be

found to be as good and virtuous as he believed her to be.

Thus encouraged, our hero quickly recovered his strength, and was soon endeavouring to discover some clue to where Deveril could be.

It had been a hot day, and our hero had fallen fast asleep in a corner of the veranda, where he was completely concealed by beautiful climbers, when he was startled by hearing the sound of voices only a few feet from him.

They spoke in Spanish, but as that was a language our hero knew thoroughly, he had no difficulty in understanding what was said.

"Basta! but this is no easy matter. He keeps so many men about the place."

"What of that? Will not Senor el Demonio come down from the mountains with *his* sailors?"

"Hombre! that is true."

"Then we are to have no fight if we can help it. We creep in—our knives are sharp, our aim good. Tut! the thing is soon done."

"Aye; but *should* they be awake when we enter, and discover us?"

"Do I not tell you that El Demonio, or *Deveril*, as some of his men call him, will be with us; he gives the signal, and in rush all his men, who are to be concealed in yonder plantation."

"Hist! don't speak so loudly. Some one may hear us. And you have discovered the way to enter the house?"

"Yes. We climb into yonder veranda—the window opens easily. You enter the room of Lieutenant Daulton. I seek out the sick lad, Conrad, whilst Deveril pays his respects to Captain Ireton.

"When all is settled we call in the followers of El Demonio, seize the place, and murder all who resist. We pack up the plunder, and are off before dawn.

"Now do you not think the plan is well laid?"

"Yes; very well laid."

"And you will join us?"

"I will. Where do you meet for the last arrangements?"

"At the Bodega Escovedo. Captain Demonio will be there, paying his respects to the beautiful Lucinda. Caramba! but it is strange he cannot win a smile from her bright eyes, and the old witch, too, protects her.

"If you come you must remember that the word by which one brother recognises another is ' Noche Triste.' Will you remember it?"

"Never fear! I will not forget it, and I will be there. Until then, adieu."

Through the trellis our hero could see two fellows, dressed in the picturesque costume of Mexico, wave their hands to each other, and then dash off in different directions through the plantation.

"Humph!" thought Conrad, as he rose from his chair. "Most men would have followed those fellows and had them seized. But they would have been wrong—very wrong. I must do more. I must catch the whole band. I must rescue Lucinda, and bring that fiend Deveril to justice."

And calling some of his men he strode to the stables, mounted his horse and rode down to the village, where the greater part of the crew of the "Sea Breeze" were.

From them he selected some fifty whom he could trust, and ordered them to procure Mexican dresses by nightfall, and to meet him just outside the town of San Francisco.

To Barnacle, and to Barnacle alone, did he tell what he had heard, and by his commands, the old sailor, with his comrades, all well-armed, were to keep watch round the house where Captain Ireton dwelt.

Then he rode into San Francisco, and having entered a costumier's shop, came out so altered, that no one would have known him; for he was dressed in the gayest Mexican style, and looked like a well-to-do cattle farmer.

He strolled about the town for some time, rolling up cigarettes, and humming Mexican airs.

Night at length closed in.

Then Conrad stole out to the quiet place, where he had ordered his men to be, and having found them there, told them to make their way to the Bodega Escovedo, enter the public room, and amuse themselves as they pleased, but to keep their eyes and ears open.

The gaiety was in full force, when Conrad pushed open the swing doors of the Bodega Escovedo, and puffing his cigarette strutted in.

It was a handsomely decorated place, and crowded with men and women, all the former of whom, and most of the latter were smoking and drinking.

Conrad saw amongst them one of the men whom he had seen talking beneath the veranda.

Calling one of the waiters, our hero ordered some drink, seated himself by the side of the man and said, carelessly—

"This is a gay scene, senor? Better to be here than toiling at sea."

The man looked sharply up at our hero, and then, after a pause answered slowly—

"Yes; I am almost surprised to see so many here, when it is such a fine night."

"*Fine night.* Well, to my thinking, to all merry men, this is a *noche triste* (sad night)."

As the man heard this he started, and looked sharply at our hero.

"Noche triste!" he muttered, what

do you know about that? Why should it be sad?"

"Basta! why should we be merry? A man who loses his fortune is not gay. But then, if one 'Firebrand' has been quenched at sea, another can be ignited on land."

"Sanatas! I understand you," cried the fellow. "Have you aught to say to the captain?"

"Yes; that is, I should like to see him. By the way, is it decided when we attack the house up yonder?" and here Conrad nodded his head carelessly in the direction of the villa.

"Hombre! do you not know?" exclaimed the man in surprise.

"I was told it would be to-morrow night," replied Conrad; "but Pedro said the time has been changed."

"Pedro! I don't know what Pedro you mean. We have so many of them. However, he is right. The time has been changed to to-night."

"To-night! Phew, you surprise me. That is sudden. But go on. What time?"

"This place closes to the general public at eleven."

"Well."

"No sooner has it closed, than the free brotherhood meet — you understand?"

"Yes—yes; I understand."

"We shall assemble here, and Diego will inform us of the captain's plans. We then leave the city and creep up to the village near the villa that this Captain Ireton has taken, and fall upon the sailors, whilst the captain and his friends—I am one of them—go up and settle the people in the villa. Is not the plan a good one?"

"Ah, yes—yes, I think so," said Conrad, cautiously.

"You do not seem half to like it. Do you think that it will not succeed?"

"How can I answer that?" replied our hero, and then he added to himself —"If it succeeds as well as I wish it, you will be surprised, and I shall not complain."

"And Captain Deveril," he continued, speaking aloud. "Does he meet us here?"

"No; he goes up to the villa. But I must be off."

"Stay! We have time enough for one glass of brandy. Ho, waiter, brandy!"

The fellow pretended that he did not care for the drink; nevertheless, he drank it off with a hearty smack of the lips, and then with a "*Buena noche, camarardo,*" strode from the Bodega.

And now our hero scarcely knew what to do until the hour for action came.

He strolled round the tables, and then he passed out into the street, and sauntered up to the barracks, where he had a short interview with the commander.

From thence he marched back to the Bodega, and as he threaded the tables, gave orders in an undertone, to the men of the "Sea Breeze."

At last the hour struck when the Bodega had to close.

The merrymakers rose, and strolled out into the open air.

But our hero noticed that some of the most stalwart villains drew into a darkened alcove of the café.

Seeing this, he rolled up another cigarette, and followed them.

"How now, senor!" cried one fellow, advancing towards him with a swagger. "What do you want here? Do you not know that this is private? What do you seek?"

"That which few men seek and many find—a *noche triste.*"

"Ha, say you so? Has the hour nearly arrived?"

"Yes; but the guard may find us, and turn us from this place."

"No; they will not do that. See, they have just turned out the last man. Now the secret door will be opened."

With a careless laugh the fellow marched up to the door, and knocked three times.

Someone answered from the other side in the same manner, and then the door was opened.

As our hero glanced in, he saw that it was only a dark entrance to a still darker passage.

But as the rest of the party entered, Conrad would not draw back, but boldly pushed on amongst the rest.

"Hist! hist! make no noise," whispered someone in the passage, as one of two of the party stumbled. "Come up the stairs as quietly as you can. The guards if they heard us, might suspect something, and we had had an idea that the house has been watched already."

" Impossible ! We have managed things so well," said the burly Mexican, who had spoken to Conrad.

" Did we not murder old Calemachio up in the plains yonder, steal his cattle, and then swoop down on Pedro, the herdsman, and make him drive the beasts in here, slaughter, and sell them ?

" Basta ! there is not a man in all San Francisco who does not believe that we are wealthy cattle owners come down from the prairies for a spree."

" True ; but should Pedro have turned traitor ? He loved his old master."

" That he loved his master, I doubt not ; but he could not turn traitor."

" Could not ? How do you make that out ? "

" Why, when he was killing and selling the beasts, two of us remained always near him. At the slightest sign of disaffection or treachery on his part he would have been killed."

" Ah, I understand. And where is he now ? "

" How should I know ? The last I saw of him he had three deep stabs about the breast, and was well weighted with shot. We rowed him out about a couple of miles to sea, and then threw him overboard."

Our hero shuddered when he heard this declaration from the horrible wretch, and he would have liked to have flown at his throat.

But policy dictated that he should restrain his feelings, and, therefore, he did so.

They had now reached a large room, and here the burly Mexican, who acted as leader, coolly addressed his friends, and unfolded to them a plot so diabolical that our hero could not believe that even Deveril could be guilty of such wickedness.

Ireton's villa was to be attacked—the people all murdered—the place plundered !

In the meantime some men were to creep on board the " Sea Breeze," which was now in port, and by forged orders, drawn out by Deveril, who knew Ireton's handwriting but too well, gain possession of the ship.

The plunder was to be conveyed by the murderers to the " Sea Breeze," and all jumping aboard, they were to set sail for Mexico, there to start afresh in their wicked life.

" Basta ! " cried the fellow, " but we shall have a glorious time of it. No ' Sea Breeze ' to hinder us there, brave boys. The captain marries the fair Lucinda, according to the pirate's laws, and from that moment we give ourselves up to pleasure. Come, lads, has anyone a word to say against this plan ? "

" Yes," cried Conrad, springing up and placing his back to the door, " I have."

" You ? "

" Yes," replied our hero, as he quietly produced two pistols, " I object to the plan."

" Angeles y demonios ! and who are you that you should object to the plan ? "

" I am Conrad Ireton—known as the Child of the Waves—and captain of the ' Sea Breeze.' "

As he said these words, every man drew his knife.

Conrad placed a silver whistle between his lips.

" Gentlemen," said, he quietly, " I do not think you will be fools enough to attack me. See ! I blow upon this little whistle."

As he spoke he did so, and a confused murmur rose on the air, as of men struggling.

" There ! Already the guard and some of my men from the ' Sea Breeze ' have seized all your men below. Be calm, senor," he continued, as the burly Mexican was about to spring forward. " My finger is on the trigger, and in another instant a bullet will be in you —that is if you dare move ! "

Muttering many a bitter curse, the Mexican drew back.

" Senor," said our hero, as he saw one man open a window and look out, evidently with the hope of escape, " it will be useless to try that way. The house is surrounded. A party of soldiers are placed on the ' Sea Breeze ' to protect her, and your plots are discovered. See ! " he cried, as he unlocked the door, " Here comes your fate in a party of the Municipal guards."

As he flung the door open, the burly Mexican leaped upon him, and as he raised his knife aloft, ready to plunge it into our hero's breast, he called out—

"To it my lads. If what this fellow says be true, we will die game."

Shaking the huge fellow off, Conrad turned and grappled with him.

The other pirates would have sprung upon our hero, had not a large body of sailors and some of the city guard rushed in. Then there commenced a fierce struggle.

Pistol bullets whizzed through the air; many fired by intention, but more by accident in the deadly struggle.

The lights were dashed out; tables and glasses upset; and amidst the bitter curses of the Mexicans, came the fierce oaths of the determined English sailors.

Silently Conrad had fought with his man until—he knew not how in the dark—he felt his knife strike something.

Then, with a deep groan, the man rolled over, never to rise again.

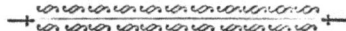

CHAPTER XXXV.

DEATH OF THE WITCH OF THE ROCK—HER CONFESSION.

No sooner had victory declared for the right, than lights were brought in, and no one seemed more surprised than the worthy owner of the Bodega Escovedo, that *such a plot should be hatched in his house!*

But the authorities did not seem to believe this; and, consequently, the landlord, waiters, and servants were all put in durance vile as well as the pirates.

Another party of soldiers were marched down to the port to protect the "Sea Breeze," and a third party also offered to accompany our hero back to the villa.

This, however, he declined, but demanded that the house should be searched; and soon, to his joy, he discovered Lucinda and Elspie—the latter wounded, and evidently dying, stretched on a bed! the former kneeling by her side and praying.

As the door was burst open, both women shrieked, and crouched down in fear.

Springing forward, our hero caught Lucinda up in his arms, and cried—

"Lucinda, my own sweet love, I am here. You have no need to fear—all danger is past, and the crew of the 'Firebrand' is destroyed."

"Destroyed!" gasped Elspie as she raised herself off the pillow. "Destroyed!"

"Yes, they have been caught in their own trap at last," cried Conrad.

"And who has done this?"

"I have, by the aid of my gallant men."

"I knew it—I knew it," moaned the old woman. "I knew that your hand was doomed to plant the blow on him whom I loved most. Listen, Conrad! I was Walter Deveril's foster mother. Oh, I might almost have said his mother; for never yet did mother love a child of her own more than I have loved that man."

"I can believe it," said Conrad, kindly.

"Well, well; let all that pass. It is over now—over now. His mother was my foster sister, and I worshipped her. She is dead, and it is better so. This girl—Lucinda—"

"Yes, yes; what of her?" demanded Conrad, leaning over the dying woman, and signing to his friends to approach, so that they might be hearers of her confession.

"Her father, the rich mine owner, Don Aleco Sigiur offended—offended— All grows dark."

"Go on— go on! I pray you go on!" cried Conrad, startled, as he recognised the name.

"Ah! yes, yes," murmured the old woman. "I stole the child to please Walter Deveril. He had her educated. Ah! but the fearful oaths he made her take that she would not speak of the past until he was dead. He would have married her, and so have gained the old man's wealth; but she refused him. She has been kind to me. I love her. Look—look!"

From her bosom the old woman plucked a small silken bag, and placed it in our hero's hands.

"Open that," she muttered; "open that. Therein is the proof of Lucinda's birth."

Eagerly our hero opened the bag and poured out a coral necklace, and several other beautiful jewels.

"What do you wish me to do with these?" demanded Conrad. If you would have me restore them to their lawful owner I promise you that I will do so. If, on the other hand, some terrible crime has been done, and these jewels will give some clue to bringing the perpetrator of the deed to justice, or to right some wronged person, I will do my best to punish the guilty and restore the injured one."

"Guilty! crime! who says such words to me? I did not say there was crime."

"For mercy sake, throw off all disguise. Whatever confession you may make to me cannot injure you. In this world you will never be called on to answer for your crimes; but in the next you must account for all. Then be wise and make what reparation you can to those whom you have injured."

"Am I so near death?" groaned the woman. "Is there no hope?"

"None. Ask yourself if you believe you can live any longer."

"No, no; I feel I cannot. Oh, that I could see Walter Deveril before I die! Where is he?"

"I know not where he is now; be assured he shall not escape me long. This night I know that he intends committing a deed out-doing all he has ever done. A deed of blood—"

"Blood!—blood!" shrieked the dying woman. "Blood! That word is ever ringing in my ears. Who would he murder now? Hath he not glutted his love of revenge enough already? Surely he will not murder Pauline whom he loved so well?"

"No; but this night, if I do not stop him, he will murder her father!"

"Fool! I have warned him that when he attempts that his own death is near. I know it—I feel it. Well, why should I care? I—I shall die soon. Murder! Ah, he would have murdered Pauline, but I prevented him. No; he cannot do that—she is dead —dead! Stay, it must be Lucinda he would slay! No, no; he must not do that. She will marry him, and all the vast wealth of her father shall be his. Save—save Lucinda. She shall not die!"

Both Lucinda and Conrad looked horrified, whilst the others leaned eagerly forward to catch the last words of the fast dying woman.

"Trust me," said our hero. "I, Conrad Ireton, will die before harm shall come to Lucinda. I love her, and she has promised to be my wife."

"Your—your wife, Conrad! Well 'tis better so—much better so."

"But these jewels?" demanded Conrad. "What am I to do with them?"

"They—they are Lucinda's. She wore them when I stole her. Oh, I die!"

"Quick—quick! some cordial!" cried Conrad. "Give her some directly. Much depends upon her confession."

The cordial was brought, and after a few drops had passed her lips the old woman seemed to revive a little.

"Take the trinkets to Don Aleco Sigiur. He will recognise them as his daughter's. He will know Lucinda. Tell him I confessed—say the gipsy Leona confessed all, and said Lucinda was—his child—and—"

She paused, her eyes became distended, and she pointed with her shrivelled hands to a distant part of the room, which the light of the oil lamp left in shadow.

"See — see — yonder!" she cried. "There—there is a black ship. It comes sailing towards me. What are the crew? They are not men. Their eyes flash like live coals Each one bears in his hand a firebrand. Ah, they beckon me. No, no; I will not go—I will not go. Save me—save—"

She uttered one long piercing shriek, and then fell back dead.

"Thus ends a tempest-tossed life of sin," said Conrad, as he threw the sheet over the face which Death, who generally softens expressions, had made even more fierce and stern. "May she find forgiveness and rest above."

"Methinks, senor," said one of the officers, who had made notes of the confession, "that a woman, who dies like that, has no chance for forgiveness."

"'Tis not for us to judge others, or to limit Heaven's mercy!"

"'DEATH TO THE PIRATES! HURRAH FOR CAPTAIN IRETON!' CRIED CONRAD."

"Hombre! I know not that. But, senor, this Don Aleco Sigiur. He is the owner of the villa and the estate which Captain Ireton has taken."

"I know it," replied Conrad, quietly. "He visits my father."

"True, senor; of course, you know it. But what is most strange, but an hour ago Don Aleco Sigiur passed through this town and went on to the villa to see the noble Don Ireton on especial business. Basta! It may be about this child."

"It may," replied Conrad, calmly. "Come, Lucinda, this is no place for you."

"Alas! Conrad," exclaimed the girl. "My life has made me quite familiar with scenes of death. But this death-bed seems more horrible than all similar scenes that I have witnessed."

"Come, darling, do not tremble so. Pray heaven the unhappy life she has led may, in some measure, atone for her sins. Let her remains receive all respect," he continued, turning to the people around. "I will pay all the expenses of the funeral."

"The senor is too good," cried the civil officer, who was only too glad to get anyone to take the expenses off the city accounts.

Leading Lucinda from the chamber of death, Conrad conducted her to a private apartment.

When he had overcome the young girl's agitation, he took her hands, and gazing into her eyes, said—

"Lucinda, dear one, you know now your birth, and the immense fortune which you must inherit. I am, or rather my grandfathers, are rich, and I shall, no doubt, be their sole heir. Still, I should be only a poor man compared to your father. Tell me, then, dear one, if you can still love me—if you will be my wife."

"Conrad," replied Lucinda, "when I was poor and friendless, you loved me. Think you that I would be base enough now that fortune has changed in my favour to desert one who has loved me so truly? No, Conrad, I who think so much of my hero, would have you believe that, weak as I am, I am strong in my love."

"I do believe it, dear one," cried Conrad, as he caught her in his arms. "I do believe it; and you have made me the happiest fellow in the world by telling me this. But your father—he is proud of his birth, and reckons himself almost equal to the highest grandee in Spain. Do you think that he will object to our union?"

"He cannot, when he thinks how much you have done for me—from what misery and degradation you have rescued me."

"You know not the pride of birth. It is a thing which I scorn; and yet, when I knew not from whom I sprang, no ambition to me was greater than to prove my ancestors were men of worth. Perchance your father may refuse. If so, what will you do?"

"I must obey him. But still I will be true to you; for here I swear that I will wed no other man than my brave deliverer—my noble Conrad."

"My own sweet love," cried our hero, rapturously. "But we must away at once," he continued, as he glanced at his watch. "This night's adventures are not yet over. Come, sweet Lucinda I will take you to a place of safety, where you shall see your foes beaten, and your lover triumph."

CHAPTER XXXVI.

THE ATTACK ON THE VILLA—AND THE RESULT.

A FEARFUL night. The rain fell in torrents, the wind roared through the forests, and bent the weaker trees almost to the ground.

Now and then the vivid lightning would rend the skies; and as it struck down some giant of the forest, the awful thunder made the earth shake.

Three men crept out from the plantation near the villa, in which resided Captain Ireton and his friends.

"*Angeles y demonios!*" murmured

one. " What a fearful night.   Phew ! what lightning ' "

" I cannot hear our men down yonder in the village," said the leader, who was no other than Walter Deveril. " But it is no wonder on such a night as this."

" Basta, senor ! I think the night is capital for our purpose," said one of the fellows.

" Why so ? I do not like the lightning," replied Deveril, with a shudder.

" Hombre ! senor has changed. I have seen you in a storm laugh with delight, and hurl defiance at the heavens ! "

" Yes, and why I do not do it now, I cannot tell. Somehow, to-night, my nerves seem shaken."

" Too much grog, captain—too much grog," growled out another of the ruffians ; " but don't be cast down ; it won't do to lose nerve to-night. Take a pull at this flask."

As the fellow spoke, he produced a flask of brandy, from which the captain took a hearty draught.

" Ah ! " he muttered, " that feels better. To-night will either make or mar me. I care not much what it is ; but I will bear this suspense no longer."

" Never you fear captain," replied one of the fellows. " We shall be able to bunk into the place as nicely as possible. When we have the crossbar in at the shutters, we wait for a flash of lightning —it comes, and as the thunder roars, we break open the shutters. No one hears us."

" Do you know how many sleep in the house ? " demanded Deveril.

" Captain Ireton, Lieutenant Daulton—"

" I want not a catalogue of their names—I asked the number.'

" Well, seven, counting the three servant men. Then there are the women, but they don't count. A naked blade held at their throats and they are as quiet as lambs."

" You are wrong, there," sneered the third ruffian. " Women are not so easily quieted."

" It matters not," said Deveril. " If we manage well, there will be no fighting. By this time all the inhabitants of the villa are, no doubt, asleep, and one blow will, if well-directed, kill the one at whom it is aimed. Ireton,

Daulton, and Conrad dead, we have nothing to fear. The rest will be soon overpowered. Besides, we shall soon have the help of our men from the village, and then to work."

Deveril drank with feverish thirst.

" Now I am ready to meet anyone," he cried, striking his breast. "Come on, my brave lads, to-night we will make our fortunes."

They crept over the lawn and reached the veranda.

Then one of the men produced a crowbar, with which he prized open the shutters of one of the windows.

Throwing open the shutters, they crept into the room, paused, and glanced fearfully around. All was still.

" Shall I strike a light ? " whispered one of the men.

" No, no ; we shall be safer in the dark," replied Deveril. " The room to the right is old Ireton's, that to the left is Daulton's. The one farther on is Conrad's. Have you your knives all ready ? "

" Yes, we are prepared."

" Mind, keep your pistols ready ; yet do not use them, but under the greatest necessity."

" All right, captain. Your commands shall be obeyed to the letter."

" Now let us advance together."

With cat-like tread they crept forward, each going to the door appointed him.

Their hands were just upon the handles of the doors when the shutters of the windows by which they had gained admittance were closed with a crash, and they could hear them fastened with an iron bar.

At the same moment the three doors leading into the room were thrown open, and the whole apartment was flooded with light.

Instantaneously the two followers of Deveril were felled by Ireton and Daulton, whilst Captain Deveril only saved himself from being run through the body by a tall Spaniard, who, sword in hand, stood in the doorway of the room the pirate had taken to be Conrad's, by springing backwards.

Seeing that the game was up, Deveril turned to fly.

But he was met by Conrad, who, with his back turned to the shutters, confronted him.

In each hand he held a pistol, and these he presented point blank at Deveril's breast.

"The game is up, Walter Deveril," said Conrad, sternly. "Throw down your arms and surrender!"

"To you?" cried Deveril. "Never! You have laid a nice trap for me, it is true, but thus do I defeat your plans!"

So saying, he snatched a pistol from his belt and fired.

Conrad only saved himself from certain death by stepping nimbly aside.

The next moment he fired both pistols at Deveril.

But, as he fired, the lights were suddenly extinguished.

Deveril was uninjured.

The pirate captain was about to turn, when he felt his arm suddenly seized, and a deep voice whispered in his ear—

"Come—grasp me tightly, and I will lead you to safety."

He recognised the voice as belonging to the tall Spaniard, Cosmo, as he was called.

Deveril did not hesitate.

Grasping the Spaniard by the waist-belt, he followed.

Two or three paces, and he heard what sounded like a heavy door close with a crash.

"What is that?" he asked.

"Follow!" was the only reply.

They crossed a landing, passed through an opposite room with the speed of lightning, and reached a window.

On the outside was a small balcony.

The Spaniard, who was a powerful fellow, without hesitation, flung the window open, and told Deveril to get out.

"Delay," he said, "and both of us are lost. It is but twenty feet. Drop it—quick, quick!"

Deveril, placing his long knife between his teeth, clambered over the balcony, and dropped to the ground.

He was at once followed by the Spaniard, who said simply—

"Run!"

Thereupon, he plunged through the thickly wooded garden at the back.

It is needless to say that Deveril kept close at his heels.

For the moment the Spaniard was chief.

Deveril, proud and haughty though he was, was content that it should be so.

Anything—anywhere so that he got out of the net which had been woven about him.

Their movements were considerably hastened by hearing shouts behind them.

Again and again Deveril encouraged the Spaniard to greater speed by promises of a handsome reward.

But Cosmo needed little encouragement.

He was perfectly aware that, if caught, he would share the same fate as Deveril.

Though the pirate captain's thoughts were concentrated upon escape, he, nevertheless, could not help wondering how the Spaniard was so well acquainted with the paths he traversed, some of which were most intricate.

The grounds were quickly left behind, but still Cosmo went on.

But at last a small inn was reached, and here he halted.

"Have you money?" he asked.

Deveril placed a sovereign in his hand.

"More," said Cosmo.

Deveril added four more.

With this sum in his hand, Cosmo entered the inn, and called for a bottle of wine.

The landlord knew him well enough, and quickly produced the required refreshment.

Cosmo handed him the five pounds.

"I want you to lend me two horses for a couple of hours," he said. "They must be fleet and powerful, and here is a deposit on them."

The landlord hesitated when he caught sight of Deveril, who presented the appearance of an assassin fleeing from justice.

"Quick!" said Cosmo, "we are in a hurry."

"But a deposit of a small amount is by no means—"

"The horses—quick, I say! Trifle not with us! In two hours I will myself return them."

The landlord hurried out to the stables, saddled the horses, and led them to the front.

Having finished the wine, both mounted and rode away, and it is scarcely necessary to say that they urged the horses into full gallop.

"Safe! safe!" said Deveril.

"True," said Cosmo. "I snatched you from certain death."

"You did, you did. I cannot tell you how to claim your own reward, but I will present you with a handsome sum. I know where to get money."

It was not until they had put a distance of five or six miles between themselves and the inn that they again paused.

Deveril looked about him.

He saw that they had halted in the midst of a mountainous spot, but where it was he had not the faintest idea.

"Presently," said Cosmo, "I will lead you to a friend, and you will be safe with him until you choose to set out again."

"Good; I thank you. But perhaps you will tell me why you, a comparative stranger, take so much interest in me?"

"I will. This, then, is the reason. I heard you say that it is your intention to leave for England soon."

"So it is. What has now occurred will cause me to quit this country almost at once."

"You say you know where to get money?"

"I have hidden certain articles of jewellery, and upon that I can raise money."

"To be sure. Well, what I want you to do, is to take me to England with you."

"Assuredly. You have proved yourself an excellent man—sharp and clever. Let us, then, for the future be friends."

He held out his hand, which was grasped by the Spaniard.

"What has struck me most," continued Deveril, "is your almost perfect pronunciation of English."

Cosmo smiled.

"Yes," he said, "I studied it in England—in London."

"Also, I am astounded at your knowledge of the villa and the grounds surrounding it."

"No doubt, but I have been there many a time before—under other circumstances."

As he said this a fierce light shone in his eyes, but it quickly vanished.

Leaping from his horse, he said, as he took the bridle—

"By-and-by I will tell you the story of my connection with the villa.

Now, dismount, and lead your horse as I do."

Deveril obeyed him, and followed Cosmo down many a rugged and dangerous path.

In some places they were able to see where they were going by aid of the moon, which ever and anon peered through the somewhat lowering clouds.

But in other places it was so dark that the greatest caution was necessary, lest a false step might hurl them down some yawning chasm.

Presently Cosmo stopped, and placing his fingers in his mouth, imitated, and with remarkable accuracy, the cry of the vulture.

After a short interval he repeated it, and it was at once replied to in the same manner.

"You might as well tell me where we are," said Deveril.

"I will now. You are close to the home of Pedro Francasi."

"Who is he?"

"What! is it possible that you have not heard?"

"If I have been told, then I do not remember."

"Pedro Francasi is the most daring brigand in the country."

"Brigand, eh? Shall we be safe?"

"Safe? Ay, perfectly. Pedro is my friend."

As Cosmo thus spoke, a man attired in a picturesque costume, carrying pistols in his belt, and a long rifle slung at his back, made his appearance.

Cosmo uttered a few words, which Deveril could not understand, and the sentry—for such he was—nodded and, beckoning to the pair to follow him, turned and strode away.

In five minutes they reached a small hut, before which five or six men—sentries—were seated, playing cards by aid of two or three small lanterns.

Passing these, they made their way along a narrow, rocky pass, then, suddenly passing between two gigantic rocks, they stood before the entrance of one of five or six caves.

Before the mouth of this were more men—brigands, all of them.

Without giving these any explanation, the sentry drew aside the heavy curtain which concealed the cave, and sounded a gong.

A deep voice directed him to enter.

"Cosmo," said the sentry, "and a friend."

"Let them enter."

The next moment Cosmo and Deveril passed into the cave.

Deveril was astounded.

The place bore a striking resemblance to his own cave, and he sighed as he looked around and saw the valuable articles with which the cave was crowded.

Lying on a sofa, which was covered with valuable skins, was a man of about fifty—tall and powerful, and elaborately attired.

This was Pedro Francasi, one of the most desperate, determined, and impudent brigand chiefs in all the country.

As Cosmo entered he rose and extended his hand, first to one and then the other.

"Speak in English," said Cosmo; "for my friend here is not much of a hand at our language."

Pedro smiled, showing as he did so, a row of teeth of dazzling whiteness.

"So, Cosmo," he said, "you have returned once more. No doubt you have thought over my last offer, which was, that you should be my lieutenant."

Cosmo shook his head.

"No," he said; "you are wrong."

"Wrong, eh? Then I am sorry. Yes, it struck me when your name was announced, that you had reconsidered my offer, and that, not only were you about to accept it, but that you had brought a friend to join with you."

"It is impossible—at present."

"Who is your friend?"

"Walter Deveril, the—"

"What! the English pirate?"

"The same."

Deveril's eyes lighted up as he saw that his name was known even in this isolated spot, and his figure became more erect, his demeanour more proud.

"I am glad to meet so important a person," said Pedro, again extending his hand; "we will have a chat together. Be seated," he added, as he brought his hand upon a silver bell.

It was instantaneously answered by a young and pretty Circassian boy.

Pedro ordered him to fetch wines and tobacco.

These being placed before the three, Pedro said—

"You have been absent now, Cosmo, for three months."

"True—it is quite that."

"Still on the same path?"

"Ay, still on the same path," said Cosmo, gloomily.

"And what has transpired? Did you track him down?"

"I did—but only to lose him just as I thought myself on the point of taking my revenge."

"'Tis ever so. He continually slips through your fingers. Where is he now?"

"On the road to England."

"To England, eh? Then you lose him for ever?"

"Never! It is my intention to pursue him. From place to place I traced him, never halting, never faltering. Then I found that I had spent the whole of my money."

"What did you do then?"

"I was forced to join in enterprises which, at any other time, I should have scorned."

"Was it at one of these that you met your friend here?"

"It was. And glad am I that I did so, for we shall go to England together."

Pedro shrugged his shoulders.

After carefully lighting a long silver-mounted pipe, he said—

"You are my friend, Cosmo—more, we were once like brothers, and I would not endeavour to place any obstacle in the path you may select—but you must remember that the laws of England—and you know them well—are severe."

"Fear not. What I shall do will be too secret for the law to discover."

Deveril had listened to this conversation with much interest, but he did not interrupt."

At last he said—

"Perhaps you would favour me with particulars."

"I will. Here they are :—

"Two years ago, when in London, where I was born—"

"Where you were born!" interrupted Deveril, in astonishment.

"Ay, I was born in London."

"Then you are not Spanish?"

"My father was a Spaniard, my mother English. My mother died in London, while my father, having lost his fortune, came here, joined Pedro, and two days afterwards, when attacking a traveller with a large escort, was shot dead."

" Ay," said Pedro, " it was a sad thing ; but it was all his fault, for he would persist in joining the party."

Cosmo continued—

" Two years ago, as I have said, when in London, I made the acquaintance of many persons of influence and position.

" The reason of this was that I represented myself to be a person of large fortune ; and in this I was supported by a lawyer, to whom I paid periodical sums to support me in any statement I might choose to make.

" At the house of a gentleman of the name of Cole, I met a young lady.

" Her name was Margaret Collins, heiress to a large fortune, and Mr. Cole's ward.

" Again and again I visited the house, and fell in love with her—"

" Or her fortune ? " interrupted Pedro, with a laugh.

" Well, with her fortune. I received, as I thought, great encouragement— certainly I was always warmly welcomed by Mr. Cole.

" Time passed on, and at last I proposed. You may, perhaps, consider what my state of mind was when Margaret fairly laughed in my face.

" I was so overwhelmed with astonishment, and felt so crushed, that I could not utter a single word.

" When I recovered myself, Margaret had disappeared ; but, nevertheless, I heard her laughter in the distance.

" I sought out Mr. Cole, and laid all before him.

" He replied--in the calmest fashion in the world—that he was astonished. Ay, *astonished!*

" Then he asked me if I had not heard that Margaret had long been betrothed to Mr. Edward King, son of a banker, and who, at that time, was abroad. And he showed me his portrait.

" What reply I made I know not, but I quickly left the house.

" One day I met Margaret near the house, and I again tried to get her to listen to me.

" She refused. I seized her hands, and she called for help. Maddened at being so snubbed and treated with contempt, I retained my hold of her."

Here Cosmo paused for some few minutes, as if thinking whether he should continue the story.

Then, swallowing a tumbler of wine, he continued—

" I did not hold her for long.

" Suddenly I heard a rush. The next instant a heavy lash descended upon my shoulders, face, everywhere— until I was nearly blinded.

" It was in vain that I cried hold.

" The hand that wielded the lash stopped not until I lay writhing in agony upon the ground.

" Then I saw a man standing over me. At once I recognised him as the original of the portrait Mr. Cole had shown me.

" Yes, it was Mr. Edward King who had thus thrashed me until the blood ran down my cheeks, and until I felt as if my body had been cut in every part with a knife."

" By heaven ! " said Deveril, " I would have killed him on the spot."

" And I would have done so," hissed Cosmo, " only I was not armed—not even with a stick."

" What did he say to you ? "

" He said but little. I remember his words. They were—' Begone, coward and impostor. Take my advice and leave the country at once, lest the law lays its hands upon you. I have made inquiries, and have learned what a fraud and blackleg you are.' "

" Was he a powerful man ? "

" Very. He stood over six feet in height, and is broad and muscular in proportion.

" For more than a month after this I lay at home very ill. When I recovered, I learned that King had married Margaret, and that they had gone abroad.

" I determined to follow, but how was I to proceed ? I had no money. Fortune favoured me. Through the solicitor who worked with me, I was introduced to a certain young gentleman of fortune.

" He, I soon saw, had more money than brains, and, in less than a fortnight, I succeeded in swindling him out of three or four thousand pounds."

Here Cosmo burst into a fit of laughter, and it is scarcely necessary to say it was echoed by the brigand chief and Deveril.

" Yes," Cosmo continued, after he had

THE CHILD OF THE WAVES. 137

swallowed yet another tumbler of wine, "I robbed the fool with the greatest ease, and then, having purchased a complete outfit and disguised myself, I started for France, for my lawyer ascertained that it was to Paris that the newly-married couple—my bitter curse on them!—had gone.

"I arrived there just as they left for Germany. I need not tell you how I tracked them from place to place; how I lay in wait to kill Edward King, and always failed.

"At last, after losing sight of them for weeks, I tracked them to the villa owned by Don Aleco Segiur.

"Thoroughly well disguised, I made the acquaintance of one of the servants, an English girl. I made her repeated presents, and pretended that I was madly in love with her.

"I learned that Mr. King was about to travel to Vera Cruz, and I laid my plans accordingly.

"I repeatedly visited the villa, and was smuggled in by the servant. May she perish miserably!"

"Eh?" said Deveril. "May she perish?"

"Ay, for she betrayed me. Every word I had spoken was repeated to her master and mistress. I have now no doubt but that, while we spoke in the kitchen of the villa, they listened and recognised my voice.

"One day the servant, whose name was— Let me see—"

"Kitty," said Pedro.

"Ay, Kitty Kavanagh, an Irish girl, told me that her master had left for Vera Cruz. The time, I thought, had come. I came to Pedro, and he, with half-a-dozen men, accompanied me at night to the villa.

"My intention was to force Margaret from the villa and bring her here.

"We encountered, first of all, Kitty. She was soon seized and silenced; and then, totally unconscious of any danger, we marched up to the sitting-room.

"I was first. As soon as I threw the door open, crash went a pistol, and a man beside me dropped dead!

"There, in the centre of the room, armed to the teeth, was Edward King, beside him two friends.

"Totally unprepared for this, we were compelled to beat a hasty retreat.

"So now, Captain Deveril, you know how I became acquainted with the villa."

"It was not the defeat which annoyed me most," scowled Pedro, "it was this: We had just scrambled out of the villa, when the body of the man who had been shot dead was hurled from the window, like dirt. Then there was a loud burst of laughter; while every time the men exposed themselves they were treated to a few shots, the result being that everyone was wounded."

"After that," said Cosmo, "Edward King and his wife left the villa, and went to the village of Marzian.

"Yet I followed them in various disguises, but at last they got clear away, and I have positive proof that they have gone to England.

"So now, Captain Deveril, since I have assisted you, you will assist me."

"I will, most decidedly. We must remain here for the present. Those now at the villa will search for me, but failing to find me, they will proceed to England.

"Of that I am convinced. Yes, they will go there, fancying themselves perfectly safe. Let them wait— let them wait!"

"Are you provided with plenty of money, Captain Deveril?" asked Pedro.

"Nay; but at a certain spot I have secreted a pocket-full of valuable diamonds. I can raise money on them."

"To be sure. But it would not be safe to go alone to get them. I will accompany you when you like, and a dozen men shall keep at a respectful distance."

"I accept your offer."

"My coffers here are full of gold, English, French, and Spanish. If we can come to terms, I will advance you money on the jewels."

"Good! That offer I likewise accept."

"It is settled then. Cosmo, I will present you with five thousand pounds in English money if you will consent to join me on your return from England."

"Readily," cried Cosmo.

And the precious pair shook hands on the "bargain."

*   *   *   *

In the meantime, those at the villa could scarcely realise what had happened.

When lights were procured, search

was instantly made all over the house and grounds.

This proving fruitless, Conrad was in a terrible state.

"Just as I thought that I should send the wretch to his last account," he said, "he suddenly, and in the most mysterious fashion, disappears."

"No matter," said Captain Ireton. "His recklessness is certain to meet with its reward ere long."

"My opinion is," said Daulton "that he is seriously wounded. But in a few hours search shall be made for him. He cannot be far off."

On the following day twenty experienced men were employed, under a man who was thoroughly well acquainted with the surrounding country, but not the faintest clue to Deveril was discovered.

He had disappeared, as if the earth had suddenly opened and swallowed him up.

"We will not further waste our time," said Captain Ireton, when, late the next night, the whole party were once more assembled within the villa. "We will at once make arrangements to proceed to England."

Conrad shook his head and looked hard at Lucinda.

Don Aleco interpreted the look.

"Do not fear," he said. "You shall not go without Lucinda. And I will form one of the party."

This was received with a shout of joy.

"Yes," continued Don Aleco, "I will place this villa and my other properties in the hands of my agents, and will accompany you to England. It is a country which I have long wished to visit.

"I may stay there for the rest of my life. Certainly I should not think of returning without my daughter, and I strongly question whether she would leave England without consulting her husband.

"Conrad, my boy, embrace your future wife. We will retire; for, no doubt, you have much to say to each other."

Our hero was too full for words.

Warmly did he shake hands with the noble-looking old man.

"Men," said the Don, with a smile, "have for years envied me my good fortune, and have coveted the treasures which, by sheer hard work, I have amassed. But who would envy me *this* newly-found treasure ?"

And he embraced his beautiful daughter.

"Upon my word," smiled Captain Ireton, as he placed his arm within Dalton's, and led him towards the door, "it strikes me that I, for one, already envy you ! "

"I am afraid I must say the same," said Dalton. "But now let us go, and over a cigar and a bottle of good wine, make our arrangements for quitting the country.

"Old England! Ha, how I long to see the dear old country once again !

"Conrad, my lad, when the white cliffs of Dover come in sight, I shall think that all our troubles are over, and that there is peace and happiness for all of us."

Conrad's face became serious.

"I would I could think so," he said. "I will try hard to think so, but I am afraid it will be a failure. So long as that double-dyed villain remains on earth, so long shall I be troubled."

"Fear not, the wretch will speedily drink himself to death; or, what is more probable, he will be killed in some drunken brawl."

*   *   *   *

In a little over a fortnight, all arrangements were complete.

The "Sea Breeze" was disposed of, Don Aleco's mines and other property were handed over to a well-known agent, and berths were engaged in a splendid merchantman called the "Queen of the Waves."

Great crowds watched the departure of the fine vessel.

Among the vendors of various articles, was a dark-skinned man, wearing a heavy beard, and attired in a ragged sailor's dress.

He had a basket of fruit attached to his waist, but he made no attempt to push the sale of it.

His eyes were continually fixed upon the "Queen of the Waves," and the pasengers who thronged the white decks.

The reader has already guessed that this man was Deveril.

When, amid loud cheers, the fine

vessel began to move, he clenched his fist and hissed—

"Wait—wait, Conrad, wait. Wait *all* of you. The day will come when I will have my revenge. Be you in England or the wilds of Africa, I will seek you out. Yes, yes, I will seek you out!

"Captain Deveril is not dead—nay, nor will he die until he has crushed you.

"Go, as you think, to happiness; but, in the midst of it, I will descend upon you with the stealthiness of a serpent."

CHAPTER XXXVII.

"SNUFFY GARVEL."

AT the period of our story, the neighbourhood of Holborn was possessed of many a vile slum, down which it was dangerous for an ignorant pedestrian to pass.

Modern improvements have happily swept many of them away, and among them "Larkhall Rents," which was a *cul-de-sac*, or blind alley.

In one of the rotten old houses lived a man of the name of Garvel.

His occupation was notified on the exterior of the house as follows—

"JAMES GARVEL,
"*Solicitor.*"

If asked, he would have found it difficult to say to whom he acted as solicitor *for an honest purpose.*

James Garvel was one of the black sheep of an honourable profession, and a very black sheep indeed.

He was about sixty years of age, short and thin, with a beardless face and bald head; and he was always attired in the rustiest of black suits, the pockets of which were invariably crammed with documents of one sort and another.

He had many strange and nasty habits, but the principal was an extraordinary strong taste for hot rum.

He was also a confirmed snuff taker. He nearly always had a snuff-box in his hand, and this obtained for him a nickname, for he was called "Snuffy Garvel."

This was the very man who had assisted Cosmo in his villainy in London.

He had been successful in placing several flies in Cosmo's web, and had pocketed a plentiful share of the "plucking."

One night, just about six months after the departure of the "Queen of the Waves" for England, Garvel was in his "office," engaged in a calculation of some sort.

The hour was not late, but he certainly did not expect visitors, otherwise he would not have had a steaming jorum of rum before him.

Suddenly a knock came upon the street door.

So startled was Garvel that he leapt to his feet, nearly knocking over his favourite drink.

"Martha, Martha!" he cried, poking his head out of the door. "Quick! there's a knock."

An old woman appeared at the head of the stairs. She was "housekeeper."

"What of it?" she demanded. "*Let* them knock; it's only them little brats who will persist—"

"It may not be," interrupted Garvel. "Go and see."

The old woman, with a string of groans and grunts at being disturbed at such an hour, slowly shuffled to the door and opened it.

Two "gentlemen" stood upon the threshold.

"Well, what do you want?" asked the woman.

"We want to see Mr. Garvel, if he's not dead."

"Well, if he was *dead* you wouldn't see him, *would* you? What's your name? Where do you come from, and what's your business?"

These questions she asked, after the manner of a parrot who had been taught to say that and nothing else.

"Say that Mr. Ronald Rosso is here."

"Here!" said Garvel—"here, eh? The devil! Show them in, Martha—show them in."

And at the risk of scalding his

throat, he swallowed the rum remaining in the glass.

The two gentlemen entered the office.

The one who had called himself "Mr. Ronald Rosso" was Cosmo, while the other was Captain Deveril.

"Here, once more!" said Cosmo, as he seated himself. "So you did not expect us, eh? And yet you had a timely warning."

"Ay, but you did not say when you would arrive, and I did not expect you for at least a fortnight."

"A good ship and fair winds lessened the time. And now that we are here, what have you for our refreshment? There is a strong smell of rum, your old favourite."

"The bottle is at your service."

And Garvel, in the most gingerly fashion, placed the bottle on the table.

"No thanks," said Deveril. "We will drink brandy if you have it, and, since I am informed that you are very poor, we will pay for it.

Thereupon, he threw down a sovereign.

Garvel produced a bottle of brandy with wonderful alacrity.

Money *always* had a most wonderful effect on his movements.

"Now, gentlemen," he said, "let us to business."

"First," said Cosmo, "what have you done in the matter I wrote about?"

"All that you required. Do you remember a man I used to employ called Leakey?"

"I well remember him."

"I engaged him to find out all you desired, and he has done so. Mr. and Mrs. King, with their one child—"

"A child?"

"Ay, twelve months old. They are living at Clevedon Villa, Clapham Common. They have been there for some time, and have no intention of again going abroad."

"Good. This is indeed excellent information. Now, as to the other matter?"

"I again employed Leakey, and, in this case also he was successful. How he managed it he has not yet told me, but from the description furnished, he has traced the youngest man of the party to Epsom. No, not to Epsom, to Banstead, a few miles from Epsom."

Deveril smiled.

"Your man is right," he said.

Then to Cosmo he added—

"That is Banstead Manor, part of the estates of the Earl of Bellchambers."

"So now," continued Garvel, "the next thing to be considered is— Who can that be?"

He had been interrupted by a sharp knock.

Martha went to the door and opened it.

As before, she was about to question the visitor.

But, instead, she was heard to say—

"Oh, it's you, is it? Come in, then, you drunken hound!"

A hoarse laugh was the reply to this, and the next moment a man stumbled into the passage, and then into the room.

It was the man the lawyer had spoken of—Leakey.

Certainly he was much the worse for unlimited potations, but he knew what he was about.

Not being aware that his employer had visitors, he seemed somewhat staggered for a moment, but quickly recovering himself, he nodded, and then, without a word, turned to retreat.

"Wait!" said Garvel.

"I'm *always* waiting," was the reply.

"What brings you here at this hour? You can speak freely, for the business you are upon concerns these gentlemen."

"Indeed?" grinned the man. "I am pleased to hear it—very."

"What makes you so pleased to hear it?" asked Cosmo.

"Because, no doubt, you will feel inclined to pay me for the—"

"Silence you infernal fool!" thundered Garvel. "How dare you insult my clients before my face?"

"Insult! Is it then an insult to ask for payment for—"

"Do not I pay you?"

"You paid me well the last time," was the reply—"yes, very well indeed—a heavy bottle fair at my head, gentlemen, as sure as I'm alive. Bash it went against that wall. If I hadn't moved I should have been smashed."

"You shouldn't be saucy, then," growled Garvel. "But tell me, quick, what has brought you here now?"

"The business."

"Out with it. What you have to say, say at once."

"I *am* badly treated," sighed Leakey. And yet, even when I had a chance of enjoying myself, I was thinking of your business.

"Well, the fact is this : I was walking along Holborn, when suddenly a vehicle stopped, and I saw a young gentleman alight.

"You might have knocked me down with a feather; for, upon my soul, I at once recognised him as the one I had seen at Banstead."

"Impossible!" said Garvel.

"Impossible! What are you talking about? Do you think I am likely to make a mistake? No fear. Well, he went into a portmanteau shop. Pretending to be fastening my shoes, I hung about the doorway.

"The young gentleman was ordering a portmanteau. I saw him pay the money, and heard him say that it was to be sent to his address at once.

"Though I tried as hard as I could, I did not overhear what the address was.

"He came out in a few minutes, and walked rapidly away."

"And you followed?" asked Garvel, now, like his visitors, in a state of excitement.

"I? No fear. I should not have cared to follow that young man. If I had done so, and he had found it out? Why, bless you, one blow from him, and all the breath would have been knocked out of my body.

"No, I waited. Don't you see—the portmanteau was to be sent on at once. So it was. In less than ten minutes, out comes a boy with the portmanteau on his head.

"I followed him a little way, and then stopped him.

"'I say, my lad,' says I, 'are you from Newberys?' 'Yes, sir,' says he. 'And,' says I, 'you are going to take that to Mr. Thomas, are you not?'

"He replied, 'No, sir.' I thanked him and walked off. I had obtained what I desired, for on the top was the name and address. Here it is."

So saying, he pulled out a dirty slip of paper, spread it out, and read as follows—

"Conrad Ireton, Esq.,
"Russell Hotel,
"Guildford Street,
"Russell Square."

Adding with a triumphant chuckle—

"There you are, gentlemen, what do you say to that?"

Deveril leapt to his feet, and almost snatched the paper from his hand.

"I say that you are a clever man," he said. "And here is a five-pound note for you."

To look at Leakey's face as the crisp note was thrust into his hand, one might have been inclined to fancy that he had just inherited a fortune.

He clutched it hard between his fingers, and seemed afraid to look at it.

Could it be a fact that he was the actual possessor of a five-pound note? He, who considered himself blessed indeed if Garvel doled him out an occasional few shillings?

"Don't go out of here with that five-pound note," said Garvel.

"Eh—why?"

"You are certain to be arrested for stealing. I will give you four pounds ten in hard cash for it."

"Hush, hush!" said Deveril, impatiently. "Drive your bargains, Mr. Garvel, when your clients are absent. The man has well earned the five pounds —seek not to deprive him of any portion of it. I wish to have a little private conversation with my friend here. Can you show us into a room?"

"To be sure. This way, gentlemen."

Garvel conducted them to a room on the same landing.

There, for over half-an-hour, they remained.

When they returned, Leakey had gone.

"We are going now to our hotel," said Cosmo. "It is probable we shall return to-morrow night, though by no means certain. Meantime, do not lose sight of this man of yours. As to the sum to which you are entitled, we will speak of and settle it to-morrow."

After a little more conversation, Garvel ceremoniously bowed them out.

"It is certain that Cosmo, otherwise Captain Rosso, otherwise the Lord knows what, has plenty of money on this occasion," he muttered, as he closed and bolted the door. "That is a good thing for me, for it will be less bother.

"But I wonder where he got it. Ha! no doubt he has been carrying on a nice game since he quitted England. And this friend of his—Deveril—De—the devil!" he suddenly muttered. "Surely this cannot be the same Deveril on whose head a price is set for piracy? But why not? It may be. Oh, oh! So, so? Eyes open, and mouth shut!"

CHAPTER XXXVIII.

WHAT HAPPENED AT THE RUSSEL HOTEL.

THE Russel Hotel was, at the time of our story, excellent property, highly remunerative, and well known as a place of departure for various coaches.

The ground on which it stood—now occupied by private houses—was extensive, but the building itself was one of the most awkward and ugliest in London.

People said, and with much truth, that the prettiest part about it was the stables, which had been designed by a military inventor, Captain Langley Taylor.

It was just after the hour of twelve that a fly, containing two gentlemen, drove up to the front entrance.

The sleepy porter conveyed the luggage, which consisted of one large portmanteau, into the hall, and the gentlemen followed him.

The manager appeared—and very affable he was—and arrangements were soon made for the pair to occupy two rooms on the first floor.

He asked them if they would kindly inscribe their names in the visitors' book.

Would they! They would indeed.

Very anxious were they to get a look at the book, and no wonder; for they were respectively Cosmo and Captain Deveril, and both were remarkably well disguised.

Cosmo went to the book first.

There, the last but one, was the name —"Conrad Ireton, of Banstead. Room ten."

But this was not what caused Cosmo to start, and almost utter a cry of astonishment.

Certainly not.

It was the last name, or, rather, names, as follows—

"Mr. and Mrs. King, of Clapham, and infant. Room fourteen."

Mr. and Mrs. King, of Clapham!

Surely they must be the pair on whom he had sworn to have his revenge!

Cosmo, with a little difficulty, for his hand trembled somewhat, signed his "name" as follows—

"Mr. Robert Ellborough, of New York."

Deveril, after one glance at the book, placed his name as follows—

"Mr. Thomas Houghton, of New York."

Then they were conducted to their rooms, refreshments were placed before them, and they were made otherwise comfortable for the night.

"We will have a bottle or two of the best wine you have," said Deveril to the manager; "and perhaps you will share it with us?"

"With pleasure, gentlemen," was the manager's reply.

He did not require it, but he knew it would not do to offend a couple of gentlemen who might be good customers.

So he joined them, and for some time the conversation turned upon London, its various sights, and so forth.

Then, by degrees, Deveril got the conversation round to hotels.

Upon these the manager naturally waxed warm.

"I have managed this house," he said, "for over fifteen years, and must say that business during the past twelve months has been fearful. We have had scarcely anyone staying here.

"Why, within the last three or four hours, we have had more visitors than for a week past."

"All ladies, no doubt?"

"Ladies? No, sir. We have but one lady staying here—and a very beautiful lady she is, truly—a Mrs. King, of Clapham. She arrived here with her husband, baby, and servant. The husband left as soon as he had seen them safe."

"Safe, eh?" said Cosmo, forcing a laugh.

"Yes, he has business to transact, he

informed me, at Epping, and would return in the morning."

"But now, gentlemen, I must leave you. If you have any further orders you have simply to ring that bell."

So the manager retired.

As soon as he had closed the door, Cosmo rose and locked it.

Then triumphantly he turned to Deveril, who had taken a pair of small, delicately-engraved pistols from a case, and was about to look at them. His disguise did not conceal the devilish smile on his face.

"By all that is wonderful," said Cosmo, "we are in luck's way, for we can have our revenge at the same time."

"What do you mean?"

"Mean? Did you not hear what the manager said—Mrs. King, of Clapham?"

"Ha! Upon my soul I did not notice it."

"That was because you were thinking of Conrad Ireton."

"Can it be the same Mrs. King?"

"Undoubtedly."

"Then you are in luck's way as well as me. Now what do you propose? So far as Mrs. King is concerned, you can have it all your own way, since her husband is absent."

"I do not wish to kill *her*."

"*I* should—and **the infant as well**," said Deveril, calmly. "I should enter her room in the dead of the night, slay her and the child, and place upon the latter's body—

"Revenge at last!—CAPTAIN ROSSO.

"What do you think of that?"

"Nay," replied Cosmo, "I will not do that. I will steal the child."

"As you will; and, after all, it would perhaps have more effect on King, because of the uncertainty of its fate."

"Exactly. If—but hark! what is that?"

"A child crying," said Deveril. "Depend upon it, it is the infant in question."

Cosmo opened the door so as to hear more distinctly.

Just as Deveril looked over his shoulder, "Room ten" opened, and a young gentleman, elegantly attired, stepped out, crossed the landing and descended the stairs.

"'Tis he!" said Deveril—"Conrad Ireton."

"True," said Cosmo. "As you know, I saw him but once; but his is a face which, once seen, is not easily forgotten. Come—let us consider how to proceed. Remember, we have no time to waste."

"It will not take us long to consider how to proceed," said Deveril.

"First, I should advise you to pocket the pistols," said Cosmo, "and keep your dagger handy. There is nothing like the dagger for silent and sure work. But what are you doing now?"

"Getting ready undoubted evidence of the hand who struck the blow," replied Deveril, who was tracing some large letters upon a sheet of paper.

He soon completed this task, and the words read as follows—

"To Captain Ireton, otherwise the Earl of Bellchambers, Lieutenant Daulton, Lucinda, and all others whom it may concern.

"I swore that I would slay Conrad Ireton, and I have done so. Now find me who can. "WALTER DEVERIL."

"When I have struck the blow," said Deveril, "I will attach this to his body,"

"Ay, ay—good. Now what I propose is this—we will first of all deal with Mrs. King. Having forced an entrance—"

"No, no. We must use no force in gaining an entrance. Remember, there is a porter on duty all night."

"Well, having gained an entrance, we will immediately silence Mrs. King by forcing a pillow over her mouth; then we will gag her."

"As to the child—well, we can stifle its cries in a blanket. Certainly the porter will not be alarmed by the crying of a child."

"Then you will assist me, if necessary, with Conrad?"

"Exactly."

For a long time the two scoundrels sat perfecting their plans.

Then they sat drinking until the clock below chimed the hour of two.

It was not until then that the pair considered it safe to stir.

They then left the room, and glided on to the landing.

Cosmo, after listening, crept silently half-way down the stairs.

Looking over the banisters, he saw the hall-porter buried in the enormous hooded chair.

He was apparently asleep.

"All is well," he said, on his return. " Now let us get what we want."

Re-entering the room, Deveril opened the portmanteau, and took from it a screwdriver, several pieces of iron bent to this shape ⌐, some screws, and a gimlet.

Returning to the landing, they proceeded to deliberately fasten the doors of each room, except their own and numbers "ten " and "fourteen."

This was accomplished so rapidly, and yet so noiselessly, as to be absolutely remarkable.

They then proceeded to number fourteen.

Cosmo cautiously turned the handle.

The door was open.

The reason was simple.

Tired out with long travelling, Mrs. King had retired early, and had quite forgotten to turn the key.

A small night-light burned upon the mantel-piece, and, by aid of its dim rays, the pair of rascals were enabled to see the nestling figures of mother and child.

Their entrance having been so cat-like, mother and child were not at all disturbed.

For the space of a few moments Cosmo fixed his savage eyes upon them.

Then, giving a thick neckerchief to Deveril, he crept to the bedside, gently removed one of the pillows, and then clapped it over Mrs. King's mouth.

Of course, she was instantly awakened.

Cosmo was very much mistaken in her.

He had been under the impression that terror would render her powerless to struggle.

But the beautiful lady thought of the safety of her child, not of herself.

She struggled frantically, trying hard to tear the pillow from her face.

But for a long time her efforts were unsuccessful.

Deveril tried to fasten the neckerchief round her, but that was a failure, because Cosmo was afraid to shift the pillow.

With the strength that comes of despair, the brave lady continued the struggle, and at last, she contrived to partially rise and so far force the pillow aside as to shriek for help.

A series of piercing cries left her lips.

Deveril started forward, and dealt her such a heavy blow that she dropped ba on the pillows unconscious.

Cosmo had just seized the child and torn a blanket from the bed, when the hurried tramp of naked feet were heard.

Deveril turned to find himself face to face with our hero.

Despite his disguise, Conrad instantaneously recognised him.

What his feelings were as he looked upon him may be imagined.

So powerfully affected was he that the pistol he held in his hand dropped at his side.

But, in a few short seconds he recovered himself.

"Deveril !" he cried.

"Deveril it is !" was the savage reply.

And as he spoke Deveril raised his dagger and dashed upon Conrad.

Our hero was unable to use his pistol, though he tried hard to.

But he had caught Deveril's descending hand, and he then closed with him.

With a mighty crash both rolled to the floor.

Conrad uttered no word, but Deveril gave utterance to the foulest of oaths and curses.

At last Conrad succeeded in getting over Deveril.

He held him tightly by the throat, while he kept his left foot upon Deveril's arm in such a way that the wretch could not use his dagger.

"Atrocious ruffian !" thundered Conrad. "This time there will be no mistake."

He placed his pistol close to Deveril's face, but ere he could fire, he received such a fearful blow at the side of the head that he was knocked senseless to the ground.

Deveril would undoubtedly have used his weapon only for the fact that three or four servants came racing down the stairs.

"Run," said Cosmo, "run if you would save yourself !"

Down the stairs ran Deveril, but half-way down he was confronted by the hall porter.

Raising his foot, he gave the man such a kick that he rolled down the stairs.

Another moment, and Deveril and Cosmo were outside the hotel, the latter bearing in his arms the muffled figure of the poor child.

"'BY HEAVEN! I WILL STAND THIS NO LONGER!' CRIED CONRAD."

With all their might they ran on for more than a mile, now darting down this turning, now down that.

At last they chanced upon a man driving a trap.

They stopped him and offered him a couple of pounds if he would drive them to Hammersmith.

The man, naturally scared, hesitated, but, a pound being offered him in advance, he consented, and the precious pair entered the vehicle.

They had no opportunity of speaking about what had occurred.

They considered it advisable to say nothing which could be overheard.

Cosmo was the only one who spoke at all during that journey, and what he said consisted of but eight words.

They were—

"Again I have saved you from certain death!"

Deveril's only reply was a moody nod.

* * * *

Meanwhile the scene at the hotel baffles all description.

The cries of the servants, the noise of those imprisoned in the rooms was terrific.

But the appearance of the manager had the effect of calming them somewhat.

It happened, very fortunately, that he was a calm, methodical man of business, and he proceeded first of all to send for a doctor.

The female servants were then told off to attend upon Mrs. King.

Strong restoratives were rapidly procured, and administered with success, for the unfortunate lady speedily recovered her senses.

Her first inquiry was for her child. And then, for the first time, its disappearance was noticed.

Spellbound the servants stood.

But they were quickly startled into activity by Mrs. King's heart-rending shrieks.

"My child, my child!" she cried, as she leapt from the bed and began, in the most frantic manner, to search the room. "My poor child! Oh, my God! where is my child?"

Search was in vain.

She quickly realised that the child had been stolen, and, throwing herself upon her knees by the bedside, she burst into a passionate flood of tears.

This, so far, was well, for had the shock had an opposite effect, it might have culminated in a violent attack of brain fever.

Tears relieved her overcharged heart, and, by the manager's advice, the servants left her alone for a few minutes.

The doctor, who lived close by, quickly made his appearance.

Conrad, by this time, had recovered consciousness it is true, but he was in a very dazed condition.

Blood was trickling from his head, and the doctor, after a brief examination, declared that he had been struck by some heavy instrument—either a bludgeon, a poker, or perhaps the butt of a pistol.

The only restorative administered to him was brandy.

Then the doctor, having attended to his wound, proceeded to Mrs. King.

The principal thing she suffered from was shock.

But the brutal, cowardly Deveril had left a mark upon her which was not likely to be effaced for some considerable time.

The left side of the poor lady's face was much bruised.

Poor thing! Her appearance almost unnerved the doctor.

"My good lady," he said, " I entreat of you endeavour to be calm. I am informed that your child has been stolen by a couple of villains, and that, I am well aware, is sufficient to throw you into the state I find you; but it is only by proceeding calmly, that any good is likely to be done.

"Tell me—did you recognise any of the men?"

"No—no," sobbed Mrs. King.

"But I did," said a voice.

It was Conrad.

He had entered the room beside the manager.

"One moment," said the doctor, as he placed a heavy wrap around Mrs. King," and we will go right into the matter. I am well aware that this is no part of my business, but still I may be of some service."

"You say, sir, that you recognised the men?"

"One of them."

"May I ask whether you are any connection of this lady?"

"Not at all. I was in bed in my room, No. 10, when I heard loud cries for help. I at once seized a pistol—for I am a sailor, and, for certain reasons, always travel armed—and ran in here.

"Then I recognised one of the men as Captain Deveril, once a desperate pirate.

"There was a struggle, and just when I thought myself victorious, I received a fearful blow from the other man."

"Whom you did not recognise?"

"I did not."

"Have you ever heard the name of Captain Deveril before?" asked the doctor of Mrs. King.

"Never, that I am aware of."

"Gentlemen," said the manager, "the two men have left a portmanteau in the room they occupied. I propose that we search it."

This was agreed to, and Conrad, the doctor, and the manager, repaired to the room.

They found the portmanteau locked.

But our hero quickly smashed the lock.

A cry of astonishment followed the opening of the trunk.

What was in it?

Magnificent clothes and weapons of various sorts?

Nothing of the sort.

All that the trunk contained was a dozen pieces of *paving stone!*

It was thus evident that it was the intention of the two ruffians from the first to leave the trunk behind them.

On a closer inspection Conrad saw that the trunk had been newly lined.

On the bottom was the name—

"G. D. Howell, Maker."

Conrad took out his knife and cut away the new lining, thinking it possible that it might conceal the *address* of the maker.

He was correct.

There, in almost obliterated characters, was the name and address—

"G. D. Howell,
"Maker,
"Broadway,
"Hammersmith.
["No. 1284."]

Again Conrad used his knife.

This time he cut the name and address

clean out, and transferred them to his pocket. Then he said, addressing the manager—

"Sir, I ask you as a favour to let what has transpired at this house remain a secret. Let the whole of this matter remain in my hands, and I assure you that I will restore that child to its mother's arms.

"The man who stole it is undoubtedly the companion of the man I recognised, and if—"

He was interrupted by a knock upon the door.

One of the female servants entered, and handed the manager a locket.

"It was picked up just where the hall-porter was found," she said.

"Have you opened it?"

"No, sir. We tried, but failed."

The manager attempted to open it, but failing, he handed it to Conrad.

Our hero tried it all ways, and then, not being able to find the spring, he forced it with his knife.

The portrait of a man in the costume of a Spaniard was revealed.

"This," he said, "was evidently dropped by one of them. See, it appears as if it had been broken from a chain. Wait but one moment. Mrs. King may be able to recognise the portrait."

He crossed to No. 14, where Mrs. King, surrounded by sympathetic servants, was still weeping.

"Madam," said Conrad, "this locket has been found below. Will you kindly look at it and see if you can recognise the portrait?"

Mechanically Mrs. King took it.

The instant her eyes rested upon the picture she started up.

"Oh, my God!" she cried. "I now see it all! Captain Rosso!"

As she said this the locket dropped from her hand, and she fell insensible in the servants' arms.

The doctor being summoned, Conrad rejoined the manager.

"She recognises the portrait," he said, "and soon, no doubt, we shall have particulars. But let me again ask you to keep this matter a secret. I assure you that you can place every confidence in me. If you will refer to these papers you will see that I am grandson to the Earl of Bellchambers."

This announcement, as may be supposed, had a great effect upon the manager.

"I am perfectly satisfied, sir," he said as, after reading them he returned the papers, "you can command me. I will do everything to meet your views."

"I understand that the lady's husband is at Epping?"

"He is, sir."

"Let us endeavour to get his address. Then I will procure a horse and set out to him."

"But, sir, the hour, and the injury to your head!"

"Both are of no importance, I assure you. In the first place, I am used to travelling in the dead of the night. In the second, I am more used to wounds than travelling. Now, let us see how the lady progresses."

Soon after this, our hero obtained the address of Mr. King, and received the warm thanks of his wife.

Leaving the hotel, he made his way to a livery stable, knocked up the proprietor, and, on consideration of double pay, at once got a good horse.

Then he started for Epping.

CHAPTER XXXVIII.

"DICKEY" DEAN OF THE "LODGE," HAMMERSMITH.

SOME years previous to the opening of our story, one of the largest owners of house property at Hammersmith was Frederick Dean, than whom a more honest and straightforward man never breathed the breath of life.

The house he himself occupied was an enormous one, and contained some of the handsomest furniture and works of art in London.

The front faced a pretty bit of common, while the garden at the back ran to the river's edge.

He died worth an enormous sum, which he left to his son Richard, as well as all his houses.

Richard, up to this time, had been kept short of cash, for his father but too well knew his disposition.

Yes, Mr. Dean kept him short, but Richard found plenty of accommodating Jews to advance him money at the rate of sixty and a hundred per cent., and he went in for it right and left.

Like the majority of empty-headed fools, he went in for gambling, betting, and so on, at all of which he lost.

More, he allowed the vultures of society to prey upon him to any extent.

The result of all this downright madness was that, when he inherited his father's property, the Jews and such " fry," closed in upon him and demanded a settlement.

When all he had borrowed was paid, he found himself in possession of his father's own house, the "Lodge," and a few hundred pounds. This was all.

He was like a poor little sparrow, after heartless boys had stripped him of his feathers.

At first he decided to sell the house and go abroad.

But there was one who put quite a new idea into his head.

That one was a man who had often fleeced him.

Our readers know him.

It was Captain Rosso, otherwise Cosmo —otherwise—well, only he himself knew.

Cosmo proposed this—that, as he had been so often fleeced by others, he should now set himself to fleece anyone who could be got to his house.

More, Cosmo suggested that the splendid building should be used as a sort of gambling club.

Richard, or "Dickey" Dean, as his lovely companions called him—at once snapped at the idea, and from that day the "Lodge" was nothing better than a gambling hell.

Everything was done on a most magnificent scale.

The brilliancy of the place attracted those with plenty of money and no brains, just as a light attracts moths.

They came, saw, but certainly did not conquer.

Oh, dear no; not by any manner of means—Dickey was surrounded by too many skilled hawks for that.

Not only men, but women of fashion and position were attracted to the place, and often thousands changed hands in a single night.

What of the police? Well, what could they do?

This was a private house, and when questioned, Dickey emphatically stated that his numerous visitors were his own "personal friends."

The authorities could only look on, and regret that there was no law to touch the place.

It was to this house that Cosmo and Captain Deveril came.

But they were not driven right up to the house. The trap was stopped several hundred yards away.

Again and again the poor child cried piteously, but neither of the two ruffians took any notice of it.

They found the "Lodge" in darkness; but after several knocks, the door was opened by an elderly, but strong-looking woman.

Cosmo quickly made himself known to her; and, as the woman knew he was an especial "friend" of her master's, she admitted both.

"Call your master," said Cosmo; "and then I can give you a task—that is, if you will undertake it."

"What is it?"

"Look," said Cosmo, unfolding the blanket.

The child's pretty head was revealed.

"Do you want me to mind that?" asked the woman.

"Ay, and you shall be well paid."

"Very well. But whose is it? Is it yours?"

"Do you think it bears any likeness to me?"

"As much likeness as the wolf bears to the lamb," was the cool reply.

At any other time the woman might have regretted this remark; but, on this occasion, Cosmo deemed it advisable to say nothing.

The woman went and roused her master, and then took possession of the child, which she conveyed below.

"Dickey" Dean soon made his appearance.

A pretty object he looked too!

He had been roused from a drunken sleep, and his brain was consequently much muddled.

But he soon recognised Cosmo, and welcomed him with great warmth; after which he expressed much pleasure at meeting with Captain Deveril.

"I thought I should soon see you," he said to Cosmo; "but did you get the portmanteau all right?"

"Yes—all safe."

"It was so ragged that I had to have a new lining placed in it. Now make yourselves at home," he added, as he pushed two luxurious chairs to the table; "I will get you wines or brandy, or whatever you may desire."

"Brandy and cigars," said Cosmo—"that is all we require at present. Then we can—but what, in the fiend's name, is all this?"

And he pointed to the floor, and to the mirror-lined walls.

On the floor broken bottles, decanters, and plates lay in every direction; while three or four of the handsome mirrors were smashed to atoms.

Dickey smiled.

"Well, you see," he said, "we cannot always get well-behaved people here. All that terrific smash was done by a lady. Only fancy it! by a lady."

"I don't understand."

"Oh, it's very easy. A lady was introduced here to-night, and, for some time, played quietly. But suddenly she started up, declaring that she had been cheated.

"The people here tried to calm her, but it was no use. She demanded her money back. They laughed at her, and, by the Lord Harry! many of them had reason to regret it.

"The lady turned out to be a very demon. She seized the bottles, the decanters— everything she could lay her hands upon—and flung them about her in all directions, scattering those in the room like chaff, and inflicting some ugly wounds.

"God bless you, I never saw such a thing in all my life before. I might have been killed, but I darted beneath the table. He! he!

"The smashing, however, was not all," he added, in changed tones. "No, not by any means all. On one of the tables was a pocket-book, belonging to one of my friends—a very clever man at the tables!

"It contained bank notes for over four

thousand pounds. This was missed. Well, everyone present offered to be searched, and the search took place. But the book was not found.

"Half-an-hour after the lady had left, a note was brought here. Here it is. Listen to what it says —

"'To Richard Dean and his hellish crew.

"'Twice has my son been fleeced at your accursed house. On each occasion he has lost over one thousand pounds. I am thankful to say that I can now recoup his losses, for, in my possession, is a pocket-book containing over four thousand pounds.

"'Adieu. I AM SATISFIED.'"

"By thunder!" said Deveril, "she was a clever woman, eh?"

"Ay, far *too* clever," said Dean. "She had us to rights. Well, I am not a loser—except as to the smashes. And now for the brandy and cigars. I suppose it is your intention to stay with me for a short time, Cosmo?"

"A few days, perhaps."

"Good. It may be to our mutual advantage."

*   *   *   *

It was about eight o'clock on the following evening that two horsemen rode up to the "Bell" at Hammersmith.

They were our hero and Mr. King, a fine, stalwart, handsome man, whose bearing was so erect and graceful that he might have passed for a trained soldier.

Both were attired as gentlemen farmers or sporstmen.

Having partaken of refreshments and left their horses, they left the inn and made their way to the Broadway.

Very little difficulty had they in finding the maker of the portmanteau.

It was a small, dingy little shop, and the proprietor himself was within it.

"Are you Mr. Howell?" asked Conrad.

"I am, sir," was the respectful reply, "and at your service."

"Can we have a few words with you privately?"

Mr. Howell was astonished.

"Well, gentlemen," he said, "really the request is most unusual. But I have no objection. I have no creditors, as I know you do not require money. This way, please."

And he led them into his parlour.

"The question we are about to ask you," said Conrad, "may sound as if we are detectives. Such, however, we can assure you, is not the case. Now, sir, will you look at that?"

And he handed Mr. Howell the piece of leather he had cut from the bag.

Mr. Howell immediately recognised it.

"This," he said, "has been taken from a portmanteau made by me. I put the name on myself."

"Can you tell who purchased it?"

Mr. Howell smiled.

"I really can't say," he said. "I sell a large number of portmanteaus— in fact, I sell more of them than anything else. The only question is, was it taken away when purchased, or did my boy deliver it. Well, we will soon find that out."

He reached down a thick and heavy book labelled "Portmanteaus," and carefully ran his finger down several pages.

At last he stopped.

"Here we have it!" he said. "Portmanteau, No. 1284; bought—no, mended—yes, repairs eight shillings—and it is four days ago. Er—let me see. Sent to Mr. Dean, the 'Lodge.'"

Mr. Howell closed the book.

"Well, upon my word," he said, "I am a fool. I ought to have remembered it without consulting the book. Yes, my boy took it to the 'Lodge,' sure enough."

"Your son?"

"Yes; I remember his mother had a strong objection to his going. Of course, you know the 'Lodge,' gentlemen?"

"We do not."

Mr. Howell was surprised.

"It is a gambling hell," he said.

This was information with a vengeance. Conrad and Mr. King, however, were careful not to express surprise.

"Yes," continued Mr. Howell, "I don't know what will be the end of it all, I'm sure; but I fancy that one of these fine nights some awful tragedy will happen, and then the house would be closed.

"Lord! how I would like to see it. I wish Mr. Dean—or 'Dickey' Dean, as his beautiful companions call him— would not send his work here. I don't care for it, I assure you; and yet I can't very well refuse, can I?"

"Not likely. So this 'Dickey' Dean, as he is called, has plenty of companions?"

"Yes, *he* calls them companions, I am told, but everybody else calls them blacklegs, and sometimes names much worse. Well, they deserve it."

"Look you, Mr. Howell," said Conrad, "the little information you have given us is of the highest importance."

"Well, gentlemen, I feel sure that you seek it for a lawful purpose."

"We do indeed, my friend. But, as we do not expect a man to waste his time for nothing, perhaps you would accept this five-pound note."

Mr. Howell would have refused, but, being urged by Mr. King, he consented to take it.

"You have children of your own?" said Conrad.

"Ten of 'em, sir," smiled Mr. Howell.

"Then you can feel for a man who has had his only child—a mere infant—stolen from him."

"Ay, sir—indeed I can."

"My friend here, then, has had his child stolen from him; and we expect that the two villains who seized it, took it to the owner of the portmanteau."

These few words had affected Mr. King very much, and his emotion was at once communicated to honest Mr. Howell.

"I now see the reason of your inquiries," said the latter. "Do you think it possible that I could assist you in any way?"

"I do," said Conrad. "You say that your son has been to the house?"

"Many times."

"Could you send him on some errand? He may get a glimpse of a few of the guests, and his description of them may be the means of determining whether either of the two men we seek are there."

"He shall go at once, gentlemen. He is a pretty sharp boy. He can go to Mother Crowe—that's the housekeeper—and ask her whether Mr. Dean ordered a bag."

Thereupon he shouted for his son, and a lad of fifteen quickly made his appearance.

"Yes, he *was* sharp—very sharp.

Not noticing that anyone was present beside his father, he cried, in loud, exultant tones—

"I've got sixpence, father. Play you double or quits."

"Be quiet, you little fool," was Mr. Howell's reply. "Can't you see that customers are present? Do you want to make me out a gambler?"

The boy was silent at once.

What he had to do was explained to him.

He was to say that someone had ordered a bag in the name of Dean. Was it for Mr. Dean of the "Lodge" or not?

While the housekeeper was asking this question of her master, the lad was to "look around."

In half-an-hour he returned.

"Well," queried his father, "whom did you see?"

"Only the housekeeper."

"No gentlemen?"

"Not one."

Conrad heaved a sigh of disappointment.

But it quickly changed to a cry of joy.

"That old Mother Crowe is a crabby old wretch," said the boy; "and beastly mean, as well as brutal."

"Brutal? What did she do to you?"

"Nothing to me. But while I was talking to her a baby cried; she went to where it was, and I heard her scolding the poor little thing as hard as she could."

"The child!" cried Conrad. "It is yours, safe enough, Mr. King."

"Yes, yes; thank God it is yet alive!"

"Go on, Tim," said Mr. Howell, who was so pleased that he was rubbing his hands together with might and main. "Go on—what else?"

"She gave me a letter to take to Mrs. Brewer—that's the nurse in Broad Court—and only gave me twopence."

"Here, my boy," said Conrad, "is half-a-sovereign for you."

"Oh, thank you, sir, and good luck. Can I do anything else?"

"It is possible that you can, if your father will permit you."

"Certainly," said Mr. Howell; "but it is likely, gentlemen, that you want to speak privately over the affair, and arrange your plans. I will close the shop and you can have this parlour, and if I or my boy can do anything to aid you, command us."

CHAPTER XXXIX.

A CHECK—THE ATTACK ON THE "LODGE," AND THE RESULT.

CONRAD and Mr. King speedily arranged their plans.

As our readers are aware, Conrad had had great experience at disguises, and he proposed that they should disguise themselves and proceed boldly to the "Lodge."

Mr. King, of course, would have accepted any plan if there was the least chance of recovering his child.

Mr. Howell was consulted as to a costumier.

He recommended one in the Broadway, and his boy was sent for him.

He informed them that he had many scores of disguises, and recommended them to accompany him to his house.

This they did, and just after the clock struck eleven, they left, excellently well disguised as Americans.

There was nothing elaborate or extravagant about these disguises, and yet the costumier was decidedly to be congratulated.

Reaching the "Lodge"—and both were considerably surprised at its imposing appearance—they stood away some distance and watched.

In less than half-an-hour no less than a dozen persons—male and female—arrived in various conveyances, and were admitted.

It appeared to them that they had only to present themselves to be admitted.

They were mistaken.

In a few more moments they went over to the house and knocked at the door.

It was immediately answered by a tall, and evidently powerful man.

No doubt he was here on constant duty during the evening and the early hours of the morning.

But he did not stand aside when he had opened the door.

No, he stood on the threshold as if waiting for something.

Then he asked—

"Well, gentlemen, who do you wish to see?"

"Our old friend, Dickey Dean."

"Have you an invitation?"

"Nay, we have but just arrived from America and—"

The man interrupted with a wave of his hand.

"If you want to see Mr. Dean," he said, "you must show me his card of invitation."

"Well, we have no such thing. But do you go and say that two of his old friends wish to see him. We will wait here," said Conrad.

The man shook his head.

"It is more than I dare do," he said, at the same time glancing suspiciously at them.

"What are we to do then?"

"Write him a letter; and to-morrow, no doubt, he will send you invitation cards."

There was no help for it.

They had undoubtedly received a check.

Conrad saw that it would be useless to offer the man a bribe.

As for Mr. King, he felt inclined to knock the man down.

"Come," said Conrad, "the man is right. We must send a letter."

Both turned away, and the man softly closed the door, only to open it the next minute to give admittance to a young lady and gentleman, who drove up in a spanking dogcart, behind which sat two small "tigers" in an elaborate livery.

"What is to be done now, my good friend?" asked Mr. King. "I cannot—will not return to my wife without the child."

"We must now put into practice a plan I have formed, but which I have not mentioned."

Meeting a man he inquired the way to the nearest police-office, and was directed to King Street.

A dingy, smoke-begrimed place they found it.

They inquired for the chief detective, and were informed that his name was Mr. Hunt, and that he would be found in a room on the first floor.

Thither they proceeded.

Through an open door they saw the man they sought studying a small picture.

He was as much unlike a detective as it is possible to imagine.

He did not stand more than five feet high, and, moreover he was very thin.

His age must have been about sixty.

Conrad requested an interview, which was readily accorded.

After some preliminary conversation our hero briefly sketched the details, to which Mr. Hunt listened with increasing attention.

Our hero concluded by stating who he really was, what he had been, and who his friend was.

"Grandson to the Earl of Bell-chambers," thought Mr. Hunt, "well, this may be very much to my advantage."

Aloud he said—

"Gentlemen, I assure you you could not have come to a better man than me. I have long had my eye on the 'Lodge,' of which I may say I know almost every brick—or rather, I should say I *did* know it.

"But I am informed that this precious Dickey Dean has greatly altered the interior. You see, the police have threatened him, and being fearful that they might at an unexpected moment make a run on the place, he has had secret doors fitted up.

"But you see there is this difficulty, I could not search the place without a magistrate's warrant, and that could not be obtained for many hours. In the meantime, the birds might have flown."

"But now that you know the house shelters the renowned pirate, Captain Deveril; now that you know that a poor child—"

"My dear sir," interrupted Mr. Hunt, "I assure you that a warrant would be necessary. But listen to my advice," and he gleefully rubbed his hands; "the back of the house," he said, "can be approached from the river. Now, about two o'clock in the morning, the visitors will have departed. With your great experience you ought to have no difficulty in forcing an entrance.

"It so happens that I have here a dozen men, and these I could use to surround the house. Thus there would be little chance for anyone within the building to escape."

"Good! The idea is an excellent one," said Conrad. "It must be carried into effect. Are you aware, Mr. Hunt, that a heavy reward is offered for the capture of Captain Deveril?"

"Quite aware of it, but if we captured him we should get nothing—being police."

"Well, you would get something from me, I assure you, and something worth having."

"Thank you, but we will talk of that by-and-by. Let us see first that the bird is securely placed in his cage. I should much like to assist at the capture of this Captain Deveril. Long ago, when at his devilish work on the sea, his description was extensively circulated. I, among others, made inquiries when it was rumoured that he was on the way to England.

"But nothing came of it. All I discovered was that, whenever he came secretly to this country, he disguised himself, and made his way to a certain inn at Greenwich. If—but here—I remember that I have a note-book containing the name of the place at which he called, and a lot of other particulars."

So saying, he opened his desk, and, after a search, brought out a well-worn pocket-book.

He handed it to Conrad, who, having glanced through it, said—

"Can you lend this to me?"

"Certainly—but I must request you to take great care of it. You see, something may happen by which I may be called upon by the authorities to produce the book."

"Rely upon it, I will take the greatest care of it."

Conrad, Mr. King, and the detective now went right into the plans for the attack on the house, and then the two former rose to go.

"We shall be in the grounds at the back, then," said Mr. Hunt. "There are so many shrubs there, that we shall have no difficulty in hiding. The signal is a whistle repeated twice. And now, gentlemen, one last word of advice—do not forget your arms."

*   *   *   *

It was close upon the hour of two

that a boat containing two persons pushed off from the opposite side of the river, and made towards the back of the "Lodge."

The two persons were, of course, Conrad and Mr. King.

They were not disguised now—that was deemed unnecessary.

Slowly and silently Conrad pulled the boat to the shore, and secured it to a stake.

Then they landed and looked about them.

Not a soul was to be seen—grounds and house were in almost total darkness.

Conrad took a whistle from his pocket and blew it softly.

It was almost immediately answered, and when repeated, the signal was again returned.

"All is well so far," said Conrad. "And now, Mr. King, since you are not so used to this sort of business as I am, follow me."

"It appears to me," said Mr. King, "that the occupants have retired."

"Ay, I don't think there is any doubt about it. If we can only manage to force an entry without attracting attention, our errand may prove entirely successful. Look—to the right. Quick!"

Mr. King looked, and saw a number of figures creep from out of the shadow of the shrubs, and go forward.

They were Mr. Hunt's men.

On now went Conrad, followed closely by Mr. King.

Speedily they reached the back of the house. Every window they found closely shuttered on the inside.

Conrad selected one of the lower windows as the best to commence operations upon.

Then from his pocket he took a diamond.

With this he succeeded in cutting a hole in the glass large enough for him to insert his hand.

It is true that in falling—which it did on the inside—the glass made a noise, but it was too faint to be heard above stairs.

Next, our hero produced a large gimlet and a narrow, fine saw.

With the former he made four holes in the shutter of the following shape—

o   o

o   o

Then he commenced with the saw, and in but a few seconds he had cut a square hole, which permitted him to insert his hand and arm.

There was no further difficulty.

The bar was quite an ordinary affair, and Conrad at once detached it, and pushed the shutters open.

The whole of the operation had taken but very little time, and but little noise had been made.

Had everyone in the house been asleep, they could not have been awakened by the raising of the window, and the opening of the shutters, but it so happened that they were not.

"Dickey" Dean had long since retired, though he found it impossible to sleep, for a few hours before he had lost an enormous sum at the table.

It was, he had said, an "accident" that had not occurred to him for a long time.

The reader will not be very much surprised to know that the successful "operator" had been Cosmo.

Dickey's apartment, since Captain Deveril and Cosmo had been at the "Lodge," was on the ground floor.

His two precious guests were accommodated on the first floor.

Neither Deveril nor Cosmo had made any attempt to retire.

Nay; they sat at the table, card-playing and drinking, and forming plans which certainly were not calculated to *benefit* our hero.

Their windows being shuttered and closely curtained, the light could not be seen from the outside.

Wide awake Dickey lay, thinking how, by the name of all that was marvellous, Cosmo could have won so much from him, when a slight noise fell upon his ears.

He listened, and the noise being repeated, he glided gently from the bed, unlocked and opened his door.

Then, of course, he heard the noise more distinctly.

What on earth could it be, he asked himself.

He crept along the passage, and at the end, again listened.

Yes; he considered there could be no doubt about it. A saw was at work somewhere.

He decided, before he proceeded farther, to arm himself.

So he returned to his room.

On his way he knocked over a candlestick, which had been placed on the floor against the wall.

That noise was heard by Deveril and Cosmo.

Both started to their feet.

"Pshaw!" said Deveril, "we are fools. 'Twas only a cat."

"I am not so sure about that," said Cosmo; "we cannot be too careful. Let us descend, and see that all is safe. If we—hush! By thunder! I hear someone moving."

"Perhaps it is the housekeeper. Children are troublesome in the night."

"Well, we will make sure at any rate."

Each secured a pistol and descended the stairs.

Just as they reached Dickey's room, a dark figure bounded out.

Instantly Cosmo fired.

A wild cry of agony followed the shot, and a loud thud denoted that a man had fallen to the floor.

Conrad and Mr. King by this time were in the room.

Hearing the shot, they rushed to the spot.

Again a shot rang out.

This time it was fired by Deveril.

The bright flash lit up our hero's features, and Deveril instantaneously recognised them.

At first he was so staggered that he could scarcely move.

Then with a fearful imprecation, he tore open his vest, and snatched forth a long dagger—a weapon without which he never travelled.

Another instant, and Conrad was upon him.

Our hero held his pistol ready, but he was afraid to pull the trigger, because Mr. King, who had Cosmo by the throat, was in the line of fire.

So he took hold of the barrel, and with the butt end, dealt Deveril a heavy blow on the head.

Then, seizing his hand, he beat it with the butt of the pistol until the dagger dropped to the floor.

It seemed as if Conrad had suddenly become possessed of double his usual strength, and that it was at last all over with the murderous pirate.

But no, he contrived to break away,

and fly up the stairs with marvellous speed.

Conrad was about to follow, when there was a rush of rapid feet, and he was seized from behind, while a brilliant light was thrown upon the scene.

He saw that this was carried by a woman.

It was the housekeeper.

In a few seconds he contrived to turn himself round.

Then he saw that the man who had thus seized him was the man who acted as doorkeeper, the same that had refused him and Mr. King admission.

A tremendous struggle ensued, and the man, finding that he was certain to be overpowered, yelled to the housekeeper to brain our hero with the lamp.

The woman, however, was too much alarmed to come close.

At last, Conrad got the man by the throat.

Then, contriving to get his right hand free, he dealt him such a tremendous blow on the head with the butt of his pistol, that the weapon was broken in two.

The man fell senseless to the floor.

The struggle between Mr. King and Cosmo still continued, but Conrad seeing that the former had the upper hand, and required no help, rushed up the stairs.

Room after room he burst open, but without success.

To the very top of the house he went, but no, nothing was to be seen of Deveril.

Throwing up one of the front windows he looked below.

Distinctly he saw half-a-dozen men.

They were the detectives.

Certain it was, then, that Deveril had not made his way out of the front.

As he ran from the room a loud shout came from the back.

Conrad immediately dashed into one of the back rooms and tore open the shutters.

Not being able to open the window, he smashed it to atoms with a heavy stool.

As he looked out the shouts were repeated, and he saw a number of men running towards the river.

It at once struck him that Deveril had managed to get out of one of the windows, and make his way in that direction.

Without a moment's pause, Conrad leapt from the window and dashed across the grounds.

"A thousand pounds to whoever captures the villain!" he shouted again and again.

The detectives, who were led by Mr. Hunt, redoubled their energies.

But they were too late.

Deveril, in the first place, had got an excellent start, and he maintained it.

He reached the edge of the river, leapt into the boat, severed the rope with a knife, and pushed off.

When Conrad reached the river, he was a couple of hundred yards away.

Our hero drew another pistol, and taking aim, fired.

Whether the ball had struck the wretch or not was not ascertained.

At any rate he did not fall.

Then his voice was heard.

"Good-bye for the present, Conrad," he said, derisively; "we shall meet again soon. Do not fear, I will kill you yet. Tell your friends this, and let those with you take this as a remembrance of me!"

As he spoke he fired.

It was impossible he could miss one of the men, for they were all collected beside Conrad.

The ball struck one of the detectives in the breast, killing him on the spot.

"This is indeed terrible," said Mr. Hunt, as he, with others, fell upon his knees to examine the one unfortunate man of the party. "I shall be called over the coals in this matter."

"I would to heaven I had a boat," said Conrad, "the wretch should not escape me. The coward—the brutal coward! But I will never rest, day or night, until I have him. Take that unfortunate man into the house. Is he dead?"

"Yes—quite dead, poor fellow."

Conrad re-entered the house, and found Cosmo lying insensible upon the floor.

He presented a terrible spectacle, for his face, neck, and hands were covered with blood, while his clothes were torn to ribbons.

"Have you killed him?" asked Conrad.

"Not quite; though the scoundrel deserved death."

"You recognised him?"

"Easily."

"As Captain Rosso?"

"Yes, though he is much altered And what of Captain Deveril?"

"I am again unlucky. He managed to reach our boat and has got away. From the river he fired a pistol, and shot a detective dead."

"Truly sorry am I to hear it. But in one way it will do good, for a warrant will be issued against him for murder, and the police will be after him in all directions."

"You are badly injured, I am afraid."

"Nay, it is nothing."

"Come, follow me, for we must secure the child."

Down the stairs both went, and they were met by the housekeeper.

"The child," said Conrad. "Quick!"

"The child? What child?"

"The child you have here."

"You are mistaken—there is no child here. And listen to me: you ought to be arrested for murder."

"For murder? Who has committed murder?"

"One of you. I dragged his body into the room, and—"

"Whose body, woman?" interrupted Conrad, impatiently. "Whose body?"

"My master's—'Dickey' Dean."

"Well, allow me to tell you that we had nothing to do with it. If he was shot dead, then it was by one of his two precious friends. Again, I say, the child!"

"I repeat that I know nothing about a child."

"Wretch! why do you stand there and tell such a deliberate, barefaced lie? The child is here, and if you do not produce it, we will secure it ourselves."

As he spoke, Conrad advanced nearer to the door.

The woman at once placed herself before it.

"No you don't," she said, suddenly producing and brandishing a large knife. "You don't pass me."

"We have no time to waste," said Conrad. "I again tell you to produce the child."

"And I again defy you to pass me."

"Refuse again, and I may forget that you are a woman."

"I have given my answer, and I will stick to it."

Conrad, with the speed of lightning, seized her wrist, and pressed it so tightly, that the woman was compelled to drop the knife.

Then, as she commenced to struggle fiercely, he seized her by the waist, lifted her from her feet, thrust her into an opposite coal-cellar, and locked the door upon her, where her shrieks, yells, and oaths were almost lost.

Mr. King walked into the opposite apartment, and there, fast asleep upon the bed, lay the child.

Certainly it looked none the worse for its extraordinary adventures.

Mr. King was overjoyed.

Again and again he seized our hero's hands, and, with tears running down his cheeks, thanked him with all his heart and soul for being the means of replacing his firstborn in his arms.

"Do not disturb it yet," said Conrad. "Presently we will secure a carriage of some sort. The principal thing to be done is to see that this Captain Rosso is secured."

"The detectives are in the house; I can hear them."

Ascending, they found Cosmo in charge of Mr. Hunt and his men.

He had recovered his senses, and was looking about in what seemed like a dazed fashion.

But our hero's experience of such men had been extensive.

"Be careful of him," he said, "and at once secure his hands behind his back."

Mr. Hunt and a couple of men at once seized his arms.

Not a moment too soon.

They found a large knife in one of his hands.

He would have used it right and left, had he been given the chance.

It was promptly snatched from him, and he was dragged to his feet.

Then his arms were tied behind his back, and he was led into one of the rooms used for gambling.

As he entered he caught sight of his reflection in an opposite mirror, and a deep groan escaped his lips.

Never before—though he had been in many a fight—had he presented so terrible a spectacle.

"Mr. Hunt," said Mr. King, "I give this rogue into your charge—firstly, for assaulting my wife; secondly, for child-stealing; and thirdly, for forgery."

"Forgery!" gasped Cosmo, now trembling violently, for he was well aware what heavy punishments were awarded in this country for forgery.

"Ay—a forgery committed four years ago, on a certain bank not a hundred miles from the City of London, Captain Rosso. You must remember the whole of the details, and you must be well aware of the fact that I shall be one of the prosecutors.

"At your trial I will take care that the whole of your fearful history—and your connection with the notorious pirate, Captain Deveril, is placed before the jury.

"I can assure you that I will show you no mercy whatever."

"No," said Mr. Hunt, "nor will the jury. You can reckon yourself booked for twenty years at least."

"No," said Cosmo, "I will never enter an English prison."

"Not of your own free will—of course not—it is not likely."

"Am I to be taken to the police office in this condition?"

"You are. I only wish it were daylight, so that you could be seen."

"I am dangerously wounded."

"I hope not. I should be sorry to see you slip through the fingers of the law. At the police office I will see that you are attended to by a doctor. Now, my men, away with him."

So, just as he was, all bloody and with his clothing torn to shreds, Cosmo was escorted from the house.

Then it was found that the shots had attracted the attention of the neighbours.

Quite a crowd of persons of both sexes were assembled in front of the house.

Mr. Hunt undertook to take charge of the premises.

Now that a murder had been committed, of course he was entitled to do so.

After some consultation, the doorkeeper was allowed to go, while the woman was detained.

"She will make an excellent witness against this Rosso," said Mr. Hunt; "for if we threaten her, she is safe to offer to give evidence. She, of course, is the one to prove that Rosso placed the child in her arms. Well, upon my soul, I am sorry Captain Deveril has escaped, but he is bound to be taken soon."

Mr. Hunt now left the house in search of a carriage.

He managed to secure one despite the hour, and Mr. King, with his child in his arms, was the first to enter it.

"In a few hours, Mr. Hunt," said Conrad, " I will return."

The coachman was then directed to drive to the hotel at Guildford Street, Russell Square.

CHAPTER XL.

THE ESCAPE TO GREENWICH—DEVERIL TRIES TO SECURE A CREW, AND FAILS.

THE reader, during the course of this story, has seen that Captain Deveril was at heart a coward.

But he has had the best proof of his cowardice in the last chapter, for he has seen that, when danger was nigh, he totally ignored his companion.

All that he thought of was his own safety.

But he also thought of something else.

Where could he go if he escaped without money?

His valuables were upstairs in a leathern case.

More — Cosmo's money, including a sum of no less than two thousand pounds, which he had won of Dickey, was in the same room.

He speedily pounced upon it, crammed notes and gold into the case, and into his pockets, and then fastened the door.

He then stripped the bed of its sheets, and his experienced fingers soon manufactured a rope, which was strong enough to descend from the window by.

In but a few minutes he reached the ground.

But not until he commenced to run was he overheard.

And then, as we have seen, it was too late.

Yet, had the detectives obeyed *to the letter* the orders of Mr. Hunt, Deveril must have been captured.

Safely in the centre of the river, Deveril seated himself, and, seizing the oars, pulled with all his might. Nor did he stop until he had placed two or three miles between himself and the " Lodge."

Then he rested, and considered what he was to do.

He quickly arrived at a conclusion.

" Since detectives are employed," he thought, " the best thing I can do is to remain in hiding for a few days, and the safest place I can go to is Greenwich.

" Greenwich, yes, that is my destination. But what will Nancy say? Hem! Well, I must risk it. After all, she may be dead—or married. I hope it may be one or the other. By heaven! if I only had a flask of brandy!

" It is of no use attempting to get it. If I went ashore I should find every house closed."

Having waited some minutes, and attentively scanned the river, he again took the oars, and went on.

Arrived, after two hours, at Greenwich, he landed unobserved, and made his way to what, at the period of our story, was a well-known tavern — namely, the " Anchor."

Of course, it was closed, but noticing a light moving about in one of the upper rooms, he knocked upon the door.

No answer being returned, he repeated the knock.

Still receiving no reply, he picked up a number of stones, and hurled them at the window.

It was at once thrown up, and a woman's voice asked—

" Well, well, who is it? What do you want? "

" By thunder!" muttered Deveril, " it is Nancy herself. Curse my luck! Well, well, I flatter myself that I can throw dust in *her* eyes again. Ah! I could recognise her voice anywhere, What a difference between hers and Lucinda's! "

Aloud he said—

" It is Walter."

"What Walter? What Walter?"

"Walter Deveril. Is it possible that you can have forgotten my voice?"

"Ha! now I recognise you. I will be down in a minute."

She was, in much less than a minute.

As she threw open the door and raised her candle aloft, she revealed a very pretty face and figure.

Nancy Turner, the daughter and only child of the landlord of the "Anchor," was about five-and-twenty, of about the medium height, dark, and blessed with a most magnificent head of hair.

But there was a deathly paleness in her cheeks, and a wild, terrified look in her eyes, which seemed to show that, day after day, she saw more trouble than usually falls to a woman's lot.

The reader will presently see that this was indeed the case.

"Walter!" she said—"Walter Deveril! Is it possible? And you have returned after all this time?"

Captain Deveril's notion of sweet tones must have been somewhat eccentric, for Nancy's voice was decidedly a sweet one.

"Yes," said Deveril, "I have returned, Nancy. And it is my intention never to sail again, until—until—well, until you consent to accompany me."

"I could never accompany a pirate, who has the blood of—"

"A pirate!" said Deveril, forcing a laugh. "Why, what do you mean?"

"I mean that I am well aware that Captain Walter Deveril is a pirate leader of the blackest dye."

"Upon my soul you wrong me. I know that for a long time past, a notorious pirate of the same name as myself has made himself the terror of the seas."

"You, then, are not the man?"

"Certainly not. What, Nancy, do you not know better than that? You must be well aware of the fact that I should never engage in so desperate a game. No, no. I was always an honest man.

"I may be a wild and erratic customer, but never a pirate—no, no. Believe me, what I say is true. Nay, Nancy, since I last saw you I have suffered deeply."

"In what way?"

"I have been a prisoner in a French prison. It was only six days ago that,

assisted by another prisoner, I contrived to escape."

"Indeed!"

"Ay, you believe me, Nancy? Did I ever tell you a lie?"

"Never," was the reply.

Then she thought—

"Infamous liar that he is. But let me control myself, and I may discover the reason he is here."

Aloud she said—

"Enter, for you look weary."

"Weary! That is scarcely the word for it. I beg of you to bring me some brandy."

This was quickly supplied, and Deveril swallowed two measures of it, as if it were no stronger than water.

"You, then," said Nancy, "are penniless?"

"To tell the truth, I am not far off it. A few pounds, which I borrowed from a sailor, is all I have."

"And that case?"

"This? Oh! that contains what little linen I am possessed of, and that, like the money, is not much."

"Let me take it. I will see that—"

"No, no," interrupted Deveril hastily, "not for the world. You see—it—there is blood upon some of it, Nancy, where I injured myself while getting out of prison. But tell me—how is it—that you are up at this hour?"

"My father is very ill."

"Indeed? How long has that been?"

"Some few days now. It is the last illness he will ever have."

"Come — come. Don't be downhearted. Hope for the best."

"I do—and the best is that he may die."

"Well. That is rather strong for a daughter."

"For a daughter who for years has been compelled to mix with the scum of the sea—is it? Your ideas are somewhat wild, Walter Deveril."

"Tell me," said Deveril, avoiding the question, "what is his illness?"

"Two bullets in the chest. He is bleeding inwardly to death."

"It is a sad business. But if he dies, Nancy, see what will fall to you. Your father, during the twenty years he has been here must have amassed an immense sum?"

"DEVERIL RECEIVED A FEARFUL BLOW IN THE FACE."

Nancy smiled bitterly as she replied—

"You are correct. He *did* amass a fortune. Unknown to me, he kept his gold buried in a cellar. But a few days ago his secret was discovered; half-a-dozen men made an attack, and my father got his wounds in endeavouring to defend his property."

"And the gold?"

"Every piece was taken."

"By Davy Jones! it was, indeed a misfortune."

"A *merited* misfortune."

"How?"

"He obtained it from thieves, and by thieves it was taken."

"He would be sorry to hear you speak thus."

"He has often heard me speak in this way."

"Well, we will talk of this to-morrow. I hope you have a spare bedroom."

"Yes; you will find one on the second landing."

"Many guests here?"

"Nay, one only. He is on the second floor."

"A sailor?"

"Ay, he calls himself a sailor—but he should add, 'and smuggler.'"

"His name?"

"Seth Beckton. If you look out of the bedroom window, you will see his vessel. It is lying right opposite to the house."

Deveril rose and made as if he would kiss Nancy ere he retired.

But she shrank back.

"I cannot bear the smell of brandy," she said, forcing a laugh.

"Ha! ha!" chuckled Deveril, as he ascended the stairs, "I thought I should have a hard job with her, but it has been the easiest thing in the world. If there is any man who can throw dust in a girl's eyes, it is Walter Deveril."

He was utterly mistaken as to Nancy Turner, however.

"Kiss *him!*" she muttered, as her eyes flashed fire and her hands tightly clenched themselves—"never! I would sooner kiss the skull of a skeleton! Wait, Walter Deveril, wait! I am not the fool I was long ago, when I was mad enough to believe that you loved me.

"Someone took your name? Pah! Abominable liar! You have been too well described by the ruffians *at the back.* No, no; *you* are the *only* Walter Deveril, the villainous pirate upon whose head a price is set."

Deveril ascended to the bedroom, and opening the window, looked out.

In the distance, to the right and left, was a mass of shipping, but in, as it seemed, the very centre of all, was the outline of a smart brig.

"Seth Beckton's, eh?" muttered Deveril, "I wonder if he would remember me? He must have got on wonderfully well to be in command of that vessel. Can he be the owner? I will tackle him in the morning. By Jove! she's a pretty little craft. I wonder whether she'd be trim enough to make the first of a second set of 'Firebrands?' I'll overhaul her to-morrow."

* * * *

In the morning Deveril had a private interview with Seth Beckton, and the result was that both set off on a visit to the brig.

They remained aboard of her some hours; in fact, it was dark before they returned to the inn.

By that time Seth Beckton had received two thousand pounds deposit on the sale of his vessel.

So, once again Deveril was captain and part owner of a vessel.

"Another and a last cruise," he thought, "and then, when I am rolling in riches, and can pay right and left, and with a liberal hand, my vengeance is *certain.* To-night I will get a crew from the Rut."

* * * *

"*At the back.*"

Nancy meant a great deal when she muttered these words.

At the back of the inn ran a long lane, with a dozen narrow turnings on the left, leading to the river.

The lane was called the "Rut," though why was not exactly known.

On either side were a number of low wooden houses, the majority of them not larger than a fair-sized cabin.

These rotten shanties had been owned for twenty years by James Turner, the landlord of the "Anchor."

When he took them over from an impoverished landlord, to whom he paid only one-third their value, they were what we may call the workrooms of respectable boat-menders and net-makers.

But James Turner who, "on the other side of the water," had had an extensive and lucrative connection among the smugglers, turned them all out, and let the places to his former "friends," upon many of whom the law would have given something to have laid its hands.

As may be supposed, these precious "tenants" turned the whole place into a "hell upon earth."

But neighbours were too far off to hear the fearful quarrels or to witness the many murderous fights among the ruffians, and so no complaint was made.

What cared James Turner for their noise or fights ?

Nothing at all.

The smugglers made plenty of money, and he compelled them to pay him double the value for articles with which he supplied them.

In fact he coined money.

If, in consequence of stress of weather the men could not proceed on their dangerous expeditions, he advanced them money at outrageous interest, and the several men he employed took precious good care that it was repaid.

It was to their advantage to collect it, for James gave them a certain commission out of what was returned to him.

Occasionally, when the smugglers had been more successful than usual, James entertained them in a huge wooden shed at the back of the house, and which communicated with the inn by a covered passage.

This rude building, fitted with one gigantic table placed in the centre, and several rough sideboards, he called the "banqueting room."

On these occasions, Nancy, poor girl, was compelled by her unnatural father to assist in attending the wants of the —well, savages—for they were little better.

It was this dreadful slavery, this compulsory mixing up with such men, that had ruined her life.

The men, of course, were well aware that she detested them ; but, nevertheless, they rarely offered her an insult.

For several days previous to Deveril's arrival the smugglers had been very successful.

They had reaped a rich harvest of spirits, tobacco, and silks.

Having disposed of the property to a few of the hawks who were ever ready to prey upon their ignorance, they decided to have a "banquet."

Therefore, they consulted, not their leader exactly, but a man they usually consulted on such matters.

That was Seth Beckton, the man who had disposed of the brig to Deveril.

Despite the fact that James Turner was sick unto death, it was decided that a banquet should be given — not at Turner's expense, since he was ill, but that each should contribute.

Poor Nancy, worn out with her constant attendance upon her father, and with having the whole responsibility of the inn thrown upon her shoulders, could not refuse to order the servants to prepare it.

So it was got ready.

Soon after his return to the inn Deveril was joined by Beckton, a huge, ungainly specimen of what we may call the "Sailor Shark."

"What's all this row ? " Deveril asked.

"Row ? "

"The shouting."

"Did I not tell you that the men are about to have a banquet ? "

"Ay, so you did."

"And you said that you had joined them more than once ? "

"True. But that was a few years ago."

"Well, if you want a crew, the time will be two hours from when the banquet commences. But I warn you as to what you say. The majority of the men you knew a few years ago are gone to Davy Jones's locker, and those who remain, like me, will not know you.

"You will have to pitch some lying yarn—say something about a buried treasure, and say you are going to weigh anchor with the first streak of dawn. But utter one word of piracy, and it is all over."

"I am not likely to prove myself such an infernal fool."

"Very good, for you are well aware that these men, though they risk their lives on the sea, would not care to risk them under a pirate's flag. And if, by any chance, they found they were being deceived — well, you may guess the result."

"Leave it to me. But will you not support me if I pay you well?"

"Ay, I will support you right enough. In fact, if you agree—and sign to that effect—that I shall have a fair half, I would join you myself."

"You would?"

"I would—here's my hand on it. I know that you have captured many a thousand pounds' worth of cargo, and I know that you are good for more. But not a word, for I alone know that you are Captain Deveril, the pirate."

"But you would not have known it had I not revealed myself."

"I have already said so. Now, do you order what you require. I must join the men, who are now arriving. I will send for you when the time comes. Meanwhile, I will send for the long boat, so that the men you manage to secure can be sent to the brig the instant they agree to join."

Two long hours did Deveril wait in his room.

He thought Nancy would pay him a visit.

But no, she came not near him.

However, he did not think much of this; he concluded that she was too busy.

Little did he dream that, while he was conversing with Seth Beckton, Nancy had been very close to him.

At the top of the partition on the left was a small hole.

This communicated with the other apartment, and, at one time, it had been used to place a thin rod with the old-fashioned "workable," or movable lamps.

They used to be hung by means of a chain from the rod, and could be pulled from one side to the other as required.

By means of this hole, then, Nancy had been enabled to hear all that had been said.

That Deveril was the notorious pirate was now fully confirmed.

But her astonishment at Deveril's impudence in making use of her and the inn for such dastardly purposes was great indeed.

But her face betrayed neither astonishment nor agitation as she left the room, and descended to see how the "banquet" was going forward.

She very calmly issued her orders to the servants, as they were called, and then said that she would visit her father.

The doctor had just arrived, and she met him on the stairs.

He was a clever, honest, and straightforward man, but the want of money and friends had compelled him to accept a practice in this miserable hole.

"Doctor Hutt," whispered Nancy, "go at once to Will's for me, will you?"

"Anything in the world I would do for you, my dear."

"Say that I have something of importance to tell him, and that he must come here without delay."

"He won't need much urging," smiled the doctor, as he left the house.

In less than a quarter of an hour he returned, accompanied by a young fellow of about five-and-twenty.

This was Will Wright, a boat builder, and one of the best scullers Greenwich had known.

He was a fine, tall, powerful man, and liked everwhere.

Even the drunken smugglers respected him—ay, and feared him too.

He at once made his way straight to the parlour, where he was joined by Nancy.

The conversation which ensued was a brief one, but it was thoroughly understood on both sides.

Will left the house again.

His last whispered words were—

Do not fear, I will be there."

Eleven o'clock came round, and by that time the mighty load of provisions which had been placed on the long table had been disposed of.

It was then "cleared for action," in other words, for a drinking bout.

Wines, spirits, tobacco and so on, were placed upon the table in shoals.

Not only were bottles set before the men, but also small casks, ready tapped.

If there was one man in that room, or rather shed, there were sixty, while several women—and such women!—and children could be seen here and there.

One glance would have been sufficient to have convinced any one that the men here assembled were of the very lowest class.

Not one of them was under thirty, while more than one was so aged as to be past all "work."

There were also three or four blacks.

Savage brutes they looked—men who might have just leapt from a pirate cutter.

And yet there was not one man in that shed who had ever crossed a pirate's deck.

It was "against their grain."

They detested the smell of powder, though they often used it when chased by the coastguard.

At the head of the table sat Seth Beckton.

He had proposed all manner of toasts, which had been drunk with enthusiasm, though the principal—"Confusion to the Coastguardsmen!" had been drunk with "three times three."

When he saw that the men were well on, he got up, and stood upon his chair.

"Boys," he said, "listen to me. What I have to say is little, but you will be pleased with it."

"Silence! silence!" was the hoarse cry on all sides.

Seth continued—

"The fact of it is, I have sold my smart little brig, the 'Will-o'-the-Wisp.'"

"No!" was the the thundering cry.

"Fact," smiled Seth, "and I will tell you to whom—a man who is honest to the backbone. His name is Richard Overton, one of the greatest travellers living. Now, what do you think he has bought it for?"

The men shook their heads, while one of the women yelled—

"To find the North Pole!"

"My friends," continued Seth, now in serious tones, "I will tell you. Two years ago, while exploring on a certain desolate coast on the—well, I must not tell you where it was—he came across a buried treasure."

At these words the men became breathless with excitement.

"A buried treasure!"

It was the constant dream of the sailor, the smuggler, ay, and the landsman.

"The gentleman, Richard Overton," continued Seth, "is in the inn at this moment, and he— But here he is."

As he spoke, Deveril passed through the doorway.

He was instantaneously greeted with a ringing cheer.

The discoverer of a buried treasure was a god among such men.

Deveril's pale face flushed as the cheer fell upon his ears.

It sounded like old times.

Old times! Yes, when, with wild yells, his bloodthirsty men had boarded some unfortunate vessel, and were about to put the crew to death!

Old times with a vengeance!

The cheers having subsided, Beckton handed Deveril a glass of spirits.

Deveril raised it on high.

"Success to all of you!" he said, a toast which, of course, was much approved.

"My friend here," said Deveril, speaking so that all had no difficulty in hearing him, "has told you a little about a buried treasure. Well, my men, let me assure you that it is no myth. The treasure is still there where I found it."

"Your pardon, yer honour," said an old man, rising, "how was it you didn't clear it?"

"Ay, ay," said several.

Deveril smiled.

"A very natural question," he said, "and I will answer it. I was alone when I made the discovery—entirely alone on the island."

"But the vessel—the ship you sailed in?"

"Was wrecked. I was the only survivor. A month after the discovery, I was picked up by the crew of a vessel which had put off in search of eggs. Was it likely that I should say anything of my discovery to them?"

The men were apparently perfectly satisfied with this explanation.

Deveril continued—

"I have purchased the 'Will-o'-the-Wisp' from Beckton. He will sail with me."

At this the men opened their eyes very wide indeed.

There must be something in it, or Seth Beckton would never have agreed to sail.

The men were very quiet, while Deveril, seeing that a profound impression had been made upon them, continued—

"I want five-and-twenty men to complete my crew. Who will join? I will pay the best wages, and, when we return to England with the treasure, every man shall receive five hundred pounds!"

There was a dead silence for some few moments.

Then a man asked—

"How long is the voyage likely to last, captain?"

"Twelve months," was the reply.

Twelve months! It was a long time to men like this.

Their "voyages" rarely extended to days.

They drank their rum and considered and conversed.

Suddenly one of the men slowly rose, and, taking his black pipe from his mouth, said—

"Ahoy, captain! What *proof* have we that what you say is true?"

This was a "staggerer."

It was a question which Captain Deveril certainly had not anticipated: and yet it was a very natural one.

But ever ready with a lie, Deveril promptly replied—

"Proof!" he smiled. "Ask Seth Beckton for the proof."

Beckton was astounded.

He nodded, not knowing what to do; and a very uneasy nod it was.

"Seth Beckton," said Deveril, with all the coolness in the world, "holds money of mine amounting to over twenty thousand pounds."

Beckton felt inclined to drop at this barefaced lie.

But what was he to do? He dare not deny it.

"That money," continued Deveril, "will remain in his hands. He will have the paying of the crew, and he will see that they have each the five hundred pounds at the conclusion of the voyage."

"I join!" said one of the men, standing up.

"And I—and I!" ran round the shed, until the twenty-five required were obtained.

Deveril was overjoyed.

His eyes flashed with triumph as he looked round the shed.

Already he fancied himself once more treading the deck of a vessel which was to procure him thousands upon thousands of pounds.

Away on the open sea he could terrify

the men into obedience, as he had often done before.

But his joy was short-lived.

Just as Deveril raised his glass and said, "Success to the 'Will-o'-the-Wisp,'" Wright made his appearance.

"What ho!" he said. "What is all this about, eh? Why, my men, you are never about to sail beneath a black flag?"

The words fell among the men like a number of thunderbolts.

"Sir," said Deveril, noting with some consternation the effect of Will's words on the men, "perhaps you will explain yourself?"

"To be sure, my hearty. You have purchased the 'Will-o'-the-Wisp' from Seth Beckton, and you intend to go back to your old business. My men," he added, in a loud voice, as he pointed to Deveril, "that is Captain Deveril, the pirate chief."

The men—every one of them—leapt to their feet.

"Yes," continued Will, "and Seth Beckton knew it when he sold him the vessel. He has betrayed you."

"You lie!" said Deveril. "Where are the proofs of what you say?"

Will turned and called—

"Nancy!"

Nancy came slowly forward.

"Nance," said Will, "who is that man at the end of the table?"

"Captain Deveril, the pirate chief!" replied Nancy, "on whose head a price has been set."

It was enough.

The men made a mad rush at Seth Beckton; and in two minutes he was lying upon the floor, bleeding and insensible.

From him they turned to Deveril.

They were about to rush towards him, when he threw back his jacket, and his belt revealed two pairs of pistols.

In an instant a pair was in his hands, and levelled at the men.

"Beware!" he said. "Attempt to touch me, and I will shoot the first man who approaches."

The men paused.

The majority of them were unarmed.

Those who were what we may call armed, had only a sheath knife.

Suddenly a heavy wooden block was hurled across the table.

It struck Deveril on the right hand, knocking the pistol from his grasp.

That block had been aimed by one of the women.

Seeing this, several men, with loud shouts, rushed forward.

Deveril kept his word.

The foremost man he instantaneously shot dead.

Then, through the smoke, the others saw that he had drawn two more pistols.

Again there was a pause.

It was undoubtedly certain death to whoever advanced, and therefore it was no wonder they paused and considered.

But, in the meantime, one of the children, unseen by Deveril, who was compelled to keep his eyes straight before him, had fallen upon his knees, and, crawling along, had possessed himself of the fallen pistol.

Unseen he placed it in his father's hands.

The man, hiding behind one of the women took aim at Deveril and fired.

But, unfortunately, he was the worse for the powerful liquids he had consumed.

The ball flew wide of the mark.

It struck one of the huge hanging oil lamps, and the oil, pouring in a stream on to the table, came in contact with a lighted candle.

The result may be imagined.

In an instant the table was a mass of flame.

The shrieks and cries of the women and children were awful to hear.

The men, ignoring the levelled pistols made a rush to the door which led to the Rut.

Deveril mistook their intention, and the first man to get near him he deliberately shot.

Will Wright now seized the table, and shouting to the frantic persons on the right side to stand away, he turned it over.

This act showed what great strength he was possessed of.

Deveril saw now that his chance had come.

Like a madman he rushed to the opposite door—that is, the one leading to the inn.

At the entrance he saw Nancy.

"Wretch!" he thundered, "it was you who betrayed me—take that!"

His pistol was pointed at her face, but before he could pull the trigger, a figure floated before him, and he received such a fearful blow in the face that he went staggering back into the shed, dropping the pistol.

But he did not fall.

No, the next moment he again rushed forward.

But this time it was to find a pair of pistols levelled at his own head.

"By the foul fiend," gasped the wretch, "Conrad Ireton!"

"Correct," said our hero, for he it certainly was. "Conrad Ireton once more stands before you."

"Ha, ha!" chuckled a little man beside Conrad. "Excellent, excellent."

It was Mr. Hunt.

CHAPTER XLI.

IN WHICH AN EXTRAORDINARY DUEL IS FOUGHT, AND DOCTOR WOOD PLAYS A TRICK.

DEVERIL, remembering that he was now unarmed, suddenly turned.

He was, of course, about to make for the other door.

But behind him was Will Wright.

"Stay where you are, captain," he said, calmly. "We don't want you to go yet."

The fire by this time had been stamped out, and the women were busy rescuing the spirits.

As for the men, they now crowded round the speakers.

"Captain Deveril," said Conrad, "you are at last caught in a trap from which there is no escape. Beside me stands a detective."

The half-drunken smugglers opened their eyes at this.

"I produce my warrant for your arrest," said Mr. Hunt. "There are many charges against you, but the chief is that of murdering one of my men. From a boat on the river you shot him dead."

"That is not all," said Will. "He has just shot *two* men dead."

At this there was a loud and threatening howl from the men.

This, of course, showed Conrad that the crowd of men were not the friends of Deveril.

" I do not know what has occurred here," said Conrad, " but no doubt you are aware that this man is Captain Deveril, the pirate chief, and one of the most brutal assassins that ever lived. For years he has sought my life. He would take it this instant if he had the chance.

"The man beside me is, I repeat a detective, but, if I ask him, he will retire."

"Retire!"

Mr. Hunt opened his eyes very wide indeed.

"Retire? What for?" he asked.

"You shall learn presently. But you need not fear. Captain Deveril will have no chance of escaping."

For some little time, however, Mr. Hunt could not be prevailed upon to retire, but at last he followed Nancy.

" Now," said Conrad, " let the women and children retire."

Wonderingly, the men escorted them to the door.

Then Conrad continued—

"Captain Deveril, the time has come to show what you can do in *fair fight*. Has anyone a pair of cutlasses?"

"I have," said Will. "I can get them in a few minutes."

"I refuse to fight," scowled Deveril.

A loud, angry roar told him that if he did not fight, it was probable that he would speedily be torn to pieces.

He continued—

"Not with cutlasses."

"Well," said Conrad, "with pistols. Here are two. Select which you please."

He handed them to Will, who, amid breathless silence, offered them to Deveril.

Deveril selected the first, but it was with a trembling hand.

" Now," continued Conrad, in such cool tones, that every man present listened in amazement and admiration, " here is a handful of money. The one who guesses the nearest to the number of pieces will be the first to fire."

And he placed the money in Will's hands.

Deveril's face was now ashy pale.

"Let him call first," said Conrad.

Deveril, with some difficulty, jerked out—

" It would not be fair. He may know the number of pieces."

"I swear I do not," said Conrad. "But let someone else place more money with it."

Will took a number of coins from his pocket, and, without allowing anyone to see them, added them to Conrad's.

Deveril was then satisfied.

After a brief pause, he said—

"Fifteen."

"Twenty," said Conrad.

Will counted them.

"There are but sixteen," he said.

Deveril, then, was to fire first.

A devilish light shone in his eyes when he knew this.

"I am a dead shot," he muttered. "After all, he dies by my hand!"

The smugglers were not at all satisfied at what had been done.

But they made no attempt to interfere then.

By Conrad's directions, the men were drawn up on either side of the shed; and Will, who was now intensely excited, was requested to give the word to fire.

"One moment," faltered Will, "have you no instructions to give? Bear in mind that, in a few seconds, you may be a dead man?"

"I have sent a long letter to my friends," replied Conrad, "Mr. Hunt, the detective, will do the rest."

Then he placed himself at the farther end of the shed, and, with his arms behind his back, stood erect, awaiting the word to fire.

What name was upon his lips as he stood thus?

The reader can guess. It was Lucinda's.

"Get ready," said Will, in low tones.

Deveril took deliberate aim.

The strain was too much for the smugglers.

The majority started forward and excitedly protested against such a duel.

"My friends," said Conrad with a

smile, "it is of my own choosing. I beg of you stand aside."

The men reluctantly obeyed, and Will, in a second or two, uttered the word—

"Fire!"

At once Deveril pulled the trigger.

The sharp report was almost immediately followed by a ringing cheer, for Conrad was seen to be still erect.

The ball had struck the woodwork behind, splintering it.

But a quarter of an inch lower, and our hero would have received the ball full in the throat.

Deveril with a curse hurled the pistol to the ground.

Then he looked wildly round him, as if seeking a chance of escape.

No, no; there was none.

Will now presented the other pistol to Conrad.

Our hero, having carefully examined it, took aim.

Deveril did not stand erect.

Far from it! he cowered back as if a dozen weapons were levelled at him instead of one.

"Fire!" said Will.

Conrad pulled the trigger as the word was uttered, and the next instant a wild yell told the breathless men that the bullet had found its billet.

Yes, Deveril had been struck full in the breast.

He fell with a crash to the ground, and was surrounded by the men.

"He is dead!" cried several, "it was a good shot."

Will pushed his way through, and, almost at the same moment, Mr. Hunt made his appearance.

He soon learned what had taken place, but he refrained from saying anything.

"He is not dead," said Will, "but he cannot live long."

"I claim him," said Mr. Hunt, "he is my prisoner. I have here a warrant, and I hope no one will dare to dispute my right to him."

"Pah!" said Will, "what is the use of a dying prisoner?"

No matter, he is my charge, dead or alive. I will give a couple of pounds to the man who will fetch a doctor."

"Doctor Hutt lives close here," said one, "I will go and fetch him."

Doctor Hutt was in the tavern, but he refused to go anywhere near Deveril.

The man thereupon went to another, a notoriously drunken wretch, named Wood.

This individual, though in a maudling state, at once seized his case and set out.

Reaching the shed, he examined Deveril with great attention, considering his state.

"He is fatally wounded," he said. "The ball has struck him just above the heart."

"There is no hope for him?" asked Hunt.

"Hope, sir? No, not the faintest hope. He is as good as a dead man already."

"Never mind," said Hunt; "I am not going to leave him. "Look, you, doctor, can he remain in your house until he dies?"

"Ay, if I am paid for it. But then, mine is only a poor place."

"No matter. Let him be taken there, and I will see that you are well paid. I am a detective, holding a warrant for this man."

"Who will carry him?" asked Wood.

The smugglers drew away.

"What!" said Hunt, "will none of you help?"

"Help?" said Will. "Certainly not. If you want to take him away, get your own men."

"Stop here," said the doctor. "I will get a couple of men."

He left the shed, and in a few minutes returned with a couple of men.

These, assisted by Hunt and the doctor, carried the dying pirate chief from the shed, and conveyed him to Wood's house, which was distant some five hundred yards.

"I will remain at this tavern," said Conrad to Hunt.

*   *   *   *

An hour passed, and Hunt returned.

"Well?" asked Conrad.

"You took the law into your own hands, sir, with a vengeance. He is dead."

"Dead!"

"Ay, and with his last breath he cursed you."

"No more than I expected," said Conrad, grimly.

"I am sorry, very sorry that you took the course you did. I don't wonder at it, to be sure, but you might have waited.

You would have had the satisfaction of seeing a rope round his neck. I don't know exactly how I am to proceed. I suppose I had better say that he met his death in a drunken brawl."

"As you please."

"What you did was in fair fight," continued Mr. Hunt, "but the law of this country punishes the duellist."

"I am prepared to stand by what I did."

"Leave all that to me, sir. Well, will you have a last look at the wretch ere you leave here."

Conrad, who was very thoughtful, started as the question was asked.

"Yes," he said, after a few moments; "I will come."

They soon reached Doctor Wood's "house," a miserable, one-storied hovel at the end of a narrow lane, and they had to knock several times before they were admitted.

Doctor Wood conducted them to his back parlour.

There, upon the table in the centre, lay the body of Deveril.

Conrad shuddered as he looked at it.

The doctor had removed the upper portion of the clothing, and the wound was revealed.

"For the present," said Mr. Hunt, "the body will remain in your possession, Mr. Wood. An inquest will have to be held, of course."

Doctor Wood shrugged his shoulders.

"In the ordinary course an inquest would be held," he said; "but, were I in your place, it should not take place."

"What do you mean?"

"This. Under your nose you allowed a duel to take place in which this man meets his death.

"Well, if you do not have to undergo an examination for that, it is a strange thing to me. Whereas, if you say that you have failed to find your man, you will not be blamed. I shall not open my mouth; and I am certain none who witnessed the fight will."

"What you say is right," said Mr. Hunt, whose face had turned several degrees paler; "it must be hushed up."

"I will see to the burial of the man, if you pay me," said Doctor Wood. "I can give a certificate that he died of some disease."

This, after some discussion, was agreed to; and Conrad handed to the doctor the sum of twenty pounds.

"Will you return to London with me, Mr. Ireton?" asked Hunt.

"Nay, I am going at once to Banstead Manor. You have plenty of time, and can accompany me. Before you leave, I can promise you a handsome present."

"I will go with you with pleasure. When do you propose to start?"

"At once. But before I forget it—here is the pocket-book you lent me."

"Thanks. Well, sir, the particulars I jotted down in that book caused us to find the villain."

"It did—easily."

Doctor Wood ushered them out of his "house" with much ceremony.

Then having closed the door, he hastened back to the parlour, seized a mahogany case, opened it, and took out a small bottle.

Pulling the cork out, he, with a quiet chuckle, seized Deveril's head, raised it, and poured the whole of the liquid into his mouth.

Nothing followed for some few minutes, but suddenly, a violent quiver shook the apparently dead man's frame.

"Ay, ay," muttered Wood, "he's all right. I will soon pull him together."

Other remedies he applied to head, arms, and legs.

In five minutes Deveril opened his eyes, and stared vacantly around him.

"All is well so far, captain," said Wood, with a grin.

"Where am I?" murmured Deveril.

"In my house, right away from your enemies, who fancy you are dead."

"Conrad."

"Eh? Who?"

"Conrad Ireton."

"Don't know him. Oh, is that the one that fired the shot?"

Deveril nodded.

"The one with the detective?"

"Ay."

"He's gone with the detective to—let me see—Banstead."

After considerable labour, in which he certainly showed much skill, Wood succeeded in completely restoring him to his senses.

Then he bound up the wound he had received.

"You feel great pain there?" he asked.

"I feel as if I were on fire."

"I don't wonder at it. But if you will only follow my advice, you will be able to move about in a month."

"How is it I am alive?"

"Ha, you may well ask that question. The fact of it is you are one of the luckiest men I've ever known. The ball struck you here on this bone—there —I don't want to hurt you—if it had been the twelfth part of an inch lower down you would have been shot dead. As it was, the ball, as I have said, struck the bone—but only slightly splintered it—and then took an upward direction.

"That is the reason you have lost so much blood."

"Where is the ball?"

"Here."

And Wood exhibited the leaden bullet, partly flattened.

"Give it to me," said Deveril.

"What will you do with it?"

"*I will return it.*"

"Nonsense. If you will take my advice, you will leave the country as soon as ever you are able. But let me continue. As soon as I heard that a detective was after you, I knew that you were not safe. Thinking that you would be prepared to pay for whatever I did for you, I said that you could only live a short time.

"You were brought here, and taking the opportunity when the detective's back was turned, I poured down your throat a quantity of stuff which had the effect of causing rigidness, and, in fact, the complete appearance of a dead man.

"You remained in that state for some time, during which the detective returned with the young man—the one whom, I suppose, shot you."

"Conrad Ireton!—and he saw me here? On this table?"

"Ay."

"And he had no doubt that I was dead?"

"None whatever—nor had the detective."

"Good. You have rendered me a service, and I will pay you well for it. Sewn in the lining of my jacket are bank notes for a large amount. I *did* have a goodly sum in my pockets."

As he spoke he felt in them.

There was not a single piece.

Who had taken the money? The men or the doctor?

Deveril did not ask. He knew that it would be of no use.

Wood then told Deveril what instructions he had received from the detective.

"I will have a funeral easily enough," he grinned. "Two men were shot dead in the shed. The body of one I will secure to-morrow night, and convey it here.

"Then I will order the coffin, and the man will be placed in it. There are several forms to be gone through, but I will manage it all right."

"I see that you are a clever man, and I repeat, I will well reward you. But you are quite certain that I shall recover from this wound?"

"As certain as that you are now here."

"Good!" thought Deveril, "I shall, then, have another opportunity. Banstead! Let him wait—let him wait!

"But what of the two thousand I paid Seth Beckton on account of the brig? I would not be at all surprised if I lose the whole. He will never remain at Greenwich after what has occurred. Well, I must talk to the doctor about it to-morrow. If I only got a thousand back I should not care."

*　　*　　*　　*

Deveril never recovered one shilling of the two thousand. Seth Beckton vanished from Greenwich, and so did the brig.

He was not likely to return, for the smugglers threatened that if ever again he was seen near their quarters, they would destroy the brig by fire, and he knew them too well to disregard the threat.

Five weeks after the duel Deveril left Doctor Wood's house.

Wood had procured him an excellent disguise—that of an Italian.

It was night when he passed out of the place, and made his way along the London Road.

Many passed him on the road, but they regarded him with very little curiosity.

It was nothing to meet with foreigners at Greenwich.

Just at the Cross Road, on the left, was a large wooden building.

On the top was a small model of a

boat, and on that was the name, "William Wright, Boat Builder."

As Deveril glanced at it, a man came out of the place, accompanied by a young lady.

Deveril at once recognised him.

It was Will, who had denounced him, while the young lady was Nancy.

Deveril's hand wandered to a long knife beneath his jacket.

But he did not draw it.

Nay; he felt that Will would be too much for him.

His wound had healed, it is true, but it had left him very weak.

But he advanced to Will, and said some words in Italian. Will shook his head and pointed down the road, as much as to say—

"Ask someone further on."

But Deveril had asked no question.

What he had said was—

"May my bitter curse be on both of you!"

He had the "satisfaction" of saying this, even though he knew Will would be unable to interpret it.

"Now for London, for a time," thought Deveril. "And perhaps I may learn something of Cosmo, though, whatever his position, I cannot help him. After that—Banstead!"

CHAPTER XLII.

THE "YOKEL" AT BANSTEAD—HOW DEVERIL WEAVES ANOTHER PLOT, AND HOW IT FAILED MISERABLY.

ON the second day after his arrival in London, Deveril, still disguised, visited Hammersmith, and put up at a small hotel.

There he had some conversation with the landlord as to the neighbourhood, and by-and-by he got full particulars of all that had transpired on the night that he made his escape by means of the boat.

"This dastardly pirate chief," said the landlord, "got away as clean as a whistle, and the detectives, up to now, have failed to find him. But he is bound to be taken. Everyone is on the look-out. Even the war vessels have orders to stop and overhaul any suspicious-looking craft. The man taken—a foreigner, I think, whose name I forget—was taken to prison. Two days afterwards he was found dead."

"Dead!"

"Ay, he had taken poison, which had been secreted about his person. So, you see, he escaped the law. Who shot 'Dickey' Dean has remained a mystery; but, no doubt, it was this—er—Captain Deveril."

"Ay, ay, no doubt."

At this hotel Deveril remained for two more days, when he left for Banstead.

It was the first time in all his life that he had visited the place, and he was astonished to find what a dreary, desolate spot it was.

But when he reached Banstead Manor, he was compelled to admit that it was one of the most magnificent places he had ever beheld.

It was indeed a small palace, standing in its own grounds of about twenty acres, the whole being surrounded by a high wooden fence.

There were two or three lodges at the entrance to magnificent avenues, and over the principal gateway was the arms of the Bellchambers, beautifully guilded and delicately interwoven with the elaborate ironwork.

As Deveril looked around him, he gnashed his teeth and breathed a bitter curse on the occupants of the manor; for he had no doubt all his enemies were within it.

Speaking broken English, he asked the keeper of one of the lodges several questions, and learned that Conrad, Lucinda, the earl (Captain Ireton), and Lieutenant Daulton were "in residence."

From the lodge he, after inquiry, made his way across the fields to an inn.

He was just about to cross a stile, when he heard the rapid clatter of horses' feet.

The next instant two riders—a lady and gentleman—came along the lane.

He had not the least difficulty in recognising them.

They were Conrad and Lucinda.

The latter's laughter rang in his ears and nearly maddened him.

He sprang into the road as soon as they passed, and snatched a pair of pistols from his pocket.

But he did not present them.

"No, no," he muttered. "I must get to closer quarters than this."

He had scarcely placed them in his pocket, when a peculiar voice said—

"Hillo, my hearty, what is it, eh? What the devil are you going to shoot ? "

Deveril turned and looked about him.

In a few seconds, he saw the face of a man peering through the hedge.

"Birds," he said.

"Birds ! " cried the man, with a loud laugh. "Who ever knew a man shoot birds with pistols? Ah ! but I see you are a foreigner."

As he spoke, he crawled out of the hedge.

A strange-looking individual, truly !

He had the appearance of a countryman, but yet there was something about him which seemed to indicate that he was not by any means what he appeared.

"Yes," said Deveril, "as you say, I am a foreigner. And you ? "

"Oh," said the man, with a silly grin, "I am a *yokel*. Are you staying in the neighbourhood ? "

"I have only just come to Banstead, and shall stay here perhaps a few days. I have been directed to the 'Hare and Hounds.' "

"I know it well—too well, in fact— and will show you where it is, if you like."

"Ay, do," replied Deveril.

Then he thought—

"No doubt this man has lived hereabouts for years, and knows all that is going on. It is evident that he is a fool—a man that would be willing to do a lot for a paltry shilling or two. He may be of immense service to me."

The "silly fool" was picking his teeth in the silliest fashion in the world; but he also was thinking.

His thoughts ran as follows—

"This man speaks very good English for a foreigner. I wonder what he does this way ? Shooting birds, eh ? No,

it won't do for me—not by long chalks. It strikes me he was about to let fly at the pair as rode by—that's two from the lodge."

Deveril lit a cigarette and offered one to the man.

The "yokel" calmly took off the paper, and thrust the tobacco into his mouth.

Then he went on, Deveril closely following him.

They soon reached the inn known as the "Hare and Hounds," and Deveril invited the man to drink with him.

He accepted ; but while Deveril drank brandy, he swallowed nothing but old ale.

Deveril had no difficulty in engaging a room.

"I hope you will make me comfortable," he said, "for I am a stranger here, and at present know nothing of the place."

"Oh, you will be comfortable enough, sir," said the landlord. "And as to the place, why Jimmie here can tell you all about it. He's been here longer than me."

He referred to the "yokel."

"Ay," said Jimmie, "I've been here years enough."

His voice appeared to change as he said this.

Waiting until the host had retired, Deveril, in the most careless fashion, commenced his questions.

At first they referred to the surrounding country.

Then he got to the inhabitants, and finally to the Lodge.

"Ah, as you say," said Jimmie, "it *is* a place if you like. Why, for years, you must know, it was in the occupation of a caretaker only. But a short time ago, the earl came back at last. He brought with him several others. One was a— But hang me, here is the very man ! "

As he spoke, a burly figure passed through the doorway, and a cheery voice cried—

"What ho, master landlord ! put your right leg foremost, and hoist me a bale of good home-brewed ! "

It was Jack Barnacle.

Yes, there he was, "All alive, oh ! " and the picture of good health and spirits.

He had not seen the "foreigner;"

nor, after drinking his ale and passing out, did he notice anyone.

"That is one of them," said Jimmie. "You can see that he's been a sailor. I never come near such a strange man in all my life. He often comes in here with another he calls 'Doctor.'"

The reader rightly guesses that this was Dr. Mc.Taggart.

"When they first came here," continued Jimmie, "the one that's just gone out—Jack they call him—told the landlord that he wanted about a dozen men who knew gardening. They were wanted for a job; so, of course, I volunteered, and I was paid well."

"You went to the Lodge, then?"

"Yes, with several others. But that was not the first time I'd been to the place. Lor' bless you, I know every inch of the grounds. Beautiful they are, too, I assure you. But what will they be in another month's time? Ha!"

"How do you mean?"

"Why, there's going to be a grand wedding there. Just before I spoke to you, did you notice two persons pass on horseback?"

"A lady and gentleman—yes."

"That's the two."

"They are going to be married?"

"Yes, in a month. Workmen are busy getting the house and the church ready. No doubt it will be a grand affair. All the neighbours—they are mostly the earl's tenants—are to be invited."

Deveril became thoughtful.

Now, indeed, was the time to strike the blow.

But was it possible that he, who knew nothing of the place, could strike that blow without assistance?

If he decided that he could not, was this man to be trusted?

"Even if I could succeed in slaying Lucinda," he thought, "the blow would be terrible enough. Conrad would never recover from it. It would be *his* death blow, and it would also break the hearts of the earl and Daulton."

Presently he said—

"Look you, my friend, can you keep a secret?"

"Ay," was the reply, "that I can."

"If I asked you to keep a secret, and paid you well for it, would you do it?"

"*Would* I? Of course I would."

"Here are five sovereigns. Now what would you do for that?"

"Do? Anything."

"Well, it is very little I shall want you to do. The fact is," he whispered, "I *know* the persons at the Lodge."

The countryman's face expressed the most profound astonishment.

"Really?" he said.

"Yes, and I am here to see *one* of them."

"Only one?"

"Yes, that is the lady. You have seen her several times?"

"I have."

"And have you not noticed that she has a foreign appearance?"

"Yes."

"Well, let me tell you that she is my sister."

The countryman opened his eyes to their fullest extent.

"Lor!" he ejaculated.

Then he thought—

"I am right. Something heavy is in the wind here. I'll be sworn that this man is not what he seems. I'd bet my head that he is a man who would murder anyone without the least hesitation. But I must continue to play the fool."

Deveril, having ordered more brandy, and lit another cigarette, continued—

"My sister has gone to live with these people without the consent of her parents, and I want to see and reason with her. But you must understand, she would not say a word to me if she could help it."

"I understand you quite well."

"Now, if I wrote a letter, do you think that you could find a means of conveying it to her?"

"Bless you, there would be no difficulty as to that. You see the workmen are all over the place. I should not be questioned at all."

"Could you take it to-night?"

"Easily."

Deveril called for pen, ink, and paper, and in a disguised hand, which strikingly resembled a lady's, he wrote—

"MADAM,

"Pardon me for thus intruding. I am a poor dressmaker, who has just settled at Banstead; but, unfortunately, up to now, I have had no orders. Hearing that you are about to be married, I have taken the liberty to beg of you to give me a little work. I assure you that I should be deeply grateful for anything. I am so shabbily attired that I dare not apply at the Lodge for permission to see you. The bearer has very kindly consented to take this letter to you, and to conduct me into the grounds. Pray, good lady, do not refuse.

"Your faithful servant,
"JANE BROWN."

This he sealed, and directed simply—
"To the Lady of the Manor."

He did not read this to Jimmie, but he explained it.

"It is safe to succeed," said Jimmie, "for I remember being told that the lady was very simple."

"At what time will you take it?"

"Say ten?"

"Ay, that will do. Will you remain here until that time?"

"Yes."

"Then order what you require. And if I succeed in seeing my sister, I will give you another ten pounds."

* * * *

It was a little past the hour of ten when Jimmie, accompanied by Deveril, crossed the dark fields and made for the fence bordering the estate.

The part Jimmie selected was at some distance from either of the lodges, and, therefore it was scarcely likely that their movements would be observed.

Jimmie made for a part of the fencing which was broken, and, having clambered up first, Deveril followed.

"It's very dark," said Jimmie, "and man traps are about, so you had better keep close to me."

Deveril did not fail to do so.

On they went through the magnificent park, Jimmie taking care to select the shortest paths.

Deveril saw that he had not boasted when he said that he knew every inch of the grounds.

Presently they came to a small summer-house.

This, like other parts of the ground, was in course of re-decoration.

Jimmie paused here and pointed ahead.

"Do you see two lights?" he asked.

"Ay."

"Well, they are right and left of the terrace. Do you think you had better go any further?"

"No; this spot will do very well."

"I will return with the lady—that is, if she consents to come, and I fancy she will."

"Go, then—and remember the ten pounds."

Away went Jimmie towards the house but, instead of taking the smaller paths, he now took one of the principal.

Yet, even this, in consequence of the deep shade of the trees, was so dark that he could see nothing right or left.

He had arrived within fifty paces of the Manor, when suddenly a heavy hand descended upon his shoulders, and a voice asked—

"Hillo, mate! What the devil are you doing here—poaching? If you are, hang me, if I don't rope's-end you until you dance like a cat on hot bricks."

The speaker was Barnacle.

"It's a good job I prowl about these 'ere grounds o' nights," continued Barnacle; "for, hang me if you aint the second pirate I've found. Now, out with it—what ship do you belong to?"

"No ship."

"Ay, I forgot. You're a land shark, eh?"

"No, I'm not. I'm one of the men you employed."

"Oh, are you? And when you were employed here, I suppose you took a fancy to something, and have now come to get it?"

"No, you are wrong. But walk along beside me, and I will tell you why I am here."

"Walk along beside you? Well, that's curious! Howsomedever, I'll walk—since there don't happen to be a boat handy.

As they went on, Jimmie uttered a couple of dozen words.

Their effect on Barnacle was something extraordinary.

He paused abruptly and looked around as if he feared that someone had overheard what had been said.

Then he whispered—

"Where is this man?"

"Beside the summer-house."

"Dressed like an Italian?"

"Ay, and he speaks broken English. But I fancy that is only assumed."

"Stand away, mate. I'll interview *him!*"

"'HILLO, MY HEARTY! WHAT THE DEVIL ARE YOU GOING TO SHOOT?'"

"Don't attempt to do anything of the sort."

"Why not?"

"You would spoil everything. Lead me before the gentleman."

"Your advice is good. Come with me. But first tip us your flipper mate! You're a good man, and—dang me—you won't be forgotten. Don't you know what I am, here?"

"No."

"Steward. Now come on."

Conrad, Lucinda, the earl, Daulton, Don Aleco, and Doctor McTaggart were seated in one of the pretty sitting-rooms.

The subject of their talk was the approaching marriage of Conrad to Lucinda—or, as her real name was, Inez.

Conrad was correcting a long list of names, those invited to the feast and the subsequent illumination of the grounds, for it had been unanimously agreed that the happy pair should remain at the Manor.

Already they had done enough travelling to last them a few years.

Suddenly there was a somewhat loud knock upon the door.

"Come in," said Conrad.

Barnacle, hat in hand, entered hastily.

It was at once seen that he was in a state of great excitement.

"What has happened?" asked Conrad, who now caught sight of Jimmie.

"Happened?" gasped Barnacle; "snakes and scorpions, your honner! something awful has happened. Do you know, I fancy that monster has returned to life!"

"Eh? What monster?"

"Deveril!"

Had a bombshell been thrown into the room, those present could not have leapt to their feet with greater rapidity.

Conrad smiled.

"What madness," he said; "did I not tell you that I saw the man dead?"

"Well, your honner, just listen to what this man will tell you."

Jimmie, though somewhat awed by the magnificence of the room, told his story, and handed over the letter, which Conrad read amid the most profound silence.

"Here, indeed is a mystery," he said, when he had concluded, "who can this man be?"

"Who knows?" said the earl; "it is possible that a trick has been played upon you, and that the Italian is none other than Deveril."

".I can scarce believe that."

"Well, my lad, doctors have been bribed before to-day. However, it is certain that, whoever he is, he is bent on Lucinda's destruction."

"Yes, there can be no doubt about that. Lucinda, do you at once procure a dress that will fit me from one of the servants, together with bonnet, veil and cloak."

"What are you about to do?"

"Personate you."

"No, no, no! You may lose your life."

"Do not fear, I shall be guarded. But be quick."

The clothes were soon forthcoming, and Conrad, assisted by Lucinda, donned them."

"Now," said our hero, "hand me a pistol. Then, Barnacle, do you go to the summer-house by another direction."

"We will go too," said the earl. "Whoever the man is, we will take care that he does not escape."

Barnacle quickly procured the arms, and with the earl and Daulton, he left the house first.

It was very fortunate he had made himself well acquainted with the grounds; for he was enabled to lead the earl and Daulton so close to the summer-house, that they could distinctly see the "Italian," and yet not not be seen themselves.

In a few minutes, Jimmie was seen coming along the centre path.

He was closely followed by Conrad.

Quickly the summer-house was reached, and Deveril sprang forward, a long dagger in his hand.

But ere he could reach Conrad—whom, of course, he made certain was Lucinda—our hero presented the pistol at his head.

At the same instant, Barnacle, followed by the earl and Daulton, dashed forward.

Deveril, with a wild, savage cry, sprang—not upon Conrad—but upon Jimmie.

He then found that the "silly fool"

was a very clever and a very active fool indeed; for Jimmie, stepping nimbly aside, turned and dealt Deveril a heavy blow in the face.

Conrad then immediately closed with him, the while Barnacle struck a light.

In the struggle, Deveril's disguise was disarranged; so that when Barnacle came close up with the light, he was instantly recognised by all.

Deveril, too, had recognised Conrad; and again and again did he frantically try to plunge the dagger into his heart.

Our hero was in the act of throwing him, when his foot caught in the dress with which he was encumbered, and he fell.

Deveril immediately turned and sped away like the wind.

Barnacle followed and fired, but without success.

Conrad was soon upon his feet, and tearing off the dress, rushed after Deveril, who was making direct for the house.

Our hero ran nearly twice as fast as Deveril, but the wretch had had a good start.

Presently the terrace could be seen, and Conrad's heart beat wildly as he saw on the steps—Lucinda!

"Great heaven!" thought Conrad, "if he reaches her before I can interfere, he will murder her."

Seeing that it was impossible to reach him in time, Conrad stopped, and taking a steady aim, fired.

The shot was effective; for, just as Deveril reached the steps, he fell.

He had been shot through the thigh.

"Curse you!" he yelled, as he fixed his fierce eyes upon Lucinda, "you shall never marry him."

As he spoke, he raised his pistol and pulled the trigger.

But there was no report.

The trigger only snapped.

"You villain!" said Conrad. "It was, then, as has been suspected — you shammed death so that you should have yet another opportunity of committing murder. But the law shall have you at last. There will be no yard-arm, but the gallows before Newgate—"

"You lie—you lie!" interrupted Deveril; "the law will never claim me. See—thus do I cheat you!"

And before Conrad could pounce upon him and stay his hand, he had plunged the dagger deep into his heart.

The sight was too terrible a one for Lucinda.

She staggered down the steps, and fell insensible in our hero's arms.

At this moment, Barnacle, panting for breath, reached the spot, and was speedily followed by the others, while the cries caused the servants to turn out *en masse*.

The females took charge of Lucinda, and conveyed her within the Manor.

Lights were brought, and Barnacle examined Deveril.

"There's no sham this time," he said; "he's as dead as a dried shark."

"Did you slay the wretch, Conrad?" asked the earl.

"Slay him—no," said Barnacle. "I was just in time to see him drive the dagger into his body."

"He found he could not get away," said Conrad, "hence his suicide. Barnacle, leave him where he is, and fetch the officers."

"I will go, your honour," said Jimmie. "I know the quickest way."

"Do. And here, my man—you have rendered us all a service this night. You shall be well rewarded. What are you?"

"Well, to tell you the truth, your honour, I'm only a man who is glad to get a job here and there. But at one time—five or six years ago—I was the landlord of the 'Hare and Hounds.'"

"*You?*" cried Barnacle.

"Ay, I was."

"Well, how did you lose your craft—I mean, how did you come to let someone else board your vessel?"

"Fact is, I was ruined by my son."

"Ruined?" said the earl.

"Yes; I had to pay for a certain thing. Er—the truth—"

"Never mind — never mind, my friend," said Conrad. "None of us seeks to know your private affairs."

"Barnacle," said the earl, "this man is to be your assistant. He will, in fact, be deputy steward."

"Very good indeed," said McTaggart. "And when, in defiance of my advice, Barnacle disposes of too much rum, this good man will attend to his duties."

Jimmie warmly thanked them, and then ran off for the officers.

In less than an hour from this, the police had removed the body to their office, and a messenger was despatched to London for Mr. Hunt.

That gentleman made his appearance the next morning, and his astonishment may be imagined when he learned what had taken place.

After examining the body and satisfying himself that it was really Deveril's, he set off for Greenwich and called upon Doctor Wood.

That " worthy " being threatened with the law, revealed the whole of the trick.

He could not be punished, it is true; but Hunt made him refund the whole of the twenty pounds.

That amount he was told to pocket himself, and the earl added another hundred.

* * * *

One month after the death of Deveril —who was buried in the unconsecrated portion of Banstead Churchyard—our hero led the lovely Inez to the altar.

Who does the reader think was " best man ? "

Well, it was Barnacle; and mighty proud he was, you may guess.

It was a grand wedding, indeed !

From the Manor to the church, the way was strewn with flowers by the little girls belonging to the parish school, while the neighbours raised cheer after cheer.

The wedding being over, a feast on a magnificent scale was given, and at night the vast grounds were beautifully illuminated, and dancing—which was led by Conrad, Inez, and Mr. and Mrs. King—was kept up until a late hour.

We have now but little more to add.

In a couple of years, the earl died, and Conrad succeeded to the title and estates; while, at the death of Don Alico, Inez inherited his large fortune— and much good she did with it.

Barnacle continued as steward until his death, which occurred in his seventy-first year.

We need scarcely add that, despite his eccentricities—his loss was a blow to all, and especially McTaggart, the " resident physician."

As the years went on, our hero rose higher and higher in the estimation of his neighbours and tenants, and he became widely known in England and abroad as the firm friend of distressed seamen.

He and his beautiful wife were frequently visited by persons of influence and position ; and our hero often entertained them with some of his adventures.

There was something in the great hall of the Manor which immediately arrested the visitor's attention.

It was a huge picture, painted by a a well-known artist, and represented our hero being rescued from the sharks by the brave crew of the " Sea Breeze."

The portrait of Conrad was an excellent one, and could not fail to be recognised.

At the bottom were these simple words—

" Nailed to the Mast! "